I0655445

Wake

of the

Raven

Graham Worthington

Wake

of the

Raven

Angry Orchid Publishing

Copyright © 2007 by Graham Worthington

All rights reserved. No part of this book may be reproduced
in any form or by any electronic or mechanical means,
including information storage and retrieval systems, without
the permission of the copyright holder, except by a reviewer,
who may quote brief passages in review.
For more information, contact the author using

ISBN: 978-0-9869306-0-7

Cover design copyright © 2011 by
Graham Worthington

For more information on Graham Worthington or Angry
Orchid Publishing, use grahamworth@hotmail.com

Other Fiction by Graham Worthington

Zorn:
A Legend of the Days to Come

By Graham Worthington with Others

Xangans

Thanks

Thanks to all the people whose dances through my life coalesced into this story.

Thanks, all you who shared with me your drink from life's tainted well, whispering horror tremulously into my ear, or rambling loud in drunken glee, or staring stoned through the haze of unhallowed smoke.

In bouncing joy, in withering grief, in sneering indifference – that you mistook for sophistication; in enthusiastic exchange of life's curious tales, you all told me your fragment.

Thanks to Sam, who said "what if…" and set the whole ball rolling; thanks to that girl – name now forgotten! – who silenced a bar with a reckless confession. Thanks to the real Major Willis, and to she who once sat on a wall.

You are all there: the good, the bad, and the ugly.

The real, the illusory, and the unknowing crowds through which you passed, unseen, unfamed, yet carrying your freight of hidden worlds untasted.

Contents

Contents continued

"The art of living is more like wrestling than dancing, in so far as it stands ready against the accidental and the unforeseen, and is not apt to fall"
Marcus Aurelius Antoninus (121 - 180)

"Light is meaningful only in relation to darkness, and truth presupposes error. It is these mingled opposites, which people our life, which make it pungent, intoxicating. We only exist in terms of this conflict, in the zone where black and white clash"
Louis Aragon (1897 – 1982

Prologue

You've been in an airport of course. I was in one myself recently, crouching on the edge of a padded seat in the main lounge, sipping their overpriced coffee as I tinkered on my laptop and watched my fellow travellers surge past.

Airports are interesting, futuristic places, with a bright touch of other world glamour to them. I still find them so, even after many a boring flight. With their high ceilings and thronging devotees, the endless halls and concourses form almost temples to the polished glory of the modern age, greater and harder than the amiable, soft-fleshed creatures that arrive to worship within them.

A forest of concrete and tarmac usually guards these palaces, bewildering the pilgrims who arrive by coach and car to struggle with the maze of roads, ramps and walkways; through, over, around and under the tangle until they reach their numbered terminals. As before they navigate with one anxious eye to the vigilant traffic police, and another to their burden of luggage and kids that must be shepherded safely through the outer melee of cars and people, and into the great spacious halls. There a rank of waiting desks displays their carrier's name, and at that point their tension begins to ease, as now it is only a matter of time to kill and directions to obey, for they have seized the great rope of commerce that will haul them surely to their destination.

For them this is not an everyday event, but neither is it new, and they know that all paths have long been prepared for them, and that a thousand unseen little precautions will ensure their safety and comfort. As their mildly anxious eyes scan the cold emptiness of space and concrete they see that all is ordered and arranged, as last time and the time before that, and they proceed through the layers of security, now cheerful and unafraid, guided by polite barriers of rope and chrome to the final departure lounge. There they can with much confidence await that last direction to pass down one of those ingenious tubes, and encouraged by the practiced smiles of those pretty and oh so competent air hostesses, board some massive jumbo for Rome, or Manila, New York or Tokyo.

While they await that final call, they may visit the many chapels within this temple: the burger stands, the bars, the newsagents and souvenir shops, and most essential, the off duty store with its bright display of perfumes and spirits, wines and tobacco. Like the rest of the eager horde, I sometimes worship there, but cautiously, for too much enthusiasm with the plastic can run up an unholy bill.

The types recur: doubtless they are all individuals, with their own lives, yet all are cut from one of the range of patterns. In one queue an energetic Chinese man in a suit still pursues his affairs over his mobile 'phone, even within minutes of a five-thousand mile journey, and in another a denim clad men of thirty something exchanges a few pleasantries with a fellow-traveller, who he will never meet again, while his bottle-blonde wife at his side clutches the hand of a small child. The child stares about him with infant curiosity, but his older sister is lost in the tiny world of a hand-held game, oblivious to the ponderous details of the journey, and about the family, like the circled wagons of Indian fearing pioneers, their armoury of suitcases, stuffed with ammunition to attack the promised delights of Spain or Greece.

As they shuffle inwards, others surge out, laughing, noisy, and re-energised: a tanned discharge of northerners returning from The Dominican Republic. Rum is cheap in that hot country, and the bleary expressions of that group of young men show they have taken full advantage. The tall one, with his hair braided for a few pounds on that far country's beaches; he looks self conscious already; he will whip those beads out before he resumes his place at the bank counter.

Yet these airports have another, grimmer side, which sometimes they show to me in my dreams. They are touched by a fearful air of final mystery, which they share with graveyards and funeral parlours, for an airport is both a doorway and a fearful barrier. If he passes through it, the traveller will be swiftly snatched to a different place, but this place will die to him, the very thread by which he could find his way back snapped by the shock of the swift departure.

On an aircraft journey, as with death, there is no time for the traveller to give a backward glance, and for the ones who remain, no slowly diminishing figure, to which extra, distant farewells can be waved. It is abrupt and final: a goodbye, a promise to 'phone, and the traveller passes through a narrow door; we catch a brief glimpse of sober looking men in dark uniforms inspecting him keenly, then he is gone. We see him no more, neither does he see us again, nor the bustling life we shared, but we can guess him to watch, from a soaring height, as the mottled world falls away beneath him.

But to return to this my latest trip, and my expensive coffee... there was a girl at the airport.

Many girls of course, but this one stuck in my mind. I glanced up as she sashayed past my table, twenty-two perhaps, tall, slender, a smooth, flat midriff bared above tight pants whose dark chocolate colour enriched the ripeness of her figure. Her face was strong and confident, her dark brown hair long and straight. I gave a glance, I had a second for brief appreciation, then she was passing into the distance, wending her way between the tables with an easy sway of her hips, leaving a trail of final satisfaction in the sight of her rounded bottom.

But there was one final note adding intrigue to the girl's charms beyond the physical. The pants that she wore, close at the hip and thigh, were flared below the knee to the ankle. There was nothing new in this, for the fashion for flares had crept back tentatively some years before, but it was the "back" that was the point. Wasn't it somewhere in the seventies that flares went out of favour, never to return till the sun should grow cold? And here this young woman could wear them with no apprehensions, for this was 1999, and my fashion conscious youth ended far before her birth.

Another girl sat a few tables away, of much the same age, but pale and angular, talking in a quiet, mousy way to an older traveller, probably her mother. There was no hint of fire in her timid glance, no eyes that challenged the world, and I pondered the difference. That passing girl: her face, her stride, her air of assurance; from what source could they spring? Possibly merely the sure knowledge of her beauty, taught to her by her mirror over the years, but perhaps also some inborn desire to be, and be of consequence.

Such women are not for the timid, for if the face is to glow with presence – that near arrogance that magnifies beauty – so that a man's head turns as the dimness of a weary day is brightened, is there not a threatened price? Can one think that such outer glow does not spring from inner fire? And will such fire always flow cool and harmless like a placid stream, and shape itself calmly to the glass to be sipped at leisure, and never scald? No. They can be dangerous, these real women. But then, so is life.

Always, when I see such a brightener of the day, it leads my thoughts to those two whose story I've long kept under my hat. At one time I would have thought their history unmentionable, but that too was long ago, and surely now the world is different, and soon the century ends, so... why not? Didn't he several times say that when the century was out, he probably would be too, but he wouldn't care much in either case?

And I should, for otherwise much will be lost. What man has not been disconcerted by the touch of his judgement's cold, pocking finger, picking at his intended deeds with anxious doubts, and wagging sternly at his accomplished follies? Who has not needed to match the record of his triumphs and failures against those of another frail human, and so plot a path across the strange country of his own life? At that time, the story of another's wavering course becomes precious, for that other life becomes ours, and grips our full attention as fear glues us to virtue, or fascination beckons us to excess.

And as no man's story should be wasted – if his life been at all worth living – I see with some trepidation that I am a custodian, who must now undertake a task. Must undertake? Perhaps not must, and it's certainly not my profession, but yet I've long wanted to take a stab at it, and if I stick to the truth as much as possible, can I go far wrong?

I dislike falsifying fact to suit convenience, but only a few judicious changes of name should ensure their privacy and honour the trust their friendship gave to me. Let me begin then, before time nibbles away my memory, and their good and bad deeds blur together, losing all distinct features. And at what better place than an airport could I start to recount their story, even though they are now such vast antiseptic palaces?

You know what an airport's like today of course, and they're all much the same. If you've seen one you've seen them all, believe me, whether its New York or Madrid, Sydney or Kuala Lumpur. But it was much different in 1951, and much different at Paa, for Paa is nowhere near a size to rival those famous cities. Yet small and petty as it is, it is in Paa that I should start.

Perhaps to those born there, this little seaport seems so big that its boundaries mark the world's end, but the greater reality of a well detailed map shows it as a mere fly speck, one amongst countless other towns clinging to the endless islands circling the South China Sea. Lost in the world's vastness, this hot, primitive place is a mere strange name, puzzling to pronounce.

It is here though, that the world turns a corner.

Many people could make a decent stab at sketching a simple map of Europe, putting such chunky countries as Spain and France in the right place. A quick triangle would do for Britain, and an easy boot for Italy, and he could probably rough out the great, distinct shape of Africa to the south, and so enclose the homely pond of the Mediterranean.

I suspect our average citizen would falter at the eastern end: Israel and Egypt probably in more or less the right place, but rather a tangle up in that northeast corner where Greece and Turkey brewed so many ancient legends. But were we to enquire as to what lay to the east of Europe, then a little more knowledge than usual would be needed to separate the far, legendary names one from the other.

I have no doubt that if we pressed our by now faltering mapmaker, we would have asked too much, and that Iran and Arabia, Afghanistan and Pakistan would find themselves muddled and displaced. Were he cunning though, our mapmaker might leap in description over them, and apply the common knowledge that beyond them lies great, crowded India, imitating Africa as it thrusts its pointed base south into its ocean. Beyond that, he would probably say, tailing off in despair, lies China, and places like that.

And so they do.

China can be entered directly from India, but only by braving the cold, towering Himalayas, and centuries ago the expanding nations of Europe took a warmer, more profitable route, sailing their wooden ships past India into the bay of Bengal, which they found to be enclosed on the east by Burma. Turning south, they passed through the narrow Strait of Malacca that lies between the Malay Peninsula and the long island of Sumatra, and there they found an end to the constant eastward progress of the Asian continent.

Here Asia's great corner turns, for the coast swings north, heading poleward from the hot equator to become China, after a detour into the gulf of Thailand, and a flirtation with Vietnam. Here on the Malay Peninsula's southern tip they built Singapore, to dip its merchant fingers into the passing traffic, and lord it over the endless maze of islands choking the seas between Asia and Australia.

So thickly do these dozen or more great islands – Sumatra, Borneo, The Philippines and others – crowd together, that they form a ragged wall against the Pacific, stealing from it The South China Sea, a stretch of water nearly as great as that Mediterranean where the lost Odysseus wandered. Were that sailor to have wandered here, he might have taken even longer to find his home, for there are over three thousand of these islands, ranging from the massive Borneo down to an uncounted host of islets. Some are so tiny and obscure that even today's satellite-drawn maps have no name for them, and traveller's myth has it that no man has ever found it worthwhile to set foot on some.

The nature of the people turns a corner too, as the features and customs of India mix and intertwine with those of the sea-faring Malays, with distant China adding to the mix of its cultures, and everywhere, entangled yet separate from their ways and customs, the influence of their one-time masters, the cold Europeans, and their cousin Americans.

The tangle of these cultures is matched by the tangle of their inhabitant's faiths, for there is no one church that dominates all others to obscurity. Austere mosques, bare of images and decorated only by hard geometry, may lie close to Buddhist temples where statues of the Enlightened One rule; and the plain icons of a Christian church may be echoed further down the same street by the gaudy painted Gods of a Hindu temple. Yet the same hot dust drifts through the doorways of each, and each roof is battered by the same monsoon rains.

In deep forests, a short step from towns striving to imitate the trendy frolics of the twentieth century, simple forest deities rule simpler people, needing neither building nor image, and in the myriad little seaports, wooden boats, built by shoeless natives to centuries-old designs, jostle smoke-stacked iron steamers, built by the riveters of Clydebank.

Paa is one such seaport, little different today from what it was in 1951, when it had an airport – of sorts.

Gary Wilson, Manchester, England, August 1999.

15

Chapter 1. Papa Rice's

The afternoon was near its end, and the narrow street onto which the bar opened was falling into shadow. Here near the equator the sun rises and sets rapidly, the first dimming of light being swiftly followed by the fall of darkness. When that happened the sun-bleached streets of Paa became black canyons, with the occasional oasis of gentle light falling from the dim interiors of its few tawdry cafes and bars.

Errol had caught the first two of his three fish already, tracking them down easily in the small seaport, but the Englishman had proved elusive. Finally Errol had retreated from the sun to the shaded lair of Papa Rice's bar, and there he sat quietly for some time, watching the hot, weary foot traffic shuffle past. He was confident that this was as good a way as any of finding his final passenger, for there was little in Paa to entertain the young unmarried Europeans of that town, and Papa Rice's dingy bar was one of their few watering holes.

The Englishman was of that kind who reserve their drinking time till after sundown, but he was winding down what affairs he still had in Paa, so there was no certainty of his schedule. And even if he doesn't come, thought Errol with satisfaction, we're still in the money with tomorrow's flight, well in the money, and he smiled in satisfaction, for the Limey was coming now, strolling down the dirty, rubbish strewn street, weaving his way through the jabbering natives as casually as if he were in London.

"Stuart!"

The calling voice was familiar to Stuart: he had heard it often, usually coming to him over the top of a glass, and he peered from the sun-blasted street, squinting into the shadow to see Errol sitting within the shadowed den, beaming and waving to him over the inevitable drink, and he left the dusty street to join him. The American was a man whose company he soon found wearing, but it would be pleasant to escape the monotonous glare of the dying afternoon sun for a while, and besides that Stuart felt the faint tickle of promise.

He eased himself cautiously into one of the tiny bar's rickety chairs, raising a finger to the ancient Malay who ran the place. There was not much need for words with Papa Rice: already he was shuffling to the battered icebox where he kept the beer. Whether they sat at his tables daily, or whether six months passed between their visits, still he knew his customer's habits: beer for the young Englishman who had just signalled to him, and something stronger for the older American. Bourbon, if it could be obtained, but more often some impostor of a rougher but equal strength.

"Where's Isaac?" asked Stuart indifferently, not particularly caring. Isaac was the quieter of the two partners, a thoughtful check to Errol's gustiness. The two usually stuck together like brothers, although Stuart knew Errol be of Italian descent, which Isaac definitely was not. Stuart wondered on occasion how the absent young Jew could have tolerated Errol over the years; still, both were from Brooklyn, and they were both insane Yank pilots, so anything was possible.

"Attending to business, like me. Isaac's looking after the details, while I attend to the grand design. Some are good at one thing, some at something else. Which side of business are you looking after?"

"Both and neither. Not being as fortunate as yourself in having the acquaintance of an excellent partner, I'm both the General and the dogsbody of all my business, except that now I'm no longer in business, so I stroll the streets of Paa, having the occasional drink with other loafers."

Errol laughed. "And this for another two days until the steamer comes, if it comes, and a bunch more days zigging about the islands till it gets to Singapore. And this is a man with money in his pockets! Limeys!" He leaned back in his chair laughing harshly, the ancient timber creaking in chorus.

Stuart began to feel the growth of irritation that Errol usually provoked in him, felt conscious of the predatory bite that lurked even in the man's humour. He had known the two Americans for some years, making their acquaintance bit by bit as their paths crossed his. Whether it was Sarawak, Singapore or the lesser towns of the crowded Malay Archipelago: always the two yanks would sooner or later show up, hauling goods here, there; always busy, often useful, mainly dependable, yet always with that air of being not completely trustworthy. Errol had darkened over the years as the tropical sun ripened the Italian in his blood. Now he seemed a creature of the South China Sea, wholly lost and foreign to his distant New York home, his bloodshot eyes peering with savage humour at the dirty streets of a host of petty eastern towns, his once lanky body becoming heavier and grosser as the years accumulated flesh.

"Told you before fly boy, you charge too much. Didn't get too much from winding up the business, so it has to spin out. No immediate prospects in England, so it has to spin out more." The glass arrived at his elbow with a clunk, and Stuart took it up with a leisurely, deliberate lack of concern, looking past Errol at the passing traffic of merchants and beggars. A better price was coming; he felt it, for he smelt the unsold goods sitting heavy on Errol's hands, and like all his race, the American saw himself as a salesman and played out his role consciously, shaking hands quickly on a deal, or grinning and rolling with the punch of rejection.

"Fifty bucks," said Errol briefly. Stuart nearly dropped the glass in shock. He had expected an improvement, but not by so much.

"How come?"

"Take it or leave it pal. Let's just say I'm having a generous day."

"If you're having a generous day I'd better leave it. Probably some plan to get me to Borneo and sell me to the headhunters. They like British heads. Plenty of capacity."

"No. No time to bargain. Tomorrow morning we're for Singapore. Full plane almost; one place left."

"Full? Two days ago you said you had nothing to go there for."

"That was two days ago my friend. You were charting the whole damn plane then, and fuel's not cheap. Now we're full, just one seat left."

Stuart took a long pull at his drink, gazing mildly through the glass at Errol. He too sometimes acted out a role: that of the cool collected Englishman, at home and untouched even in the jabbering tumult of an eastern town. It was an easy mask, an often useful way of dealing with the world, and it worked well on Errol, amusing him as the uptight reserve of the British often does Americans. Nor was it far from the truth, for at twenty-six Stuart was not yet as lost to his origin as Errol. He remained at his core a calm Englishman, deftly handling the swirl of eastern language and primitive culture while remaining separate, always conscious that he was an out-flung piece of that damp, cold, superior country that had extended its grip well-nigh over the entire world, then in amiable muddle and uncertainty relaxed that grip, and diminished back to a small island.

"Well?"

"All right." The opportunity was too good to miss. At that price, better than two days heaving about on a boat with coolies, cattle and God knows what else, even if the boat came on schedule, which probably it wouldn't. "What time?"

"Seven. And don't be late. I've a bunch of people that that can't wait to get to Singapore, that's why you're lucky. If you're not there – we're gone!"

"Seven it is. But who else is on the plane, who're your important people who need to get to Singy so badly?"

Errol beamed. Usually he was secretive, but success had put him in an expansive mood. "Not who, what. Boat put in at Panwey, left a bunch of crates for some factory. Machine tools and stuff. Boat left for here, they opened the crates, guess what? - wrong crates! So they wired to Paa, can we pick up the right crates when the boat docks here, fly them to Panwey urgent? Factory can't run without its parts."

Errol smiled contentedly, and Stuart guessed that their need had called up a stiff price from Errol. Not an unusual thing to happen out here though; he had bawled and shouted after more than one lost cargo himself. Some coolie had boobed, and now someone else would have to pay out the shekels.

"A muddle," he commented, "but you said Panwey, not Singapore."

"Panwey first, throw the crates out, then straight up again for Singapore, quick, before our Arabs start grumbling."

"Arabs?"

"Yer. We were down at the dock waiting for the steamer, and up comes some fat Arab guy in a hurry with another one dancing behind him. Got to get to Singapore now, big hurry, business man, needs to close some deal. I told him we could get him there tomorrow, but we had to go to Panwey first, then we'd turn back south for Singy. And if they didn't like it..." Errol waved his hand in the air dismissively, "so they decided they liked it. That's where Isaac is now. Crates to the plane this evening, fly out early tomorrow. North and West for Panwey, then south to Singy, and we'll be there before dark, and hit the town." He smiled. "Better ending the day in Singapore than Panwey."

All was now clear to Stuart. Errol had already made his profit twice over, and was now trimming it with a few more bucks. "So that leaves you with the grand design part. You came to bar land looking for me to fill the last seat. Very kind of you Errol."

"I am indeed a kind man, but there are others beside you wandering these streets looking to leave this great city. Father

Bryne and Roger Dawson, both of who I have successfully seized by the ear."

"Roger the journalist," asked Stuart, "a reddish-haired man?"

"The same. You know him."

"I've met him once or twice, that's all. Didn't know his second name. So that's three of us and the Arabs"

"Four. You, Roger, and two from Father Bryne. He's not going anywhere, just arranged a passage for two from the orphanage. A nun, and some kid. You behave, you've got a nun watching you."

"With nothing more than a nun on board I wasn't thinking of doing any miss-behaving."

"We've more than a nun on board. The Arabs have a girl with them, a looker." Errol leered as he spoke, an expression that suited the fleshy coarseness of his face well. "Their secretary. White girl, another Brit. A bit skinny for my taste, but okay for you I guess. I like them stacked. Tits like temple gongs, that's the main thing."

Stuart grimaced. "I must remember that expression for future use," he answered. A strand of him relished the vigour of coarseness, but it was entwined closely with another, which set women on a pedestal of respect. He found them strange creatures, but fascinating, from another world almost. One couldn't do without them, or, more correctly, without some of them. Certain ones it was very necessary to do without, as he had learned, to his cost. His eyes had brightened all the same.

"Yeah, and remember there's a nun watching you," Errol reminded him. His tone was jovial, that of the fellow conspirator in the man's world where women were a quarry, but he was watching the younger man with regret, conscious of the void of opportunity between them. Here he was nearly forty, and he drank too much, like Isaac often told him. The face that looked back at him from the mirror got grimmer and flabbier every day, he could see that, and the crazy girls that he had known – so many of them, so anxious to be with the handsome young fly boy – they didn't seem to be around anymore.

This Brit though, he still had it all before him. He wasn't tall or bulging with muscle, just average, but he had that slim, wiry, compact kind of body that swung into a cockpit easily, like he, Errol, used to have, the kind of body where it was easy to have a girl swinging on your arm, or two. And tough under that cool, soft manner, and probably clever and educated as well. He had been an officer in Burma, hadn't he, and the Brit officers always kept their titles, even when they went back to being civilians. Probably his family had a pot full of money, and he was going home, and he wasn't dumb, wasting his money away. His short dark hair was all one colour as well, and this especially roused Errol's envy, for he was finding streaks of grey in his own thick mane.

Errol dismissed his thoughts brusquely. He was getting soft thinking this way. They would make a pile on this flight, and that would stop Isaac's whining for a while, always "the plane needs this and the plane needs that." Errol sat up briskly. He wasn't all that old, and he was still a dammed good pilot; even Isaac admitted that. "Papa Rice!" he called, and held up two fingers. Damn it all, he'd buy if the limey weren't going to offer.

Stuart sat awhile and casually tried to pump Errol for the British woman's name, but Errol turned perverse and merely wagged a reproving finger. Probably he doesn't know anyway, thought Stuart, but I'll find out tomorrow, despite him; it'll liven up the flight a bit. He was not intimidated by women, for though he had no illusion of being a Don Juan, yet he knew himself to be presentable, and capable in the kind of conversation that he had found his kind of woman to prefer: intelligent without being heavy, witty without being too smart.

If he had been asked to describe his looks he would have laughed a little in embarrassment, and said he had a nose and all the other bits, but they didn't fit too well. This was too modest, for though his features were unremarkable they were neat and regular, with a stubborn mouth contradicting mild brown eyes. Women with a taste for a great show of masculinity overlooked him, and this did not trouble him, for they were rarely his type; but those who looked for a man who was steady, without being boring, they found him a catch, and several regretted that he had already been caught.

Darkness had still not dropped its swift curtain by the time Stuart left, for whilst he found Errol's gusty rogueries amusing, he could only swallow so much of his wind. Besides, he had a few preparations left to complete, though not many, for all that he had built up over the years he had turned into cash some days before, and had been merely killing time, awaiting the uncertain arrival of the steamer that called on its way to Singapore. Now he was leaving a little sooner than expected, and he must make a few last goodbyes before filling his single suitcase and winding the little travelling alarm.

Tomorrow would bring the end of Paa and all the other places of the East in which he had worked, the end of the draining tropical heat, the end of the dirty, bustling towns and cities where a dozen languages strove together in tumult, the end of the life he had toiled to make there. He would miss it, but he was glad to go. It was time to move on, time to fly for a colder, calmer land, even as Jennifer had done.

Chapter 2. Paa

Small as it was – and in those days, it was even smaller than today - Paa had an airstrip. True, it was little more than a single dirt runway, separated from the surrounding forest by a sagging wire fence, and barely large enough to carry the few light aircraft operating from there; but since it was scraped together in the days of the struggle against Japan, it had been a Mecca of excitement to the native boys, drawing them magnetically from their simple villages to trek through the surrounding forest and cling to the fence.

There they swung, monkey-like and jabbering in excitement, until in parts the flimsy barrier was beaten almost to the ground. Some of the planes had a hangar of sorts, but most, when not in flight, sat scorching under the Pacific sun on the area of beaten dirt at the runway's end. Here also were the workshops and parts stores, huts of rough-hewn local timber from which the paint - if any - had peeled some years earlier.

Central to these structures was The Clubhouse, a long, low wooden building, dignified with glass in some of the windows, that gained its name from its main function: a place for the owner-pilots to enjoy a quiet drink together – although often not so quiet – and supplement Paa's meagre entertainment with the occasional wild party. True, one corner was partitioned off to form an office from which the loose cooperative of pilots ran the airstrip's affairs, but as their management had little more facilities to worry over than the dirt runway itself, the office saw little use, and as Paa had no prying officials to check their records, they kept none.

On this day however, in January of 1951, The Clubhouse's rowdy nights were forgotten, and it assumed a certain dignity, for it was a waiting room and sun-shelter for the small group patiently awaiting The Raven's readiness.

This particular aircraft sat at the end of the runway a stone's throw from The Clubhouse. It was a Beech 45, a small twin engine plane, one of fifteen-hundred or so that had served the U.S. military as unarmed transports, one of the myriad items of equipment and humanity that America flooded into the Pacific in its efforts to throw back the might of Japan. Afterwards, like many another of those items engaged in the great conflict, the plane never returned to its home in the land of the Eagle, but mysteriously remained in that of the Dragon.

America had been reluctant to join the spreading global conflict, but once in had not stinted spending its great wealth to pound the enemy. The war being over, celebration had been general, and discipline became redundant. There had been a serious fire at a small base, and an officer was assigned the task of checking the equipment listing, and signing to confirm what had survived, and what was to be jettisoned as scrap; a dreary task that he bustled through hastily, before dashing away to what promised to be a very wild party.

The non-commissioned clerk who had toiled to prepared the list sighed wearily when he was gone, and shook his head at the folly of officers, for had this one not signed to confirm that a certain plane was part of the fire's debris? And even now, as he looked through the window, could he not see the plane standing sturdy and unmarked only fifty yards away? The clerk laid the report to one side, for it was late, and tomorrow would be soon enough to grip his patience firmly, and gently point out the error to the officer.

But although tomorrow came, the officer did not. The party had indeed been wild, with no disappointing shortage of drinks or girls. But alcohol does not always mix well with chasing giggling Filipina girls down flights of concrete stairs, and the officer had tripped, and with the morning came the news that he now lay in the morgue, his neck awry.

The clerk again shook his head, and thought wearily of the bullshit to be gone though again, and how he was glad to be going home to Tulsa in a day or two. Then he became very still, as still as the cold stone figures he had seen meditating within these foreign temples, though inside a hot tremor began to lure and terrify him, for he had remembered the cost of that little hardware store his brother had written to him about, and their regret at how short they were of the price.

He rose slowly from his chair, his hands suddenly damp. The base was being wound down: everyone was in transit, and security was as lax as foam. There were two pilots that he knew well, and knew that they too had come to the end of serving Uncle Sam, and were at a loose end, chewing on plans as futile as they were grandiose. More important, he knew their swift and reckless natures, and which bar he could find them in.

Later that evening a bored sentry admitted three men in a jeep to the base with a casual wave. He did not know them, for he too was in transit, but it was enough for him that they wore uniform, for he, like the clerk, was soon to go home, the nightmare of war behind him forever. Not long after that, the C45 rose from the base and headed south. It was never seen again, nor was it missed. The clerk's palms remained sweaty for some days, until he climbed thankfully onto a truck, the first step in a homeward journey.

In some filing cabinet, a forgotten report lists the plane as destroyed, and a dead man's scrawled signature attests to this lie. The trifling sum of dollars that paid for this convenience was well spent, and the spender stands behind his counter in Tulsa, the transaction long forgotten, as are Errol and Isaac who scrapped together the dollars. Both being pilots, and the East being exciting, they planned to work up from one plane to many, serving the short flight traffic of people and goods that abounds in the South China Sea. Errol was not particularly a reading man, but he affected to admire Poe, and in his pride he called their acquisition The Raven, and painted a black silhouette of that bird's head on the transport's nose.

The Raven had flitted busily about the myriad islands and towns of the east for many years now, but its brothers never arrived, for there were too many contracts they could not take, too many places they must avoid, and too much hard earned money spent on good times. Instead, there came the gradual deterioration of parts and moral, till today, out of earshot of their passengers, Errol and Isaac again argued over the capability of their craft for the coming flight to Panwey. But the money was paid in cash, as were all Paa airstrip transactions, and it was needed, and the passengers had all arrived.

*****

Julia, if he had heard correctly. Stuart had caught her name across the room, from the fat one of the two Arabs, though he was not sure that it wasn't Judy. If Roger hadn't spoken at that moment, he would have heard for certain. Roger might know her name – journalists had their noses in everywhere - but he wasn't the type who knew when to murmur discretely, and so Stuart shelved the question, and turned his attention back to their conversation.

He and Roger had been talking for an hour, having arrived together well before Errol's seven a.m. deadline to find the two Arabs and the woman already at the clubhouse, huddled defensively in one corner. The Arabs looked at them stonily, so without comment they chose their own corner and fell into conversation on the current doings of the world in general.

Stuart had wondered vaguely where his promised nun was, but soon the door opened to admit her robed figure, surprising him a little, for she was unusually tall for a woman, but slow and weary with age. A girl of eleven or so followed obediently in her trail, like a captive moon, and the two of them settled silently in a third corner, the nun as impassive as a Buddha in her robes, the girl round eyed and docile in the green stripped cotton uniform of the orphanage.

Since then the time had dragged past, and it was well past eight, and he was tiring of hearing of the joys and sorrows of a journalist's life. The Arabs – if that was what they were – were becoming impatient, grumbling to each other in guttural undertones, whilst Julia sat still and resigned by their side. Stuart guessed that she was unable to understand their language. Like her, the ancient nun sat patient and silent, occasionally smiling indulgently at the girl, who had lost her awe of this mysterious place and kicked her sandaled heels against the chair legs, bored.

Stuart rose and went again to the window, as if to inspect the plane or the distant jabbering children, but really to take a closer look at the young woman as he passed. How old was she? Twenty-five? Perhaps a bit more? Her skin was too remarkable pale and creamy for her to have spent much time in Paa: probably she was passing through. Or did she perhaps work in Paa, spending her days sheltering in some shady office, with the big fan swirling slowly? Was she one of that legion of secretaries serving the many British business interests of the East, the kind you often met in the front office, always busy typing, but if the visitor was young and good looking, or even merely presentable, always ready to smile and flirt with the a man who might relieve their boredom a little.

For a woman, Paa – and most of the east – was a wretched place, where she could grow old as the sun sucked the youth from her skin. How many of these secretaries were looking for a man, who might be their ticket to a better life?

But wasn't that how he met Jennifer?

Stuart grimaced at the thought and turned abruptly from the window. A sharp cry of pain came from the region of his armpit and he stepped back, flustered, making a hasty apology; he had trodden on the foot of the schoolgirl, who must have come silently to the window by his side. A pair of eyes wide with hurt and on the verge of tears looked at him from beneath the shelter of a new straw hat, and she murmured some vague word before limping back to resume her seat.

Blasted kids, he thought silently, yet he felt ashamed at hurting the child in his clumsiness. The secretary was looking at him; she gave him one of those sympathetic little smiles that men need in order to recover from some minor stupidity, and Stuart responded with a wry look of regret, and walked back to his seat.

Even in disaster a little good can be found, he thought. The petty accident had broken the ice a bit, and perhaps conversation could come later. Her boss – for surely the fat man sitting by her was her boss – had given the incident a brief, cold glance before turning to resume an earnest conversation with the third member of their group, a younger, slimmer version of himself.

Definitely Julia – if that was here name – was his employee, for the faint air of deference was there, and not the familiarity of a wife or mistress.

And the younger man? His quick nods to each point that the elder seemed to be forcing on him declared him also the fat mans junior. Both men were of some Arab-European mix, and their features said brothers, although the younger man was slim and mild, whilst his overweight elder had the gesticulating, assertive manner that Stuart particularly detested. Both were dressed as though for business in a fan-cooled office rather than for travel; did they like to announce their importance in this uncomfortable fashion, Stuart wondered? More fool them if they did, for the sticky heat of the day would rise as the morning progressed, and he had preferred shorts.

Julia by contrast looked cool and at ease, and now Stuart's interest warmed, for she was studying her watch in a manner that told him that she was aware of his covert attention, and that his attention was not unwelcome. How elegantly she stretched her hand out now to examine her nails! And with what an air of casual sophistication she appeared unconscious of him. It was a slim, shapely hand that bore the delicate little watch, delicate like the fine chain around her slender neck, a neck supporting a face of more than ordinary prettiness framed in long, lustrous dark hair, a chain resting on fine collarbones, with the vee of her open necked blouse beneath. A vee in a blouse of dark blue, opening like an invitation to the swelling breasts stretching its material. A blouse that ended where the wide belt of a cream skirt melded to her hips, thighs before giving way to smooth calves, ending in shapely feet bare beneath her sandals – the door opened abruptly to admit Errol, as darkly jovial as ever. It was time to leave.

Stuart, startled, had to dally in his chair a little and walk out last of the group, for a sudden swelling had begun to press out the material of his khaki shorts, and threatened embarrassment. Lie down buddy, he thought, its not your time yet, if ever, so not in front of the ladies, please! We might manage a bit of chitchat later if you don't make me look silly now. He slowly followed the others to the door, thinking earnestly of polar bears as he went, and his troublesome part subsided. Funny how it always takes you by surprise, he thought, as though it hadn't happened before.

He waited, running his eye over the plane as the others boarded through the narrow doorway in the side. He had been on The Raven once before. Looks okay to me, he thought, not that I know a thing about them. Solid looking machine, nothing fancy about it, and the yanks had a hell of a lot of them, and they liked them. Engine on each wing that looks big enough to haul it all the way back to the states, double tail plane – I suppose that helps – and they changed it about a bit inside.

There's a crapper in the rear if I remember right. Thoughtful of Errol: amazing he didn't fix up a bar instead. But he's a damn good pilot; everyone who knows him agrees on that, so what's Isaac's problem? He's not happy with the plane, but isn't that always the way with everything out here? And it's only a few hundred miles, and Isaac always was the worrier of the team, so – here we go. Thinking this, Stuart hoisted his case and climbed last through the narrow hatch.

The small group of travellers had little luggage, and Paa airstrip had less formalities. Within a matter of minutes the boys swinging on the fence were cheering as the roaring twin engines of the Raven drove the parrots shrieking from the trees, and it swept down the runway to lift steeply into the clear morning sky. Only a few hours to Panwey.

Stuart had regretted at first that his little embarrassment caused him to enter the plane last, for he found only one choice of seat left to him. Down either side of the passenger cabin ran a row of seats, four to the right and three to the left, each by its own square little window, with a narrow isle between them.

The bulky Raoul had stomped impatiently to the plane at Errol's call, snapping at Julia to hurry, and they boarded first, taking the two front seats behind the bulkhead separating off the pilot's cabin, Raoul on the left and Julia on his right. Andre claimed the seat behind Julia, and Stuart reluctantly took the seat to the younger brother's left, resigning himself to the sight of the back of the Arab's podgy neck.

He would have preferred to sit across from Roger, so that they could continue their chat in some imitation of comfort, but the journalist had taken the third seat, behind him, and the child had occupied the seat on the right, opposite him. The nun had taken the final seat on the right, behind the girl, and the fourth seat on their side had been removed, leaving him no choice. At least Roger's close behind, he thought, so I can always twist back and have a natter with him. Not that there's much privacy: it's like a bloody dog kennel.

Once settled in his place Stuart had found his seat to have an advantage, for it gave him a slanting view of Julia's shapely legs. He wondered idly as to her eventual destination. Certainly there could be no real intimacy between her and her boss, to whom he had by now taken a strong dislike. On boarding they had all sought for places to stow their bags, for the rear of the plane was crammed with wooden crates, and she had picked up her employer's briefcase, at which he had snarled angrily and snatched it from her irritably, to thrust it beneath his seat. Julia had merely taken her seat with a feigned expression of indifference.

Probably she had to put up with a lot of that, Stuart thought. It would be difficult to attempt conversation with her on the plane, but at Singapore.... That might be possible.

He ran through various gambits in his head as the engines roared into life, and the plane commenced a bumpy taxiing that culminated in the shaking headlong rush down the uneven runway. The cabin tilted as the plane heaved itself into the air, and more than one voice uttered a sigh of relief as the noise and vibration of takeoff fell away. Stuart noticed the child massaging her toes absently as she gazed enthralled through the window, lips parted in excitement, obviously on a plane for the first time ever. Behind her, the nun too looked out at the distant ground, as it fell away and yielded quickly to the sea, but she made little sign that the passivity of her sanctified old age had been disturbed.

The plane climbed rapidly to the thousands of feet at which it would race before the rising sun to Singapore, and as the sight of the sea grew monotonous, Stuart turned his attention to the slantwise contemplation of Julia's charms. After a while even her smooth legs palled, and he turned his gaze absently back to the panorama of sky and sea beyond the tiny window, for considering Julia had caused the unseen chain in his mind to rattle, and he was chewing again on the misfortunes that had lead him to this flight, and away from Paa.

Chapter 3. Raven

Stuart was twenty-six, and till recently his years, though hard, had been a parade of ever increasing successes. He was not yet twenty when he joined the British forces struggling against the Japanese in Burma, and afterwards he served in the troubles in Malaya. He entered the these conflicts an uncertain, half-formed youth, and emerged moulded into a leader with a lieutenant's pips, fingering a pencil thin moustache as he viewed a future of assured success, a series of ascending steps placed before him for his firm treading. But on one of these steps he stumbled and suffered a bruising fall, and the step's name was Jennifer.

Theirs was an old story, and simple, but to him and her it was new, for they were new. New to each other, and new to the ancient venture of life-long commitment. They understood this, for it was too obvious for comment, but they did not consider that they were also new to life, little more than untried runners at its starting gate. This point they would have denied indignantly, firm as they were in the completed wisdom of their twenties.

In their early days together there was little to suggest the strife to come between them. They met at an officer's dance at one of the small bases where they served, Jennifer like him being army. After a rapid courtship they married, Colonel Haig giving away the bride in lieu of her parents. For a year or more all went well, during which time Stuart resigned his commission and turned to making their fortune in trade, becoming one of the legion of confident young men striving to build a business in the wide-open arena of islands and sea.

The rift between them seemed at first a matter of petty differences, till with a shocking swiftness it grew to the final angry separation, and Jennifer left both Paa and Stuart abruptly, heading for her family's home in Kent, and for all Stuart knew she was there still. He had cared little as he recoiled in disgust from the ruin of their marriage, but as time passed he thought more deeply.

There had been girls before Jennifer of course, and the memorable ones seemed to him like bright windows through which he gazed onto the wide skies of beauty. Stuart had little time for philosophies of moderation: the world to him was a broad adventure in which all things had their own sweet or bitter flavour, not to be avoided, but to be savoured or spat out according to judgment. He was not alone in this: six years of war had taught the raw facts of hovering death, and left little space for delicate scruple in many minds. But with the coming of Jennifer, he closed the shutters on all windows but her.

When it was his choice to roam freely, he had admitted of no restraint to that choice, but when he had chosen to bind himself to only one, he had allowed himself no option but that single person. He had prided himself on his faithfulness, and was stunned to find that Jennifer had ceased to regard herself as so bound. She had revenged her grievance with a casual love affair, and so he was stabbed with an unforeseen dagger, of bitterly poisoned blade.

His rage at discovering his betrayal frightened even himself. Words were shouted of such violence that the blows he struck the man seemed minor details to the uproar, and Jennifer fled hastily for England.

He had dismissed her with swift anger from his life, bellowing that he was happy to see the back of her, and a thousand times better off, and he threw himself vigorously into his business. The months passed and lengthened beyond a year, and had business gone well his acceptance of the break would have seemed vindicated as the wisest course of action. As his animal good spirits recovered, her image would have faded, till their separation entered the ledger of his memory as a decision well taken. But success eluded him: the quick footwork of his decisions faltered as he found that his bond had become his shackle.

The failure of his marriage had not quenched the longing for the feminine other-than-self that burned in him, and other chances at partnership offered themselves as he strove to remake his life

Again he mixed with the young European women of the towns that business took him to, of which Paa was only one. As before they welcomed the attention of an apparent young bachelor, a dashing ex-lieutenant, and as before he dinned with them, danced with them, and sometimes in his bed they met in that other-worldly meeting, that lone adventure that is shared by two, a journey wherein the traveller voyages in the land of another traveller, who journeys with him not only as a companion, but as the land of adventure itself.

How private that journey is! How can a thing so common, so much the property of all, be yet such a thing of secrecy and concealment? Stuart pondered this mystery often, and for him it added yet another layer of charm to womankind. It irked his soul that he had regained his freedom, but found it a false freedom, for if with any of these women he felt the warm possibility of a deeper relationship, then the drag of his unseen fetter tainted his emotions, and cool restraint hampered him, as it had not done before.

For now there was a spoiling as not before. If he should meet the one who counted, the one who was the final one, what then? Now he was a free man who was a bound man, a lone man who was a paired man. Open and direct by nature, he was now constrained to deception, for Jennifer although half a world distant was still in law his wife.

Doubt had begun to trouble him. Was it possible that this was a failure of his own making, which he could and must repair? He probed the sore to its roots, pondering how Jennifer and he had drifted so far from each other. They met, they loved, they married; a reasonable, everyday fairytale, which surely every man was entitled to. But then they quarrelled, fought, and finally parted.

Why for him that unwanted everyday ending? He had done his best, he had been faithful, he had striven for their betterment, so how could this betrayal come? Neither married nor free, he turned the question wearily in his mind until he achieved understanding, but not satisfaction; for with understanding came an awakening to his own folly: he had not understood that her wants were not his, even as she was not he.

Too late he saw that a vision of further, greater goals had always beckoned him, and he had considered this normal, but this vision she did not share. To him the struggle to achieve was itself a joy in life; the battle was the victory, the strength to win a part of the prize, and he was contented to strive. But to Jennifer only the thing sought was the goal, and the effort to attain it a chore to be endured. Raised in a comfortable middle class family, she had longed to return home wearing the trophy of her warrior husband, and settle to the life of the familiar and cosy so long denied to her. But to Stuart this dull picture held so little value that he barely comprehended its existence, and brushed aside her needs, thinking them whims, until they became the chasm into which their marriage plunged.

Often the weakness and downfall of reason is that it cannot measure its own limits, cannot fathom it's own inadequacies, and Stuart, though a man of much passion, was also a man of much reason. In his small way he had shared the tragedy of many leaders whose vision was greater than that of their followers, who in striving to grasp their crock of gold outstrip the ambition of those they would pamper, and by their effort to be angels of plenty, become seen as devils of fanaticism. This little known rule he had discovered the hard way.

Stuart would have put it into less grand terms. There was no mighty task that he wanted to achieve, no heaven's gates that he wished to storm, only to be active and follow the projects that beckoned his eager will. He saw himself as no angel, and even less as any devil. When friends commiserated with him on his loss he would simply say, " She wasn't as ambitious as me." But he knew that to be wrong, for Jennifer too was ambitious, but not for the striding success that he sought. Her vision was for her life to be softly blended with reputation, and with polish, and these she saw her young lieutenant has having attained. This was sufficient, and henceforth some smaller sphere of domestic duty should be his lot.

But Stuart was in love with the course that he had chosen, and clung to Paa and the trading enterprise to which he had bound so much of his will, given so much of his energy, fastened so much of his determination. He realized now that in Jennifer's eyes his dream was her rival. Yet was his error so great that she should answer it in this fashion, he wondered? Could he forgive her, and should he, even? But what if he were to meet with her at the place of their roots? Might he not then see clearly?

Like some schoolyard bully, this uncertainty had tormented him with ever-increasing strength, and finally joined hands with his growing business frustrations. His sense of purpose was thrown down by these two foes, till bitterness tainted his days, and doubt of all his courses began to drift through his thoughts, gathering like dust on his judgment. The bustling streets of these exotic towns became dreary to his eyes, till even as the strange vistas of the East had entranced the untried young soldier, so now the homely fields of England sang to the older veteran with a song of quieter, long forgotten beauty.

And so he came to be on a plane that would take him cheaply to Singapore, from where he would go onwards over the thousands of miles to England. There he might attempt to glue together the broken pieces of his marriage, or if that were not to be, then he would sever his shackle legally, completely, and strive in freedom for a place in the new world rising from the war's debris. He did not know which of these two intentions was uppermost in him, only that he must close a wound of uncertainty that yawned open and infected.

Stuart aroused himself from his reverie with an almost physical shake. The memory of her betrayal still burnt him, and lately he had fallen too often into these depressing thoughts. He yearned for a cleansing action, for the flight to be over, for the entire journey home to be ended. He might have to endure some delay in Singapore. Perhaps to walk its streets for a day or two would be a healthy change, for he felt that his muscles like his mind had become slack, and cried out for use. More, it was a far bigger, busier place than Paa, as England was, and that might help him to order his intentions.

As though in response to his thoughts, Julia rose gracefully from her seat and walked to the tiny cabin that housed the chemical toilet at the plane's rear. As she passed she cast Stuart a smile that sparked him into brighter thoughts, for by this time he felt certain that she would not repulse his attentions. It was too public in this crowded cabin for any but the most banal of words to be exchanged, and none of them were to leave the plane at Kampong Panwey. Singapore was probably the end of her journey, but for him it was only a staging-place. A pity. She was pretty, but also he saw in her a fresh and natural charm beyond that of many of his recent liaisons, and it struck him as ironical that he should meet with such a one in Paa, even as he finally quit the place.

Presently Julia passed him again as she returned to her seat, and to his delight paused a moment, for the Raven was swaying a little as it passed through turbulent air.

By necessity or design she steadied herself, resting her hand on the top of Stuart's seat. "Have you been to Kampong before?" Her unexpected question came easily, as though they were already friends.

"Yes," he answered readily, though taken by surprise, "to several of them actually."

"Several?" Julia knit her brows in a charming expression of puzzlement.

Stuart smiled to take away any offence from his little joke. "Kampong simply means village. There's quite a few Kampongs about. I guess you haven't spent much time in Malaysia?"

"No.... well... I heard our pilot call it Kampong Panwey though?"

"He was joking. Errol likes his little jokes. Panwey's too big to be called a kampong, but it's a little small for Errol's taste. That's why were going to end the day in Singapore, not Panwey."

"Aaah...." – how delightful this kind of girl was when they made that long "aaah" of understanding, thought Stuart – "now I hope that I'm not going to make a blunder pronouncing Singapore's name. I'm sure I've heard it called Singy on a few occasions, and so I've done the same. Probably I've been talking about the wrong place entirely, and upset no end of people"

"No, not to worry." Stuart felt the world to be a cheerful place again; her rich, plumy accent said London, and money in her family, and her humour implied the pleasant ability to inflict a little self-mockery. "Same place. Although the more precise will never call it anything but Singapore."

"Curious. What do you call it?"

"Well I studied map-making, so I should say Singapore, and be one of the precise. But I've found too much precision to be bad for the health, so sometimes I do the lazy thing and just say Singy."

Julia laughed in an easy, unaffected way, and Stuart was pleased to see that her teeth were white and even. "And are you just passing through Singy, or are you making a map of all of Singapore?"

"Neither. I might stop a few days to see what the opportunities are, or I may go straight on to England."

This was a half-lie at worst. If something appealed to him strongly in Singapore, he might remain a little while.

"And you," Stuart now asked in his turn, "Are you going to become one of the good citizens of Singapore?"

But at that Julia's face clouded a little, and she hesitated. "That's not certain yet..." for an instant her cheerful composure faltered, and her eyes made the quickest of darts to the bulky Arab. She clutched Stuart's seat as the plane made a violent bump, and possibly took this excuse to evade the question. "I'd better sit down before they start to do summersaults," she said brightly, and then she was gone, leaving behind a considerably perkier Stuart.

He watched her settle easily into her seat a mere two yards distant. Raoul neither spoke nor moved as Julia resumed her place, but from the rigid immobility of his thick neck, Stuart imagined a radiated message of disapproval. He smiled a little. It would be nice to stick a pin in Raoul, for whom he felt an instinctive antipathy. There was some mystery here, some contradiction between the openness of Julia and the tense bearing of her travelling companions.

Tension there certainly was, for Stuart now caught the flicker of Andre's eyes examining him furtively before turning fixedly forward. The little Julia said had been for them too much. Too bad for them; typical of wogs: always possessive and secretive if they were around women, and that was probably all there was to it.

After this pleasing encounter, Stuart absorbed himself in studying the occasional islands that they passed, for although Paa stood on an island, it was a large one. Journeying within its interior, or immersed in its petty life, it was easy to forget the dwarfing sea in which it lay, which was dotted with uncounted islands, small and great. Stuart had flown over many of them before, taking their beauty for granted, but now he realised with regret that he might never see these tropical jewels again; and jewels they were, not least in that from this height they were clean of human strife and problems. Often they were untouched from any height, for many were uninhabited, and sometimes not even the size of a good farm.

Some were hills of smooth green, rising steeply from the sea that broke against them as though angry at the insult of the up-thrusting land. At their bases, the soil and rock had often been torn away to form high cliffs, falling sheer to the creaming white surf, and great boulders sometimes lay at the feet of these cliffs, emerging soaked with the retreat of each wave only to be drowned again by the next.

Others islands had a lowland of jungle surrounding the central hills, as though to shelter them from the water's jealousy, and these islands seemed to agree better with the sea, for the dense forest met with the waves as though by polite introduction, the trees yielding to gently slopping beaches, whose smooth sands received the lapping kiss of the waves. Not always, for some beaches were mere narrow deposits of grit, where the salt water struck almost at the roots of the trees, and these Stuart could scarcely see, but others were wide plains of sand empty of even the footprint of human life.

Most islands were fringed or ringed about with coral reefs; banks of living stone that grew upward beneath the water at a distance from the land, until on approaching the light the tiny coral building creatures ceased to thrive. Within the shelter of these reefs the waves were tamed, and the waters formed a calmer lagoon, as though the rearing central hills had thought of yet another courtesy with which to meet the anger of the waves.

After a while the supply of islands petered out, and though Stuart strained his eyes the sea seemed empty in all directions. He regretfully turned from the window, realising he might never see such a sight again, unless it were the harsher beauty of some cold isle of the Hebrides. The hot, noisy interior of the plane was wearisome, and he had nothing on him to read, and Roger was dozing in his seat.

There was a half written letter in his pocket, telling his father of his intention to return to England; senseless to finish it now, when he would arrive home long before it did.

It was at this moment that the Raven's engines coughed and fell silent, and Stuart stared appalled through the tiny window, seeing but not believing as the blur of the propellers faded till the blades stood motionless and useless in the air.

Chapter 4. Flotsam

There was a murmur of consternation in the cabin that rose to cries of fear, cries to know what was wrong. Stuart stayed rigid in his seat, willing the engines to burst back into life. He felt the attitude of the craft change, heard in the absence of the engine's noise the flaps creak as the pilot adjusted the trim, and realised that they were now gliding through the air and must be steadily descending.

Roger leapt suddenly to his feet and headed for the door to the pilot's cabin, but the door opened first and Isaac stood there pale. "Keep in your seats!"

The plane began to bank to the right and Isaac was gone again, the door crashing to behind him. The bank became more extreme; Roger lost his footing and fell sprawling across Andre, who fought to throw him off. Raoul was shouting, demanding to know what was happening, and from the rear came a grinding as the stacked boxes shifted.

Stuart saw Julia staring at him, face ashen, and the girl screamed in a child's high pitch and struggled against the angle of the plane to leave her seat. The nun alone seemed calm; she had reached forward to grasp the child's arm reassuringly, and as Stuart's eye fell on her he saw the foam-flecked sea through the window beyond her. The ancient woman's eyes met his; stern and clear, they made a wordless demand of him.

Then the plane was levelling out again, and Roger fell with a crash from Andre's lap into the isle. Again the door sprang opened, and Isaac ran the length of the plane, clutching the seats to keep his feet, and rummaged frantically amongst the cargo at the rear.

Stuart found that terror was gripping him, as it had not since that desperate night when the Japanese had overrun their camp. With a sudden spurt of anger at the pandemonium around him he threw his fear off, and headed for the cockpit, thrusting first Andre then Raoul back into their seats as they blocked his passage. "Bloody civilians," he grunted, his urge to do whatever could be done calling back his officer's nature.

He stopped in the cockpit doorway. The plane was level now, but the sea was visibly closer, and they were descending fast. Through the windshield he saw ahead an island perhaps two miles distant, their speed making it appear to race across the sea towards them. "What's happening," he asked, forcing his voice to calmness, but dreading to hear the answer.

"Get back," Errol shouted without turning, his attention riveted to the controls, "get back in your seat."

"What's happening?" roared Stuart, "they're all over the bloody place back here."

"We're going down. I have to put her down. Oh God's shit we'll lose her! Get back dammit."

"In the water?" demanded Stuart.

"No in the bloody cocoa you fool." Then sense asserted itself; "get back and break up the seats, they'll float. I'm putting her down in the water just off the coast"

Stuart turned and collided with Isaac.

"Where's the inflatable," Isaac shouted.

Errol hesitated, then "In Paa," he said.

"In Paa!" howled Isaac in incredulity.

Stuart had heard enough. He shot from the cabin and ran the length of the plane to the crates. Seizing a hammer from an open toolkit he began to break the lids from the heavy wooden boxes, whilst a melee of people struggled to rip off the upholstery of the seats.

"Back in your seats! Back in your seats!" came a cry from the cabin.

Stuart ran for his seat, seeing through the open door the island impossibly close, a confused glimpse of bare rock and forest wrapped hill that seemed to rush across the gleaming sea towards them. He fell into his seat as the cockpit door slammed, cutting off the voices of the two aviators that were raised in frantic argument. Raoul was babbling in some language unknown to Stuart, and he heard the nun murmuring steadily in Latin. The child had thrown herself onto the nun's lap and was whimpering softly. Stuart seized the back of the seat before him and lowered his head.

He waited.

In the cockpit Isaac had ceased to curse Errol for the missing inflatable. He could hardly speak as the plane, dropping fast, headed for a long outcrop of rock that ran far out from the island to stretch before them, a barrier they surely could not clear, a barrier into which they surely must smash. "We'll make it, we'll make it," hissed Errol to himself, his face shining with sweat.

"Turn out to sea, turn out," Isaac shouted. But Errol feared the sea. Even the reckless and carefree have their inner dreads, and his confidence in the air was matched by his fear of the clinging water. He had seen this island before, and remembered that its east side was one long bay of calm water, enclosed by two outreaching arms of rock to north and south. They were gliding down, descending rapidly towards the southernmost of these arms, with the island to port and the open sea to starboard, but to reach the bay the Raven must pass over a flotilla of lone rocks at the island's southern tip, then over the low, jagged, wave-lashed barrier beyond.

The Raven was dropping fast; its airspeed was falling, and for good or bad he could no longer turn, but must trust his judgment: they would clear the final wall of rock, and then he must hold the plane steady as it slammed belly first into the water beyond. Errol's judgment was good: a gusty taker of chances in life, he was a skilful pilot, and Isaac clenched his jaw to silence as the final wall rushed towards them. Then they were over, with only feet to spare. But Errol's memory was

44

imperfect, and they saw too late the fearful sight of still more rocky teeth, scarcely breaking the bay's surface, but amidst which the hurtling Raven must now fall.

The Raven's belly slapped down on clear water, but it's speed carried it onwards, a great wake of foam racing out to either side; within yards the right wing struck a pier of rock and was torn away. The impact slewed the plane around as its starboard side ground against the rock, ripping open the fuselage from the wing-stub to the tail, which the rock bit into and tore away. The maimed body of the plane ploughed clumsily onwards into the clear water that Errol had sought, and there it halted, its speed exhausted, settling rapidly as the salt water rushed into the yawning caverns of its injury.

Within seconds the water rose to devour the maimed hull, to drown the narrow windows, to throw spray playfully across the upper structure. Then the waves met across the last remaining metal, and the great bird disappeared beneath them and was gone, leaving only the radiating waves of its death, and some bobbing scattered remnants of its entrails.

The rending din of impact had driven the birds of the forest shrieking in dismay from the trees; one of their great silver cousins that passed over at lordly height had fallen noisily to its death amidst them. But soon they returned to their usual haunts, for the clamour was ended, and the intruder was no more. The waves rolled gently as before, sparkling, creaming as they licked the dark sands, and the bay was as before, its waters the serene prisoner of forest and rock, unchanged, save for a scar on one of the great rocks, and some clumsy land-beasts struggling amidst the blue waves.

*****

The blow of the Raven striking the water shook them, and a cry breaking from many throats filled the cabin; Stuart was never able to remember if his voice was one of them. But that was mild, for an instant later they were hurled forward amidst

45

a deafening explosion of noise and blast of spray as the starboard cabin wall vanished like a paper screen. In its place there was hurtling rock that seized and consumed Andre, seat and all, and then it was gone, and so was Andre, snatched away like a rag doll. A final, world-shaking hammer blow hurled Stuart from his seat, blinded by brilliant light and salty spray.

Stuart found himself sitting on the floor waste deep in water. The whirling motion of the cabin had ceased, and he tried to rise, but a struggling body lay across his legs, and a rolling mass of water picked up the body and threw it against his face, even as it buried him powerfully. He found himself on his back underwater, holding his breath and struggling to stand as an entanglement of limbs impeded him; then he was up, hauling someone upright with him, and standing on the floor of the Raven's cabin chin deep in water.

It was Roger, he realized: limp, helpless and moaning faintly. Stuart drew a hasty breath as the ceiling came down firmly and pushed him under again. Through the blur of the water he saw the great rent in the hull before him, saw the last bubbles of air fleeing nimbly, and knew that their tomb was sinking.

The irresistible inrush of water had ceased, and he jammed his feet against the seat behind, and thrusting hard propelled himself and the limp man through the jagged-edged gap. A tooth of torn metal seized his shoe, and he felt the steady pull of the sinking plane on his leg, drawing him down to death; then his foot came free, and grasping the injured man about the chest Stuart kicked hard and drove up towards the rippling light of the surface.

Stuart surfaced gasping onto the heaving face of the water, half blinded by salt and the reflected brilliance of the noonday sun. Roger seemed barely conscious, but he was breathing hoarsely. To Stuart's horror they faced an empty sea, and he clumsily trod water, bringing their joined bodies around to see nearby rocks newly gouged from the violence of their arrival. Flotsam rocked on the waves in between, and with burning eyes he made out a mass of torn seat upholstery, a hat, one of the lids that he had wrenched from the boxes. But no swimmers, nor any drifting bodies.

Roger moaned, and Stuart saw that the water around them was laced with tendrils of blood. He twisted around more, and to his relief saw the beach behind him, perhaps two hundred yards away. Diving his head beneath the water, he glimpsed through the drifting murk a confusion of irregular shapes that may have been great boulders, and a torn gleaming shape that might have been a plane.

But Roger was struggling, and Stuart broke surface hastily to find him choking, for he too had been pulled under. Stuart looked around wildly; there was nothing in the water to lash him to, no other swimmer to entrust him to. We are alive, he realized. The others, have none escaped? Julia, the poor little girl, the nun? But the man in his arms was moaning again, and Stuart, caught the word, "leg..." and saw the water was now even bloodier. He could do nothing more than help this one, he decided, and adjusting his grip on the injured man he struck out for the beach.

Kicking his legs in a backstroke, Stuart was able to keep the man's head above water, and raising his own head, he scanned the bay again for other survivors. Nothing, but in the water behind them there was a steady trail of blood, and Roger was now completely unconscious.

Stuart ceased to look back, for the effort of hauling the limp body through the water was tiring him rapidly, and the sun was blinding in his brine soaked eyes. He felt his strength ebbing, and swallowing water once at a miss-timed breath he felt panic, until a twist of his head showed the beach close. But there was no movement from Roger, and by the time Stuart felt the sand beneath his feet he knew that he hauled a corpse with him.

He dragged the limp body up through the shallows and laid him on the sand clear of the waves, seeing for the first time the bloody rents in the man's trousers, and tearing the material open he saw the ragged slash that severed the main artery of the thigh. Stuart dropped to his bottom and sat exhausted on the sand, peering through bleary eyes at the scarred rock that marked the Raven's grave.

The waves of the bay rolled playfully in before him, running briskly up the beach to lap his feet, then retreating again, hissing softly. To his right, they broke grumbling on a long, natural pier of rock that enclosed the bay, and occasionally there came a cry from the birds circling overhead, who sometimes swooped low to inspect him, but otherwise a peaceful silence reigned. Of the Raven there was no trace, and even the drifting debris seemed to have vanished.

Slowly Stuart got to his feet, finding that a host of aches and bruises now inhabited his body. He felt drained by the panic and fear of the disaster, but an anger remained small and throbbing, and a mourning for the others arose and grew in him, a reluctance to accept that he alone had lived, and their stories ceased. He swept the sea again with his eyes, noting that some current must move across the bay, for now he saw the odds and ends of debris, drifting slowly toward the seaward end of the rocky arm to his right. He scanned the rocks for any other survivor might have clambered onto them. Nothing.

And closer in, nearer the beach... He started, for there a head was raised briefly from the waves, and now an arm rose and fell in a stroke, and he ran limping and stumbling along the beach to meet the swimmer, who must soon gain the shallows. Again the head, cresting a wave. From where had the swimmer come? But no matter from where, it was another survivor.

He ran painfully, glancing down repeatedly to avoid the stones and lumps of driftwood marring the smooth wet sand of the water's edge. Now he saw the swimmer's head more clearly, her hair streaming thick and dark. Julia? Had she too escaped the wreck? And he forced a little more speed into his faltering legs. The figure reached the shallows and knelt there as though unable to rise, and now he saw it was not Julia, but someone too short and slender to be a grown woman.

He splashed into the shallows as the child rose and staggered forward, exhausted, bent, and reaching for him. Stuart grasped her by the hand, and she stumbled forward from the hungry waves and looked up at him with a bewildered, speechless face. Suddenly she heaved violently, and vomited a stream of salt water that splashed hot onto his feet, and then she sank onto all fours on the sand and crouched there retching. The prim cotton dress was now plastered to her frail body, and her neat straw hat was gone, leaving her face shrouded by her water-dark hair.

Stuart gripped her thin shoulders in comfort as she heaved. But that would pass, and he walked out again into the waves, looking in despair at the now nearer arm of rock where the flotsam was gathering. Nothing. Nothing but minor odds and ends of debris. Now, so close, he was sure. "Waste," he said bitterly, and turned from the sea in sorrow. He became aware that he was clutching something caught between his fingers. A strand of red seaweed had been tangled around the girl's hand, and had transferred to his. He pulled the weed from his fingers and threw the puny missile defiantly into the indifferent waves.

The girl had risen, and was staring out at the bay. "Sister Therese…" she said dully.

He paused, reluctant to speak, seeking words: what should he say? "Gone," he said finally, too numb for tact, "all gone."

Chapter 5. London

It was well past ten am, but the chairman had not yet arrived. Before each man at the long table lay a manila folder, bearing only a number as its title.

Colonel Haig had stared at his folder for a while, playing a little game of trying to guess its contents. The game, which he had played before, was not entirely for his amusement only. He found that it focused his mind onto subjects that it could be dealing with, and from there onto subjects that he would like it to deal with. Quite often he was wrong as to his guess, but the exercise was no less illuminating for that. To form the idea that beneath a cover lay the final report solving a long standing mystery... a proposal to implement a much needed change... an urgent warning of danger from an unexpected quarter...

By the time such a folder was opened, often to reveal some banality, his mind would often have held its own conference, determined its own course in some other troubled area. This satisfied the colonel immensely, for in his game his mind ran ahead, independent of the slow process of discussion and opinion, and his impatience with the waste of his time was evaded. And in any case it would be quite improper to open the folder before invited to do so.

Or at least improper in the eyes of many of the others around the table. Sinclair for example. Colonel Haig had grown to dislike and mistrust Captain Sinclair. The man was too priggish, too certain of himself, too lacking in perception of his own shortcomings. Worse, he was not trustworthy. His allegiance was to... what? That was something that the colonel had not yet completely defined. To his own ambitions? No. Sinclair was ambitious, and Colonel Haig had no quarrel with that, for what was a man without ambition? It was something beyond that, something that the colonel had met before, and learned to mistrust.

His offence in Haig's eyes was that he gave his allegiance to some inner, arrogant set of values that was too often at odds with common sense. There was a fanaticism in him that told Haig that he looked constantly down his nose at other, weaker mortals. This was not uncommon; moreover, a little of it was valuable, but an excess was not, for then it needed the excuse of great ability, and this Sinclair did not have. His mind was sharp, certainly, but sharp to what end? When facts were known, and the power to act lay within his hands, then Sinclair swiftly seizes on the relevant and acted decisively, without hesitation. But when facts were doubtful and a subtle tact was needed the captain seemed to wander, blind and bullish, and as he grasped the known but irrelevant for support his judgement frequently became impatient and rash.

And that, thought the colonel, was the crux. Too much certainty lead to too little inquiry, a useful trait in the unthinking heat of a battle, but now in the quieter more sober field of the intelligence war a fatal flaw. And in his certainty and excess of self-possession, Sinclair had several times strayed unwittingly into conflict with the colonel, who found himself unable to infuse understanding into the captain on these occasions.

So definitely the colonel did not trust Sinclair, did not admit him in his mind to that companionship of those whom he had accepted over the years. And this was a pity, considerably more than a pity in fact, for Captain Sinclair was the colonel's personal aid.

Colonel Haig raised his eyes sharply from the folder. Was this today's lesson? Was this what the dull manila was teaching him? Would the wearisome Captain Sinclair become more than an annoyance, like the chalk box fixed beneath the long blackboard, a chalk box that seemed never to hold chalk? Did the assured young captain perhaps see himself as wiser and more competent than the greying colonel with the thickening waist? Wiser, and more suitable to be in control of the colonel's department, more suitable perhaps to sit in the colonel's seat?

Haig's awareness sharpened, and he became conscious of the younger man seated at his side. He gave no outward sign other than to tap the folder lightly in thanks, but mentally he nodded to himself in satisfaction. At that moment the door opened and the chairman entered.

By ten forty the meeting had reached a halfway mark, and the mess of reports and maps that the folders had concealed lay before each man at the table, sorted neatly or scattered loosely as was each man's character. The chairman had explained the matter methodically, referring to each numbered sheet in turn. It was as Colonel Haig had half expected: Kenya again.

For some time a situation had been developing in this East African country that looked ripe to grow into trouble. The Kikuyu, the dominant black tribe of Kenya, had been protesting their right to farm their ancestral land for years, but to little effect, and the white settlers had slowly denigrated them into little better than medieval serfs. Now came rumours of secret political meetings where oaths were taken, oaths accompanied by the drinking of blood and sacrifice of animals.

Much of this was mere gossip, but here too were lists, garnered by agents and informers who were often discretely referred to only by a number, lists of men who were or might become involved, reports of suspected caches of weapons, reports of planned acts of violence, of murder and of rebellion.

All of these lay before the committee on the polished wood, and together added up to a picture of unrest, of danger in the making. Here lay the indications of many little sparks that might glow a while, and then fade as sparks do. But also they might gather and multiply until they flared suddenly into a blaze of violence.

This was not a new thing in Kenya, nor in any other part of the vast empire that the once little nation of Britain had built, but this year there was a difference. It had been thought wise to oil again the machine of colonial policy, and that next year His Majesty King George VII should visit Nairobi, the capital of this East African country, and from there fly onwards to Australia and New Zealand. To add more delicacy to the situation, the King's worsening health would almost certainly mean that his eldest daughter, Princess Elizabeth, would undertake the tour on his behalf.

Therefore any suspicion of insecurity must be treated with the utmost concern, for as the chairman finally rounded off his briefing, "it would be a scandal of major proportions if the probable Future Monarch should be seen to be unable to safely visit one of the Jewels of Her Colonial Realm."

The chairman sat back in apparent satisfaction at the linguistic flourish with which he had ended his briefing, and drawing his pipe from a side pocket commenced to fill it methodically. To those who knew him well, this was the signal for a change of pace, for slipping down a gear from the polished formality that he found necessary to imparting graveness. Now they would move at the slower, more workmanlike speed of deliberation and proposal.

Cigarettes and pipes made their hesitant appearance in some hands and the chairman waved one hand airily in permission. "Questions, ideas," came his voice, muffled by the pipe stem as he struck a match.

Haig sat silent and made notes on the pad before him as the to and fro of words began. Questions, sometimes to be answered by the chairman, sometimes to be deflected by him to another at the table, and occasionally the promise from someone to find out the facts on this point, or draw up a report on that. Notes onto scratch pads, memos to aids, tentative suggestions that this or that action be taken.

The colonel as usual asked few questions, but took brief notes on the answers given to others, reserving his comments for later. His area was to advise on the use of specialized military units in situations that fell short of actual warfare, and his strength came from a deep knowledge of the past effectiveness of such methods. Military and political history was both his specialty and his hobby, and his gruff, measured voice was second only to the chairman's in swaying the decisions of the committee. This Haig knew well, and marshalled his thoughts in silence, leaving untidy queries on details to lesser mortals.

The committee had fallen into separate knots of discussion, and the chairman knocked impatiently on the table. "Proposals gentlemen. Do we need to advise measures? If so what measures?" As usual at this point, his eye fell first on Colonel Haig. "Colonel. Do you have any suggestions?"

Now was the time that Haig would unhurriedly lay out his thoughts on the subject. He had a reputation for seeing what others missed, for outlining plans both sober and decisive. But today he in his turn drew out his pipe and pouch before passing on the question. "Captain Sinclair. What do you think?"

Sinclair was surprised but not flustered, and neither had the colonel expected him to be other than ready with an opinion. As Haig had taken his notes, as he had asked his own questions, he had also covertly watched the younger man, had seen what points amongst the host of considerations had drawn Sinclair's attention, had seen those facts amongst the whirl of information to which the captain had been indifferent.

"Obviously it's an urgent situation with a great deal of time pressure," Sinclair stated decisively. "We must identify the ringleaders quickly and incarcerate them before the royal visit." He paused briefly. "There may be a problem with what charges to lay, especially if the evidence can't be obtained, so possibly there will be a need to stretch the usual powers of arrest."

There was a faint stir of unease, but the captain continued onwards. "That shouldn't present any problems that will come to the attention of the public until after the visit, and by then the situation will have changed. We're not dealing with British subjects or courts, and a successful visit by the princess should generate a great deal of goodwill. That will tend to smooth over any irregularities that may have occurred."

Not bad, thought Haig silently, noting the buzz of approval from some members of the committee, but not good enough. He sucked on his now lit pipe and waited, festooned in smoke.

Sinclair had said his piece and was sitting back with a sense of worth. The members of the committee were practical people living in the real world, and this was Princess Elizabeth's honour and safety. There would be no prolonged objection to any illegalities that might occur; of this he felt sure.

A voice came from down the table. "But identifying the ringleaders might not be easy. The speaker held up one of the sheets. "This list is sketchy to say the least. Could we be sure of getting them all?"

To the colonel's great satisfaction, Sinclair spoke again. "That's a matter for our people out there. If they need more manpower that could be supplied, the visit justifies the expenditure. And we don't need to get them all, just sufficient to cripple their effectiveness. Those that we miss will go to ground until it's over."

"Might it not be better to cancel Her Royal Highness' visit until this situation is resolved?" came a suggestion from the other end of the table, provoking an immediate outcry of protest. "Unthinkable – laughing stock – natives."

The chairman tapped the table again. "The cancellation of Her Highness' visit is not an option, or at least is an option that we very much wish to avoid." He looked again at the colonel, and Haig knew that it was now his time to speak.

"I agree that we must definitely avoid that option," he said, slowly but firmly. "Won't do at all for Her Highness' own subjects to be seen to be pushing her around." Haig paused in a haze of blue smoke as an immediate murmur of agreement ran around the table, the indignant heads nodding vigorously at this simple expression of their feeling.

"But we can't handle a situation of this sort by bull headed tactics," he continued, raising his voice markedly. He gave a brief, dismissive glance towards Sinclair, as a man might to a waiting dog that he does not wish to feed. "This isn't a military campaign where you can fight once and win completely. By all means cut off the head if you're dealing with an army. Destroy the leaders, confuse the chain of command, win the war. But this isn't war. We are not concerned with a simple case of winning a battle, we are maintaining a peace. The difficulty here comes from discontent giving birth to a popular movement that seeks leaders to listen to, not from officers leading an army. Arresting demagogues in a situation like that proves the value of their grievances to the people who were listening to them, and a day later you have twice as many troublemakers."

Haig paused a moment, resting on the murmurs of approval that respect for his record gave him, whilst the committee digested both barrels of his shot, both his analysis of the situation and with it his rebuke to his junior. "If you go around arresting people without good cause" – and here he turned to look directly at Sinclair, infusing his manner of hearty common sense with a tone of disdain – "then you'd better be damned sure that the British public don't get wind of it, because what you stir up will be worse than before you started."

Colonel Haig paused again, remembering how the British public had warmed to Gandhi during his visit some years earlier, a man the British government had repeatedly imprisoned.

"And in any case what matters primarily is the effect on the situation in Kenya, not what gets printed in the papers here. Arrest the leaders without good cause, or more likely arrest who you think are the leaders, and by the time Her Highness arrives you'll have a whole new set to contend with, probably more than there are now." And the colonel sat back in his own unseen flourish of triumph, conscious of having both irrefutably defined the situation and crushed Sinclair with one volley.

Now the table was again alive with talk, but the chairman cut through it. "What alternative do you have in mind Colonel," he asked, frowning slightly. He did not approve of the colonel using the meeting to discipline his aide, who now sat rigid and motionless at Haig's side, his set face betraying no emotion, yet flushed with suppressed anger.

"A strategy needs to be adopted that will achieve both the needed objectives" replied Haig promptly, unabashed by the chairman's displeasure. "Firstly it would be ideal if we could remove the reasons for discontent, so that the situation cools. But almost certainly we can't do that, so we must appear to be working towards removing the grievances, or at least appear willing to move in that direction. If we can do any of this convincingly -and it has to be done visibly- then popular feeling will reverse and can be kept reversed until after the visit."

He considered briefly; "If we have to start with arrests and increasing police presence, we're moving towards failure. The political boys need to get some talks going, get the known agitators involved, pull in some of the newer names, make them think we're genuinely assessing the possibility of change. Get a talking shop going in fact. If in the worst case it does come to arrests, then at least some of the people who should be arrested may have emerged from the woodwork."

"And what do you feel the second objective to be, Colonel," continued the chairman, a little too smoothly for Haig's liking.

"After the visit we have greater freedom of movement. Then deal with the situation on a long term basis," replied Haig, wary of committing himself in what he knew to be a pure political matter. It was his private conviction that only a genuine redressing of colonial injustices would work in the long run. But in this room his private conviction was best kept private.

Wilson, the quiet one, spoke from the end of the table. "You may not be aware of this, Colonel Haig, but opportunities for discussions of this nature with the native Africans are constantly being pursued, unfortunately often without success."

Wilson was the political liaison chap, and Haig dammed him silently. Justice, he thought to himself, feed me the same balderdash that I'm suggesting we give to the wogs. Valour stirred in him and overcame discretion. "Well if you were saying anything to them that they felt was worth hearing you wouldn't need to pursue them because they'd come running," he snapped, "the root of these problems is injustice, a desire to be done with us and our governing. We can contain that for a while, but eventually it'll burst out, just like in India."

"The policies of His Majesty's government are beyond the scope of this committee Colonel Haig," broke in the chairman sharply, though not altogether unkindly. Like most old soldiers he disliked the slipperiness of politics, but the committee had been formed to advise on practical forms of action, not to criticise its masters, and by that mandate the colonel had stepped way out of line. "Our task is to ensure security, to maintain the rule of law and order so that government can proceed effectively. We cannot expect to be allowed to make policy, Colonel, attractive as that may sometimes seem," he concluded with unexpected humour.

"Well I'm not hung yet then," thought Haig, relieved that his impropriety had drawn only this diluted rebuke. But he had not been too concerned in any case, for compared with the jungles of Burma there was little to be feared from this roomful of tongues, certainly little to be feared from the clever captain, who now seemed to have no more to say. But the meeting was hung, for after this point the opposed ideas of talks and arrests were argued across the table to no conclusion, and in the end a recommendation was postponed, pending further study.

The day at an end, the colonel drove to his home on the outskirts of the city. As always the traffic was heavy, and this evening the rain slashed down spitefully, driven by the icy January wind. At this time of the year it was long past the fall of darkness, and in bad weather like this the journey was a dreary trudge, an endless, monotonous ritual of brakes, clutch, gears. One of the wiper blades was worn and left a blurred trail across the windscreen with each squeaking swipe, swipe.

The road mirrored the lights of the city confusingly, and at one set of traffic lights the colonel braked too late and sharply, causing the car to slide squealing into the junction. He had seen the lights change but had impatiently pressed forward, then changed his mind. He reversed cautiously and sat fuming, angry with himself, as the traffic crossed endlessly before him, headlamp after headlamp creeping densely forward, tires hissing on the flooded tarmac. The daily routine of the drive was wearing on his nerves, the London traffic getting heavier each year, and the weather filthier.

Arriving at his home he ran through the blustering rain to open the garage door, flinching as he received a cold baptism from the damaged fall pipe that he had neglected yet again to repair since the last storm. When the door of his house closed solidly behind him he paused dripping in the warm dark cave of the hallway, the dismal sigh of wind and spatter of rain now faint and muffled through the timber, the rain rattling, cheated, against the stained glass panel over the door.

Before him was quietness, and the flickering glow of the fire showed reassuringly under the door to his left. Colonel Haig had again attained his lair. He extended a hand expertly in the gloom to snap on the electric light, and blinked in the glare as the hallway sprang into sight. He loved the swiftness of electricity, but yearned sometimes for the dim glow of the old gas mantles.

From the door to his left came a call, "Nigel, is that you?"

"Yes." And who else would it be, Haig thought silently, and after hanging his wet coat on the horns of an ancient coat stand, he passed through to the living room to hear how Mildred's day had been.

Later he sat before the fire, absorbing the final bad news of the day. Raymond had dropped by during the afternoon, and as usual news of Raymond's doings brought the colonel no pleasure. At twenty-two his eldest son was long past the age at which Nigel Haig expected him to firm out into some kind of a worthwhile young man. National service had not toughened him, nor had education sharpened him.

Raymond was a branch from a family tree rooted in solid, quiet achievement, but he was a weak and wayward branch, swaying leafless in the world's winds. He was clever in his studies, yet had none of that firmness of intellect called character. No strong desire seemed to arouse his interest, no well-formed purpose called him to action. He was tall, but without that carriage of his height that should make him imposing, strong, yet vague and indecisive. Neither the army nor the city had fired the growing youth's will to more than feeble effort, and slowly, grudgingly, the colonel had admitted to himself his understanding of his son: the finished man was without direction or goal, and always would be.

Once his only child had been part of the pride of his life, but with the passing of the years the boy had slowly drifted from him, had pawed with disinterest at the dreams that the colonel had dreamt for him. And now the son who he had once proudly named had grown to be a stranger to him, and the cold ache of disappointment lay not only in that he was a stranger, but in the gulf between the bright vision of what was to be, but now was not.

For there was an abundance of strangers in the world, and they caused the colonel no grief. Being strange, they were strange to his guarded affections, and became, if they crossed into his world, the interesting pieces in his chess game with life. But this man had been a boy whom he had held and in his cool, precise way cherished, for whom he had seen a future of proud manhood, where he, the colonel, strong and victorious, would be joined on the pedestal of achievement by his younger equal, by the man who had sprung from this boy. But it had not worked out that way, and now it never would. His son was as he would be, unless some great change should occur in him, and of such a change the colonel had long ceased to hope.

And now, today, what great news had arrived from this son by route of his mother? The colonel grimaced at the dancing flames. Only that the boy had quit another job; nothing unusual in that. "No better than a coolie," Haig growled to himself, but this expression of his feelings did not purge his disgust, instead it lead him deeper into his sour mood. What the colonel needed he did not have, yet he could neither obtain it nor resignedly accept the lack, and in the fire-lit room his personal blackness grew. Better that the boy should not come around. Better that he had never been born. The self-righteous Sinclair irked him, but at least... but the colonel could not define why Sinclair should be better, and this angered him still more.

Well then blast them both, he thought.

Better than thinking of either of them was to remember the real men that he had helped to build, like Soames or Ellis. They had had their faults, they had been raw green hands, but all had in the end emerged from the war amounting to something. The memory of the war years cheered him, and he leaned back into his armchair with a creak of leather, rubbing the balloon of his brandy glass reflectively. Yes: Soames, Ellis, Lister. Where were they now? Lister had attained the rank of major, and Ellis was still out in Malaya, or was it the Philippines?

Ellis had taken the least expected route, setting up as a trader. That to Haig's mind was a step down from the life of an officer, but fortunes had been made out there, and once the big war was over soldiering had bored Ellis, and so the colonel had regretfully wished him good luck. Ellis would succeed. A pity about his wife though; left him, or so the colonel had heard. Silly chit of a girl. Another good man bedevilled by a woman.

Soames had married the daughter of a successful Birmingham manufacturer, and gone to that city to help run her father's business. The colonel hadn't heard from him for a while, but at the last news he was doing well, apart from the usual trouble with the trade unions. As the girl was an only daughter, it seemed that someday he would own the business as well as run it. Well, they had all done their bit when it counted, and if Soames made his bundle, the colonel didn't begrudge it to him.

The thin chimes of the clock on the mantel struck the hour, and the colonel found that he was on the point of nodding. Slowly he drained his glass, and positioning the guard carefully before the dying coals, he braved the chill drafts of the hallway, and following his wife's earlier route ascended the stairs to his bed.

Chapter 6. Jest

Many years before, a great palm had fallen, torn from its roots by one of the typhoons that often sweep the South China Sea. Mightier than its neighbours, it stood at the edge of the forest, where soil gave way to sand, until it crashed heavily to the sand to lie stretched at the feet of the other, still living trees at the beach's highest point. For years it had lain there, its saps drying as the life of the island teemed around it, and to the scuttling crabs and insects it had no more significance than the thousand other pieces of fallen timber.

But the human eye seeks order and seizes on the familiar, and when Stuart turned from the water's edge he saw in that hulk of dead wood a familiar thing, a thing that some landscaper working with nature might have put in that place for the relief of a weary traveller. The bleached trunk, although indifferent to the two people at the wave's edge, offered the only welcome to the Raven's two orphans, the sole promise of sustenance.

The girl stared at him dully when he spoke to her, and he pointed to the great log, and taking her gently by the arm drew her with him in a slanting course up the beach to the only comfort he could offer her, the natural seat that the typhoon had long ago provided. There the dense forest cast a cooling shadow onto the beach, as the fire of the sun, now past its zenith, moved into the west.

The girl sat like an automaton at his bidding, and watched him mournfully, expectantly. What now, he thought, noticing that his own hands were trembling, where to go from here? Where were they? They were in a bay, perhaps half a mile of narrow sand trapped between the waves and a wall of greenery, bounded at either end by an arm of the island. They were closer to the southern end of the bay, where again he noticed debris drifting to the enclosing rocky pier. He was loosing hope of other survivors, but what of bodies? And had she not appeared as though from nowhere?

Still the girl did not answer when he spoke, and he told her gently to wait, and left her seated on the log, trembling and silent, staring shocked at the water as he paced hastily down the beach. He clambered cautiously along the rocky arm, swiftly examining each fissure and inlet into which a body might have drifted, unable to accept that only he and the girl had escaped the sinking plane. But he found no one, and the long arm was treeless and barren, hiding nothing. Beyond it to the south lay neither beach nor land, but only the open sea over which they had flown. Useless; surely there was more to this place?

Looking back down the beach, he saw that its northern boundary was a higher, tree-topped cliff, an arm of a tree-shrouded hill that rose from the further forest. There was no sign of human life within the bay, but what lay beyond it, beyond the trees? The hilltop was bare of trees; it would be a good place to see from, but he dreaded how little he might see.

He returned to find the girl still sitting, but now sobbing quietly, and he gazed helplessly at her, and at the water and the newly scarred rocks beyond, trying to comprehend the sweeping disaster that had placed him there. He struggled to accept that the Raven and its dead would not rise again from the blue waves, as though to announce that it was all some jest, for which playful fate would now apologise. But more than that, he struggled to accept what he had known even as he glimpsed the island through the windshield of the Raven: it was small, and such islands were rarely inhabited. Were they alone on some small rock with little more than the clothes that they stood in, and neither food nor water? He forced the knowledge back in frightened denial; there might be a village, he must find it, and the high ground would be the place to look from.

"Won't some people come?"

Stuart started and turned. She had not spoken since saying her companion's name, and he feared that she might enter some form of permanent shock. He saw enough problems without a hysterical schoolgirl, and chose his words with care. "It may be some time...can you walk?"

She nodded, staring at him dumbly, eyes too bright and wide.

"We need water." He must move, get the two of them moving, put something together before the girl realised that the crash was only the start of their disaster. "We might have to wait awhile...and we'll need water." Even as he spoke he felt thirst beginning to nag him, felt the slow deadly lick of the tropical heat. He pointed into the dimness of the forest. "There's a hill behind all these trees. We might find water there, seeping down from the high ground. I could go..."

"No." The girl jumped to her feet, startling him with her sudden energy. "I'm not staying here."

"Come on then, we need to get things done before it..." he choked back the "gets dark," and set off north along the beach. Coconuts, he realized as he passed a palm; they contained milk if there was no water, and the tall, leaf-headed trees dominated the tree line the length of the beach, though the climb up the great, smooth trunk was no joke. The girl had followed him closely, but now she halted, staring beyond him fearfully, and Stuart realised that she was looking at the corpse that lay not too far down the beach, almost forgotten by him. He had seen many corpses. "We can't do anything for him now," he said, realizing his error and forcing himself to speak gently. "We have to look after the living. That's us."

She nodded but did not move, and he grasped her firmly by the arm and turned their course into the forest to avoid passing any nearer to the dead man. He was thankful that she followed without fuss, and he aimed their footsteps northwest, steering by glimpses of the sun flickering down through the canopy of leaves, heading towards the low hill now hidden from them by the forest. It seemed cooler here, and he was glad that the hiss of the surf was muted by the denseness of the trees, hiding its useless, maddening message of nature's indifference. "What's your name dear?" he asked, feeling that he must somehow encourage the girl's recovery and restore some normalcy to the world.

The answer came back softly, "Tania."

"Well I'm Mr. Ellis. Stuart Ellis." Something scuttled grunting through the undergrowth behind them, and the girl leapt forward with a squeal of alarm and stumbled over a fallen branch. Stuart caught her by the arm as she nearly fell. "That's nothing. Sounds like a pig," he rasped impatiently, almost snarling.

God, this was an impossible task, he thought. On a damned island God knows where with sweet bugger all and a kid to look after too. Why the sodding hell had this happened to him? If there were no drinkable water to be found then what the hell would he do? And if no one ever came to this island? He was used to the jungle, and knew that food could always be found, but water! The girl stumbled again behind him, and he rubbed a hand over his brow as though to massage away the weight of the problem. What if she went into some screaming hysteria? What would he do then? He remembered only too well Jennifer's ridiculous fear of spiders. Better if one of the others had survived instead, then he would have someone to fall back on, then there would be more chance of making it, then... But this was how it was, so there was no use to "what ifs."

He glanced back at the girl walking a little behind him, and felt a tinge of shame. She was eleven at most, and barely up to the height of his collarbone; the skirt of her dress was torn to shreds on one side, and her eyes were swollen from crying. He stopped, for he had noticed for the first time a gash on her shin, caked with dried blood. "Here let's look at that dear," he said, stooping, for he had realised that she had been limping since they left the beach. "Does it hurt?"

"No, not much. I hadn't noticed it. It must have happened on... on the plane," she finished with a quaver.

"Yes" he said. " It was bad." He knelt silently for a while, taking a few long, slow breaths, realising that he must now undo the knot that the crash had tied into his nerves, that frightening as it was for him, it was worse for the kid. "It must have been very bad for you," he added. Her eyes were brimming again, whether from sudden realisation of her cut or from the memory of the crash he did not know. They had walked away from a mess that had killed others, and he had been too hasty in counting that as uninjured. "Have you got any other cuts?"

She shook her head. "No, nothing big. Will it make a scar?"

"I don't think so" Stuart replied, "it looks superficial. Not very deep that means."

"I know," she said, "I've heard superficial before."

She sounded almost resentful as she wiped away a tear with the back of one small hand, and Stuart felt that at another time he might have smiled. "Come on then," he said, straightening up quickly, for he could see that the kid was beginning to discover the host of minor cuts and grazes she had collected, and feel the ache and sting of them. "Don't worry dear, I'll look after you." They moved of again, and she followed him, silent but uncomplaining. "We'll be all right." He searched his memory. "What did you say your name was dear?"

"Tania. Tania Webster."

She was bearing up; perhaps they would be okay. "Well, you call me Stuart."

The water at least was soon found. Arriving at the rise that was the beginning of the hill, they turned west to work their way around its base, and came to a fissure running deep into the hillside. Much of the rain that fell onto the island's northern hill gathered into this narrow ravine, dripping from ledge to ledge to finally form a tiny stream that trickled down, running clear over smooth stones to end in a dark pool, from which the hint of a stream seeped away westward amongst the trees.

It was this pool that they came across, and they gazed dubiously at its leaf-crusted surface, beneath which the water looked murky and stagnant. But a faint tinkle of falling water came from the ravine, and passing by the pool they entered the ragged crack, and followed the wet fallen rocks of its rising path to find a miniature waterfall trickled from the edge of a great slab. Wholesome or not, the separating drops of the trickle sparkled in the sunlight as they fell and splashed musically into a little pool below, their quiet beauty forgiving much doubt, and Stuart cupped his hands beneath the tiny Niagara and drank. The water tasted thin and clean after the heavy salt of the ocean, and lacking the means to boil it, he had little choice but to trust it.

In turn they drank and drank again from the falling water, the girl gathering handfuls from the falling trickle and washing the dried salt from her face in a neat, cat like way, Stuart following suit with a more vigorous rubbing. He sat back onto the wet stone, enjoying the cooler air of the ravine, feeling that a corner had been turned, that some measure of safety had been achieved by this small re-establishment of order.

A question had risen to his mind once or twice, and now he voiced it tentatively, ready to let it go if the girl's reaction was too painful. "How did you swim ashore?" She looked at him blankly. "I mean I didn't see you when I was in the water, I was looking around but I had to get the man ashore."

The kid's eyes became wide. "She pushed me out. Sister Therese... she pushed me when the water came in..." the girl stopped, shuddering at the memory, and then the words came out in a cleansing rush. "And the water was choking me... I was under the water... and I came up and I saw a rock, and I swam to it but it was all rough and hurt my hands and I swam round it to where I could hold on at the other side. I could see over and I saw you swimming to the sand holding the other man and I shouted but I couldn't shout and you didn't hear. The waves kept pulling me off and I thought that you would leave me so I let go and swam after you, except I swam to where the sand was closest."

Stuart nodded. She had probably clung to the very rock that the Raven had torn itself upon. "Did you see anyone else? Besides me and the other man?"

She shook her head. "No." She squeezed her eyes shut tightly. "That native man who was with the fat man and the lady. When the plane got all smashed up, he got... pulled out."

"Yes," said Stuart, "I saw that. I think he must be dead"

"I saw him," she continued, " I think it was him. He was in the water but he was all... smashed up. He was all covered in blood and he was under the water drifting. I saw him when I was under the water, I think it was him."

The girl had opened her eyes wide, and Stuart saw the horror of the memory in them, heard the shrillness in her voice. He reached out and took her by the hand quickly. "That's alright, forget about it now, you're alright now." He held her hand for a while and massaged it clumsily, conscious of the trembling of her fingers.

"Why did that man die?" she asked suddenly. "The man who you got to the sand?"

"He was bleeding," Stuart answered, "his legs were cut in the crash and he bled to.... he bled too much whilst we were still in the water, before we could get to the beach."

"Oh the poor man." He noticed vaguely that she had produced a sodden handkerchief, which she twisted anxiously into a tight knot as she spoke, wringing it until salt drops fell. The picture was to stay in his mind, as many petty details do, and he was later to wonder how she had managed to hang on to such a commonplace thing. "Could you have bandaged him up or something if you hadn't been in the water, you know, stop the bleeding somehow?" she asked.

"I don't think so," Stuart answered, "the cuts were very bad. The big artery in his leg was cut."

"Artery?"

"Vein dear, like a vein."

"Oh. Where will they bury him? I mean, will they take him back to Paa? Or will they take him to England. He was going home to England."

Stuart rose abruptly and helped her up. The knowledge of where the man would be buried and by whom had been in the back of his mind, growing and hardening to a certainty for some time, and he should avoid encouraging the kid to chew on the mess. She was recovering, and like all children, seemed to have a host of questions. "We have to go on a bit farther," he temporised, "let's look at your hands." Her hands were covered in minor scratches, but they were clean, like the one on her leg, and he reflected that salt water was supposedly an antiseptic.

They left the ravine and started to climb the hill, Stuart pushing ahead eagerly. He would be able to see farther from the summit, and as they ascended the trees thinned out, until the ground levelled and they emerged onto the flat hilltop. There was no sign that it had ever known inhabitants. Smooth and barren, the tangled grass stretched before them to the north, a gentle slope, broken only by the occasional straggling bush. They were again in the full glare of the sun, but at this slight elevation there was a faint cooling breeze.

Looking back, he could see over the jungle through which they had passed to the great C shape of the bay, and he strained to locate the plane amidst the jumbled shapes of rock and coral that choked the rippling waters. But the jagged piers of rock defeated him, for the surge of the waves around them confused the eye with foam and shifting reflections.

Turning from the bay he marched the scant fifty yards to the west side, the girl bobbing at his elbow, and here he stopped, as unspeaking as dumb stone, for the sight was worse than he had expected. They were looking down the other side of the island, and it was no more than a tree-shrouded slope that ended in the empty sea. He could have thrown a cricket ball into the waves without taking another pace.

They had more than half crossed the island already, east to west, and he doubted that they had travelled as much as a quarter mile. There was no hope in the south. There, the island was even narrower, for this new, western coast swung in towards the bay, and the island tapered, until the two sides joined in an jumble of sand, scrubby bush and tumbled rock, from which the long, stony arm enclosing the bay sprang out, like a yawning, skeletal jaw, completing the great bite of the bay's arc. Only the north remained unseen, and so far he had seen no trace of human life.

The girl was wandering, turning uncertainly from side to side as she took in the narrowness of their world. Suddenly she spun and ran like an arrow, heading for high northern point of the slope.

"Hey wait," Stuart cried, and hared after her in pursuit, "don't run... wait," for fear rose in him that she might plunge into another crevasse, or over a sheer cliff edge. Outrunning him, she stopped suddenly at the hill's high point, and catching up to her he too was forced to an abrupt halt, for the north end of the hilltop fell away steeply in a crumbling, treacherous slope, in tier after tier of minor cliffs and landslides that ended in a final cliff edge twenty feet or so below. He could not see the waves that struck its base, but could hear them pounding dully, and see the white cream of their defeated retreat, and beyond that drop, beyond those waves, again the open useless sea.

"It's LITTLE!" she cried shrilly, and he grasped her shoulders firmly with both hands, fearing that worse might come. But she sat down abruptly on the grass.

"I think he will be buried here dear," he murmured, "I think I will have to bury him. There isn't anyone else here but us." But this he murmured only in the lowest whisper, for it was only for himself.

Chapter 7. Ceremony

He sat with the girl at the cliff's edge for a long while, encircling her shoulder securely with his arm, and rubbing her hands occasionally as though to massage the world back to rights again. He talked to her softly, explaining that they must be patient, and not get upset, for in a day or two help would come, and they would be safe. They sat at the very edge of the grass, their feet grazing the treacherous slope, and as he spoke he kicked the loose soil occasionally, sending dirt and pebbles scurrying down, and though the child did not join in the game she became calmer.

Perhaps he had said the right words, or perhaps it was the atmosphere of peace there, where the silence was broken only by the cries of birds and the dull crash of the waves below, and the careless beauty of tree and rock, grass and sand leading on all sides to the turquoise and blue of the ocean, distancing and diluting the savagery of their arrival.

As the mild, neat prettiness of a graveyard soothes the grief of the mourners to a duller ache, so the vista of unhurried nature blunted the urgency of their distress, and gradually they became aware that though calamity had snarled at them, it had not bitten them to the bone. There must be no haste now, he thought to himself as he spoke, no haste, no panic. They were alive, and if he were methodical they would come through unscathed.

She nodded as he spoke, though her eyes were hard with strain, and she twisted about anxiously, scanning the empty skies for the searching planes that he suggested. His own mind cleared as he became more assured of her calm, and he took her gently by the arm and led her as they made a circuit of the hilltop, looking for the tell-tales of a worn pathway, or a faint plume of cooking-fire smoke rising from the forest below. Neither was to be seen, so they returned to the northern peak of the hill and descended its steep western slope, keeping the rocky northern terraces close by their right hand, and emerged from the trees onto a narrow beach where the waves lapped almost at the feet of the trees.

A few yards to their right, the western beach ended in a tangle of jagged boulders, the waves fighting between them to lick the foot of the cliff. Neither by walking nor climbing could they circle the island in that direction, so they turned away and followed the narrow, log-fouled beach south, peering into the forest for any sign of human dwelling on the hill's slopes. Within a minute, the land seen through the trees levelled as they left the hill behind, and they passed a wet ooze, seeping from the forest into the sand, which he guessed to be the end of the stream. The beach widened, and the tree-line curved steadily to the left as he strode methodically on, the anxious girl at his side trotting briskly to keep up with his march.

The island was narrowing towards the low southern point that he had seen from the Raven's cockpit, and he guessed that the log that marked their starting point now lay through the trees a mere two-hundred yards to their left. Finally the wave-smoothed sand steepened and the beach narrowed again, the trees petering out into low scrub and rearing pinnacles of rock.

As the waves broke at their feet they were forced to turn their steps left into the broken area of rock, bush and sand, for it was the island's southern tip, and they picked their way cautiously through the tangle, stumbling over boulders sometimes slippery from the close crashing of the waves. They did not have far to go. Within yards they could see ahead the out-flung arm of rock that Stuart had scrambled on in his final search for survivors. Reaching it they stopped, finding themselves again on the beach, and they gazed silently in dismay at the bay that had received them, and nursed the ruin of their plane.

The log lay little more a hundred yards before them. They had nearly circled the island, and it was beyond doubt that only they dwelt in this tiny kingdom. The girl said nothing, but looked up at him with a face that seemed age by grief beyond her few years, and he bit his lip and strode forward again until they passed the great log.

"Let's see the lot, right to the far end," he said, summoning resolution, and grasping the girl's arm he steered her firmly down the beach and past the sprawled body, giving it a wide berth. This time she made no protest, but gripped his arm tightly as she trotted past it briskly, keeping pace with his impatient stride.

The central part of the bay was free of the thicket of rocks that chocked the southern, but ahead at the northern end the waves creamed as they washed over a jumble of reefs. Beyond them was a low cliff, no more than thirty feet in height, that seemed to be one side of a narrow, stony spur, springing out from the hill before ended in its own final cliff.

The beach grew steeper and narrower as they approached this cliff, and suddenly he saw what he had hoped for. Set in a narrow gap between the trees was an angular, unnatural shape of poles bearing a sagging mass of thatch. Stuart broke into a run, the girl following close at his heels, but as they approached the hut he slowed. The leaning poles, the collapsing thatch; both spoke of age and neglect. They entered the hut's open front to find that it had obviously been years since the place was inhabited, for within there was nothing more than a litter of discarded rubbish, half buried under the thatch, which had fallen in great swathes.

"Horrible place," muttered the girl tearfully, backing out of the entrance, "and nobody lives here."

Stuart picked his way through the debris, and gave a grunt of satisfaction as he left through the rear opening, for he had entered an ancient, overgrown garden. "Yams," he announced, starting to dig with his hands, "someone lived here long enough to grow yams." He dug up several of the ugly roots, and returned to scour the abandoned debris. There were several crude wooden bowls in a corner, caked with long dried food, and between them lay a strangely shaped jug, glazed, and bright with yellow and blue flowers, but spoiled by a piece broken from its wide mouth.

He puzzled over its strange shape whilst the girl sat forlornly outside the entrance, and turned it over to discover the name of a Staffordshire pottery on its base. It's a vase, he thought, made to hold flowers in somebody's home, and somehow it ended up out here. It must have been a prized possession to these native people, but it got broken, so they left it. But left for where? Nomadic islanders perhaps, wandering these scattered islands as the fancy took them? Would they return?

Stuart brought the vase eagerly from the hut, explaining that people came here and sometimes lived here, even though they were only natives in canoes. The commonplace piece of pottery with its familiar trademark felt like a link to the lost real world. People had been here, and they would come again. More, it would hold a day's water, and so he bore it in triumph down the beach and scoured it in the sea, together with the yams, before leading the way back to the spring.

It took time to fill the jug, for the slow trickle of water seemed less even in this short time, and the narrow canyon was falling into shadow as the sun descended towards the west.

"We have to make camp somewhere," he announced, holding the precious jug carefully before him as they picked their way from the canyon.

The girl looked at him in horror. "Where?" she protested, "there's only that hut, and its horrible. It must be full of fleas."

Stuart didn't feel the ancient hut attractive either. "We'll have to sleep on the beach," he said, "we have to sleep somewhere."

"Can't we..." she began helplessly, and stopped, no more capable of finding an alternative then he.

"We'll be all right," he assured her, "when I was in the army we had to sleep in the jungle night after night sometimes, and it was full of Japs. There's nobody to bother us here – unfortunately," he finished ruefully.

But still she looked doubtful. "We don't have any choice," he said firmly, "if you don't like the hut we can sleep by the big log. We'll have to pretend we're camping out or something," he added ingeniously, "and in a day or two somebody will come for us." He hoisted the jug aloft and set off for the beach.

Keep going, he thought. Keep doing the stuff that has to be done, and we'll get through. It's no good worrying about tears; they'll pass. This is no time for committee meetings. But still, he realized, a gentle hand as well as a firm one. He had chivvied patrols of grown men through far worst than this, but this was a slip of a schoolgirl, and it seemed unfair to expect the same kind of stoic endurance from her, but what choice was there? But to his relief the girl followed him meekly, though on reaching the beach he fell sombre again, for the patient corpse still awaited him. He lowered the jug carefully to the sand, conscious of the girl hanging back timorously.

"I have to bury him," he said gently, gesturing at the corpse. Already it had lain for hours in the sun, and by tomorrow it would be bloated hideously, but it was best not to tell the girl that. "This is a hot country dear, and you have to bury people quickly. That's the law."

"Where?" she whispered.

"I'm going to take him right down to the end of the island, where we crossed all those rocks and sand. There's no need for us to go down there again. The water's at the other end, and the natives lived up there so that's where everything must be. I'll have to carry him down. You stay here..."

"No. I can come with you."

"Okay then dear. Bring the jug. No, better leave it here for now, with these yams."

With a struggle, he hoisted the dead man awkwardly onto his shoulders, while she watched round-eyed, and resigned himself to bearing the weight to the southern rocks. The girl followed in solemn procession a pace or two behind as Stuart laboured stiff legged beneath the corpse's weight, his feet biting deep into the sand at each slow stride across the lengthening shadow of the trees. Twice he stopped, lowering his awkward burden gently to the sand, conscious of a need to treat the dead with what respect he could before an impressionable girl.

By the time he reached the dunes he was exhausted, sweat streaming from him, and seeing a hollow close between two low rocks, he lowered the body gently in with the last of his patience, and dropped gratefully onto the rock beside it. The sun hadn't stopped its descent though, and he soon rose and commenced the dismal task of feeling through the pockets of the unfortunate journalist's clothes, making a neat pile of the few possessions, and lastly attempting with difficulty to remove the wedding ring from the dead hand. It was not the first time that he had performed the unpleasant task of making such a final tally of a man's life, but he girl's presence made him uneasy, for it weighed on him that this was not the kind of thing that children should have to see.

"We have to take his personal things back to his family," he explained briefly, having the ridiculous feeling that the girl might think that he was robbing the body. Again the solemn nod from a very church face, but she winced as Stuart spat on his fingers, and moistening the dead finger finally succeeded in slipping off the ring.

"His wife will want this," he concluded, placing the gold band on the pile. The wallet yielded a few papers, one of them a press card bearing a photograph and name. "Roger Dawson. This is Mr. Roger Dawson. We have to do... the final things for Mr. Dawson." She looked around at the scrubby grass of the dunes.

"I know it's not like a proper churchyard, but we have to bury him today. Nobody might be here for days but us." He dropped the last sentence out with deliberate, brutal frankness; the half-pretence could not go on forever.

"I know. I know there's no one else here yet. We have to do everything."

He was pleased at the reaction. He would give her something to do. "Do you know any prayers dear?

"Yes. We said lots of prayers at the Institute. But I don't know which to say. Don't you have to be a priest to say prayers at a funeral?"

Stuart was arranging the limbs and grooming the tangled hair as best he could. "When people got killed in the fighting sometimes they had to be buried where they died. Then I had to say the service from the prayer book."

"Were you a soldier?"

"Yes, I was an officer. And officers have little books for things like this. But I don't carry mine anymore so I'll have to remember the service as best I can."

"Oh. What if you get it wrong?"

"Well, in that case I guess he might jump up again." But that was wrong; her shocked stare told him so. "Only a little joke dear. Sometimes you have to make a little joke, even at serious times. It helps sometimes you know."

"Sister Agatha said that…" the girl began and then stopped.

He straightened from his task and came slowly to her side. Together they stood over the shallow grave in unconscious imitation of the countless mourners who have stood at countless graves, pondering as to what proper thing to do to tidily mark the untidy end of a life.

Finally Stuart spoke, reciting as best he could from memory the service for the dead, fitting in words that he felt appropriate where memory failed him. Then he fell silent again, and held the silence for a while in his mind, unknowingly offering a place to be filled by an understanding that he did not expect to come, from a God in which he did not believe.

He looked at the girl. Her eyes were closed and her lips moved silently for a while, then she fell silent and looked at him.

"I have to get stones now to cover him," Stuart explained, and pointed to a patch of wave-rounded stones. He came back with as many as he could heap within his arms, and began to place them on the body.

"This is what you have to do when you don't have spades to make a proper grave," he explained, for the girl again looked doubtful.

She turned away, and he paused and followed her with his eyes as she went to the nearby bushes. There she started stripping the great broad leaves from some fern-like bush that Stuart could not name, and he abandoned his task to fetch more stones. He returned to find that she had piled the leaves by the body.

"They're soft."

He understood, and gently covered the pallid face with the leaves, then went with the girl, and they tore and carried armfuls of the leaves until the still figure was shrouded generously, as might have been an island king. When he went again for stones the girl accompanied him and bore back what she could, laying her burden by the green mound for Stuart to put in place.

"I don't think you should have come dear," he said, pleased none the less at the girl's actions. "This isn't a very nice thing for a young girl to have to see."

"I wanted to come," she replied, "he should have somebody at his funeral."

Stuart looked up from his task in astonishment, a tinge of respect for her colouring his mind. She looked at him with a timid but level stare to which some life had now returned, and he noticed that her eyes were a clear green, and her face held the promise of beauty to come. "Yes he should dear. When I see his wife I can say to her that a young girl came to his funeral and said some prayers for him." A funeral, he thought, a funeral, like most people have, and this was a person, this is Roger, not just a body to be got rid of before the heat turns it nasty.

Finally the cairn was completed. They stood for a moment contemplating it, then turned away in the slow, reluctant, backward looking manner that mourners have on leaving the unwanted ritual, and returned down the beach, dark now in the long shadow of the forest, and left behind the headland of harsh rock.

The girl hesitated and hung back as they approached the log where their few possessions lay. "I have to go…"

After a moment he understood. "OK, you… go. Don't go far though. It's too dark for getting lost"

"I'm not a baby," came back low but tart as she disappeared between the trees.

Stuart nodded tiredly and went for the jug. Children could be difficult at times, or so he'd heard. He and Jennifer had never got to that stage. He had a penknife in his pocket, and he started to laboriously pare the gnarled skin from the yams, carefully, for in the fast growing darkness he could scarcely tell yam from fingers. There was a better knife in his bag, and he stopped his peeling at the thought and cursed softly. Everything was in his bag, not just his knife, but – damnation - his money too, and the glass that he needed to start a fire.

He groaned aloud, for tomorrow he had a task, and not an easy one. If the bag was in the plane that was bad enough, but if it had drifted away… he let out a vigorous curse and shook his head. There was nothing he could do tonight, and the bag should still be on the plane, for he'd had enough trouble getting out himself.

The girl returned through the near darkness, and he held out a piece of the raw yam, but she rejected it with a dismal shake of her head. He was not so hungry either, he realized. He hadn't eaten since early morning, but he was not yet ready to insult his stomach with the tough, uncooked root. He laid it aside and scraped the soft sand into a hollow with a raised hump for a pillow, whilst the girl resignedly imitated him.

"We shall have to sleep here tonight. It'll be okay if it doesn't rain. This island's not big enough for dangerous animals, so we should be okay."

The girl sat for a while silhouetted against the stars now appearing in the growing blackness. Finally she lay back. "Do you think they'll come tomorrow?"

"They know the Raven's missing already. They'll come. Don't be frightened. There's nothing dangerous here."

"I'm all right," she replied, but he heard the quaver in her voice.

"Tomorrow we'll build a fire on the beach and make it smoke," he said assuringly, "then when a plane passes they'll see the smoke."

The girl was quiet for a while, then; "there's a lot of bits of wood on the beach, and there was a lot in the forest."

"Sure there is," he replied, encouraged. The kid was finding things to be cheerful about, so hopefully there'd be no tears or fears, and they could get some sleep. "Lots of it, and we've got water, so there's nothing to be scared about. It'll be light again before too long."

All was coming back into shape. The kid was calm and no real trouble, they had no real injuries, they had water, there was food, by tomorrow the search would start... His mind ran down the inventory as the stars blazed brighter overhead. Over the hiss of the surf, he heard the rustle of the girl removing her sandals and arranging them to improve her makeshift pillow, as he had done with his shoes. He prattled some disjointed words of comfort for a while, but she did not answer, and he lay back silently, willing her to sleep. Tomorrow... water... search...bag.... Restlessly his mind repeated the anxious tally, until sleep like a waiting predator seized and devoured him.

Tania lay back quietly, but sleep did not come quickly. A numb alertness seemed to fill her mind, and as though from a distance she surveyed the day's events dully, until a burning anguish to be back in Paa suddenly flooded her; to be back and all this not to have happened. Sister Therese was gone, lost there in the horrible water, and she was here on this horrible little island full of dead people and this man who trod on her foot and buried people. And they had to sleep here all night in their clothes – my case! The thought shot into her mind. It was gone too, with all her things in it! Mum's photo and Dad's photo! And her clean underwear! But the man was clever, and he might be able to find it. He would fix things. But what if she died here! He would bury her too, under lots and lots of stones! He must have buried lots of people, he knew all about it! And he'd shouted a dreadful swear word in the dark. Perhaps he was really a ... one of those people who buried people!

She looked fearfully at the black hump of his shape. Was he asleep already? Did he sleep quickly after he had buried people? But he had run down the beach to her, and he had found the nice place where the water trickled, and he would get a plane to land even if it took days. He was clever and he would look after her. If only it were morning. And so thinking she too drifted into a restless sleep.

In the night she cried out hoarsely, and reared upright, confused by the starlight beach and the grumbling surf. But the man sat up also and spoke to her. She stared at the dim form, not knowing who it was that spoke soothing words. Then she remembered and lay back "I had a dream...." But her words were a thick mumble before she plunged back into the confused depths.

She was dreaming again. The dead man had come to her with Sister Agatha, and they were both dead, and they lectured her on how to do a funeral without loosing your case. Then they got hold of her case and pulled it and pulled it and pulled it.... She awoke again with a cry, but this time knew it all to be a dream. The man was asleep. Or was he dead now and she alone? He did not move, and she could not hear him breathing, only the surf hissing. She reached out tentatively, wondering if she dared to poke him, but he was too far away. He grunted and stirred slightly and she lay back quickly. Again sleep came, this time deep and unbroken.

Chapter 8. The Deep

Clunk. Again. He had heard it before. Clunk. This was bad. There was a clunking, and a growing light was probing his eyes painfully. He covered his eyes with his forearm. Clunk. And clunk. His arm was gritty; his back ached. Clunk.

Remembrance flooded in, and he sat up swiftly in dismay, his eyes springing open to a vista of sand ending in rippling blue sea, framing the brilliance of the rising sun. He was trapped on an island, and it was morning.

Clunk. There was a pile of wood on the beach close by, and the kid was throwing more on top. Then she scurried back to the trees, and he rolled stiffly onto all fours, discovering his body to be a continent of aches. He assembled himself slowly upright and watched blearily as she returned with an armful of dead timber and dropped it onto the pile. Clunk.

The girl stopped and regarded him gravely. "Mr. Ellis, is this the right place for the signal fire?"

He nodded dully. "That's okay. Good girl. That's good," and staggered woodenly into the forest, his bladder bursting. Had she hurled them into the sea his answer would probably have been much the same.

Returning, he dropped back onto the sand and reached for his toes, his muscles first protesting and then yielding into suppleness.

"How will we light the fire Mr. Ellis?" she asked him as he stretched, his shadow long in the rising sun.

"Magnifying glass" he mumbled dully – damnation, even his tongue seemed to be aching – "I can use a magnifying glass to focus the sun."

"Do you have a glass?"

"There's one in my case."

"Your case. But where's your case?"

"On the plane."

"But the plane's in the water."

"Yes. So soon I will be in the water. If I want my glass that is."

"But how..."

"Tania. I shall swim. Be quiet a bit now please." She turned silently away and went for more timber, and he continued to twist this way and that, driving the ache and stiffness from his body in preparation for his task. Soon he rose and snatched up the jar. "Tania, I'm going for water. Stay hear and if a plane comes run up and down and wave your arms."

"Will it come this morning?"

"I don't know," he said impatiently, "but be ready." Then he was gone into the sparse jungle, retracing their steps of the day before. The brief walk to the fissure was soon completed, and he filled the jar and immediately set of back to the beach, noting gloomily that the trickle was now considerably less than it was the day before. Surely a plane must come, he thought as he hastened, but he had been betrayed by too many certainties in the past to depend on this. Fixed routines and schedules were almost none existent in this part of the world. It would take time for their none arrival to be noticed, time for the first lazy inquiries to be made, time for someone with a sense of responsibility to become involved and prod the uncertain engine of search into motion.

Back at the log, he found the girl fingering the yams doubtfully. His head had cleared and his body felt looser after the brisk walk. He dumped the heavy jar onto the sand and sat beside her, studying the fatal rocks and making estimates of his abilities. He was not too happy with his assessment. A few years ago the exertions of the day before would not have left him with the aches that he felt today, but civilian life had eroded the edge from his former hard fitness, and he dreaded the task before him. Failure or worse was possible.

"I must get my glass. I've got a glass in the case to light a fire, and a knife. We need the glass as soon as possible." He was talking as much to marshal his thoughts as to inform the girl. "We can light a fire, a small one, and keep it alight. Then we can light the big fire from it quickly if a plane comes. So I shall have to swim out and try to dive or there's no fire." He paused, his face abstracted as his mind pierced the layers of water and danger to the sunken Raven, and entered the jagged hole of the metal tomb. "If it's stuck or the plane's turned over... we shall have to do without it. I can light a fire some other way, but... there's other stuff we need." He visualised the seat he had occupied lying opposite to the great gash. The bag should be under the seat. Could he descend so far? And if it were stuck, could he pull it free?

"My case is on the plane too," the girl said quietly, breaking into his musing.

"Yes dear but what's in it?"

"My things."

"Well they're not too important are they?" he murmured abstractly.

"They're important to me!" she flared unexpectedly.

Stuart looked at her in astonished resentment. "We have to be practical," he snapped in annoyance, "I may not be able to get down there at all."

"And Sister Therese she's down there too," the girl continued unheeding, "you can't leave her down there!"

Stuart jumped to his feet. "We're lucky we aren't down there with them," he barked, "if I get the glass that's all we need."

He started down the beach angrily. God! How impossible the kid was. She followed him and stood at the water's edge as he waded out.

"Mr. Ellis..."

"Yes," he called back tersely over his shoulder.

"Please... if you can get it..."

He looked back. Her eyes were tearful again and he softened. "I'll try. But I might not be able to. You look out for planes," and he dove shallowly forward into a steady breaststroke, aiming to the left of the scarred rock to which she had clung, swimming rapidly to warm his body into a confidence that he did not feel.

"Be careful." Her voice drifted out to him like a lifeline, and hearing the words he forgave her obstinacy.

It was not a great distance, and he had been a strong swimmer since his early teens, but he knew little of the sea and feared sharks or some other watery predators. The sandy bottom fell away rapidly as he left the beach, and soon he was peering down through the water after every few strokes, dipping his head beneath the surface to seek the smooth geometry of the man-made amidst the rough, coral encrusted shapes that loomed up at him through the steadily deepening water. Shoals of brightly coloured fish twisted sinuously through the valleys of the sunken landscape, and aquatic plants waved lazily at him, but so far nothing threatened. Occasionally a single larger fish would dart beneath him, but nothing moved larger than his hand.

His reckoning was out, for as he approached the scarred rock he saw no sign of the plane. He turned before the rock and headed north for some yards before turning again for the beach. And suddenly it was beneath him, a long fish-like shape, spoilt by the deformity of the remaining wing with its stubby engine. It lay nestled amidst the rough irregularities of the bottom as though hiding in ambush, but the torn side seemed clear of obstruction and the depth less than twenty feet.

He paused for a while, resting and breathing deeply and steadily, fixing his mind on the widest part of the great rent through which he had escaped, gathering both air and courage. Two hundred yards away, the girl stood minute and motionless at the water's edge. Suddenly he drove down his head and extended arms, throwing his legs upwards and driving for the place where the missing wing would have been.

His skills were rusty, and he found himself descending clumsily at too shallow an angle, which brought him over the nose of the plane, passing through clouds of browsing fish, which unimpressed by his performance parted languidly to avoid his touch. At the nose he paused, turning about in the water with a deliberate slowness to waste time and breath, and so rein in his anxiety to rush and snatch the needed goods. With slow strokes he approached the cracked glass of the windshield, and peered in through the blurring water.

In one seat a strapped body lay with the head thrown back as though sleeping. The pallid face was gashed and tiny fish busied themselves at the wounds. The other seat was empty, and Stuart sought with his hands to gain a grip somewhere on the fuselage and hold himself steady as he studied the mystery. Then he saw high up against the glass, within inches of his face, a pair of flying boots, and he realised that one of the two in he cockpit had died undrowned and floated to the roof of the cabin. He brought his own feet to rest on the windshield and thrusting hard shot to the surface.

Stuart took his time breathing deeply and recovering from the sight. He knew there would be worse within the passenger section, but now he felt more confident. Positioning himself a little off the side of the plane, he took a deep breath and dived again, steepening his angle as much as he could until he found himself at the centre of the great rent where the wing had been.

Again slowing deliberately, he felt carefully at the jagged edges of metal, remembering the slashed legs of the journalist. He meant to do only this and rise again, but through the blur and gloom he saw his seat with the bag beneath it, a mere two yards away, and in a sudden decision pulled hard on the torn metal, propelling himself into the semi darkness of the plane. The scavenging fish scattered tamely as he entered, and fine tendrils of some drifting black fabric parted before his face and stroked gently down his back. Ignoring all else he seized the seat leg with one hand for stability, and with a feeling of triumph drew the leather case easily from beneath the seat. Its weight helped him to stay low and turn smoothly to face back to his entrance.

As he turned, he found himself looking at the dead and bloated body of a woman floating against the roof of the cabin. Mercifully her face was turned away to the roof, but the swirling black hair that he had admired hung down in a curtain, billowing slowly in the current he had caused, the contrast of its beauty making the sight even more hideous. Holding the case before him he shot low through the exit hole, cringing at the touch of Julia's hair.

At the surface Stuart found himself gasping and fought down an urge to vomit. The case was heavy, but he swam with it slowly to the rock and laid it on the flat top. Like the girl before him, he found no easy place to rest, and he swam round to the other side and hauled himself onto the rock. It was over. The worst was over. He had the glass and the knife too.

Easier than he had expected. Julia's body had shaken him though. It was bad enough that men should drown, but a woman... And a woman who only a day ago had been beautiful to him, and was now a thing of horror. He found himself trembling despite the scorching sun, which was now climbing higher as the morning advanced. "Come on," he murmured to himself. He had seen death before. And at some time someone would want an account of the accident, someone would want a tally of the dead, and there were two not accounted for, the fat man and the nun. Sister Therese the kid had called her.

He looked over the rock at the tiny distant figure waiting patiently on the beach. The kid was fond of her, and they were travelling together. Perhaps the old nun had been a special friend to her. He slid back into the water and swam back towards the location of the plane.

They had been fortunate, he told himself. They were uninjured and soon would be rescued, and the plane that could have lain hundreds of fathoms deep was only in about twenty feet of water. Now, though still tense, he felt more confident, and the exercise had chased the stiffness from his limbs. Again he dove and entered the sunken tomb a second time, the fear of being trapped in this deathly place gnawing at his mind.

Forcing himself to ignore the dead woman, he grasped his seat again and looked to the front of the plane. The fat man was there, entangled in the buckled wreckage of his seat. His mouth was open and his eyes stared dully at the cabin roof. One more, thought Stuart, and turned to the rear of the cabin, seeking the final corpse of this ghastly cemetery. But both seats were empty.

Puzzled, Stuart pulled himself forward and encountered an obstruction on the deck, which his questing hands resolved into two cases. Feeling his breath running short, he heaved both in turn through the rent, and following them resurfaced, to take only a few breaths before diving again and retrieving the smaller. He added it to his own on the rock. It was a small cheap cardboard case with the initials T. W. stencilled on the side. Tania, he thought, and again returned and dove to the plane.

Again he entered, and searched the rear gingerly, the fear of being somehow trapped receding a little, but despite the half darkness and the confusion of scattered cargo, it was certain that the nun's body was not there. He ran his hands gingerly over the jumble on the deck and traced out the shape of a steel container, hinged and clasped at one end like an ammunition box. It proven heavy, almost too hard to lift, and a memory came to him of watching Isaac sweat as he loaded a series of such boxes onto the plane. Machine tools! Errol had said machine tools.

Stuart snapped the fastening open quickly and raised the box with an effort, upending it to pour out a silent stream of the small sharp cutting tools. The container was light now, and he pushed it easily through the narrow rear end of the rent in the plane's hull. There were several of them, and some kind of tarpaulin or sheet here also, and that he seized by a corner, hauling it energetically free before he exited the plane and deftly pinned it beneath the heavier case.

On surfacing Stuart waved to the distant girl jubilantly. They could light a fire, and they had steel boxes to cook in! Filling his young lungs he dove again, and seeking the boxes he came across another small suitcase that he quickly pushed through the rent, then groped again through the now familiar debris until his hands found the tool box in which he had frantically rummaged as the plane hurtled to its end. This he hauled out of the Raven bodily through the wide central opening, and dropped it to the sandy bottom before rising to the surface again.

With repeated dives, he found tools that had spilled and – heavens! – a coil of rope, and hidden beneath it a machete. All went quickly to the growing pile outside, and finally he smartly emptied two more of the steel boxes and thrust them through the narrow rent close at hand.

He had perhaps become overconfident, and stayed almost to the limit of his endurance, for turning and kicking out a little too abruptly he jammed his ankle between a seat leg and some unknown piece of debris. For several long seconds he fought in vain to free himself, the rigid metal biting into his ankle, his lungs crying suddenly for air. Panic entered him and raced hot and frantic through his body, until almost accidentally he turned in the right direction, and his foot came loose. Frantic for air he swam hard at the opening and shot to the surface, where he gasped and cursed for a while as he swam slowly forward, recovering.

No more, he told himself as his composure returned with his breath. That was enough. They had all that they needed now, more than enough. It would be foolhardy to seek for more, not courageous, and the child on the beach would not survive without him. He would not enter the Raven again. They had all that they could use, other than a radio, and even if he could recover the massive weight of the cockpit radio, they had no source of power. If it was damaged that would be beyond his skill in any case.

No more. The rear of the plane was bad, but the cockpit would be a death trap. If the two Americans had a flare pistol they could keep it, and play with it through eternity, and their pricks as well, pair of idiots. The sunken dead would have to remain there for now, and if they stayed there forever they would be none the deader, so goodbye.

By now he had swum a little more to seaward than previously, and he gave a start as he glimpsed far below him a dark shape. A shark? No. But some kind of great manta ray? It was spread black and winged on the bottom. Then the shape resolved, and he recognised the black flowing robes of the old nun. But how did her body come to be outside the plane, he wondered? A woman so old and so resigned to her God? Had she too struggled for life at the end? Taking a deep breath he dove again.

The nun's body lay wedged face down between two rocks, the black folds of her habit rippling softly. The floor of the bay had fallen away steeply in these few yards beyond the wreck, and the depth was almost too great for him. At the limit of his endurance, he seized the back of her robe, and drew her body from between the two rocks, but the water seemed to pull upon her heavy garments, and after raising her body only a few feet he was forced to let go and surface again.

As the body sank, he saw it drifting as though caught by a current, finally coming to rest several yards from its original position, in deeper water still. Surfacing, Stuart checked his position against the rock and saw that he was even more out to sea. Here, where the shelter of the south wall ended and the water deepened, a current was definitely at work, and the seabed was sloping rapidly to a greater depth. Again he dove, but the current had grasped the body again, and it seemed to flee tauntingly from him, slowly drifting before him with a gently serene motion down the unknown slope, into a dim depth that he could not attain, the black robe decorously concealing the dead limbs as in life.

There was a chill in the water here, and the current tugged gently at him as though enticing him to follow her. His lungs ached for air, and the water, thick and darkening, seemed to encase his limbs heavily. He ceased the struggle to force himself deeper, and bidding the ancient woman a silent farewell, he rose to the surface, and returned to the rock where his case lay drying with the girl's beneath the steadily rising sun. Pushing it before him he headed thankfully back to the shore.

Chapter 9. Fire

The waterlogged case had drained on the rock, and the air now trapped within gave it a little buoyancy. Stuart was able to progress by pushing it before him, sometimes thrusting it ahead to relieve his stiffening arms with a couple of strokes of free swimming, sometimes swimming on his back to drag it beside him. The trip was neither fast nor easy, but he was rewarded, for the girl met him at the water's edge as he emerged streaming, and looked at the case in awe.

"You got it!"

"Yes," he answered, "we were lucky."

"Was it difficult?" she asked timidly.

"Yes. We were very lucky. It's only in about twenty feet of water." He broke off to point out to the place. "If we'd crashed at the other side of that rock we could forget about getting anything. The water gets deeper suddenly."

He threw the case down by the woodpile, and opening it rooted through the sodden contents until he found the magnifying glass and knife. He shaved some chips briskly from a piece of the dry wood and used the glass to focus a spot of burning light onto one of the chips, until a spot of it smoked, and then glared red. Finally a tiny flicker of flame rose, and Stuart cautiously laid other minute slivers of wood within the flame until they burned together in a bonfire no greater than his thumb. Laying larger chips on this flame, he made a fire that soon sent a wavering tendril of smoke rising into the clear morning air.

The smell of the burning wood and the faint crackle of the fire seemed to announce a victory, and he sat back with a laugh. The girl must have felt it too, for she was smiling for the first time since he had met her. "I got your case too," he said, quietly satisfied at his achievement.

"I know. I saw it."

"You must have sharp eyes then."

"It's not so far," she answered.

"Nearly too far for us though," he reflected aloud, "you must be a good swimmer."

"Mummy taught me. She was a champion swimmer." Now she looked sad again.

"Where's your mum," he asked, knowing the inevitable answer already, but feeling that he must ask.

"She died. She died when I was eight," she said matter of factly. Stuart fed more wood to the blaze.

"What about all the people on the plane? Are they..."?

"They're still there dear," He answered. He had made up his mind as he swam back. "But we shall have to leave them there until someone comes with proper equipment to get them out. I couldn't get very far into the plane." He hesitated, considered her youth, but not wanting her to think that all things would come easily. "Some of them are caught up in the wreckage. In the broken metal that is."

"Urgh..." she hid her face with both hands. Obviously he had said quite enough. "It must have been horrible."

"Yes. Very. I almost got trapped."

The girl tore her hands down and looked at him with the unashamed horror of a child. "How?"

"I got my foot trapped."

"Where?"

"In the back, when I was looking in the back."

"Not when you were looking for my case!"

"No, after that. I was looking for... something else."

"Sister Therese?" she whispered.

"Yes. But she wasn't there." Stuart thought it best to leave it at that, but the girl persisted.

"Where was she then?"

"She must have got out of the plane." He hesitated to go on, but she would want to know. "I found her farther out, out where the water gets deeper." He gestured out to the rock again. "I think she got out of the plane but... she was probably too old to swim. I found her farther out, and I tried to bring her back but the water was too deep. And she drifted farther out still. I'm sorry. Was she your friend?"

The girl nodded, looking sad and thoughtful. "She was nice. She was my favourite. She used to tell me stories about the Pyrenees. They're mountains. That's where she was born. It's in Spain." She paused. "What will happen to her? Will the people be able to find her when they come?"

Stuart chewed on the awkward question for a minute. "When people die at sea, they bury them at sea. I mean when they die on a ship the captain will bury them at sea." The girl considered this. "Perhaps that's better," he went on, "perhaps it's better to be in the sea than buried in the ground. It's... freer. The sea's a lot like mountains. She might have liked that, perhaps." he finished lamely.

But the girl understood. She nodded, and for a while was solemn and absorbed. "What about the lady? The one that you liked?"

Stuart looked at her sharply. "You mean the lady with the two men?"

"Yes. The dark haired lady. You liked her didn't you?"

"Yes. But how did you know that?" he asked, wondering if he was really so transparent.

"I just thought you liked her," the girl replied quietly, and turned hastily to fiddle with the fire. "I saw you talking to her," she added, "did you know her before we got on the plane?"

"No. No I hadn't met her before. She was just someone I talked to on the plane. But ... she's down there too I'm afraid. It isn't very nice at all down there dear. It's best not to talk about it." He rose and considered the sky, which was still empty of any sign of hope. "Now I'm going to bring the other things back. Keep the fire going and if you see a plane put some bigger pieces on, but don't smother it." He went to the tree line and returned with a mess of green leaves. "You can make the fire smoke more if you put this on," he explained, throwing some of the greenery onto the blaze. "In fact build it bigger and keep it smoking."

He left the girl again busily collecting fuel, and swimming out to the rock returned with her case. She pounced on it eagerly and snapped open the flimsy catches, as Stuart busied himself spreading his wet possessions by the log. He had not burdened himself heavily for the flight, for in many ways the frugal habits of jungle campaigning were with him still. A few shirts, a second pair of shoes, and he smiled with satisfaction at the sight of his razor —a sudden wail of anguish startled him; had the girl burnt herself? He ran the few paces to where she knelt over the case, her face twisted into furrows of misery, her knuckles pressed to her mouth.

Laid in the case amidst a tangle of sodden clothing were two photographs in cheap frames. One was perhaps of a man and a woman, the other perhaps of a woman. Both were stained and blurred by the salt water that sparkled merrily on the glass.

Chapter 10. Caviar

It was mid afternoon, and again the trees were casting their lengthening shadows onto the beach. They sat together silently within the shade, their backs to the great log. By each lay a scorched steel can from which they had ravenously scooped Stuart's cooking. It had only been yam, but at least it was stewed to softness. Farther down the sand the fire still burned, half choked with a covering of fresh leaves that sent a column of thick white smoke into the still air. Stuart glumly watched the waves drag a branch back and forth, knowing he would eventually retrieve it; they would need a lot of fuel. It was mid afternoon, and as yet they had seen no plane, no ship.

The girl was silent and downcast, and Stuart made no attempt to break her silence. Her grief over the ruined photographs had disturbed him in a way that the disaster of the crash had not, and even now he feared almost to speak in case he reawaken her sorrow.

She had cried bitterly over the two pictures. No, not cried, but howled like some wounded animal, and he stood by her uneasily, unable to find words to sooth her grief. Her sorrow came in great racking sobs, as though from some intense world within her, where their passing feast of death and fear was made trivial by a grimmer, stronger brew of endless loss, drunk unwillingly by her heart to its bitterest depths. Her pain was primal and unmasked, violating and shaming him. Here was something that he could not solve nor deal with, could not cure with the brisk hammer and nails of his ingenuity, and he was reduced to standing in clumsy tongue-tied embarrassment by her side as her slight frame shook to the hoarse noise of her pain.

Finally he had placed an uncertain hand in comfort on her shoulder, and she twisted swiftly away from his touch, and snatching up the pictures stumbled from him to the log, where she wiped them tenderly dry with the ragged skirt of her dress.

He had left her to the privacy of her distress, and returned to the water to ease the nag of his helplessness with further salvaging. He was hungry from the morning's exertions, and their newly found cooking pans still lay sunken beside the plane. But he had scarcely waded knee deep before there was a pounding of feet on the sand and the girl was splashing into the waves after him.

"Where are you going? Don't go!" she cried and seized his arm, her nails biting his flesh in her agitation.

"The other cases, Mr. Dawson's case. It's still on the rock. And some other stuff," he explained, wincing.

"But you might drown. You might drown out there. Don't leave me. I'm sorry."

He detached her grip gently from his arm and coiled the arm around her shoulders, holding her tightly for a while, feeling her tremble, and murmured confident assurances to allay her fears.

She looked up at him from eyes bright with tearful fear. "But you might get trapped again, you might drown. I'll be here alone. We don't need anything. We'll be leaving soon."

He put her from him gently. "I'm not going into the plane again. Everything I found is on the bottom by the plane. There's some cooking things. If we eat this yam raw we'll be ill." Still she looked at him, pleading silently. "It's all on the bottom, and we must have it. I don't have to go inside. Promise."

Finally she had let him go, and in trip after weary trip he ferried most of their salvage back. The girl, though she now seemed to loath the touch of the water, entering the waves unbidden to her waist, and taking the articles from him as he wearily turned for the next load.

He had returned with the final haul tired and faint, and set water to boil in one of the steel cases as he chopped the coarse yam into it. The yam being boiled to softness, they sought the shade and dipped their hands in eagerly. He ate ravenously, and the girl's hunger matched his as they snatched chunks from the still hot water and sucked their scalded fingers. Finally he laid his can aside and relaxed back into torpor, allowing the steady hiss of the waves to lull him, drowsing into a brief sleep from which he awoke with a nervous jerk. He had dreamt briefly that he was still in Paa, but he was not, and the horizon was empty, and the fire sent up its smoke in vain, and the girl sat with her head bowed.

Slowly his drained strength crept back to him, and with it the confidence that comes from the satisfaction of a difficult task achieved. We have food, he thought, we have food and fire, and we won't starve, and I'll start to boil everything, the water as well, and we won't get poisoned either. I don't need to go down to the plane again. Now we have to wait. A grunt came from the trees, reminding him of a possible meal. Not such good news for you little piggy, he thought, not if we're here many days. Saved again Ellis. Cheer up, it's like the Ritz Hotel here.

The girl had raised her head at the sound of the pig, and he gave her a contrived smile, but she remained silent, and he sensed the pain still moving within her.

They were only photographs, he told himself. She would get over it soon. Just a child who had been through a rough experience, and naturally she was upset. Her friend was dead and her few photographs were spoilt. But silly to carry on so when they were lucky to have lived through the previous day's disaster. Better to think of the plane or boat that would eventually appear on the horizon and take them away. Then all this could be forgotten, for she would be safe with people who understood how to look after little girls, and she could sleep in a proper bed, not on a dark gritty beach, and eat proper food from a proper plate. When she got back to her own people they would throw away her torn dress and give her a new one.

And he, he could go on to Singapore and then on farther to Gloucester. He closed his eyes against the monotony of the sun as his mind, yearning, reached out and roamed the streets of the far off city of his birth. His father still lived there in the old house, and though his mother was gone, there was auntie Janet who he had always been close to, and her children, Robert and Jane. They would be nearly twenty now, both of them. It would be nice to see how they had grown, especially scrawny Jane. And Jennifer... but his dreams shied from Jennifer. She was not home, not his salvation. She was an uncertainty, an intruder who had pierced and scarred his life and then fled, perhaps forever. He turned deliberately from the thought of her, the boil in the flesh of his mind. She was not his home, she was alien to him, as alien as this island that now confined him.

Despite their quarrels, his father was now his home, and the house in which they had lived and he had grown from a child. The long forgotten friends of those years stood out suddenly in his mind, seeming now to have been the best of companions. He would seek them out, he would meet them again, they would laugh together again. He had survived. He was young. The depths of the bay were not for him, were not to be the final end of his travels. He had again met the beast of disaster and evaded its clutch; he had survived and was only delayed. He would go on.

He would raise a glass in celebration in Singapore, raise more than one, and he would have a real meal and curse all rickety airplanes, and then he would go on. And once home he would raise a glass again in the familiar smoke stained pubs of his extremer youth, and curse all crazy Yank pilots to hell, and all this would then become a story, just as the war had become a story. He would tell the story, the story of his last mishap in the east, tell how he had survived the crash, and survived on an island alone, apart from some young girl.

And the girl... And the girl would go on too.

His thoughts came back from the great distance, and he glanced at the girl sitting cross legged on the sand at his side, chewing steadily on a piece of the still stringy yam. She looked up, and seeing him watching her forced a weak smile, then turned her gaze back to the yam. Her smile encouraged him. The minor tragedy of her photographs was over, hopefully.

Yes. She would go on too. But... He hesitated on the verge of a question, but refrained still from speaking. Where would she go on to, he wondered, watching her from his eye corner. To whatever place the orphanage had been sending her to of course, where they would give her another cheap cotton dress like the one she wore now, with a row of buttons fastened primly to the neck, and perhaps another straw hat with a ribbon to add polish to her bondage.

He had seen the girls of the orphanage occasionally in Paa, walking in a sedate crocodile under the watchful eyes of the nuns, the little ones holding hands, and the older, soon to be young women, with longer skirts as if in imitation of their holy captors, their hint of youthful bosom lost beneath their uniforms. The nuns, he had noticed with amusement, kept these older girls the closest to their side, vigilant to ward off the taint of the world. How would they fare after the orphanage, he had wondered. Would they at sixteen or seventeen be bent to the ways of the convent? Or would they flee gladly into the outside world, finally to end as good wives to suitable young men, raised like themselves in the true faith. "If any can be found," as he had joked once to a friend when they passed such a procession on the streets of Paa. But this one was not so old by several years. Beneath the thin material her chest lay flat, and it mattered little that she had opened the front by a button in the sticky heat, revealing her slender collarbones.

For the first time he noticed a glimpse of gold at her throat. A fine chain rested on the pale skin, curving over the delicate bones, incongruous with the plain material from which it peeked. Stuart studied it for a while, then seized on the opportunity to break the gloom. "That's a pretty chain dear," he ventured.

She raised a hand quickly to her neck. "It was my mum's. She gave it to me. I'm not supposed to wear it though. Sister Agatha kept it for me in her office." She fingered the chain guiltily. "She gave it to me when we left the Institute. I was supposed to put it in my little brush case and give it to the sisters in Singapore." A faint but triumphant smile crept over her face. "I put it on though and they couldn't see it under my collar." She leaned over to the case that lay close by, and pulling out a box opened it. "I was supposed to keep it in here with my personal things." She took out a hairbrush that had seen much use and pulled hairs from the bristles fastidiously for a while, then tried to brush the dark blond hair that hung tangled to her neck, her free hand pulling at the knots.

Glad of the improvement, Stuart went to his case and fetched the small round mirror from his shaving kit. She positioned it on the log and sat before it, shuffling back to get the proper distance, craning her neck from side to side, a child in untaught imitation of womankind. Feeling much encouraged Stuart ventured another shot. "My mother used to have brown hair like you."

"It's blond," she replied with a touch of severity.

"Oh" He didn't argue the case.

She broke off from the brushing and looked at him apprehensively. "You won't tell the sisters about me wearing my chain when we get back will you?"

"No" he shook his head in genuine promise "I don't talk to nuns much."

She worked at her hair a while, cajoling it into some kind of order. " Are you a Catholic?"

"No" Stuart replied, "I don't go to church much. My family wasn't very church going."

The girl brushed on. "You might go to hell then," she commented finally.

Stuart looked out at the scarred rock, and the indifferent waves rolling over the hidden wreck to lap the scorched beach, and refrained from the obvious reply that came to his mind. "Are most of the nuns older than me?" he asked instead. The girl paused and looked at him judiciously. She probably thinks I'm fifty, he thought.

"Yes, lots older. Most of them."

" Then they'll probably get there before I do," he capped the exchange smartly and jumped up. An idea had occurred to him. Taking one of the branches from the pile, he went some way north along the beach, past the trampling of their footprints, and digging it into the sand began to gouge out a long curved furrow. The girl followed him and watched, puzzled, until the shape became clear.

"It's an S" she exclaimed, "are you writing your name?" He laughed and started to scrape another line close to the first, broadening the great letter.

"No. Something more useful. S-O-S. Save our souls." Then seeing that she didn't understand, "it's an international distress signal. Everybody understands it."

"Will airplanes stop if they see it?" she asked, and at his "yes" ran to fetch her own stick, and thicken the S still further as he went on to add the great circle of the O. "Save our souls," she called to him, scraping determinedly, "is it a prayer?"

"No, it's just easy to spell in Morse. S O S. Three short, three long, three short." He peep-peeped a while in imitation, determined to improve on the revival of their spirits, but the hoped for laughter did not come. The simple message completed they retreated from the roasting sand to the shade. He felt reawakened now and started to gather branches of the leafier type and pile them by the log. Here the irregular line of the jungle's edge was notched back to form a little sand floored bay, an extension of the beach onto which the tide did not rise. The trees lay on two sides of this little V shaped area, and the shade was deeper here.

There were clouds on the horizon, and he knew the storms of this sea could be severe. If rescue was not today, then they would need shelter, and this space was already half-roofed by the outstretched branches. If he could complete that roof it might prevent even more discomfort, and so thinking he began to twist his materials this way and that, laying gathered branches and fronds between the overhanging branches of the living trees.

"Do you like living at the Institute?" he asked presently.

"No, not much."

They worked on for a while in the deepening shadow, the girl watching his design and passing branches to him. He tried again. "What about the nuns, the sisters, whatever you call them?"

"Some of them are all right," she answered. "I don't like one or two of them. But my friends live there as well. I had to leave them." After her reply she fell silent again. "But I wasn't going to live with them for much longer," she volunteered unexpectedly after a while.

"Who are you going to live with?" Stuart asked. But she made no answer to this question, and he did not pursue one, for of course there was no other place for her but the institute. Instead he took the knife and began splitting green branches into long pliant strips in hope of making some form of bindings. As yet he did not want to cut the rope.

The shadows lengthened with no sign from the outside world. They had busied themselves through what was left of the afternoon, feeding the steaming fire, struggling to master the unaccustomed task of thatching a shelter over part of the space, sweating as they scavenged yet more wood to feed the fire. And always their eyes and ears strayed to scan the empty skies yet again, to imagine yet again that they heard the drone of an engine.

By nightfall they were weary of coughing as they reeled back from the smoke of the fire, weary of twisting stubborn foliage into place, but at least they had shelter of sorts. It was not pretty, and it was less than Stuart had hoped to achieve, a mere untidy heaping of branches and leaves that centered on the tree growing nearest to the log, but it would turn some of the rain when it came. The sheet had proved to be a cotton sail, and he spread it beneath the crude roof to ease the gritty discomfort of the sand, whilst the girl made a neat pile of their few things. Perhaps this bit of dolls-house work pleased her, he thought as she sat on the sail, hugging her drawn up knees as she watched him poke at the fire, he feeling hungry again but too weary for the chore of cooking. The girl looked as tired as he felt, her face a primitive sketch of ruddy flesh and deep black shadow in the red glow of the fire. "Are you hungry?" he asked, groping reluctantly about him for the containers.

"No." She slumped back onto the sheet. "Can we find something else to eat tomorrow?"

"Tomorrow we might find a plane," he replied, laboriously attempting lightness. He turned from the glare of the fire and looked up at the brilliance of the clear tropical night, the myriad stars overhead painting the narrow strand of beach with a soft dim light, the wet sand glimmering faintly after each withdrawing wave. Behind them, the thin jungle was an impenetrable mass of darkness, and to the north the cliff was a black wall, cutting off the bright display of the sky. "Tomorrow we might get caviar in Singapore." There was no reply. The girl slept.

He sat a while looking at the stars, musing on his new status of lost traveller as he drank in their sharp beauty. The salvaging operation had been fruitful, bringing them the means to live in some kind of decency, raising them from gnawing raw yam and sleeping on sand. And they had water. They would survive, of that he was now sure, and despite his bone weariness he felt a dull content.

He thought of Singapore, not too far away surely, yet farther than The Raven had proved competent to carry them. Caviar in Singapore. Did they have caviar in Singapore? Probably not, but then he had never had caviar anywhere. Had it not been a vain prayer, he would have sworn never to want it, nor even a proper bed, nor anything else if only he could have the sight of a boat, a plane.

After a while the stars eased him, as food could not, and he rose and crawled beneath the low shelter, to stretch out on the lumpy canvas near the sleeping girl and descend swiftly into darkness.

Chapter 11. Club

The colonel would not have thought of himself as belonging to that species often referred to as "club men." He detested the camaraderie of inane opinion that infested so many of the London clubs to which he was often invited as a guest, and so avoided them. He belonged to one club though, a small, unfashionable, dimly lit place, with its own complement of the ill informed, and a mediocre kitchen. None the less, he enjoyed its quiet atmosphere, provided that he could choose his own company.

On this occasion the company was to his liking, for he had met by arrangement with Brook, a fellow colonel, and they had secured two of the leather armchairs in a corner by the window, with the convenience of a low table before them.

If these two chairs were free they were the inevitably the target of the two colonels, for in this farthest corner of the room they could talk undisturbed, yet look down and watch the passers by; for the room in which they sat was elevated a little above the level of the pavement, and the heavy, dull green curtains of the window shielded them partly from the eyes of those same pedestrians.

In the brief warm sunny period that London called a summer, they would turn their chairs more to the tall bright window, the room appearing black to their eyes in contrast to the light streaming in, and their eyes were drawn naturally to the strolling, sunlit world outside. Then even their deepest conversations would pause as some young woman passed, her summer dress offering white shoulders to the sun's blessing. Her passage would briefly cast fuel onto their two fires, which still burned, though no longer with the rage of youth. Then they would joke, and remember past follies, of which Haig had performed a few, but Brook less. And in the club's refrigerator there was ice for their drinks.

Autumn was pleasant too when seen from their snug eerie, for the leaves from the few trees carpeted the pavement in rotting glory, rich red and brown, or scampered dry and rustling in an October breeze. Then the pedestrians would scurry past, moving briskly to warm their blood, the men gripping their hats prudently, heads bowed against the thieving wind, whilst women in headscarves strode out erect.

Strange, Haig sometimes reflected, that men wore hats as a mark of their propriety, and a little wind would rob them of their dignity, yet the frivolous sex would knot a scarf against that wind and be enhanced in stature as they marched into it. And as the chill wind scraped the face of the building, the drink lay warm and brown in the glass on their table.

But now it was winter, and the evening was black and wet, and the walkers were dull ghosts, dimmer than the wet gleaming pavement that they drifted upon, with blurred grey faces that might turn upwards to peer with damp envy at the two men seated behind the high, bright window. So the two colonels had not demurred when the club servant had drawn the curtains against the chill of the window and the early dark of the winter, and their world was closed and narrowed to themselves, and their table, and their glasses, and their gossip.

The two had fallen into the habit of meeting each Tuesday, and their talk would often revolve around past battles, for Colonel Brook shared Haig's passion for strategy, and more importantly, shared his method, for his mind was lucid and dealt in facts and thought, not in the parroting of pre-set formulas. And so he was an indispensable part of Haig's world, and their windowed corner a favourite part of his kingdom.

On this occasion Haig had it in mind to quiz Brook on the situation in Kenya, a country of which Brook knew much, and Haig little, but had the Kenya situation not arisen he would none the less have been seated here with Brook, for this was

Tuesday. For the last quarter-hour Haig had eagerly lead the conversation through the simmering politics of Kenya, and Brook had followed, but absently, until Haig sensed that other issues troubled his fellow officer. Colonel Haig's enthusiasm paused a little, and he was groping for a way to politely give his friend an opening through which he might unburden himself, when Brook himself took the lead.

"Nigel, do you remember Willis?"

Haig did indeed remember Willis. "Yes. Of course I remember him. Haven't seen him in years though."

"I hadn't seen him for a few years either. I met him yesterday though. Met him in here as a matter of fact."

"In here." Haig was surprised. "I didn't know he was a member here."

"No he isn't, he came as a guest. My guest. He called me on the telephone and I invited him."

Colonel Haig nodded and waited. But Brook's face had taken on a pained expression, and Haig was obliged to help him along. " How is Major Willis?" he asked with soft directness, knowing that Brook would be reluctant to discuss a fellow officer, even though that officer had made him uneasy. Brook was that kind of person, solid and reliable enough as a soldier during the war, but hesitant with people in these softer days.

"Not in too good a shape I'm afraid. Not in as good a shape as I would like to be in." And there Brook stopped, and might have stayed stopped if Haig had not prodded him back into motion.

"Out with it Tony, we might as well hear about the good major now that his name's come up."

Colonel Brook was glad of the instruction. He leaned forward, his free hand stroking the air to knead his feelings into speech. "Looks old Nigel. Looks older than he should. I know we've all added a few years since the war, but he seems to have added twice as many. Grey too, gone completely grey. What hair he has left that is. And vague, vague in a way, in a way I can't put my finger on." Brook paused and sat back. "I wouldn't want this to go any farther Nigel, but I feel very uneasy about the man, and I want to talk to someone about it."

Haig merely nodded in affirmation. Brook would need no assurance to know that a confidence would go no farther.

"He wanted a loan. Seemed desperate. Quiet about it, but desperate. I had to turn him down though. Money isn't as plentiful with me as I'd like."

This was unexpected to Colonel Haig. Money was a touchy area, certainly one that he had never discussed with Brook, or with any other officer. "I didn't know that the two of you were that close. Close enough to ask for a loan that is."

"We aren't. We were in the same regiment in Burma. We were both majors then. Since then we haven't seen much of each other."

"And Willis is a major still. The old thing then. It didn't wash off."

"No. Apparently it didn't wash off." And Brook sat back and lapsed into silence, his eyes unseeing as he stared into the past.

A waiter glided past, and Haig made a sign for two more brandies, conscious suddenly of the shabbiness of the room, of the ceiling stained dark by nicotine, of the too many vacant chairs. He felt impatience with the foolishness of people, with the slowly piling weight of past folly. Major Willis. He had not thought of him in years. He too had known Willis, although not as well as Brook did, but he knew the significant event of the man's history.

There had been an incident, small in comparison with all else that had happened there in Burma, yet great according to the unwritten code that moulded the lives of officers in His Majesty's armed forces. It had occurred shortly after the end of the war. Willis had been in charge of a certain kitty, a portion of the mess room funds, and that kitty had been found to be less than it should be, or missing altogether. And there had been talk of trouble with a woman, and a need for money to solve that trouble. This was a rumour that could have preceded a court-martial, and junior officers imprudent enough to echo it found themselves brusquely rebuked to silence.

The upshot of all this had been an inquiry, quiet and informal, conducted by Willis's immediate superiors. Nothing official had come of the inquiry, and the affair became deliberately smothered in vagueness, and then quietly buried, with no blame laid formally to anyone, and therefore marked plainly as a mystery to be forgotten. And so Major Willis had remained a major; but he had also risen no higher than major. Or so Colonel Haig had heard, though he had not been privy to the full facts at that time, nor did he inquire more deeply later. But whatever the facts he had little sympathy with Willis, for the man was in any case a poor example of an officer.

"Also it's not major any more. He resigned his commission."

Colonel Haig grunted. "And now he's finding there's a surplus of ex-majors I suppose?"

"Exactly. Although exactly why he needs money he didn't say."

"Then neither should you lend. Let the man sink or swim Tony, sink or swim. No one dies from poverty, not in this country."

"Yes. Disturbing though. He can't be more than forty-five, and he looked more like sixty."

Haig grunted again. He was fifty-one and proud of his physical condition. "Worry. Nothing to age a man like worry. Especially if it's your own fault. If it's not your fault you can live with it. Time and effort, and you can turn a bad situation around. But you have to have the gumption. Willis never did have it. Now shall we forget the unfortunate major?"

Colonel Brook agreed, and having cleared his mind of Willis, pleased Colonel Haig with his succinct version of the situation in Kenya, until their talk turned homeward from the colour of Africa to the daily routine of their winter shrouded city.

"How are you finding Captain Sinclair of late." This was from Colonel Brook, settling deeper into his armchair as his brandy did its work.

"Sinclair! I'm not finding much progress there, not at all. The man's a damned pain."

"You'll straighten him out Nigel. You always straighten them out in the end."

"That might have been true in Burma. Not here though. It's a different world now. A different ball game as the Americans say. Before the war we knew we had to have a war. During the war we had a war. Now we hope there'll never be another war, and we get these bloody people with too much classroom."

"Don't quite follow you there old chap."

"No. Don't follow too well myself as a matter of fact. I mean it seemed clearer before the war. There was no avoiding it. Hitler gave us no choice, and we had to face it. Twenty-one years of peace, nearly twenty years of me being a peace time soldier, then that madman forces us to a war that we didn't want. As if the first go wasn't enough. But we fought it, and we fought it because there was no choice. And when it was over we were glad. And now some of these young puppies – and its Sinclair that I mean, he's a perfect example – they behave as though it was, was normal in some way! Normal! As though it wouldn't bother them if we had another tomorrow."

Brook smiled ruefully. "It would bother me. One was enough. One was enough for all of us."

"Yes. And that's their trouble Tony. Until you've been in one you don't know that one is enough. In fact when you've been in one, a real one like the one we had, you know that even one's too many. And that's the real task Tony, avoiding wars, not winning them"

"But surely Sinclair's not a war monger? A bit too know it all perhaps, but that's all?"

"No of course not." Haig waved a dismissive hand at the suggestion. Captains did not rank high enough in the scheme of things for their opinions to earn them such descriptions as warmongers. "But he's got that attitude Tony. Head down like a bull and force his solution, whether it works or not. You'd think he'd listen more to those who've been through it."

"Young men Nigel, young men."

"But more than that. If he were too impetuous then that can be used. Marry some good advice to young energy and you can end up with a good officer. But what scares me is this attitude that they don't need advice on fundamentals. And the fundamental here is that you can't live with conflict Tony, you can only try to end it. War's a failure of method, not an application. We don't need it, we don't want it. It's not a part of what's normal, it's a breakdown of what's normal. You can't go riding rough shod over all over the world anymore. Not since the bomb Tony. Not since Hiroshima."

"No. Not since Hiroshima."

"And not before either. You're no deader with the bomb now than you were with a bayonet before. If you've been there you know that."

"If you come back you know it. If you come back." Brook had said this quietly, and Colonel Haig remembered that his friend had been close to his brother, and that brother had been one of those who did not come back.

Chapter 12. Guilt

In their weary sleep they did not see the clouding of the starry sky, nor hear the first slow fall of the rain, but they awoke blearily as it increased to a downpour, and were tormented from rest by the chill trickles that penetrated the skimpy roof and fell on them through the pitch darkness.

They crawled to the back of the shelter, where he had built the roof most strongly onto a tree trunk, and there they huddled helplessly side by side with their backs to the tree, drawing the sail over them to turn the water that came through even there. They endured the remainder of the wretched night in fits of sleeping and waking, as the crude thatching sagged and slid, until a little before dawn the rain ceased abruptly. By then the shelter was half collapsed, and at first light they crept out blearily into the dripping world, and Stuart scrabbled vainly in the timber pile for dry chips.

In the never-ending summer of the equator their soaking was no great disaster, and soon the steady rising of the sun cheered them, and promised to restore their sodden timber to its bone-dry state. Soon the fire was sending its smoke aloft, and their plea for rescue was again drawn huge on the tide-washed sand. Then it seemed that there was nothing to do but wait, for all they needed that the Raven could provide lay jumbled within the shelter.

Eat they must though, so they heaped the fire with greenery till it smoked sullenly, and walked the few hundred yards north to the old hut. Stuart had it in his mind to raid its sprawling garden for more yam, but curiosity turned him to explore the abandoned hovel again, and he noticed that what he had taken for uprights before were actually a collection of crude spears, leaning bent against the wall, warped by age and weather. They were surely fish spears, for most of them were tipped with odd scraps of metal or thick wire, bound into place.

As he brought a pair out from the gloom of the hut, his eye fell on the maze of reef and fallen cliff that chocked the bay before him, and smiling in comprehension he passed a spear to the puzzled girl.

"Fish!" he announced, "better than yam. Can you catch fish?"

She looked at him astounded. "No. I've never caught fish."

He marched hungrily out into the surf, jabbing at the wave crests in practice. "You just watch for them, and stick the spear in them as they pass," he called back to her. "This must be a good place; that's why they built the hut here."

"But it's in the water."

"That's where the fish are usually dear," he replied, wading onwards. "Stay there if you want. It doesn't seem to be deep. I'm hungry."

The girl hesitated at the water's edge, looking back at the distant rock with its fresh scar. She had hated the very touch of the water since their escape, but this was a long way from the place where... she shuddered at the thought, and then sat decisively and began to take off her sandals.

"Better keep them on", shouted Stuart, looking back. "This coral's sharp. You don't want to get cuts in your feet."

"They're new!" she cried after him.

"Stay there if you want to," he called back.

She looked at the stained leather, already scratched from more adventure than they were intended for. "They were new," she murmured. They had looked so nice when she got them, she wasn't due to have a new pair for ages, but they gave them to her because she was going to the other place, the sandals and her new hat. Now she had to fish in them. She shrugged, and scrambling to her feet followed him into the water.

The water was no more than waist deep between the islets and sunken banks of coral encrusted rock, and as he had guessed the fish clustered there thickly. Stuart had fished with a native spear before for the sport of it, and soon had added fish to their menu, whilst the girl thrashed vainly at the water in a willing attempt. It'll keep her mind of things, he thought, as he methodically skewered his catch, and as they returned briskly down the beach he was rethinking the design of the shelter, for he was unwilling to endure the night's sodden ordeal again.

The girl had caught the already ragged skirt of her dress on the coral of the fishing ground and rent the flimsy fabric nearly to the armpit. She had emerged from the water clutching the wet material demurely together, and as he cooked, she sought in her case and disappeared into the trees, returning in an identical copy of the Institute dress. The neatness of its un-ripped condition was a shock after the makeshift life of their past two days.

"You changed for dinner," Stuart joked laboriously, glancing up from turning the crackling fish before the flames. She blinked solemnly at him.

"I had to change. I can't wear the other one any more, it needs mending."

"Mending! I think it needs throwing away dear," he replied.

"I can't throw it away. I've only got that one and this. I have to keep this one clean or the sisters in Singapore will be really angry. Do you think we'll have to fish again?"

And Stuart certainly thought that they would have to fish again, and that more than once, though it galled him to admit it; but he had by now seen both items of the girl's wardrobe, and so hauled the trove of adult luggage from the shelter. Again the girl disappeared into the trees, to emerge transformed into a piratical figure, a belt of rope gathering together the waist of a pair of Stuart's khaki shorts, her slender torso lost in one of one of his tropical shirts, which belled voluminously about her. Only the sandals and neat ankle socks remained.

After their meal, lassitude seized them both, for they had had little sleep, and Stuart forced himself to the rebuilding work. But a restless anger began to nag him, a feeling that the effort was wrong, that in placidly building the shelter he admitted the certainty of the fear that had been with him since he had first stood on the beach by Dawson's corpse: they would not be found quickly, for there was no search. The tide of luck that had swept him unscathed through the war had slackened with his marriage, and finally abandoned him as useless on this strand.

He grew ill tempered as the morning worn into the afternoon, needing no watch to know that it was now well past two days since they should have stepped from the Raven's hatchway onto the tarmac of Singapore, two days since the two dead Americans should have unloaded their urgent cargo. But with the change of clothing the girl seemed to have brightened and become talkative, or perhaps it was the improvement of food that had done it, and now she chattered and strove to assist him, impeding his sullen efforts more than she helped, and he became surly and snapped viciously at her.

She looked at him in hurt bewilderment, and turning away wandered a little distance down the sand. There she sat gazing out to sea, hands clasped around her knees, raising her head occasionally to look at the indifferent sky that yielded no hint of rescue. After a while she returned, keeping her face averted from him, and quietly taking a spear walked back to the fishing ground. Stuart watched her go, wondering if he should call her back, but he refrained. There was little danger there, where the obstructed waves were calmed to a mere gentle surging.

He laboured on grimly until the poles of the shelter stood wider and firmer than before, and his success soothed his black frustration, except that he now felt uneasy about the girl. He had kept an eye on her distant figure as she moved about the hidden reefs, and finally unable to ignore his concern he left the work unfinished, and taking his own spear, he went to join her.

What bit of her chatter was it that had rubbed on his raw irritation? That they should make a big sign on the hilltop, as big as all the hilltop. And he had snarled at her, for the work would be an enormous task, ridiculous! It would take weeks, and he was not to be penned here for weeks; he was here only until the authorities in Singapore got their act together and came for him.

And so he had shouted at the child as though she was a stupid recruit with a dirty rifle. He must keep a grip on himself. Be patient. They were lucky to be alive. And the kid was no trouble, hadn't howled unceasingly at their predicament as he had feared. Hadn't taken it badly at all in fact. And now she was out there plunging away at the fish. What if she had run off and drowned whilst he was angry with her? He looked up at the hill's flat, bald head. Why not? It could be done, and what else was there to do? More, such a sign would only be visible to airplanes, and thus to civilized people. Attracting a ship could as easily bring danger as rescue.

And how could he rely on the authorities in Singapore – what authorities there were. Most likely they had written off the plane as lost in the great watery expanse between themselves and Paa. Then what else was there to do? Build a boat? Jerry rig some kind of boat together and set out into this changeable sea, where a storm could appear from nowhere?

The idea appalled him. He knew nothing of boats, and they might be a hundred miles or more from the mainland. He was no sailor, and such a voyage was no way to learn. What else could they do but make the island itself a sign. Was there anything to do but that and stay alive? The girl's idea was as useful as any. But he had called her stupid, and now he felt a little ashamed at his impatience as he waded towards her through the shallow water, and she ignored his approach.

Later they walked back with their second catch and the girl was again talking to him. He had not ventured to apologise, for one should not apologise to children, but instead pursued the mindless fish of the reef as he shouted amiable questions across the water to her, brightly making enquiries about her life in Paa. Relieved that the big man was no longer angry, she answered, and the overlooking cliff echoed with a piecemeal description of her life at the institute.

Thus he began to learn of the doings of a young lady called Danielle, and of Betty, and of the quirks of the various sisters who ruled the girl's lives. It was all minor stuff, the petty complications of a child's daily life, yet as he half listened, he felt his good humour stir back to life, and replied as appropriate with expressions of surprise or sympathy. As they walked back along the beach he sought to obliquely make his amends, casually delivering his shrewd judgement that marking the hill was actually a good idea, but that it might take some time.

Here he received his rebuke, for the girl smiled up at him knowingly, and then surprised him by laughing in a mildly triumphant way. He had not known that she could laugh, and it tickled him that she should see through his cunning. And he laughed too, and the knotted tensions that came from worry and the horror of bloating corpses slackened their deathly grip on him a little, though he, tough man, did not realise this, and throwing his arm around her he squeezed her shoulders briefly and walked with a lighter step.

Later they barbecued their catch in the lengthening shadows, and seeing the girl's eyes wistfully turn to the dimming empty sky, he remarked optimistically that if the sign did not catch a plane, why then they would build a boat and sail west to Singapore. She looked at him in wonder. "And you can be the cook like Long John Silver," he added. But the girl did not known who that was, and groping to remember the schoolboy novel he told her in broken chunks Stevenson's story of the one legged pirate, as the early tropical night fell about them. From there, their talk turned back to life in Paa, the girl probing shyly as to what he did there, and then, was he married?

"Yes," said Stuart briefly, and would have left it at that.

"Why wasn't she on the plane? Is she still in Paa?"

"She's in England dear. We're separated," he added, feeling that though it wasn't the kind of thing that one was really required to tell a young girl, it would forestall further questions. But the girl looked puzzled, and he clarified his answer. "We don't live together at all. We didn't get along, so we separated from each other."

The girl digested this for a while. "My mum and dad separated," she said suddenly. Stuart made no answer, not wanting to open whatever sad story lay behind her comment, and the girl added no more to it.

It was warm, and there was no need of the fire, but he fed it for the sake of its ruddy light that drove back the empty darkness and embraced them in its womb-like glow, making for them the illusion of a place that they might call home. So the third day ended sweetly enough, even though it brought no promise of rescue. Stuart, musing, realised that severe danger had ended with the detestable salvage operation, and that he had suffered from its built up tensions. It would be better, he thought, necessary in fact, to take things as they came, and keep up their morale by doing useful things, without letting ill temper take the upper hand, for certainly he could do little else.

Colonel Haig had always stressed the importance of moral. "If you don't stay cheerful, then you get turned aside too easily. It all gets too grim, and you slow down, and everything gets stagnant." That was what he said, more than once, or some words very much the same, and even more to the point – "Pretty soon quarrelling starts, they you don't trust your fellow officers to watch your back, and your men don't trust you, because you're just another task master. Remember what we're fighting for – a world where we can have a laugh, if it's a reasonable one. Besides, it's a lot better being cheerful."

I forgot, thought Stuart. There was a war, and I thought that advice was just for wartime, and really it's always true. And now I know we have food, and the water supply's good, so I should start the sign without delay, and build the signal fire on the hilltop whilst I make it. The girl can help. She can run up and down and do something, and that'll keep her mind off things. We have to wait. And – he added reluctantly to himself – hope.

They slept that night beneath the bare poles of the shelter, each choosing a side and making a crude pillow from the clothing of their lost fellow passengers. The neglected thatching was unfinished, but the rain was not repeated, so they slept in skimpy luxury, though still their bruised minds filled their sleep with dreary, wandering dreams.

Chapter 13. Surveyor

His resolve awoke with him the following morning, and before the sun rose much above the horizon they left the fire smoking on the beach and climbed briskly to the hill's flat summit. They emerged hot and sweating from the trees at the lower southern end of the bare, sloping top, for they had come heavily laden.

Stuart had filled one of the steel cases with smouldering wood and slung it onto the end of a fishing spear, and the girl carried this over her shoulder, a second can with their days food in her free hand, whilst Stuart sweated beneath a bundle of dry wood lashed around with many turns of their precious rope. They went first to the hill's highest point at the farther northern end, and there Stuart quickly built a second signal fire, within feet of the descending tiers of land slip falling steeply to the ocean below.

When this fire in its turn sent its thin column of smoke into the clear sky he felt easier, though the skies remained empty of promise, and he turned his gaze down the sloping rectangle of grass that was to be their canvas. This was the only area of clear land on the island, for all other parts were shrouded in tree or bush, and the beaches, though easily marked, were narrow, and twice daily swept smooth by the rise and fall of the tides. From this aerie Stuart could see that the beach lying within the great C of their bay was generous in width, compared with the steep, narrow beaches fringing the west side of the island.

How much land, he wondered to himself. Half a square mile? No, probably not even that, not even a quarter, the whole damned island. He knew that it took a certain minimum of land to support a single hunter, but less to feed a farmer. What about a fisherman who could only fish the coast? If all of the

Raven's complement had survived, could they have fed themselves indefinitely? And if he and the kid continued to fish the bay each day might they exhaust the reef-dwelling fish? No, certainly not.

The size of the native hut indicated several people, and the presence of the hut itself meant that they had lived here long enough to justify building it, and so a continued food supply should not be a problem. But the size of this sign that they needed... suddenly the hilltop looked as big as a football field.

He took a stick from his pile and screwed it into the soil near the centre of the northern cliff, a little way from the edge. "Let's get it measured first," he said resignedly, placing one end of the rope on the ground by the stick. "Put your foot on this and I'll drag the rope out towards the middle of the other end."

"Is it long enough?" she asked doubtfully, pressing one sandaled foot on the rope's end.

"No, nowhere near long enough. But we can put another stick and run it out again from that." He took the free end of the rope in his hand, and fixing his eye on a bush at the centre of the southern end, he marched towards it with the solemn exaggerated stride that measures a yard.

"Hold the end down dear, keep it there and don't wander about near that edge. I don't want you falling over."

" I won't fall over. Mind you don't get lost," came back the prompt answer.

Stuart made a grimace of satisfaction at her riposte, though he did not reply, for he was counting as he went. Better than tears, he thought: sharp words would help them get through, and wailing wouldn't. Some day some man would have a handful though. From the stories she had told him yesterday it seemed that the nuns had not found her to be the most obedient of children, but from the little he had seen he felt that though she could be quick and tart, there was no lingering spite in her. He appreciated that in people, for he knew himself in this: that when a dark mood was on him, the sharp wit of his irreverent good humour could sour into acid, and he had often regretted the pressure of bitter sarcasm that had welled to his lips.

"You've got it all," her shrill voice sang, and he slowed as the rope came taut, and placed its end to the turf.

"Forty-eight yards plus two feet!" he cried to her. "Remember that in case I forget." He glanced back at the rope laid in a long straight line from his feet to the girl's. Might as well start with as much accuracy as I can, he thought. It'll need to look as regular and artificial as possible: no wiggly lines. "Bring the sticks, and your end of the rope as well."

The girl's feet pounded up behind him, and she dropped a bundle of sticks beside him, one of which he screwed into the soil at the rope's end. She applied her end to the base of the stick, and he resumed his pacing, his eye still fixed on the bush. When then had gone through their ritual four times, he stood close to the shade of the southern trees, and a line of markers ran down the middle of the bare hilltop.

"Four times forty-eight yards and two feet," he announced as the girl joined him. "That's a hundred and ninety-two yards and eight feet. We'll only count another ten feet of this last bit, then we're nearly into all these trees here, so that's one-hundred and ninety eight yards." He squatted behind his final marker and shuffled sideways until his eye lined it up with the now distant one by the fire, grunting with satisfaction to see that all five sticks were in a near straight line. "Not bad. Very good first go. I should have been a surveyor, just like dad wanted."

The girl squatted and imitated him. He had explained the method before they ascended the hill, and she had caught the idea quickly and eagerly, as though their daunting task were a jolly game. "The third one's a bit to the left," came her judgement.

"Now you have a job," he replied, and she ran back quickly to move the offending stick. Damn but it was getting hot up here, he thought.

"How's that?" came her call, and he set his eye to the stick again. "Good. That's okay. Go to the next and move it just a little to the east."

"East?"

"Bay side dear. That way. Just a few inches." And the girl ran eagerly to the next stick.

A little mathematics told him that the half way point was five feet to the south of the centre stick, and there he set yet another stick, then measured westwards to the sharp ridge, then east to where the curve of the slope steepened as it descended down to the tree line. He found these distances nearly equal, and returned to the stick, to honour it with the single word "centre." Now I've found the middle, he thought, and it looks as though I have the width. How do I space them out? Letters are a bit taller than they are wide, but there's a space between them, and that makes them wider, so I'll say they're as wide as they are tall. So I need three squares, three boxes. Divide it into three then, and that's sixty-six yards each box, and I don't have that much width after all. Damn.

He went from north to south along the centreline, pacing the distances of clear land on either side, the girl wandering a few paces behind, and determined that there was always at least twenty -five yards on either side.

Then I'll go with fifty-yard square boxes, he decided; shorten the line to one-fifty, and that gets me clearer of the trees. Make three boxes, and put a letter in each. Start with the O first, and make it a circle, fifty yards across. Just a circle; that'll be easy to mark out, and no fancy calligraphy. He tied a loop in one end of the rope and cast it over the central stick, and as the girl held the stick firmly in place he paced out twenty-five yards from it, knotted the rope to keep his distance, and began to circled the centre, every ten paces or so stopping to screw a stick into the ground. This proved to be a longer task than he had expected, but at the end of his circling the sticks sketched a great O upon the hilltop, fifty yards wide.

The girl looked at the apparent miracle in awe. "Where did you learn to do that?"

"Oh that's nothing. Just a little geometry. I do this every time I get stranded on islands."

"No really. Did you have to take lessons?"

"No. I don't remember really. We had to do things in geometry class with lines and angles, so I suppose I did take lessons. That was a long time ago though. I just worked it out." As he spoke he strode to the high point of the circle where it nearly touched the west ridge, and he kept his thought hidden behind an impassive face as he surveyed the great sketch. Christ, he thought, it's enormous. We need a tractor, and we haven't even got a spade. But she was looking at him expectantly, so it was time for the next miracle.

"Now we need another circle inside this one, and if we dig out the soil between the two, we've got an O," he declared. But could they get away with something smaller, he wondered? With the sod and bushes hacked away, the dark soil would show as a giant O against the green of the grass to any plane passing over. But only if it passed directly overhead, for from a distance the angle would spoil the effect, unless the plane was very high. They needed all the size that they could get. "Inside circle dear," he said, with forced cheerfulness. "Same procedure as before, only smaller."

With his earlier drawing he had determined that the lettering needed to be heavy. If the outer circle was to be fifty yards across, then the inner needed to be thirty, giving a ten-yard breadth to the giant pen-stroke. By the time he had finished the inner circle the sun was directly overhead, and they were bathed in sweat. The finished design looked even more formidable than at its start, although the girl looked pleased at their handy-work, and started to gouge at the wiry turf with a screwdriver.

Was it really necessary to make it so large, he wondered, and a test occurred to him. The journalist's luggage had yielded a screw-capped bottle of ink and the other tools of his trade, and

Stuart had brought them, expecting calculations. A notepad had sun-dried to a grey block, and on this he marked out an O with the rule, and filled it in with ink, making it one solid black letter, and passed it to the girl. "Hold it up dear, and we'll try an eye test."

As she held it before her, he retreated backwards until he could no longer distinguish the letter easily, then paced forward counting. "20 yards to see one inch. So 240 yards to see one foot, 720 for one yard. And the thing will be 50 yards across. 7,200 times five. That's thirty six thousand yards. The girl looked baffled. "One inch high and I can see it at twenty yards. So if its fifty yards wide I can see it at thirty-six thousand yards. There's one thousand seven hundred and sixty yards in a mile so... he stood for a while, his lips moving silently, then gave up and worked it out on the paper. "That's over twenty miles!" he announced finally, "so if it was fifty yards wide a pilot can see it at twenty miles. We don't need to make it so big. These small planes don't go anywhere near so high. Two or three or maybe four, I don't know. We can make it smaller, and that won't take as long. Half the size will be plenty."

The girl looked doubtful. "But we haven't seen a plane even."

"No." Frustration surged in him momentarily, but he pressed it back resolutely. "No, but one will come, sooner or later. And if it does it probably won't pass straight overhead. So the pilot will see the letters at an angle. The higher the plane the less the angle, the further away the more the angle. And the more the angle, the harder to read. Blast."

"What if it flies over that side," the girl said, pointing to the north, "or the other side? Then they'll see it from the end. Will they be able to read it then?"

Stuart pressed a palm to his brow. Stay cool, he thought, it's a reasonable question. "You, are a Job's comforter," he pronounced with mock severity, though the mock was painted thin.

"Who's Job?"

"A little girl who talked too much."

"Job's a man's name. I know, cause it's in the Bible, and it was a man's name."

"It was her brother then dear."

"And I don't talk too much. If I wasn't here you wouldn't have anyone to talk to."

"I'd catch a parrot."

The girl pulled a face and went back to her digging.

"Wait dear. We have to decide if that's the outside or the inside of the O."

"I'll dig a line between the sticks while you decide," she replied, taking up the screwdriver again with determination.

He wandered up the slope, turning the puzzle over in his mind. At twenty miles their sign could be seen, and they needed the distance, for that gave them twenty miles on every side, and surely a plane would sooner or later pass through that area. That was possible, but that one should pass directly overhead, that was asking too much. But at twenty miles distance, a pilot would be looking at the island practically edge on, even if they were two or three miles high, and the letter on the nearly flat top would be foreshortened to unreadability. Really they could do with a sign on the eastern slopes, and others on the west and south.

But there was no way to clear those areas other than using fire, and how then would they make a colour difference amongst the ashes? Impossible! The hilltop sloped though, and that would present their sign a bit more flat on to the distant eye. At least, it would to the east, and to the south, for most of the clear area sloped to the east, and a little to the south. To the west - that wasn't too good, for on that side there was only a narrow stony slope before the tree line, and the almost vertical rocky terraces to the north were impossible.

Best then to stick to his original plan. As big as possible, and with sharp, clear edges. What air and sea traffic there was in this area was surely travelling east or west, and what went east must come back going west. He strode back to where the girl was struggling to cut the turf, calling as he went. "We'll make a thin line first, all the way around following where the sticks are on the inside circle. Then if it's hard we'll use the line for the outside and put a smaller one inside. If it's easy we'll use the outside line, and have this for the inside."

The girl looked up from her hacking with immense seriousness. "It's hard," she announced.

Within an hour he was in full agreement. With what seemed like a thousand cuts of the machete, he had hacked out a few pathetic few yards of shallow trench between two of the sticks, tearing the minced sod free with his hands, whilst behind him the girl beavered away with a claw-hammer, extending the dark trench in the other direction. They had not eaten for several hours, and as hunger added its clamour to the sun's pounding he proposed a break.

Then he found to his dismay that their task involved more difficulties than that of mere work, for he discovered his hands to be blistered. The skin of his palms was both broken and dirty, and an infection could be fatal here. He turned in concern to inspect the girl's, and though she made no complaint she spread her hands painfully, and he saw that they were worse than his own. The heat was now becoming intolerable, and he called a regretful halt to the work, and they left the hilltop, Stuart gazing back ruefully to see how little of the circle was marked.

At his insistence they went directly through the bush to the beach, and scrubbed the dirt away with the salt waters of the bay. As they turned along the sand towards the shade of their shelter the girl looked at the raw patches on her hands and broke into sudden tears. "We won't be able to do it. We've got tons to do and we won't be able to."

"We'll do it, we'll do it," he replied, infusing a manly confidence into his words, though he almost felt that it would be nice if he could weep himself. "We just have to find a different way, that's all. And we can make it smaller; it's too big, much too big."

"But there's so much to do, we have to go back," she sobbed, and twisting wildly around would have plunged into the bush.

"Tania!" He caught her by the shoulders and pulled her back. "That's enough. Leave it now."

The girl's sudden burst of nervous energy collapsed and she crumpled against him, sobbing and murmuring confusedly. "It was a silly idea. You said it was stupid."

"No dear, no it wasn't. It was a good idea, a very good idea. We just need better tools, that's all. Gloves." He held her to him and rubbed her back vigorously, thinking that this marooning business seemed to involve a lot of back rubbing, and realising vaguely that he seemed to be placing a lot of trust on its curative powers, along with that of salt water. And it seemed to be a good idea, for the girl clung to him, and she was calming down.

Too much sun up there of course. He himself felt washed out: no wonder that she was. Certainly she had showed enough sass earlier, and he liked a little of that in a child, although he would have curbed it sharply enough in one of his men. And she would need some sass to get through this, plenty of it. He could feel her tears warm on his chest, but now she was pulling away and wiping back her hair from her face.

"Sorry."

"That's alright dear. It was very hot up there you know." He put an arm around her shoulder and they walked on the beach quietly, to his relief, for in fact he was beginning to feel more than a little ill, and there was only so much of the kind uncle in him. "And in any case we should have taken a break at mid-day. Can't go ploughing on in the full sun."

Plough! Of course, that was it. He must make a plough! But not today, not now. The beach seemed to be moving beneath his feet. Reaching the now shadowed hut, he threw the sail over the bare poles, and they crept thankfully beneath its shelter. "Salt," he murmured, falling back, "we might need salt. Must make some like the natives do, or.... fish." And then he, like the girl, fell into an exhausted sleep.

The shadows were lengthening on the beach when he awoke. He felt recovered, but hunger gnawed him, and he went quickly to the fishing ground, leaving the girl sleeping. She emerged from the shelter as he returned, and as the beach darkened into night she cooked, whilst he scratched in the sand, designing his plough and working out the acreage of his strange farm.

The darkness thickened about them, and he tossed his twig aside and attacked the barbecued fish. It was good. "You're becoming quite an expert," he said across the fire to the girl. She smiled, pleased. She had never been an expert at anything before.

"Sister Agatha says I'm an ungrateful nuisance," she ventured shyly.

"Was she at the, the place in Paa?" he asked, "you know, the orphanage?"

'Yes. It isn't an orphanage though, it's an institute. The Malcolm McGraff Institute,' she recited as though taught.' 'We called it The Mal though. Sister Agatha was in charge. She used to decide everything, and she used to call people to her office and tell them off.'

Stuart waited. The girl's story had ceased, and across the flickering fire he sensed more than saw her hesitation.

"She was always sending for me. She said I was a trouble maker."

Stuart laughed lightly. How much trouble could one small girl make? Blasted nuns. "Well don't make any trouble here dear, we've got enough already," he said easily.

"I wasn't though," she protested, "she just didn't like me. She didn't like anybody really, but she used to pick on some of us."

"Well, I've known a few people like that myself," he agreed.

"We've been here three days today," she said. "She'll wonder where I am. She's sure to say it's my fault."

"I'll tell her it isn't."

"How long will we be here?"

That was a less agreeable subject for conversation. "I don't know. They were expecting you in Singapore, so they'll be telegraphing to Paa to find out if you left, you and Sister Therese. Nobody was expecting me. I don't know about Mr. Dawson or the other people, but the people who wanted the stuff in the crates... Oh God." He stopped abruptly, feeling as sick as if had been struck in the stomach. 'Panwey,' he whispered in dismay, "we were going to Panwey and everyone thought we were going to Singapore."

"What do you mean," the girl said, alarmed by his sudden profanity, "we were going to Singapore, weren't we?"

"Yes," he replied hollowly, feeling that perhaps he could say just this one thing before he died, "after Panwey. Everybody wanted to go to Singapore, and that's where they paid for, and that's where we were going to, but after Panwey. We had to go there first, and drop the crates off, then fly south some more to get to Singy. And Errol, the," he chocked back a word, "he wouldn't tell anybody unless he had to, in case they fussed and wanted to go to Singapore first." He sprang to his feet and stomped down to the waters edge, feeling he must either curse the drowned pilot or explode. But he did neither. "Of course we haven't seen a plane," he whispered to the waves, "if they're looking for us at all, they're doing it two hundred or more bloody miles south."

Chapter 14. Pirates

The rising sun cast its brilliant spear from the horizon to stab his eyes, and he groaned as he awoke, and crawled resignedly from the shelter to light the signal fire.

They were completely lost, not half lost as he had thought, but it made no difference: they still needed the fire, and the little beach sign too, and there were fish to be caught if they wanted to eat. And now it seemed that he must make a plough. He started to scour the woodpile for something to make the plough from, but it was all scraps. The girl crawled out after him, and he sent her to the fishing ground with instruction to be careful and do her best, for he had lots to do if they didn't want to be here forever.

She looked at him round eyed, but he told her firmly to scoot, and away she went, concealing her nervousness at the weight of responsibility that had fallen onto her shoulders. Food was something that an adult gave you on a plate, wasn't it? Apparently it wasn't, not any more. But Mr. Ellis had a lot to do, and he'd told her she was a smart girl, so off she went. Before she was much down the beach she felt a little pleased at her new role of huntress, for wouldn't it be great if she could catch their breakfast all by herself?

He watched her go, wondering if he had asked too much, then decided he had not. She was no fool, and unoccupied she would wander beside him, bored and annoying. He turned his mind to the plough, and soon Tania heard the whack, whack of the machete as he strove to trim a thick branch into a long base. He glanced her way occasionally as he worked, but each time was reassured to see her stalking or plunging away valiantly, and resumed his task.

If I can fit the machete in as a blade, he thought, and get some wooden parts to follow it, like wedges to prise the soil apart, then we can really tear up the turf. The kid can steer, that's not too hard, and I'll have to be the horse. He grimaced at the thought, but there seemed to be little other choice, for he was now convinced that no one was seeking them in this area. Either learn to be a plough maker, or learn to be a boat builder, he decided grimly.

He dreaded that it might come to a voyage, for the storms closed in often, and without warning, and besides the treachery of the waves there were other dangers. It was good that the sign would only be visible to aircraft, for aircraft meant civilization, while a ship could as easily bring danger as rescue.

The South China Sea was not Brighton Bay. Long before the Japanese had cast their eyes on its resources, and wrestled with the Allies for its wealth, it had been a hotbed of piracy and slaughter, and the final triumph of the white man with his iron ships and crackling radio had not completely removed it from the age of the sword. True, there were steamships plying its trade routes, and planes droning overhead, with the whole might of civilization to back them up, but these passed unscathed through this part of the world only by virtue of their repute and power. Their dominion lasted only as long as their shadow, and for the remainder of the time the traditions of savagery ruled still.

It was not unusual to hear of murder, of petty village warfare and mutilation, of lives ended for the possession of a woman or a pig. For a white man to walk the main streets of a town like Paa was as safe as strolling through an English country village, but the back alleys at night were best avoided. A troop of chaperoned girls might also safely walk those daylight streets, and if old enough haggle with the market people; but at night let them be behind locked doors.

Here on this island there were no doors to lock, and no one to call out to for aid. What if some grimy wooden sailing ship was to pass by closely, its half dozen or more crewmen pausing from their work to eye the lonely island? Might it not be better to douse the fire and retreat into the woods, patiently trusting to their sign?

Stuart had seen the crews of such wretched ships before: people with nothing but the meanness of their impoverished lives, and a willingness to use the curved Malay knife at their belts. It was bazaar talk that even today the slave trade still lived, and why not, for it was known that headhunters still operated in the deeper jungles of Borneo, far to their east. If the captain of such a ship was a good man, then they were saved to the nearest port at no more cost than the reward of a few dollars. But what if he were evil, little better off than his ragged crew, and if the girl took their eye, then what could one man do against them, even though he might have been a lieutenant in His Majesty's Army?

He glanced down the beach at the diminutive fisherwoman. She was of no age to a civilised man, but that would be nothing to many of these savages, and there were no friendly bobbies to call out to here. As his mind ran over these dangers he unconsciously touched the heavy knife sheathed at his waist. He had used this knife before, as they retook Burma, and for more than chopping branches.

They had been moving through the forest for two days, following the faint, narrow trails that led from village to village. At first they wore the usual garb of tension, their eyes constantly scouring the greenery that pressed in on all sides, weapons always at the ready, swinging to cover each new vista, muzzles peering like extra eyes at the dense forest, and menacing each innocent shrub. But nothing had burst from the dense forest, no one had contested their progress down the narrow trails.

The shrieks of birds, the chatter of monkeys: these had assaulted their ears, set their nerves jangling, caused them to stiffen, to crouch, awaiting the danger that the noisy greenery must surely conceal.

But there had been no danger, no sudden burst of gunfire, no eruption of howling nips from amongst the trees. Gradually their awareness had eased, had left the jagged edge of newness and softened into a contempt, almost an irritation, that the forest would yield no foe to them, but instead gnawed on their patience with its damp heat, its flies, its eternal squelching mud seeping into their boots.

On the second night they made camp in an abandoned village, if a dozen huts could be called a village. They saw the village at dusk, a mere hint of lashed bamboo poles glimpsed ahead between the pressing trees, and they approached cautiously, bodies low and crouching, weapons again at the full ready. But the village was deserted, though the signs were there of recent occupation. The track that they had crept in by broadened into a mean dirt street as it passed between the handful of huts and pig pens, then at the other end of the village it narrowed again as it lead of into the jungle.

They posted sentries, two at each end of the village, and warily settled for the night, unsure why the villagers had fled. Thus they were not unprepared when the attack had come about midnight. A sentry crouching in the shadows at the south end of the village felt more than heard that something was moving down the trail, and suddenly the night seemed infested with small, stealthy sounds, sounds that individually could be nothing, but menaced their straining nerves with the suggestion of figures creeping about their camp, coming closer, on this side, or was it on that?

Stuart did not afterwards remember waking any of the sleeping men, for all seemed awake as though from some subtler call, gliding quietly into positions of defence at either end of the crude street. Stuart took a position at the southern end, where the narrow street was broadest, and strove to pierce with his eye the maze of shadows down the path. Time passed, and the faint sounds from the forest neither gathered into one definite threat nor ceased, and it began to seem to Stuart that it was nonsense, that they had read too much from the usual faint, inexplicable night noises of the jungle.

Then down the trail a figure showed itself briefly, flitting ghostlike, and there was the crack and flash of a shot from the path, and the crash and glare of gunfire from his men around him shook the village suddenly, and he too was firing, firing at the blue spurt of muzzle flare, hearing the enemy's bullets cut the foliage, hearing them splinter the timber of the flimsy huts, seeing a figure fall heavy and sack like across the path not ten paces away, feeling the crouching soldier at his side fall limply back without a word.

Gunfire crashed out from the other end of the village, with a scream of pain amidst it. He ran crouching half the length of the village, boots dragging in the mud, fumbling in a pouch for cartridges as he went, but fierce shouts came from the jungle on his right as two figures burst forward from the trees with bayoneted rifles extended.

Stuart aimed at the closest and squeezed the trigger at almost point blank range, but the hammer of the revolver fell uselessly onto a spent cartridge. As the long bayonet licked towards his stomach he skipped away frantically to his left, striking at the long blade with the useless pistol; metal rang against metal, and the bayonet flashed past his side, within inches of skewering him. Stuart let go the pistol and grabbed desperately at the rifle with both hands, his right grasping onto the long barrel close behind the bayonet. Immediately the metal was half-wrenched from his fingers as the Jap swung the wooden stock at his face, and Stuart caught the slam of the hard butt with his left forearm, his feet slipping from beneath him in the soft mud. He fell to his knees, and this saved him, for the Jap overbalanced, and would have fallen onto him if Stuart had not seized the rifle's centre with both hands. For an instant he held the man's weight, then he dropped his right hand to snatch out the keen knife and thrust it up beneath the rifle, feeling the blade pierce cloth and sink into the soft flesh beneath the ribs.

There was a gasp, and his opponent fell back a little, his hand clutching at Stuart's knife arm. Stuart dug his boots into the slippery mud, and thrusting hard regained his feet and pressed forward, striving against the grip of the Jap's hand to drive the embedded knife farther home, until they were staggering rapidly back across the clearing, locked together, Stuart striving to drive the knife deeper into the retreating man, the disputed rifle falling now unwanted to the side as the Jap clawed with his free hand at Stuart's eyes. Stuart seized the clawing hand by the wrist, and their dance ended as the Jap's back struck against a tree.

For a second the two of them strove together, Stuart seeing for the first time the glare of eyes beneath the helmet, feeling hot rasping breath in his face. Then the Jap's strength faltered, and Stuart braced his feet and drove in the knife to the hilt, feeling blood run thickly over his clenched hand. The man sighed and seemed to nod wearily as his arms fell away slackly, then he was sliding, sliding down to rest at the tree's foot, and Stuart had pulled the knife free and turned away, panting.

The firing had ceased, and at both ends of the village his men still held their positions. In the middle of the clearing a figure cursed furiously in English as he clubbed savagely again and again with his rifle at the twitching figure at his feet, and someone was crouching over a moaning comrade, opening the fallen man's tunic. The attack was over, and most of them lived. He went to retrieve his revolver from the mud, and realised that he still gripped the knife tightly. It was difficult to open his hand, for the congealing blood had welded his tight-clenched fingers to the hilt.

The attack was not resumed, nor was there a further sound to indicate the presence of the enemy; none the less, they did not venture from the village the few yards necessary to count the enemy's dead. In the morning they had no injured to burden them, for the wounded man had passed from soft moaning into unconsciousness, and died quietly on the earth floor of the squalid hut in which they had lain him. There were two others dead, one of them Wilson, who had died at Stuart's side, a single neat hole punched into his forehead.

As the light grew the jungle seemed empty of further threat, and Stuart went to the body that sprawled against a tree at the village's edge, the hands limp and harmless on the dirt, the swarming ants feasting on the bloodstained tunic, the dead eyes closed almost to slits in the pallid face. It was a quiet reflective face, thin, and the chin was innocent of hair. He was perhaps eighteen or nineteen years of age.

Stuart searched the pockets of the tunic, fighting down an undefined feeling of revulsion. There was a cheap leather wallet in an inside pocket, European, for a maker's name was embossed inside in French. There was nothing in it that he recognized as money, but various official looking pieces of printed paper in Japanese, and a folded letter in that script. Amidst these, wrapped in many folds of a fine, soft paper, was a photograph of a Japanese man and woman posing stiffly for the camera.

The man was about forty or more, with a thin pencil moustache, wearing a dark western suit, like a businessman's. He was staring with Victorian seriousness into the camera, but the plump woman in a kimono at his side was smiling pleasantly. They did not look like evil people. Later Stuart examined the rifles of the two men who had worked their way through the trees to attack on their flank. The magazines were empty. It was true then; the Japs were running out of both ammunition and men.

They buried their dead near to the village, but the bodies of the Japanese they left where they had fallen. Stuart kept the wallet and its contents for some time, strangely reluctant to throw away the final sum of the dead youth's possessions, even as they had discarded his unwanted corpse, feeling vaguely that he should preserve this link to parents who did not yet know of their grief. But later he found that it grew to trouble him, and he destroyed it and its contents.

With the war's end, new, clean, smarter uniforms had replaced those worn and torn from jungle service, and ink began to stain officer's fingers more frequently then blood. The blood had been bad, but necessary, he felt; but ink he considered a slow poison, and he had returned to civilian life.

As he shed uniform for the last time he had hesitated, wondering if he should leave the knife behind with all the other paraphernalia of killing. But the steel was clean, and had no memory, and his conscience was clear too, for he had only done his regrettable duty. He had kept the knife, and it had become part of his luggage, a memento of what he had once been compelled to do. Now though, he was glad of its presence, and the machete too.

The plough was well advanced before the girl returned, bearing two fish proudly before her. "Well done," he cried as she arrived, "my expert fisher-lady," and she beamed at his praise. He had to clean them himself though, for that task she firmly refused, praiseworthy or not.

Chapter 15. Timber

"Serves me right for working on the day of rest," Stuart said. The plough was not a success. He had worked on it into the night, until the darkness had forced him to stop, and at dawn's first light had set to again, and completed it by midday. This almost involved tears, for he had realized that it would be difficult to fit the machete as the blade whilst using it to work the wood, whereas a whole pile of sharp lathe tools lay on the bottom beside the plane's wreckage.

He had said nothing to the girl, but waited till she had gone to the fishing ground, and then swam out to The Raven. It was easy. The little square metal spikes lay where he had dumped them by the plane, and he rose from his first dive clutching two handfuls. They were not heavy, and he crammed them into the pockets of his shorts, and dove again for more, avoiding peering into the plane's great wound as he did so. He had no wish to see what further ravages time and the fish had made on his late fellow passengers.

Despite his haste he arrived back at the beach to find the girl waiting for him, agitated, her eyes tearful and accusing.

"Stuart, why did you go out there? You promised you wouldn't go again."

"No dear, I said I wouldn't go again, not promised. But look here," he unloaded the ugly little spikes as he spoke, dropping them onto the sand, "we needed these. These are very hard steel, for cutting metal. I can use them to make a blade for the plough. I left a whole pile of them outside the plane."

"You didn't say you were going out there. I was frightened."

"Well, now you know why I didn't say. Where's the fish?"

And that had been the end of it, for the girl reluctantly went back to her fishing, casting suspicious backward glances, and he heated a screwdriver in the fire and bored sockets for the lathe tools. After they had eaten the girl's catch he hoisted his creation triumphantly onto his shoulder, and bore it sweating to the hilltop, thumping it down where the previous days hacking had ended.

He had eagerly donned the rope harness, whilst the girl gamely seized the steering handle. He did not found it too difficult to pull, nor did she find it too difficult to steer, but the teeth failed to bite into the sod, and merely tore at the grass. Although they went back and forth over the same spot, they removed no great gouge of sod, but only great handfuls of grass blades, and dirt loosened from between the roots.

It had taken many passes, until finally the roots themselves came away from the repeated clawing. They had spent an hour hacking the few yards the day before, and after one hour with the plough he saw even less ground marked. It was then that Stuart said enough, and throwing down the rope harness, he squatted on his heels and eyed the plough grimly, recalling that it was Sunday.

Tania looked at him woefully. Things were not going well. They were in trouble, and Stuart hadn't managed to fix things yet. He had spent a lot of time making the plough, and it wouldn't work. Would he get angry? She wished there were something she could do to help, but she couldn't think of anything. He was very nice most of the time, and she felt safe with him looking after her, but sometimes he could be very fierce.

He roused from his reverie to find the girl standing before him, regarding him solemnly. He raised his head, trying to smile cheerfully, and wondering if his smile looked as haggard as he felt.

"Don't worry Stuart," she said quickly, like someone who hands over a simple parcel, with no fancy wrapping. She didn't say why he shouldn't worry, but her words revived him, and he stood slowly, stifling a sigh. She was dependent on him; he must not weaken. Were she not here, still for his own sake he must not weaken.

Stuart kicked the wooden frame lightly. "Now we have a seat for when we eat up here." He was handy with tools, but no craftsman, and he had tackled the job knowing this, and prepared for shortcomings. But not this; this was useless. The failure stung, but he must take it calmly and minimise it for the girl's sake. "We really need something that digs in," he said, hacking at the obstinate grass with his heel. "That's why some bright spark invented the spade I suppose. You can dig it in, bring out a big chunk all at once."

"Didn't they have a spade in the plane?" ventured Tania.

"No, no spades. I don't think Errol did much gardening. A pick perhaps, something with a blade where you can whack it in."

"Do he have one?"

"No. But I can make one." He picked up the rear of the plough and slammed it down. The spikes were driven easily into the ground, and he twisted the whole frame around in a circle, gouging out the most successful piece so far. "Back to the shelter. We'll get into the shade there, and I'll make a pick." He scanned the horizon. "Six days. Not a thing. We must be off any of the trade routes. And – it looks as though there's a storm coming." The north-eastern sky was thick with cloud of a dark, dirty hue, with the wavering blur of rainfall beneath it.

He lead the way to the hill's peak, from where they could see the entire circle of the horizon. Certainly there was rain out there, and it seemed to be approaching.

"Stuart, are we a long way from anywhere?" Tania asked. "I mean a really long way, like hundreds and hundreds of miles. We seemed to fly such a long way on the plane."

"No, I don't think we are. This is a big sea, but we aren't in the middle of it." He pointed west. "Somewhere over there's Malaya. I don't know how far, but it can't be much more than a hundred miles. And Singapore's right at the southern tip of Malaya. If we had a boat we could sail there. If we had a boat."

"You were saying we'd build a boat if no one came."

"So we shall dear, if there's no other way."

As they descended the hill Stuart turned this over in his mind. What if building a boat was easier than he thought. It would be better to at least take a practical look at it, before hacking away at this enormous sign. As he had dodged about the East over the years he had of course seen plenty of examples of the kind of thing they needed, but realised that having a rough picture of a boat in his mind was different from knowing how one was built.

He lacked the tools and skill to make a watertight hull for his boat, so it must be a raft, which depended on the sheer volume of wood for its buoyancy, not on a watertight space of air. That meant a lot of wood and therefore a lot of weight, so it must be made at the water's edge, with some way of launching it into the water that didn't require an elephant to haul it in. He vaguely remembered the story of Robinson Crusoe laboriously carving out a canoe in the jungle, then finding it too heavy to drag even an inch to the sea. A little planning might save a lot of futile effort.

If it were of solid wood, then they must sit on top, and so must their food and water, so some form of shelter would be good, both to protect their provisions and themselves. The raft would be broad and square-ended, and thus hard to drive through the water, so they could not hope to do much with oars, and a sail was essential, which meant a mast.

If they were on it for even one day the sun would bake them intolerably and increase their water need, so again shelter was necessary; some kind of thatched roof perhaps? But this could be swiftly destroyed by a gale, so if their sail was central and set low they could go to the shade side of it instead. The triangular sail that carpeted their shelter would be of service here.

How much timber would it take? He weighed over one-sixty, and Tania must be eighty or ninety; that was two-fifty, and the weight of 15 litres of water, for they had six cans, and their food and other bits. Well over three hundred. And don't forget the mast and sail. So the raft must carry three-fifty or so easily, and at the same time maintain its deck clear of the water. Lots and lots of timber. He eyed the tall palms dominating the tree line: plenty of them, but they were no good.

A bore had once grappled his attention at a party, explaining to him in great detail that palms were really a form of grass, or ferns, or some such thing, and that their wood was heavy, or full of tubes that would waterlog rapidly, or both. The details escaped him, but the main point he had retained. But what about all these more tree-like trees, how well would they float? Wasn't there was at least one kind of real wood that didn't float at all?

With a mutter of "Ironwood," Stuart started to throw various pieces into the waves, and test them for buoyancy with a downward thrust of his hand, whilst Tania puzzled as to whether "Ironwood" was another swearword from his vocabulary that she had not heard before. One especially large log he hauled grunting into the water, and with grim expression made determined efforts to mount it like a horse, while the girl watched him astounded, uncertain whether to cheer him on or flee from the madman. He plunged repeatedly into the water as the log spun beneath, returning to his study doggedly until he had a feel for the timber.

As to what it was he had no idea, for if he had been placed in an English field he could not have told a beech from an oak, but obviously it was not his dreaded ironwood. Nor did anything else fail to float, from the fallen trunks that he dragged sweating from the forest, to the thin branches that the girl ran willingly to the water with. So everything floated.

Good, but how was he to cut down the trunks of the trees, for there were few fallen trees in the tiny forest, and he could not build from twigs. Their only real tool was the machete, that and his knife, and the latter's proud edge was already dull enough for butter duties. One problem at a time: he must first get a better assessment of how much timber, and that meant somehow measuring its flotation power. Well, he could measure it. They had a rule, and with a little sand drawn maths he could get a volume, then see what kind of weight that volume would carry before it was entirely submerged.

The log that he had ridden was of fairly regular shape, and he dragged it from the water, measured it and calculated its volume minutely, then hurled it back into the waves.

"A weight, something that we know how much it weighs," he said, momentarily stumped. "How much do you weigh?" he asked the girl to her alarm, for he had become fearsome in his antics.

"I don't know" she replied, "do people weigh themselves?" It had never occurred to her that people might weigh themselves, as though they were flour or something, and they wanted to make a cake. "The doctor said I was normal weight for my age," she added helpfully.

At some other time Stuart might have exercised his wit on her answer, but he was too distracted for that, for it had occurred to him that perhaps the proper way was to measure how much of the piece broke the surface. That posed another problem, for the log rolled about merrily in the waves, and he sought in vain to estimate how much of its rounded shape broke the surface at any time.

"Calm water!" he announced, "and let the calm of God beee upon the waters, and upon me too, for God's sake." And having shocked the girl a little by this – for despite her dislike of all things nunish, she had acquired a vague propriety regarding anything that sounded religious – he drove the log inshore and upended it in the water, diving it on end into the sand to get his shoulder under its centre. Finally with a great grunt heaved it onto his shoulder and trudged towards the fishing ground, the girl following him, silently impressed.

Between the coral reefs he found pockets of stiller water, but not still enough for his purpose, until it occurred to him that water had depth, and he leaned the log steeply against the reef so that it floated nearly upright, with little of its weight supported. Now he could make an easier estimate of how much length broke surface, and finally deciding that one-third of the piece was above the water, he desisted from any more measuring, being satisfied with this crude approximation.

As for the weight of the log, that he guessed at about one hundred and twenty pounds, and he set to again to scribble on the sand. If they weighed three hundred with the their mast and water and other stuff, and if the raft were to float one-quarter out of the water, then... and he scribbled on...

It was only a wry, passing thought to him that he might have attracted divine disapproval, but as he had worked his mathematics the dark clouds had advanced steadily upon them, and now rain began to fall. By the time he had deposited his specimen log above the high water line, it was coming down heavily through the deepening gloom.

They retreated hastily to the shelter, but the unfinished thatch let down spouts onto them, and finally they left it and ran through the deluge to the old hut. Much of its thatch had fallen over the years, but it was roomier, and one corner was dry. "We need this," he said, looking out at the downpour approvingly, "the stream was getting smaller and smaller. This will fill it back up again."

"I hate rain," Tania answered.

"We need it. Its two days since we had any, and the stream's nearly gone."

"Four," she corrected, "it rained the day after we came, in the night. This is six days today."

He thought about it. "You're right. But it rained mostly on Thursday morning, before the sun came up, so that's really three."

"Where would we get our water from if it didn't rain?"

"Boil the pool water I suppose," Stuart replied. He was not too anxious about the water. The slope of the hilltop drained its captured rainwater into the stream, and rain occurred frequently in this part of the world. "It rained yesterday morning," he said, remembering a brief sprinkling as he was starting to work on the plough.

"That was nothing though, just a bit. If the pool dried up, what would we do?"

"We can boil sea water and catch the steam. That gets rid of the salt, but I'd have to set up a lot of stuff to catch the steam." But we don't need yet another task, he thought, just keep it simple and dig the sign. "We'd better dig the pool out a bit, make it hold more" he concluded loudly, "but it doesn't look as though we need to do that just yet."

The rain was lashing down now, and a rising wind was driving it in through the empty doorway, and shaking what was left of the thatch. The sky was darkening to the colour of ink, and the usually mild waves of the bay were rolling in strong and angry, their crests grey and furious in the failing light. Distant sea and sky had become one blur of dingy grey-blue, and the noise of pounding rain and falling water was mounting to an uproar. "When this is over, I'll make something to dig with," he shouted through the din, leaning towards the girl. A shift in the now howling wind hurled a sheet of water across the hut and into their faces, "and I'd better do some thatching as well", he added, wiping his face, "just as soon as this is over."

But the storm did not end with the daylight, but carried on past the unseen sunset, growing in fury as the light failed till their very faces were lost in blackness, with neither sun nor moon to show them the wet, raging world about them. Blindly, they crawled together, and he put his arm around the girl in the darkness. She pressed to him as they waited for life to resume, and they endured the wet, noisy blackness, that denied them speech, or sight, or hearing of anything but its useless, tormenting din. Occasionally he put out his hand, groping for the walls, unable to believe that they still held, for it was impossible to tell them from the doorway by sight.

Only touch existed, and it began to seem that the land itself must have been swept away by the force of the rain, that it was gone, could not have survived, and that they huddled in a memory of an old hut, long gone, the reality of its timbers long washed away, its two ghosts trapped in an eternal moment of wet squalor, dimly remembering the light of a long extinct sun, unaware that they were long dead.

Then with a cannon-crash the thunder burst overhead; the sky glared white and savage into their eyes, the streaming uprights of the hut stood silver about them, the fringes of the torn thatching danced frantically in the sudden light; then the brilliance was gone, and all was dark again. The girl pressed against him in the blackness as though to enter him like a warm castle, and he squeezed her reassuringly and damned the storm silently, and they endured.

Finally it passed. The wind died, the rainfall ceased. Faint points of light appeared overhead, grew brighter in places to outline the retreating clouds, and they crawled tentatively onto the beach, surprised to find that the sand still lay there, not washed away to the bare bones of volcanic rock.

They crept gingerly down the beach, like escaped prisoners, fearful of pursuing dogs, and found the shelter to have survived. It was as sodden as the hut, but it was their own place, and they touched their cans and cases, reassuring themselves that what they had left of the world still survived.

With the morning, Stuart began to methodically rebuild the shelter. He felt strangely patient, as though the repeated failures of the last week had totalled up to victory, for he understood that, in reality, they had. In his determination to reverse his disaster he had accepted his survival briskly, as though it were his right, and in the forcefulness of his character had swiftly denied the insult to his freedom, and thrown himself into action. It was good: that had been right.

What victories he had won in his life, he had not won by allowing himself to be used as a punch-bag, and though it was years since circumstances had struck at his very life, he had hit back strongly. He had put up his fists without wavering and had his three brisk rounds in the ring, but now he had to admit that whilst he had not been overcome, the past week had schooled him with a series of bloody noses.

His efforts had not been wasted, for he now accepted the solidity of their imprisonment, and had learned much of what could not be done, and of what could. Their imprisonment was neither an insolent joke nor an illusion, but a solid fact, and would not be overcome in a brief skirmish, but by a prolonged war.

They could survive. That he had long known, but they would be tried, and must preserve their strength. They could not go on being threatened by thirst the one minute, and tortured by storm the next, and so he began work on the shelter, re-planning its crude design, tearing out and rebuilding until he could trust its solidity.

But though he chocked back his frustration, his eyes swept the horizon and sky frequently, and his keen eared young helper hid many a shocked grin at the colour of his muttered curses.

Chapter 16. Skater

Carew was retiring shortly. His desk was already cleaned out, and for what duties still remained to him, he might well have spared himself the daily grind of driving to the office. But change is hard on a mere human, especially the one of ceasing to be a useful cog in a great machine, and becoming instead answerable to no one but himself, and so he was easing into the change. He had been part of the machine for many years, back before the war, back almost to the war beyond that, the one called the Great War.

The machine had grown over those decades; technology had seen to that. There had been a time when information had meant something that an unobtrusive butler had memorised from a carelessly exposed document, or that some traveller had observed, and whilst it was useful stuff, it was no longer the material that war was spun from. Now there was a need to be more methodical, as bringing death to a country's enemies could be done with greater ease, yet to be seen to be the clean, justified hero became more essential. Numbers, formulas, blueprints showing the workings of the latest devices; they were more essential than the sacks of flour and barrels of black powder on which an army had once fed.

More than a generation before, the first crude tanks had clanked their way onto the battlefield, built under the guise of being water carriers, and the last remnants of the world's great cavalry armies were rudely shown that they were overdue to hang up their spurs. The first wood and canvas airplanes had droned precariously over troops who watched them in awe, until it had occurred to their pilots that grenades could be hurled at the watchers.

Now war ran on petroleum and diesel, and the USA sprawled across its continent like a great satisfied lion, licking its lips over the allies' global victory, hiding its nuclear secrets beneath its fur, resting its paws on the defeated nations, yet uneasily eying the great bear that had arisen to challenge its final mastery. In Europe a host of cities still worked to clear away the rubble of this latest, greatest struggle, and Hiroshima and Nagasaki were new words for ultimate terror.

A new age of reason had come, for war was no longer a general's adventure, and the now literate masses could no longer be counted on to snatch up their swords and muskets for the politician's brawls. Great Britain had growled at the little man in a loincloth for a while, then bowed to his quiet arguments, and India was hers no longer. In Russia and China the slogans cried for the rule of the people; now might had to also be seen to be right, with just cause on its side, or cease to be quite so mighty. And the quiet war grew, the war of what was known, of what could be learned, of what the public might safely be allowed to know. And with it had grown the numbers of those unnoticed men and women who work in obscure offices, for departments with vague functions, all of whom fought daily this quiet, unseen battle.

And Carew was one of those.

There were many sections within this machine. Some answered to each other, some never truly knew to whom they answered. Some were permanent, and could trace their ancestry back to the days when the red-haired Elizabeth ruled; others were mere temporary arrangements, created to fulfil a newly arisen need, and often they duplicated each others work, for it was not the policy of the rulers of the machine that any part should know the totality of the whole. It was unusual for any of the machine's members to depart in a blaze of glory, but Carew had been one of its minor Sultans for a long time, and his seasoned wisdom would be missed by many of the older hands, who felt that some little send off was in order.

Colonel Haig was one of those who qualified to be seen as part of that group. At the war's end a need had been felt for men who could think, as well as do, and certain reports written by the colonel had marked him down as one such man. Six years of war, following on nearly twenty of previous soldiering, a sharp, cunning mind and a lifetime hobby of studying military history; these qualities had been noted, and little by little the colonel had entered the world of those who know, but are not known. Though his years in this world were as yet few, the reputation that he had established was solid, and so Carew was glad to see him in the crowded office where his obscure farewell was to be celebrated.

Captain Sinclair was also there. He was neither senior nor respected, but he had the dogged persistence of one who has assured himself that he will rise, and someday command from a great height, and his recent close association with Haig had given him an introduction to many of the unofficial watering holes of the machine. Sinclair was therefore also one of the crowd who found themselves at midday clutching a glass in a dingy office, and he wasted no time before finding ears into which he could pour his wisdom.

"Your man looks like one of those who intend to go far," remarked Carew, regarding the young captain through the haze of smoke.

Haig didn't answer immediately. It was a social event, a time to re-air past glories, though shop would inevitably crept in, and he had been telling Carew of Burma, a place that his listener had never seen. Haig was not a gossip, for he felt that events were difficult enough to deal with, without the added burden of petty intrigue. It was people who held the key to any mess, but it was also people who firstly made the mess. However...

"Yes I'm afraid he might," the colonel replied shortly. "One of the new breed. Given his head, he'll go as far as he can."

"A very young man to be as far as he is," observed Carew. "I suppose they tucked him under your wing for a little nurture."

"Nurture. He needs more than nurture." Haig shook his head at the thought, "best not to talk about it here though. Not the time and place."

Not much more of either for me, thought Carew. A desire to dispense some final wisdom rose in him. "He reminds me of a few I've seen over the years. Army, but really ought to be in politics."

"Unlike yourself, politics, but should have been in the army."

"Thank you Colonel, but what service I saw was more than enough. However, a few reports of this young man's career have drifted to me," - he had lowered his voice – "and I've a suggestion to make. If he's as bull headed as I've been told, make an end of his advances in this area. As I said, I've seen a lot of his type over the years, and they're best weeded out early."

A wellwisher advanced on them, and Haig drew back a little to give space for the final handshakes. This was not a new idea to him, but Carew's comment had crystallised his thoughts. Sinclair was not for this kind of work, but someone had the bright idea that he was, and he, Haig, was uncertain as to whom that someone was, except that he was much further up the pecking order. There was nothing that he could complain about directly, for thus far there was only a difference of opinion, and current thought decreed that such differences had to be worked with.

Haig nodded vaguely to some remark made to him, for he was covertly watching Sinclair, who had fixed his eye on the tall figure of McIntyre. Surely Sinclair didn't know him? No, for the man at Sinclair's side was obviously pointing McIntyre out to him. In a few minutes, thought the colonel, Sinclair will try to push himself into conversation with him, and much good he'll do himself.

McIntyre was a listener. Tall, with a flowing mane of white hair, he gave the impression of an eccentric college don. It was his habit to listen without comment, his head thrown back a little, watching the subject of his interest calmly down his long nose, and giving little hint of his own opinion. He had disconcerted Haig a little at their first meeting, but later the colonel realised that he had gained McIntyre's approval, and that was fortunate, for McIntyre was a man with the ability to assess people accurately at the outset, who rarely found a need to later change his judgement. And he moved at exalted height, and his word carried weight.

If Sinclair talks to him he'll need to be very canny, thought the colonel. If McIntyre had a fault, it was that he was too moderate; got in Churchill's bad books for it in fact, too much in favour of appeasement before the war. If Sinclair said too much in that quarter...

Colonel Haig decided that he needed another drink, and headed towards the array of bottles that stood on a table. It was convenient that the table stood between McIntyre and Sinclair, and that Sinclair acknowledged him as he approached.

"A lot of years of service here, Captain," commenced Haig amiably, speaking in the slightly wistful tones often heard at such sentiment inspiring moments, "a lot of years, and a lot of changes seen."

"True," replied the younger man, a little guardedly. He was well aware that Haig disapproved of him, but this knowledge didn't trouble him much. He thought the colonel a fossil of the old days, lacking in understanding of the modern world. But if Haig wished to indulge in a little chitchat, then he didn't mind unbending a bit. "Carew must have been here longer than most people in the room."

"Oh yes, he goes back a long way. So do a few others, Jackson over there, that fellow in the blue suit, can't remember his name. And McIntyre of course." He stopped at that point, and to his delight Sinclair took up the thread.

"Sir Henry McIntyre. Won't he be interested in the Kenya business? I believe he lived there for a while."

"Well yes he may be. Probably will be in fact, unfortunately." Haig had put a little edge into his voice, just a little, but he was no longer the sentimental old man with a glass. "That'll be just the ticket for you. I've heard he's quite a believer in the firm hand, whatever you fellows mean by that," he continued, becoming a little of the old ruffian who couldn't be bother to hide his opinions, or his contempt.

That was sufficient. He could throw no more hints without showing his cards, and perhaps it was it now time for him to rejoin Carew. Haig's angel must have been hovering close, willing to give matters a hand, for at that moment McIntyre turned and glided a pace or two his way.

"Colonel Haig. Nice to see you again."

They exchanged pleasantries, Haig half giving his back to Sinclair, who stood quiet and attentive, conscious that he was as yet a mere captain. But pleasantries can only last so long, then the flow dries up, and as it did Haig saw the tall man's eyes flick beyond him, felt the expectant pause. At such an informal gathering it would be quite natural for him to introduce his assistant, and rather rude not to do so.

"I don't think you know Captain Sinclair," he said, with no enthusiasm, but with nothing worse than neutrality in his tone, "he's also involved with the Kenya affair."

To immediately withdraw would have seemed most odd, and therefore very bad strategy, but to be close might impede the flow of Sinclair's tongue. For a minute or two he strove to open the subject without giving his opinion in any direction, and then his angel took a hand again, for the chairman appeared in the doorway. Obviously there might be a matter that a man like the colonel needed to communicate to the chairman, and it was the work of a moment for Haig to remember one. He excused himself and turned away, hearing behind him McIntyre's quiet voice asking a question of Sinclair.

Colonel Haig merely crossed the room, showing no emotion, but inside he felt something of the glee of a schoolboy, muffled in sweater, coat and winter scarf, who runs confidently at an icy pavement, and leaping onto it, slides without falling to the very end. It was all in Sinclair's hands now, and he would write his own future. He had been warned. If he heeded the advice of his superior, who could not be rid of him, then he would moderate his tongue, and perhaps there was room for more improvement. If not, then he would now show his unsuitability to one who could deal with him, and he, Haig, might be rid of him. The colonel was not a gambling man, but he would have risked a fiver that Sinclair would not.

The affair wound down; the crowd thinned. Haig had a report to read, and felt it wiser to be absent at the end. If McIntyre were perturbed he would not raise the matter here, but later, and privately.

A little after six that evening Captain Sinclair walked briskly from the building and down the now dark London street, feeling a need for the tonic effect of the chill winter evening. Alcohol was something that he used sparingly, and alcohol at midday he had no time for. The send off had put him behind with his work, and he had stayed late to finish, finally leaving the building feeling dull and muzzy. The cold air and the brisk walk cleared his mind, and he felt satisfied with his day. It had been a spur of the moment decision to attend the little function for Carew, and he had nearly stayed away, for he disliked such functions, but it had intrigued him to see the winding down of one of these pillars of the service.

Carew! Perhaps the man had been acceptable in easier times, but now he was a relic from the days when the world was a great dim unknown, and the telephone was a miracle. And hadn't he been shell shocked in the trenches of the Great War, and had to spend time lying low in a hospital to recover? Not the kind of fibre that should qualify a man to work in intelligence operations, which had proved so vital in the next war. Now that old breed of amateur soldiers were nearly gone, and hopefully the host of public school boys who directed them would soon be gone too, them and their old school ties.

Kenya beckoned to him. It was one of the last bastions of the British Empire, one of the few remaining pieces that hadn't been blundered away, but would be if some of these old women had their way. Why could they not learn the lesson taught by the loss of India, taught by the failure of Chamberlain's appeasing policy? Of what use was it to weakly hand over the ordered countries that had been created from a mishmash of savage kingdoms, in a world that needed to unite its resources against the threat of communism?

Foolishness. Weak, short sighted foolishness held the reins. They were too fond of their past, that was the cause of it, too fond of their traditions, their medals and their stories of past victories, and too fond of their titles and their petty authority.

There were too many of these old boys running things, too blinded by their gin soaked eyes to see that this was a new world, one where order should be achieved methodically, through organizing things firmly, not the occasional lucky outcome of muddling through. They fumbled with things, too concerned with not offending this person or that, unable to see the ebbing away of power, and unwilling to act to retain it. Compromise had the last word all too often, and compromise was little different from inaction.

Sinclair turned up his coat collar against the dampness of the air. There was a mist growing, haloing the street lamps, softening the outlines of the few other walkers. A woman was coming towards him, emerging slowly from the mist, walking with slow, short steps that took her nowhere, but marked her as living thing amongst the still scenery of trees and columns. She was dressed in black, and looked at him hopefully from a pale, damp face as he drew level with her. She did not speak, and Sinclair avoided her eyes as he passed and hurried on, hearing the slow clack of her heels behind him.

Streetwalkers! He snorted slightly, though he did not know that he had done so. Part of the useless mould that clung to this city, just like the droppings of the pigeons smeared on every window ledge. These women flouted the law here at the very centre of the empire, and no one stirred themselves to deal with the disgrace. There were laws, so why weren't they applied? Slack, good-enough ways, which permitted such people to ply their trade before the very offices of government.

And when he had commented on the disgrace once, Haig had laughed, as though he were blind to the shame of it, and made some ridiculous joke about the prostitutes in Singapore, as though that were anything to do with London. Buffoon. It would be good when he was free of the man and his jungle-sense nonsense. How did a year or two of falling over vines in the jungle qualify him to run anything in peacetime? All that was just the spadework, and could be left to those with brains for nothing else. Might as well place a man in charge just because he knew where to dig for the drains.

But McIntyre now, he was obviously a man who could get things done, and he had the authority to act. People deferred to him automatically, as though he wore about him a circle that magnetised all whom he passed. It was good to have met with him, though Haig would have avoided introducing him if he had been able. How easy it was to side step these old wooden blocks, once you had determination. McIntyre had said little, but he had listened with interest.

Sinclair shuddered suddenly as the cold began to strike through to him. He turned and retraced his steps, wondering if he should cross the street to the other side. It would be distasteful if the woman thought that he was trying to overtake her, and she was not far ahead of him. She had stopped beneath the one of the streetlights, and he would pass her before he came opposite to the place where his car was parked.

Even as he considered, a car pulled over, and she moved to the window. It was too distant to hear any conversation, but after a moment a door swung open and she climbed nimbly in. The car pulled away as Sinclair strode sourly on. Disgraceful, he thought, and who was to say that these women didn't get some of their clients from amongst the ranks of the very people he had to work with? It was something that should be looked into. If ever he saw any such incident again, and it involved anyone that he knew, then he'd see that something was done about it. Damnation, there were enough bad security risks about without this kind of traffic outside the very doors.

156

Chapter 17. Shark

She waited, motionless, as the stubby shape moved slowly through the water towards her, wandering from side to side as it came. It was one of the big blue and gold ones, the ones that tasted so good to eat. The fish turned towards the wall of coral on her right, and she twisted gently to the right to help her aim, raising the long wooden spear a little higher. The fish made a leisurely inspection of the coral, its tiny fins stroking gently, before turning again to the centre of the narrow channel between the two banks of reef. The girl turned fractionally again. It would come, they always did, and she waited, the rising sun hot on her upraised arm, her legs hidden from its fire in the coolness of the water.

She stood waist deep in the water of the bay, and the gentle rise of the waves billowed out her baggy shorts, then fell, collapsing them back again to her slender thighs. The fish resumed its course towards her, and she held her breath, measuring with her eye the final foot of distance that would place it within her reach. Now she could see its eyes, black, unwinking, bulging... At that instant a bead of sweat ran briskly from her hairline down her forehead, and turning aside at the junction of her brow and nose ran stinging into the corner of her eye. She gasped in annoyance and thrust the long spear down. The point drove into the sand and the unharmed fish shot forward in alarm and darted past her leg.

Tania gave a howl of disappointment and turning swiftly stabbed the water repeatedly, but it was too late. Some twenty yards away Stuart looked up and grinned briefly before turning his attention back to the water. Tania fingered the treacherous sweat from her eye and resumed her vigil between the two coral banks.

More fish were coming, this time a school of the smaller ones. They were harder to spear, but there were more of them, and she waded forwards to meet them and struck repeatedly with the spear. The school of tiny shapes scattered unharmed, and she retreated backwards to her place. Tania had not expected to hit any of the small ones; they were just a nuisance. She squatted, plunging her heated body to the neck beneath the water, then arose dripping to patiently wait for the next large fish to enter the channel in its wandering search for food.

Here at the north end of the bay there were a lot of these chunks of rock in the water with lots of these coral things growing on them. Mister Ellis said that they were pieces of the cliff that broke away or got left behind when it wore away. They had found the long spears near the old hut where they found the big jug, and when they found them they had come straight into the water and tried to catch some fish. They hadn't caught any at first, but then they had come right up to the cliff and found all these coral rock things hidden under the water and the fish swimming round and round them. That was days ago, more than a week, and they had caught fish every day, but Mister Ellis caught most of them.

When they left the fishing place they had brought the spears with them, and Mister Ellis had cut some rope into string with his big knife, and tied up the little spiky bits at the end tighter. Next day she had been frightened that he might want to fish there by Log City, but he had started along the beach to this end and she had been glad. She didn't want to catch any fish by where they lived because the plane was there and all the people in it were dead.

There was a splash to her right as Mister Ellis struck for a fish, and a low "damn" told her that he had missed. Tania smiled. Sometimes Mister Ellis swore. Today she would catch a big one, bigger than any of those he caught yesterday. Then she would wave it at him.

The thought of yesterday's catch brought a memory of the flavour of roasted fish, of the crispness of the blackened skin, and her mouth watered as she shifted impatiently, feeling the sand grind beneath her bare feet. Of course, if she didn't catch one Mister Ellis would. He got three big ones yesterday, and she had helped him to cook them. He was clever at catching fish. He was clever at everything.

She looked at him occasionally from the corner of her eye. He was very slim, and the muscles of his stomach made a nice lumpy pattern with a little hollow at either side. There was hair on his chest, but not too much. Betty said that all men had lots of thick hair on their chests, but Betty was stupid. She said that if a man didn't have a lot of hair on his chest he wasn't allowed to get married to anyone, and that's where they got all the priests from. She was really stupid. Father O'Brien had hair in his nose, lots of it, and on his ears, and he was a priest, and if you had hair in your nose you had to have hair on your chest. But he was old and fat and nobody would want to marry him even if he had tons of hair.

Father Colin didn't have hair in his nose, or on his ears. He was nice, and he smiled a lot even though he was very serious. His chin was very smooth, and Silly Betty said he didn't have to shave because he was so holy. But he did shave, he smelled of something that men put on when they shave, and she had smelt it when he talked to her. Father Colin told her to come to his office when Sister Agatha was mad at her, just before they left Paa, and he had sat down whilst she stood so her eyes were on a level with his. He had nice brown eyes and his voice was soft. He told little jokes and made her laugh, even though he was supposed to get mad at her for disobeying Sister Agatha.

She didn't dare to look at his eyes too much; it made her embarrassed and she wanted to giggle, so she looked at his chin, and it was really smooth. She wanted to touch it and see how smooth it was, but she didn't dare. He had said a lot of stuff to her about obeying Sister Agatha, but she didn't take any notice, she knew he just had to say that. When he'd finished talking, he had put his hand on her shoulder and wished her good luck, and hoped that he would see her again.

She wished she had asked him if she could touch his chin, but after that it was too late. Now she would never get to touch it. He had put his hand on her shoulder though, and she remembered that. It was nice. Father Colin didn't touch anybody usually; he always seemed to have a pen to play with or something. He was always nice though. Father Colin wasn't his real name; he just liked to be called that. Sister Agatha would always call him by his real name of Father Bryne, and that was the name on his office door, under Father O'Brien's.

A cry of triumph from her right broke her reverie. With one swift thrust, Stuart had skewered a fish and upended his spear, hoisting it from its sunken world to flap wildly in the air. Raising the spear aloft like a Centurion bearing the standard of his legion, he waded to the beach and pulled the fish from the barbed point to throw it onto the hot sand, well clear of the water.

Tania watched him enviously as he ploughed his way through the waves. He was good at fishing. And he was lucky too because he could do what he wanted. He could go where he wanted when they left this island, he could be with who he wanted. When he got home he would go and see his wife and live with her. She would be crackers if she didn't want to live with him, she was probably wishing that she hadn't left him already.

He had told her that he lived in a city with a long name near London, and his father still lived there, and he went to school there when he was a boy. So all his friends were there of course, and he would see them every day. All her friends were at the Institute in Paa and she would never see them again. All except Sister Therese of course. She was dead, and she was buried at sea like a sailor.

Another fish was meandering towards her. Tania wiped the gathering sweat quickly from her forehead and adjusted the woven hat that shaded her face. She would get this one, she would remember about the water making it look to be in the wrong place, she would go right down with the spear and pin it to the bottom... She struck, and one of the points caught the fish through the tail, then it twisted free and was gone.

She uttered a word that she had heard Mister Ellis mutter once, and then in horror at what she had said looked guiltily across the water to him. He hadn't heard though. He was cleaning the fish and throwing the guts bits down the sand. Good. What would he have said if he had heard? But the fish, the fish was still there! It was twisting about hurt and not going away, just going backwards and forwards!

Tania raised the spear and plunged into an orgy of spearing as the injured fish swam erratically before her, harder to hit than when it had browsed for food, but now too confused by injury to flee the clumsy spear. As it twisted at random through the water the fish left the shelter of the reef, and Tania followed it across the sandy floor of the bay, striking again and again, legs high stepping to escape the drag of the water, spray flying out from her efforts, her hat falling off into the water and narrowly escaping being skewered.

On perhaps the twentieth thrust the multiple points of the spearhead struck the fish squarely and she pinned it to the bottom and pressed down hard, driving the points securely through the shining body. Then cautiously she in her turn hoisted her catch triumphantly aloft. Mister Ellis was sitting on the sand laughing though, and as she raised the fish he stood up and clapped. Tania marched forwards with all that she could muster of a conqueror's dignity, but the effect was spoilt as she struck one foot against a hidden rock and fell to her knees in the surf, at which he dropped back on his bottom on the sand, overcome with hilarity. When she emerged from the water he stood up though, and came to meet her, sobering down and examining her catch solemnly.

"Where's the shark?" he asked. Tania looked at him in rage. "I thought you were having trouble with a school of sharks and killing them all." He dodged quickly to the side as the girl hurled the fish at him, and ran in a circle around the cleaned catch as she pursued him, brandishing the blunt end of the spear before her.

But it was too hot for this kind of game, and throwing down the spear she retrieved her fish and dumped it by the others. "Mine's nearly as big as yours," she stated proudly.

"I doubt it," Stuart replied, still laughing, but then thought better of his humour and assumed a sober face. Tania looked at him suspiciously. He was making some kind of joke. "Yes it's a nice fish," he complimented her judiciously, "as big as the one you got yesterday. And you got two." Picking up the knife he started to clean her catch, and she turned away grimacing.

"That's horrid."

"Not as horrid as eating the nasty bits," he replied, hurling said bits down the sand for the incoming tide to deal with. Yesterday he had thrown some of the insides at her in fun, but the girl had been genuinely upset, and he would not repeat the joke again, remembering his own childhood nausea at seeing a chicken killed.

"That's a big knife. Do you do a lot of cooking?"

"No, it's not a cooking knife. It's an American army knife. One of their officers gave it to me during the war." He wiped the heavy blade clean with leaves prior to sheathing it.

"That was a long time ago. Did you fight with it?" The girl's eyes had widened in excitement.

"I carried it all through the war. The Americans had good knives. We did too, but I preferred this. We had side arms as well. Guns that is. Revolvers in holsters, and other stuff."

They each threaded their catch onto the shaft of their spears and went down the beach to remove the sand with a brisk dip in the sea, then set of back to Log City, two island warriors, each with a spear resting on one shoulder, the fruits of their success swaying at the end. Stuart had thrust the Bowie knife in its sheath into the waist of his shorts, and the girl's eyes rested on it with interest as she scampered at his side, matching his longer stride. "Did you kill anyone with it?"

He didn't answer at once. "Killing people isn't much fun. Most of the time you're frightened that you're going to be killed yourself."

"Yes but... "

"No. No I didn't. But I might kill you if you burn the fish."

"I never burn the fish. How dare you. I burnt my fingers yesterday cooking your fish."

"Well don't burn them today, we've got digging to do. Come on, I'm hungry," and they broke into a trot, their catch bouncing wildly.

They ate well, and plunged briefly into the water to remove the grime and sweat of cooking beneath the rising sun. Then gathering their equipment they turned into the shade of the jungle, heading first for the stream then upwards to the hilltop where lay their great project, mightier to the two castaways than the vast pyramids of Egypt.

Chapter 18. Log City

The once bare hillside had seen a lot of activity in the ten days since they had first marked out the sign, perhaps more human activity than it had seen in the thousands of years since it rose in volcanic fury from the sea bed, only to cool and dwindle slowly beneath the rain's erosion to its present puny state.

Such islands of soft volcanic rock do not last long, as geologists measure time. Another few thousand years and it would be gone, hill, trees, bay, pigs and all. But Stuart and the girl did not intend to be there that long, and each day found them busy on the hilltop, scurrying back and forth with their tools, and over the days, foot by foot, great patches of measured dark-grey grew to rule the irregular green plain.

Stuart's laboriously constructed plough having failed, he had attempted a mattock, boring the end of a branch with a heated screwdriver, and setting a row of the machine tools into it. This simpler tool proved excellent, and patiently each day they enlarged the great SOS, he hacking the sod away in chunks, Tania gathering the chunks into a woven basket and tipping it down the hillside.

Their early days of effort beneath the sun swiftly taught them the art of weaving, and they now worked behind a screen of broad-leaved foliage, woven into a frame of branches. As their marking progressed slowly across the hilltop they moved the screen with it, using poles to prop it upright, slanted low when the sun was high in the sky, so that they worked almost beneath a roof, then propped more steeply as the sun descended and the screen's shadow lengthened. It had taken time and patience to construct the screen, but now, though they sweated from the heat, they did not have to endure the whip of the sun's direct glare.

Fate had thrown them a minor tribute to this ingenuity, for Tania's keen eyes one morning spotted something round and golden, bobbing against the rocks at the south of the bay, and she ran swiftly to retrieve her straw hat. That and her increasingly battered sandals were all she cared to wear of the orphanage uniform. For the rest she preferred his spare clothing, though it flapped around her baggily, and Stuart humoured her, feeling sorry that one so young should be put to this trial. He wondered occasionally how dismal orphanage life must have been, that she took to this wild existence with so few complaints. Her official duty was sod disposal, but she turned her hand cheerfully to all tasks.

The business of shelter had eaten several days of their time, for after the storm Stuart improved their shelter, trying various ways to strengthen the flimsy uprights, which had no firm foundation in the sand, and shifted maddeningly as he added the weight of the roof thatching.

Finally had he reversed his thinking, realizing that the roof needed no supporting walls, for the surrounding trees that formed their little notch could hold it aloft. He lashed a criss-cross of branches between the trees at the height of his head, firm and strong, and from this he suspended a long pole to be the centre of the roof. To this ridgepole he fastened the lighter branches to be the rafters of the roof, and carry the final sloping thatch. The ends of these rafters he supported by binding them to uprights, which determined their height, like normal walls, but would not buckle beneath the weight of the roof, for it was suspended, and the top ends of the uprights he stabilised further by binding them to the criss-cross of branches.

The framework was strong and dependable, and he was able to lay a heavy thatching of greenery onto the rafter branches to withstand the regular downpours. It was less important that the walls withstand rain, and they were easily formed by weaving thin branches between the uprights. The final shelter far outdid his earlier efforts, for it neither sat clumsy and collapsing on the sand, nor was it a sagging roof, trying vainly to span the too-wide space between the trees, but was a firm, square little hut, with a well thatched ridged roof, grasped firmly in a spider's web of scaffolding that married it to the trees.

Occasionally he had received a visit from the building inspector, in the form of a small pig that wandered from the forest to snuffle for scraps and eye his work. It was shy of them, bolting clumsily on its short legs if they approached, but occasionally it allowed Tania to pet it, and sometimes she chased it for sport. Don't get too friendly with the grunter, he thought, a barbeque will make a nice change when we get a few things out of the way.

As the hut had grown towards its final satisfactory state, it occurred to him that the girl had no private place of her own, and she was past the age of being merely a small child. In the toil and deprivation of the first few days he had given no thought to the matter, thankful enough that they lay on the sand for sleep, when their bed could have been the ocean bed, and he had assumed that the uncomplaining girl felt much the same.

But as the frame grew, he wondered if he should give the point some attention, and leaned a couple of spare poles speculatively against the ridge, saying that he could divide the single room down the middle if she liked. He asked reluctantly, for the sign would take many weeks to complete, and each day that it remained a mere row of sticks was a day when a plane might pass over sightlessly.

But she had been amused at his suggestion, and joked that he needn't build a city, as long as they didn't get rained on at night anymore. He suspected that she was a little afraid to be on her own, so he dropped the idea, glad to avoid the extra work, and laughed a little at himself for thinking of building an inner wall to a hut that had only the flimsiest of outer, and that he should consider such delicate points when they lived the way they did.

They slept in what they wore, and wore what they slept in, and their laundry and bath time were one with their fishing. That rough side of their life seemed to bother the girl as little as it did him, for she was a good few years short of that age at which the title of Young Lady would have any meaning. If anything she grew more tomboyish with each day, and Stuart noticed an increasing gaiety in her manner, as though their marooning was becoming a welcome adventure to her. She might have been on holiday with a favourite uncle, and he, relieved that he was not to be tormented by a whiney child, responded, and often they softened the hard day with a little horseplay, and laughter returned to their lives

Pleased at his final success, he had stood admiring the hut for a while, walking back to judge its lines from a distance, until the girl cheekily asked him if he needed a camera. He answered only vaguely though, for he was trying to remember the date, and he could not.

This disturbed him, and after some counting on the fingers he reluctantly hacked the score of their days into the bark of a tree. Nine. Their days of confinement had exceeded a week, and neither the sky nor the sea had been marked by a sign of life. But though they had abandoned hope of swift rescue, they now had the consolation of comfort, for when the rain fell in the night they lay beneath the dense roof dry and untroubled, occasionally stirring from sleep to listen to the heavy drops pounding the layered leaves, and through the sketchy walls watch the water pouring silver in the moonlight from the shaggy eaves and spattering noisily onto the sand.

From that morning on Tania had called the hut Log City, and fell into a habit of inventing names for the features of the island. She was cheerful and useful, and as he would now have admitted easily, her presence made this isolation tolerable. It proved pleasanter to continue sharing the hut, for when they settled at night on either side of the wide spread sail they could chat, and on the back of their words take flight from their narrow prison, and roam through the world that for a while was denied to them.

With nothing to do but await drowsiness, they told each other of the mosaic of small and great incidents that made up their lives before the island, and in the silences watched the stars that hung brilliant beyond the door-less entrance. Often Stuart found himself pausing in his stories and editing his words, for like all men there was much in his life that was not proper for a schoolgirl's ears, and in the harmless darkness it was easy to forget his companion's age. She drank in his words, and strove to match them with stories of her own, and he was surprised to find himself laughing at the petty doings of girls and nuns.

With the completion of the hut, they had set to the task of digging out the sign in earnest, and each day laboured stolidly at it, doggedly cheerful, determined not to give way to despair. On the twelfth day they had seen the speck of a distant plane crossing the sky far away in the East, and had run anxiously back and forth on the beach, feeling impelled to do something, yet in reality unable to do anything other than will the distant pilot to turn his craft and take a closer look at this island. Other than that, nothing. But at least the outside world still existed, and they had not somehow fallen of the map.

It dismayed him that the sign had progressed slowly, but the grass was tough and wiry, and much of the day was eaten by their eternal search for food and firewood. At least they had the hut finished, he consoled himself, and the screens, and the time wasting plough idea was behind them. Nearly two weeks had passed, but now he had it all under control. His main worry had been water, but though the spring could wane rapidly during a dry day, it swelled to new vigour with each of the frequent rainfalls. They could survive, and it was possible that the nomadic natives might visit the island again.

It seemed that with the commencement of the sign cutting they swiftly fell into a routine, which irked him more with each passing day, yet strangely became easier. Why it should be easier, he could not have said, unless it was that life was simple and the girl amusing, but his irritation was that there seemed to be too few hours in the day. The sun mercilessly roused them each morning, and progressed swiftly across the sky, to drop less than twelve hours later into the western sea, leaving them blind in the tropical night until the next day, and what had seemed a simple task of a few days dragged, for a thousand small difficulties hindered them.

The hours of their hot slavery on the hilltop seemed long and cruel, yet were too short, for too many of them were devoured by the petty tasks of survival. The unworried fish would not hasten to their deaths, but swam lazily between the coral reefs, and he schooled himself not to fret as they awaited them patiently, spears in hand. The water was to be fetched, and boiled, for though they had suffered no sickness from the falling trickle, he made a rule that they drank no water, nor ate any food that had not been boiled.

And this imposed another task that became harder with each passing day: the gathering of wood for the fire. They had exhausted the driftwood to be found at the high water mark on the steep sands, and had turned to scouring the forest for fallen branches. They had made a great collection of timber at the foot of the trees, just clear of the hut, and organized it into different piles. Fine slivers and pieces that would take flame easily from the glass, or from dying embers, larger pieces that would add quickly to the bulk of an already strong fire, and finally great logs and branches.

These latter they never used entirely, but in the long evenings would lay them across the fire to be divided into pieces by the gnawing of the flames. When they tired of sitting and talking he would roll the burning log from the fire pit and souse it in seawater from one of their many cans, and they would leave it hissing in steamy protest on the sand as they crawled beneath the thatch of their shelter.

Often he re-drew the calculation of his sign, crawling on the sand before Log City, scratching with a twig, and once – to amuse himself, or perhaps to know his prison better – he attempted a crude map of the island. At first he thought that a great letter C would best describe it, a simple semi circle of land enclosing a bay, but then saw that this failed to describe its elongated nature.

Drawing repeatedly, he decided finally that the island had much the shape of a pear, an upside-down pear if north were to be the top of his map. The northern highlands were the base of this pear, solid and rounded, formed by the hill and its treed slopes, promising to endure centuries of the rain's erosion. The southern lowlands were its tapered upper part, narrowing to the ragged point where he had buried Roger, and as though to complete this similarity, the spur of rock ran out nearly from this point to the east, giving the island a stalk like that of a pear, bent awry from its pointed end, as often pear stalks were.

And now with his scratching stick he could hack out this pear-island's dominating feature. Nature had taken a massive bite from this fruit, one-third devouring it, hacking into the hill's eastern side to form the steep forested slopes behind the old hut and the northern cliff beyond, and devouring deep into the central lowlands right down to the southern spur, and so forming the arc of the bay, walled and sheltered at either end. "And here we sit," he murmured, rising from his sketching, "well eaten."

Tania had wandered over to look at his map. "That's like a pier," she said brightly, pointing out to the barrier rocks, as the long southern spur had somehow come to be named.

"Yes. Brighton bloody pier. Mind you don't go climbing out there again. The top's flat enough to make you think its safe, but there's all kinds of cracks and dips."

"Fusspot. I got my hat."

"I know, but we don't want any broken legs. No doctors here, I've only been out there once myself. No point in going again."

"If you'd fallen I could bury you, and put a sign 'Humpty Dumpty'." And she pocked at him with the stick until he was obliged to chase her giggling down the beach and administer a punitive tickling, for moral must be kept up amongst the troops, himself included, and their little amusements refreshed his mind.

It was not often that he thought of Jennifer, for she had become the least of his worries. Sometimes she seemed to him as unreal as a character in a fairy story set on a distant planet, but at other times she loomed suddenly to the foreground of his mind, angering him in the way that a half-wanted piece of lost property angers, being neither capable of use nor possible to be forgotten. At these times he found himself cursing her as though this imprisonment was her fault, as though her betrayal had summoned him across the water to fall into this sandy trap.

Occasionally he speculated on Julia, if that was her name, and felt pity for the drowned woman. She must have had her dreams, her secrets, but they were gone, sunken with her at the bottom of this bay, and the subject of his brief flirtation was now of interest only to fish.

Yet though she was dead, and when he thought of it, by now well rotten, and his legal wife lived, yet if his harassed thoughts wandered briefly into the erotic, it was Julia who he caressed in his inner vision. She was one of those women who live eternally in the memory of a man, because they do not exist as a person, but as an event. They are a moment when the place was right, and the mind receptive. Then, though not the greatest of beauties, the woman who speaks the right word, who casts a passing smile in the right manner, she is immortalised, and though perhaps never seen again she enters the ranks of the lost gods.

And with the coming of each new day he would throw the sand mingled ashes into the rising or receding waves, whilst the girl again ignited some sun-dried chips. And at the end of each day, the sign had grown. But only a little.

Chapter 19. Saint George's Day

This morning he couldn't face the drudgery of the sign. It was coming into shape well, the outlines cut according to his endless measuring, the turf torn away over the days until the first scanty patches had become great swathes of raw soil. Already its meaning must be clear from the air, and he wondered if it were not futile to add to it, hacking and carting as though in grim service to sky gods that aloofly ignored their worshippers.

The girl had put the hat on it as dusk fell on the previous day. "This ought to be here in a hundred years," she had declared, hurling the day's final basket of soil down the hillside. He had not replied to her, for her words had rubbed on his frustration. Nearly three weeks. Sixteenth of January they had crashed, and this was the fourth of February. Over two weeks of toiling on the three giant letters, and who had seen it but themselves?

Twice they had spotted the fleck of a distant ship moving slowly across the water, and once more the speck of an aircraft arrowing high and silent through the sky. Seeing these distant promises, he and the girl had swiftly heaped more wood onto the smouldering fire and excitedly run waving on the beach, or leapt with out-flung arms on the hilltop, shouting into the great blue green void of air and water that separated them.

But no echo of help had come back through that void, for each time the petty distance defeated them. Each time the incident seared his heart with hope and frustration, and he stared intensely at the distant vessel, as if by will he could reach, reach through those miles of empty air, reach across the blue of sky and ocean, touch the eye of the distant traveller, declare "We are here! We are here!" and magnetically draw to himself the inattentive world.

But each time they had gradually fallen silent, their arms drooping back to their sides, and watched helplessly as the ship slowly faded into the faint line of horizon, disappear as it had appeared, until again they were alone. And the higher, faster speck of an aircraft served them no better, vanishing heedless into the haze from which it had emerged. The third such incident had happened only yesterday, and he had finally vented his feelings by shouting wry sarcasms across the waves, and the girl catching his mood had shrilled her own witty chorus.

It was the angle, the angle and the distance. For a ship to see it, it must pass to the East, for the hilltop sloped a little to the East, but not enough, so he could forget about ships. It would be a plane that would finally see their plea, of this he was certain, and then it must pass nearly overhead, and the pilot must look down.

Stuart had pictured him relaxed at the controls, bored perhaps, glancing casually over the wing at yet another scrawny island, then stiffening in surprise at the huge words bold in raw grey-brown soil on the green of the hill. And then he would speak, would radio, would point it out to his co-pilot, would bank the 'plane in a great arc to look again at the unbelievable message, would loose altitude and see the two frantic human ants scurrying on the thin ribbon of sand.

Or would this speculative pilot do none of these things? Would he, laden with his fair share of the inertia that flawed so much of human affairs, would he ponder dull-witted on how the island came to be thus marked, and continue on his way?

No. That was ridiculous. Criminal to think that way. They had not yet been seen, and therefore they had not yet been rescued. When they were seen, then they would be rescued. This was by no means the greatest disaster in the world, and he must on no account act so weakly as to let the girl think it was.

That wouldn't be too hard. He need have no anxiety there, for he had come to realize that to the girl it had become a great lark. She talked of their rescue as earnestly as he did, and shared enthusiastically his dreams and schemes of far away Europe, but for her that was tomorrow's chapter in an escape that had already happened, for her charitable captors had gripped her more securely than this narrow island could hold them.

But despite all of his counting of blessings, it remained a fact that the 'plane had overlooked them yesterday, and today he felt deflated and sour.

Twenty days at it in all, he thought, and every day like slaves, till I can't think of anything else but dirt. Take a break and let your head clear, before you go mad, and then you'll be able to start again, fresh, and he threw down the mattock in decision. "Holiday time. Lets take a look at the caves at the North end."

She looked up in surprise. "We're nowhere near finished."

"We are for today. If anything goes overhead – well if they can't see this, then they can't see anything. The second S is a bit ragged, that's all, and we'll straighten it up tomorrow, then we'll start making them thicker."

"Is it a holiday?" she asked, puzzled by his sudden announcement.

"Yes, definitely. It's Sunday today, I think, and if it isn't, then it's Saint Georges Day. Anything. We need to take a break."

And the girl threw down her basket and followed him willingly, but the caves could wait, for it was time for food, and today being a holiday, a siesta was permissible, and presently they lay dozing in the shade of the shelter.

She awoke muzzily, to find him doing a little spring-cleaning outside the shelter, and childlike followed his example, emerging to shake out the accumulated sand from the bundle of her pillow. Part of the pillow she would not have so used a few weeks ago, for it was the torn dress in which she had left Paa. She flapped it briskly and held it out before her, pulling a hideous face and murmuring that it was the ugliest garment she had ever seen, and hating the thought of ever needing it again, she rolled and knotted it into a ball and kicked it down the sands.

To her great delight Stuart sprang on it and delivered a kick of his own, at which she chased it, squealing in mock dismay, and so a football match commenced that zig zagged along the beach until they arrived hot and winded before the native hut, and plunged laughing into the sea. They had played at football before, but last time they had used a pair of his shorts. It was fun, and the water was really cool and nice. She started to swim steadily out to the further reefs where the sheltering cliff ended.

"Can you make it?" Stuart called.

"Of course," she answered. He fussed sometimes, as though she was a little girl, and not twelve next. She felt confident in the water, for she had done a lot of swimming between the reefs of the fishing ground, and once or twice had been out beyond the cliff end and seen the cave he had told her about, with the waves entering roughly and surging out again angrily. But that was as far as she had been, for the water was deep and rough past this point.

She had been frightened to swim down by Log City for a long time as well, because the dead people were under the water out by Tiger Rock. That was silly though, because Tiger Rock was a long way out, and in any case the people were all eaten by now. She pulled a face at the thought, hoping that none of the fish from that end of the bay swam up to their fishing ground. She would never, never fish down by Log City, or eat a fish if they caught one there.

Now they were out beyond the shallow water where they fished, out from the shelter of the cliff, and they turned left to the North to follow the last stretch of the island's East coast, that already was curving away to form the Northern point. The waves were much stronger out here, but she could manage, and Stuart swam alongside her as they headed for a level apron of rock that ran out a few feet from the foot of the cliff on the near side of the cave. She crawled onto the flat surface gratefully, for she was tiring and had not wanted him to see it.

They found that the ledge ran narrowing to the cave mouth and turned in to the dim interior, so that they could enter without braving the surge of the water that thrust in and out of the ragged opening. Within they were able to follow the ledge to the back of the cave, but there was little to see, only that there was a rise in the floor, so that at the very rear there was a space clear of the water, though the constant spray kept all wet. The light here was dim, and until their sight grew accustomed to it they crept along by touch. When they emerged again the sea struck their eyes with brilliance.

Leaving the cave they tentatively tried to round the northern point of the island a little more by climbing up the sloping cliff face and passing over the top of the cave mouth. At first they were successful, for there were narrow ledges and footholds, which they inched along until they passed over the cave, the green water rushing and sucking beneath them. It was not too difficult, and she felt a thrill of keen excitement at being perched over the ruthless surge of water.

Stuart felt it too, and wondered at himself that he should take even this minor risk in a place so remote from help.

But they were on holiday, and his mind tasted the long past flavour of being a small boy, scrambling over the remoter rocks of some English bay, tiny metal bucket and spade clutched in one hand, the other steadying him against the rough, slimy surface that grated beneath his sandals, watching the green slimy weeds rise and fall with the cold English waves, seeing the patient black mussels constantly covered and uncovered. Then a clumsy step on the uneven rock would bring his shin sharply down onto its hard roughness, and with a cry he would retreat from that sport to the smooth sand, to splash water onto the injury and gingerly touch the stinging bright red abrasion.

Raising his eyes from the throbbing injury, he could make out his parent's distant deck chair, and in a few paces he would pass into the host of other holidaymakers drawn to the beach by the brief glory of the uncertain English summer. Pale men in swimming trunks, the sun glistening from the sweat of their balding temples, their wives dumpy in flowered swim suits, peering through dark glasses into bags where sandwiches lurked. Unknown children like himself running shouting between the deck chairs, the thomp of footballs kicked by boys in their glorious teens, who leapt and fought for the ball with warrior shouts, the sparse soft beginning of beards on their young chins.

He would traverse this horde of babbling humanity, as always mistaking the place where his parents were, until he found them suddenly. Then his mother would fuss over the graze, but he would pull away impatiently, his eye fixed on the gaily coloured booth a mere fifty paces away, for surely it was time for another ice cream, and could he have one of those with the stick of chocolate in it?

He forgot the details, but his mind tasted the flavour, and for happy moments he savoured this petty scramble, forgetting that there was nothing beyond it but a few bare, lonely acres of trees, grass, and sand that had never seen the imprint of a deck chair.

This was a change, Tania thought. Stuart could do all kinds of things like climb trees and swim, but he didn't usually unless he had a plan and it was something serious. She hadn't seen him swim out into the rougher water for ages, not since he dived down to the plane last time for the stuff, and now they were climbing up on the rocks for fun. When they were on the hilltop he got nervous if she went up to the high point and looked down at the rocks, and now they were climbing about on them. She had always wanted to see what was in the cave, but there was nothing much there. Still it was cool and dark, kind of spooky and secret. Danielle would have liked it. She loved ghost stories and stories about dark cupboards.

They turned back, for the cliff grew steeper a little beyond the cave, and they were faced with a choice: to plunge back into the water and return to the bay, or to press on, swimming out farther to clear the rocks, then swing west to round the high northern cliff completely, then south to gain the western beach. He stood for a while looking first at the shorter return crossing, then west.

"Can you make it?"

She felt nervous, but it wasn't so far, and if he were with her she would be safe. "I think so,"

They entered the water at a leisurely pace, steadily heading out, feeling their unstrained ability carry them beyond their wall-less prison, until they were well clear of being dashed against the cliff and its attendant half-drowned crags. Turning, they beheld the rounded vee of the North cliff like the prow of a great ship towering arrogantly over their petty journey, the water creaming at its base, the several caves like the wounds of cannon balls, the heave and fall of the waves making the whole mass of land appear to rise and fall majestically before them.

They struck out again, turning west, but a clumsy stroke caused her to take the crest of a wave in the face, and she struggled for a moment, choking, whilst he dog paddled beside her. Then she had recovered and they were swimming again, though now she felt a little scared, as for a little while she hadn't been able to get her breath. But like him she maintained a steady calm stroke, and the headland inched past them until they could see around it, could see the trees that crept down to the water's edge on the west side, and they turned more decisively south, for they had rounded the scattering of reef and fallen rock and the water before them was clear.

She was growing weary, but knew now that their energy would be sufficient, and it was interesting to see all this from so far out, and she could catch glimpses of the ground between the trees on the slope of the hill, and they turned victoriously in to meet the trees.

"Race you!" he said as they saw their destination growing close.

"Not fair. You're bigger than me." But she desperately increased her pace in the next instance, and he teased her mercilessly as he easily kept even, till in the last yards he gracefully fell back a little, and shrieking with delight she surged dripping from the water onto the narrow wisp of sand, and seized the nearest tree trunk in triumph.

He surged out laughing behind her and pursued her down the beach, for now it was indeed a holiday, and overtaking her with a shout he grasped the girl by the waist and swung her giggling into the air.

That was fun. She had been a bit scared, but now that they had got to the West beach she was glad that they had swum round. If Stuart had asked her twice she would have said that it was too far, but now that they had done it, it seemed easy. Funny how the island looked different from the water, more interesting. And he was fun to be with. She remembered that her dad used to pick her up and carry her on his shoulders. No one had carried her for years though.

"Ice Cream. When we get to England we'll have ice cream every day," he said suddenly.

Yes. Definitely that would be nice. Cool, cool ice cream. They were right down at the south end of the beach now, where it widened out, and soon they would be among all that rocky place where Mr. Dawson was buried. She didn't want to go there just now, though she didn't usually mind being there, in fact she would sometimes go to look at his grave. It made her feel quiet and thoughtful somehow, and she was glad that the waves hadn't moved the stones. But they were heavy stones, and it would take a real storm.

"Let's go through the wood." There were a lot of interesting things in the wood, little flowers and birds. She wished that she had a sketch book. Sometimes at the Mal she had tried sketching. But she would need some coloured crayons, because what was really good was that the birds had bright colours, and they stood out in the green leaves. The flowers too. Most of them were tiny, but they were so pretty, like this one.

"Stuart, do you like these?" it was a little red and purple flower, so little, that always seemed to hide in the grass. It was her favourite.

"What do they call this?"

"I don't know. I've never noticed it before."

"Which do you like best? This, or these yellow ones here?"

"Which do I like best? I don't know. I never noticed either of them before."

"Blind man. I'm alone on an island with a blind man. Please help me God."

"I'm not blind. I see things that you don't"

"What? You don't see anything that I don't see," she announced, leading the way between the trees.

"I see things that you can't."

"I can see any thing that you can see. What can you see that I can't?"

"Your big backside."

"Ooooooh." That was an insult. She snatched up a twig and chased him around a tree, but he was too agile, and she hurled the leafy weapon after him, then continued on her way.

"Just wait. I'll tell Sister Agatha what you said. She'll lock you up in the kitchen at the Mal and make you wash dishes."

"She'll lock you up as well, and you'll have to sew that dress back together."

"Never. No more nasty dresses. No more Sister Agatha, no more Mal." And in celebration she broke into a wild parody of a curvaceous movie star, lurching her skimpy hips hugely from side to side as she threaded her way through the greenery.

Wicked man. He was fun when he was like this. Danielle had an uncle who did all kinds of silly things, and she used to tell stories about him in the dormitory at night. Once he dyed his dog's tail green and said it was a special kind of dog that cost a lot of money, and once he got drunk and tried to get into the wrong house. His key wouldn't fit in the lock of course, so he went in the garden and slept there all night. They all loved Danielle's stories about her uncle. All except fat Helen. She said that Danielle didn't really have an uncle, she just made him up to feel important, or else why didn't he take her away? But Helen was always nasty like that.

They came across the tiny brook, little more than a damp mark between the trees.

"Stuart, why doesn't this run out at the beach anymore?" she had seen the thin trickle cutting its way down the west sands on other days.

"Not enough water. It hasn't rained for two days, so the stream must be drying up again."

They followed the muddy trickle to the crevasse.

"We should build a bigger pool. Dig this little pool out and have a proper pool. Then if the water stops running down the hill we have a lot of water."

"True," he replied "but what we've got in the little pool would last a long time. We just have to boil it"

"Yes. But if we had a big pool we could wash in it properly, and it wouldn't matter because we would have to boil it in any case if we had to use it. Let's make it deeper. You've said we should make it deeper."

"Work time again," he protested.

"Yes, but this is different. This is fun," she responded as she gouged at the bottom with a stick.

Danielle knew things. Not that she was always right, but she seemed to hear things before other people. It was Danielle who told her about Rosalind and the man in the bazaar, and Danielle who got her to shout the naughty word out of the window.

Yet Danielle never seemed to get caught or get into trouble, whereas she was always in front of Sister Agatha's desk. And Sister Agatha hated her, but she was always nice to Danielle. But it was Danielle who invented the Sisi Club.

It was something that Sister Mary had said, when she did those special classes. Usually they had Geography, and History, and English and stuff, but sometimes they had funny classes that weren't about anything with a name. Sister Mary had said that they must have some special lessons to prepare them for life, and usually she did that in the Religion class, but it was all sort of mixed up, and she talked about When They Would Be Adults, and about Men and Women, and it was all very important except that she didn't really say anything. But it all sounded really mysterious, and seemed as though she had said something.

Once she had been talking about growing up, and said that then a lot of things happened, and it sounded as though she was talking about the private bits, only she talked about them as though they were wicked and called them Secret Sin. Or she said that the bits did Secret Sin. That was sometime last year and she didn't remember exactly, 'cause it was all so vague.

But that night Danielle was telling stories, and she said that the sisters called your thing a Secret Sin, and there was a long story about it with Adam and Eve wearing aprons, and while she was telling it somebody kept pretending to be a ghost and whispering Secret Sin, and it got to be See See. After that if anyone in their club wanted to mention that bit they said Seesee, and it got really scary, because some girls kept saying "Seesee" at silly times, like hissing it in class, or in prayers, and she was sure that the sisters would know what they meant.

She wondered sometimes what the real name for it was. She couldn't remember calling it any thing before they gave it a name, but it must have one, like a head or a foot had. All the other people in the world couldn't call it Seesee, 'cause that was their private name that they invented, and no one else knew it. So what was the real name? Would it be in a book somewhere? And what did men call theirs? Did they all have one the same or did priests have a different one? Danielle said that priests had long ones that weren't safe, but it was okay because they dropped of after two years of being a priest, but sometimes Danielle made things up. She wasn't certain what Danielle meant by long ones, and she didn't like to ask.

She glanced at Stuart covertly as they dredged the soft mud. He would know of course, but she couldn't ask him. Well, not directly of course. But he said all kinds of interesting things, so she could try.

"Do you know any priests?"

He glanced at her. What was coming now? "I knew Colin Bryne. You know, your special friend Father Colin."

"I told you before, he's not my special friend. Besides him do you know any?"

"No, not priests. I knew a few padres in the army. They're sort of like priests, army priests."

"What were they like?"

"Like? I never thought about it really. They did their job, but it's a funny job in a war."

"Were they funny?"

"Sky pilots? I suppose they were a bit. We didn't usually take them seriously."

Tania squinted at him, puzzled. Before now, she hadn't heard an adult – an important one that is – talk about priests as though they were nothing, or silly. But that wasn't what she was interested in. This is getting me nowhere, she thought, and neither did any other of her oblique questions, until they noticed the light dimming about them, and leaving their task returned hungry to the hut.

She carried her muddy stick with her in imitation of Stuart, for he bore his before him like Moses' staff, his mind grasped by sentimental memories of leaving beaches at the end of long days, tired but content, his bucket and spade in one hand, his mother's in the other.

Chapter 20. The Mal

As dusk fell they returned to the hut. The day had been long and hard, for Stuart had been determined to justify their holiday with renewed effort, and they had stuck at the wearying toil of cutting the stubborn turf throughout the long, hot afternoon, until the glowing descent of the sun towards the western sea relieved them of their duty. Now came the end of the scant twelve hours of light that seemed too short for their task, and the brilliance of the day would be matched by twelve hours of thick, velvet darkness, when nothing could be done, neither fishing nor digging.

The shadows of their marker sticks lay long across the hilltop as they scooped the remains of the signal fire into the firepot. A few minutes of contemplation from the high point, Stuart looking at the letters slowly taking shape from their efforts. He was content; they had done their best; but the girl's thoughts were unknown to him as she stood gazing at the bright east, where the setting sun cast a spear of gold across the waters to their island. Then they turned and descended through the dimming forest to the stream, pausing briefly to fill their water jug and wash the dirt and sweat from hands and face.

At the hut, Stuart scrapped the dead black ashes from between the stones of the fire pit, and the girl upended the burning timber from the firepot into the centre of the blackened sand. Untold she took a hand full of small pieces from the woodpile and fed the weak flames, whilst Stuart hauled their cooking pot from the hut and positioned it carefully on the ring of stones. The remainder of the cleaned fish from the morning were inside, covered in water. That way they were kept reasonably cool, and boiling the whole mix should kill any bacteria. Or so Stuart had reasoned, and so far they had suffered no stomach problems.

He took his broad ash-scooping stick back to its place, and like the girl sat on the sand and gazed patiently at the rising flames as they licked the can. Housekeeping was complete. In the morning he would scoop the ashes from the fireplace into the pot that they now cooked in, and hurl them into the cleansing waves before scouring the can with sand and seawater. Then he - or more likely Tania - would take the glass and ignite a sliver of wood, and from that shaving build a fire. The girl had taken over that job, having developed quite a talent with the focusing glass.

But for now there were no more tasks, save to wait patiently until the water bubbled, and watch the last faint halo of light fade over the hilltop, watch the dim features of the northern cliff darken into a solid black shoulder against the stars appearing in the now purple sky. He rolled onto his back, shielding his eyes from the red glare of the fire, and stared up as the constellations emerged faintly from the dark heavens, gaining steadily in brilliance until the night sky was transformed into a theatre of elf-lamps, their remote brilliance mirrored flickeringly on the murmuring waves.

Occasionally there was the clunk of the girl feeding the fire, and from the trees came the muffled noises of the roosting birds. Otherwise, there was nothing, nothing but that great armada of remote stars hanging motionless in the clean depths, far and unreachable. Neither spoke as the minutes passed, for both were emptied by the day, and words were feeble things, crushed to futility beneath this roof of glittering splendour.

It was almost a violation when the bubbling of the water drove the savour of fish to his nostrils, and the prone girl sat up in interest as he fetched the cloth to lift the steaming pot from the fire. With food their weariness fell away.

"Twenty," said the girl, mumbling around fish, breaking the silence as they ate. "That's twenty days today that we've been here."

"Yes I know. Twenty-one if we count the day we crashed."

"Is that why you cut the marks on the tree?"

"Yes. Six cuts, and one across makes seven. And tomorrow I'll put one across the last six, and that's three weeks."

"So we've been here three weeks tomorrow, or today? I've lost count."

"Today. I'm counting the day we crashed. I think it was busy enough to count. In fact I'm sure it was busy enough."

"Then you should put the seventh mark tonight. Before we go to sleep."

"I usually do it in the morning, but I forgot. It's too dark now. If I do it tonight I might cut my finger."

"You've got nine others."

"Yes but I need them all. I might need to spank somebody."

She pulled a face across the fire between them. He said things like that, but he was very good tempered, most of the time. He sort of liked to be smart about things, and he was a bit sarcastic, but in a nice way. It was his way of making jokes. She thought that he was going to be angry when she knocked the cooking pot over a couple of nights ago, and he was a bit, but he didn't say much, and he soon forgot about it. She'd said sorry, and he said not to worry, 'cause things like that passed, but it was the things that didn't pass that you had to worry about.

Then he looked all sour and serious for a bit, like he did sometimes, and she knew that he was thinking about his wife again. Once he'd said something about her, then said that he didn't ought to have told her about that. It was funny here, because with nobody else to talk to, she'd found she was letting a lot of the big secrets out, the ones she'd sworn to Danielle never to repeat, and he must be doing the same. It didn't matter too much though, because Stuart didn't seem to like nuns much, so he'd never tell on her.

He got mad about things sometimes, but he wasn't mad at her much. Usually when something made him mad he looked really grim and went really quiet, except that he muttered a bit. Sometimes he muttered quite bad words, then looked at her to see if she'd heard. At least they sounded like bad words, but some of them she hadn't heard before. The sisters never swore of course, except for holy swearing. But they were always mad about things. Always fussing about something.

"If you cut the next one tomorrow, that will be about the time I got up at the Institute, and that's when we started, really," she resumed brightly.

"That's when I started too," he answered "and a great pity." He threw a bone into the dark beyond the fire's red enclosure. Each morning since he had completed the hut he had cut another narrow slash into the bark of a nearby tree, often with a muffled curse, feeling the absurdity of the act.

"Like Cary Grant or somebody," he said absently to the flames.

"Who?"

"Me. Cutting marks in the tree. Like somebody in a film. Cutting marks to keep track of the days, like Robinson Crusoe."

"I've never seen a film," the girl offered excitedly, "not since we lived in England. Mum and Dad took me when I was very little."

Stuart looked at her in surprise. He had somehow formed the idea that she had always lived in Paa.

"It was a big place, huge! Hundreds of people. I can't remember what the film was about though. I think we only went once."

"How old were you?"

"I don't know. But I was six when we came on the ship. We came to Paa, and I went to school there. I was at school before."

"In England?"

"Yes. It must have been England. I wasn't there long."

"Why did you come to Paa?" Stuart asked, perplexed.

"I don't know. Dad had a job or something. Then he left. Him and mum used to quarrel a lot." Her voice had trailed off, and Stuart kept silent. In her few years the kid had somehow lost her parents, and occasionally the pain of it surfaced abruptly, as it did with his own loss. "He went back to

England," she resumed abruptly, "Or France. France is very close to England."

"Very," Stuart agreed.

"I stayed in Paa with mum. She was a teacher at the school. She taught English and French. That's how she met my dad. She was teaching in England."

Stuart waited, but the girl's story had halted for now, and she threw chips into the fire. "What happened to your dad?" he ventured finally.

"He wrote to me. He wrote to me for a year. Mum used to read me his letters. Then she said he stopped writing." Stuart remained silent, musing on the dismal story. "But I think he wrote to me," the girl burst out suddenly, startling him. "He wrote to me but the sisters keep the letters!"

"The sisters? Why would they keep the letters? How do you come to be with them in any case?"

"They took me there! They were there when mum was sick, always praying, but she got sicker and died. Then they took me to the Institute and told me I had to stay with them. I asked them to write to my dad, but they said they didn't know his address, and I had to stay with them till they got his address." The girl stopped and knuckled the tears that had appeared suddenly. "They put me in a room, and later they said they needed it and put me in a dormitory with a lot of other girls."

She sprang up and ran to the hut. Stuart sat silently, saddened by her account. He had assumed the girl's father to be dead, perhaps from some accident that had taken the mother at the same time. Now it appeared that he was alive. But the girl's idea that the nuns had kept his letters... No. That was the girl's fantasy, her youthful shield from the bitter truth.

In reality he had simply gone, gone like Jennifer had gone. Gone to make his own life, excusing his flight with promises of love by mail. Then as the years had passed, the face of the distant child had shrunk in his mind, until one day it seemed permissible not to write again, to forget the child along with the woman he no longer wanted. Or perhaps he knew, perhaps word had reached him of his wife's death, and he had made no answer. There was no way to know. Best to keep silent on the subject, to agree with the girl and let her keep her illusion.

She returned to the fire, tucking a handkerchief into the pocket of her shirt. "I'm going to find him." She stared across the flames at him with an expression of scared determination, half defiant and half begging his permission for her defiance.

"Well that's possible dear," he said evenly, "but he's a long way away."

"He's in Accrington," she replied.

"Where!"

"Accrington. It's in England."

"I know it's in England, but what makes you think he's in Accrington?"

"I heard them talking. Sister Agatha was talking to one of the other sisters, and I know they were talking about me. She said he's in Accrington. So I looked it up in the big Atlas, and I wrote it down and remembered how to spell it. And I'm going to get to England and go to Accrington and find him"

"Accrington! Well good luck!"

"Have you been there? What's it like?"

"I don't know dear, I really don't know. I've never been there, but I've heard of it." He racked his brain. Accrington? He couldn't even say which county it was in. "But England's not a big country. If you're anywhere in it you can soon be somewhere else."

"I know. You have to get to France first, and then get across the water to England. Me and Sister Therese were going to the Institute in Singapore, and that's on the real land. You can go on land all the way to France, then you have to cross the water again. There isn't any water all the way to France though."

"No there isn't any water. A few hundred rivers perhaps," he exclaimed. "But it's thousands of miles! You can't walk all the way there."

"Why not?"

"Why not! They won't let you, for a start. The nuns I mean. They aren't going to let you just leave, whether you're in Singapore or Paa."

The girl was quiet for a moment, then, "they won't stop me. When we get to Singapore I'll be hundreds of miles closer. Then I'll just keep getting closer till I get there. I studied it all on the big maps in the classroom. It's all west, and we're going west."

They were both silent for a while. He knew the kid by now. When she was quiet like that it was more deadly than when she stormed. He had no doubt that she meant what she said. And westward was the direction to return to anywhere in Europe. But it was ridiculous; the child knew nothing of the vast countries that were to her just shapes on a map. And never mind the distance, what about all that lay within that distance.

A picture came into his head of a classroom, some stifling classroom full of little girls sitting bored and docile at worn desks, and a black-clad figure tapping with a long pointer at the coloured patches on the hanging map, the droning voice reciting the names of countries. Then the figure chivvying them out, and sending them chattering down the sheltered halls to the lunch table, and crying havoc as some shrill voice protested at a malicious pinch. Later, at night in the dark dormitory, grievances whispered between the beds, dissection of the petty injuries of the day, until rebellion stirred, and some frail form vowed, not for the first time, to flee this place, until finally sleep drowned the half formed determination.

Through the netting over the barred windows there drifted in the night sounds of the small dark town: the occasional growl of a car, the laughter of some drunk bantering the street girls, the distant quarrelling voices that rose to shouting and ended with a scream and the shattering of glass. But in the morning the sunshine streaming in, and the brisk sister hustling the girls into the day with bleary eyes, and again there was food on the breakfast table, though the calendar was another leaf thinner, and each girl an imperceptible day older.

The day was new, and again the halls would echo the footsteps of their safe routine, whether paced willingly or sullenly.

In the morning streets outside, beggars creeping to their places by the market and stretching their hands to the world as it bustled past to buy and sell, the heavy carts grinding down the narrow streets, the stallholder's voices raised in stormy haggling with their shrewd customers. In the dirty little cafes adjoining the market the whole menagerie of petty officials, penniless drifters, desperate schemers, exchanging worn jests as they sipped their thick Arab coffee, watching the passing world with keen, acquisitive eyes, weary eyes that had seen too much, but could still crinkle at need in a false smile. And in some corner beyond the market a scrawny dog nosed cautiously amidst broken glass, sniffing hungrily at a fly infested stain that could be vomit, or blood.

And the girl would cross not merely this narrow minefield, but the thousands of miles more like it. Stuart shook his head.

"Tania, how far out of Paa town have you been?"

"I'll run away. When I was in Paa there wasn't anywhere to go, 'cus it was an island. But Singapore's on the real land, and I can just go from place to place."

"I think that you're a little young yet dear."

"Don't tell me that! That's what the sisters always said! I wrote a letter to the Prime Minister and they wouldn't send it, 'cause they said I was too young."

"Prime Minister! Well that's more than I've done. What did you put in your letter?"

"I asked him to please find my dad's address and send it to me, then I could go home. And I asked the sister who teaches English to post it for me, and she gave it to Sister Agatha, and Sister Agatha sent for me to her office."

"Was she angry?"

"Yes. She's always angry. She gave me this big lecture, on and on and on, and told me that I was ungrateful. She said lots of girls without parents were starving all over the world, and I was lucky that I wasn't one of them, 'cus they became bad people, and I had to stay with them, or I would end up being bad."

"Well dear, some of what she said was true," he began steadily, with a vague notion that it was his adult duty to defend authority, but feeling none the less a measure of heat, for this was not the first report of the good sister's world view that he had gleaned from the kid. "If..."

"It was a lot of shit."

"What was that!"

"Well it was. Just shit. She said my dad was bad."

Stuart did not speak for a while. Log City was a hot place tonight, that was for sure. But the kid had put her finger on the point of the matter accurately.

"You said it in any case. When you dropped the jug and it nearly broke."

Stuart groped the air with his hands, seeking excuses, but finding none there he lowered them again. "It doesn't sound very nice when young girls say it," he managed finally.

"She isn't nice. She said my dad was bad and I was too young to understand. I hate it when people say that. They're always telling me I'm too young. I hate it. She said that they didn't need to find him because I had to stay there till I was grown up, and when I was older I'd understand."

"Didn't she do anything to find him?" he asked gently, feeling strangely that he must tread as though through a field of mines.

"I don't know. She told me he was in Paris, and all the bad people were there. Then she said she didn't know where in Paris. And she said that she was going to keep a special eye on me, to make sure I didn't turn out bad."

"Perhaps she said that to a lot of people," Stuart commented, still striving to be just despite his conclusions.

"She didn't. She said I was her number one to watch. She had this horrid little sneak called Gillian, and Gillian told stories on me. If anybody told her any stupid story she believed it and said it was me, and then she told Sister Agatha."

He had never seen the girl so stirred up before, and realised that he too was now angry, angry at the stiff robed figure that had formed in his mind from the jumble of the girl's stories. He rarely liked Holy Joes of any kind, and this one sounded typical. What a thing to say to the kid! It seared him that this arid woman should stand the lonely girl before her heavy desk, and seek to hack away the father from the girl's mind, even as death had hacked away the mother.

He too had been angry once, even as she was now, angry with the father who belittled his dreams. Many of his father's cautions had proved to be solid, and that he would readily admit, but where had been the other thing, the gateway, the encouragement to be more than nothing.

And now, now that he was a man, here he met it again. All over the world were they not to be found in plenty, different names but yet the same people, the confidently ignorant, the preventers who could not be doers, the stiff moustaches, the stern faces, the petty titles shouting orders? And what easier a mark to flex authority on than a half-grown child, what better victim for their dim ideas than an orphan. But not this child, not any more. This young girl had... She ... And his heart recognised her, and grasped her warmly to itself, for she was the sole sharer of this his now narrow world, and her troubles had become his.

She was the person who was here with him, his only worry, who laughed at his little jokes, who annoyed and entertained him, and stopped this island from being a hell of loneliness and despair. She had not yet a dozen years, but she was resilient where he had expected hysteria, fiery where he had expected nothing but tears, and her chatter had entered his heart and mingled with his thoughts. He would not forget her when she passed from his care to her own world. She deserved. Like him she longed for life, like him she would struggle to go on.

The thought of her loss to these people made him aware of his affection for the girl, and warm determination swept through him, for all was in his hands. She had no own world, for she was lost twice to his once, lost beyond this island in the impossibilities of distance and youth, and in Singapore they would again crush her in their grey hands.

No. If the two of them could contrive to escape this place it was surely a lesser matter to evade that dreary fate, and he would not allow them to wring from her the juice of hope.

Tania watched him, a little uneasily. She had never said so much about her plan to an adult before, and she had sworn in temper. Now he was staring into the fire like some stone god with a stern carved face, all harsh in red light and black shadow, and she was sure that he was very angry. His eyes sprang up suddenly from the fire to hers. "When we get off this island I'm going to help you find your father," he announced, and thrust a lump of wood hard into the fire, as though nailing his words to the flames.

Chapter 21. Saturnalia

It was evening and they were back at Log City. A sprinkling of rain had fallen, politely waiting until their evening meal was complete, and they had retreated into the shelter to sit watching the flames splutter and dull.

The girl had been very animated and chatty all that day, and he understood that his promise of the evening before had gained him a devotee. Normally he didn't like women who talked too much, but this was different, for she was only a kid and he could always tell her to be quiet for a while, and when he did she generally was, and didn't seem to mind. At least for a while, until something else occurred to her, then she would be up and bubbling on again. A paragon if she stayed that way when she grew up, for he didn't like them too quiet either. But what was the kid's question? England, not his likes and dislikes in women, which she wouldn't be for a good few years in any case.

"What's it like in England? You like it there don't you?"

He struggled for a moment to think of what he liked most, but the girl forestalled him. "Tell me something there that you don't get in Paa."

"Well snow of course...."

"I've never seen snow. Well I suppose I have but I can't really remember. Sister Therese used to tell me about the snow in the Pyrenees. What's the snow like in England?"

The kid was resting on one elbow, looking at him with that level stare that in an eleven year old warns of a need for instant answers, admitting of no confusion.

Stuart closed his eyes and tried to picture it. "When it falls everything's white. The trees are all black and the snow's white. The sky's blue of course, but pale, and if it's clear the sun makes the snow sparkle. But the days are short. I used to go walking in the snow, and if it was nearly time for the sun to go down the snow's colour would change to a pale gold. And the side of the drifts that weren't facing the sun, they would go purple"

"Why were the trees black? Do they change colour in winter?"

"No, of course not. But all the leaves drop off in autumn so you can only see the bare branches, so they look black. Or dark at any rate"

"All the leaves drop off! Why do they do that! If all the leaves drop off the tree would die wouldn't it?"

"No, they sleep in the winter. All the leaves drop of and the trees slow down and look as though they're dead. Then in spring you see little points of green on the branches. That's the new buds of leaves growing. It gives the trees just a little bit of colour, like a blush when you look at them from a distance"

Tania considered this awhile. Buds. He meant buds like on plants of course, but there were other things called buds. Sister Agatha had lectured the girls once about the dreadful day when their buds would appear. On that terrible day they would have to begin a struggle – forever! – to keep themselves pure from the naughty men who would look at them in the streets of Paa. Bad men who smoked cigars and did things that no nice girl would want to talk about.

Or rather things that no-one knew about, for the girls did talk to each other of these mysterious things, whispering dark secrets to each other at night, hissing scandalous speculations across the narrow space between the hard beds, ears straining for the approach of the sister on night watch. Danielle had the bed on Tania's left, and she had sworn with eyes huge in the dim light that Rosalind had been spoken to by such a man, and he had walked with her in the bazaar where the girls were forbidden to go, and he had kissed her! No-one had seen Rosalind for a week after that, for the nuns had made her do penance and like them live alone in a little spooky room at the top of the building.

"Where did he kiss her," Tania had hissed back. Surely not in the bazaar where the natives would see it! Danielle's eyes had widened in supreme incredulity at the horror of the question.

"On the mouth of course! You don't think Danielle would let him kiss her on, on...." And she had fallen back aghast at the thought.

"No, I meant..." said Tania, a little puzzled, but it was too late.

After that Tania had a reputation for deep wisdom in these matters, and it was remembered that her mother had been French, and her father ran away to chase fashionable ladies in Europe. She was for a while much sought out and confided in by other girls, even girls of twelve or thirteen. These girls asked Rosalind things too, but Rosalind turned away and ignored them. She was all of fourteen and had her own, older friends, girls who like her had buds and mysterious problems with their underwear.

And here was a country where the trees had buds each year, and looked as if they were dead all winter! With bare branches! Yes he had used that word – bare!

"Christmas comes in the winter as well," Stuart continued methodically with his account, "but it usually comes before the snow, when the days are short but the weather hasn't turned really cold. Then people have parties and give each other presents, and everybody forgives their enemies for a while. People like it to snow at Christmas because it looks like the Christmas cards."

He laughed at a sudden memory. "I was once at a party where some of the people had too much to drink. When they left they had to hang on to each other because the snow was so slippery. One of them fell, so the whole lot went down in a drift of snow, and they just lay there giggling till they were wet through. Half of them were ill with colds for ages after."

Tania howled with laughter and threw herself back onto the sail, pummeling the sand beneath it with her fists. Stuart felt pleased with himself for amusing her; it was a long time since a woman had laughed at one of his silly stories. Not that she was a grown woman of course, but the feminine was there, shining all the cleaner and brighter for lacking the clog of adult polish. And it was good to see the kid happy, for God knows the last few weeks had been enough to send a grown man mad.

But Tania was already seized by another question. "How can the days be short?"

"England's farther from the equator, so the days are short in winter and the nights long."

Yes, of course. They had explained that in geography class, and now it came back to her with understanding. Long days in summer, short in winter. Walks in parks with dogs in a sunny July, walking through the snow to sing carols on a cold winter night. And parties!

"But don't they pray all Christmas? I mean how can they go to parties? It's a *religious holiday.*" This last phrase she brought out with a rolling cadence, as had the nuns.

"Well, people do go to church but they like to have some fun at Christmas as well." An urge prompted him to act the teacher and wash out some of the claptrap that had been poured into the kid. "Before Christ the Romans used to celebrate Christmas" – he stopped the obvious comment that surged onto Tania's lips with a ferocious glare – "but they didn't call it Christmas *of course*, they had some other name for it."

"What?"

"I forget. But they celebrated because the days had stopped getting shorter, and now they were getting longer. They had feasts and all the masters had to act as servants for a day. They drank a lot as well." He reflected briefly. "If the masters had to look after their servants they probably needed a lot to drink."

What a strange man he was! No one had told her this before, but Tania had no doubt that this strange story was true. A spirit of daring rose in her, urging her to be his equal in this irreverent world and pushing her to break the boundaries of a nice young lady. Her heart pounded suddenly as daringly she burst the words out "Then the Pope came along.... And he made a BUGGER of it."

Stuart hid a smile as he scratched his cheek. Some English here that the kid didn't get from the nuns. "That's more or less it."

"We should have a feast. I'm sick of these yams."

"Yes we should. We might be able to catch a pig." The idea had been entertaining him for some time, and it would be easy to catch one of the fat scuttling beasts.

"There's only one. I thought there were two, but it's the same pig. It's got a little mark on its snout, like a moustache."

"Moustache eh? Like the Fuhrer."

"Who?"

"Like the Fuhrer. You know, the German leader. Hitler, Adolph Hitler."

"Oh. Dad mentioned him when I was little. Did he have a moustache?"

"He did." So Hitler was ancient history already, was he, after less than six years, him and all his rant. She would only have been five then though. But that wasn't good news about the singularity of the pig. He'd gotten the idea that there were two or three knocking about, but now he realized he'd only seen one at any time. Tania noticed these things; if she said there was only one, she was probably right. Damn. "If there's only one, we'd better keep him for emergency supplies," he said, "but the day we leave here, little Adolph...."

"You can't eat him, he's friendly. He follows me sometimes."

"He never follows me."

"That's 'cause you want to eat him."

"I never told him so."

But Tania's mind had leapt back to the Romans. "Sister Agatha had a bottle of brandy. That's like wine, isn't it? She said it was for *medical purposes only*. She used to give some to the older girls on a spoon. She gave some to Rosaline once," Tania stopped fearfully. What if Stuart knew Rosalind? What if he was the man who kissed her? What if he was to tell the story of that mysterious kiss? And what if it were true that he kissed her on some naughty place, not on her mouth!

But Stuart was a teacher again. "The Romans drank wine. Made out of grapes," he added with a vague idea that only water existed in the nun's world. "Let's keep an eye open for any other pigs that don't have moustaches, and aren't our friendly little Adolph." Their diet was monotonous, though they ate well, and he found himself seizes by a desire for a pork chop.

"Not Adolph though."

"No, not Adolph, not if he's the only one, but," – he assumed a mask of sternness – "if we were to run out of fish...."

"We won't, there's plenty."

"Right." Stuart sighed, "fish again tomorrow."

"Stuart, do you know anyone from The Mal? I mean the institute I was in."

"Anyone? No, just Colin. Don't know him that well either. Nobody else but Father Colin. Never been inside the place. Why?"

"I just wondered."

"Wonder about finding a non-Adolph pig. Now I think it's time we got some sleep"

But he did not mind that as they settled back on their makeshift beds, Tania's questions continued to come, some sharp, some naïve. She was pleasant and intelligent, and as sleep approached softly, he watched the stars peeping round the edge of the leafy roof as he again amused her to laughter with a story. The hissing surf seemed against reason a reassurance that all was being cleaned for the morrow, when all would be well and there would be no greater problem than to show this talkative child how well he could cook a pig, if they could find a spare. It would be easy enough to catch, for these Asian village pigs were not much bigger than dogs, and usually nearly as friendly.

For a while longer their conversation drifted on as Tania probed the mysteries of a far country, but to her inquiry on the nature of a mince pie there was no answer, and she knew him to be sleeping, and a hiss in his ear did not wake him.

Sleep was not yet close to Tania though, for thoughts of the tall Rosalind and her wild adventure in the bazaar were now passing through the young girls mind, and in these thoughts the image of Rosalind's wicked lover solidified, took form, and his face became Stuart's. He moved assured and masterful through the crowded bazaar, his arm linked with that of Rosalind who Tania now was, and steered her willing to some quiet room where – where - the details evaded her, but her hand had for some time being gently stroking the soft skin of her inner thigh, radiating a comfort of touch and setting a rhythm of delight to her thoughts. Now her hand crept upwards, pushing aside the baggy shorts till her fingers stroked the swollen lips of her vagina that seemed now to be swelling and itself crying out for – she did not know. This had come upon her recently a few times at the orphanage, and as before she felt a moisture gathering as though at the summons of her thought.

Now her more rapidly stroking fingers had slid into the cleft and the little hard stub was touched, and rubbed, and moistened, and burning, and aching, and Stuart was kissing Rosalind and Stuart was feeling the young breasts of Rosalind and Stuart was kissing the breasts of Rosalind and sliding his hand between the legs of Rosalind and she was Rosalind and his hands were on her and sliding over her and sliding over her and stroking all her limbs and sliding between her legs and sliding where her hand now rubbed and sliding in her juice and her juice was on her fingers his fingers he kissed her he - he - he - his... a tremor shook her briefly.

Were Stuart not to have been already deep in sleep, he might perhaps have heard amidst the hiss of the surf a faint gasp of pleasure. Tania withdrew her hand slowly and smoothed her ragged clothing into decency, a faint smile curving her young lips before they relaxed into dumbness as she too fell softly into sleep.

Stuart slept deep and dreamless by her side. Neither would wake till the dawn roused them to the next days challenge.

Chapter 22. A Fine Thing

It was not really his kind of place, but he had already pushed the door open and stepped into the pub, and it would be embarrassing to turn and leave. The room was bright, and too many of the faces within turned to inspect him too openly. Sinclair preferred his own kind, who glanced at you discretely, then minded their own business. Working class people, as he should have known from the district.

But he was a little past the niceties this evening, and so he strode to the bar and ordered a whisky. He would not normally be abroad alone, but he felt some awkwardness at going home, and his usual haunts were barred to him, for there he might bump into someone who knew both himself and Catherine. If he met any of them they would ask the usual questions that come when a couple approach marriage, which he didn't feel inclined to answer, for he and his fiancée had quarrelled.

More precisely, Catherine had disagreed with him, and this was so entirely a new experience that it had disturbed him a little more than he would care to admit. It was not so much that she had disagreed with him, as that she had taken her father's part against him. He had made some remarks a few evenings ago about the validity of royalty in this modern age, which she had apparently repeated to her father, who had not agreed with them, and said so vigorously. When he had driven around to pick Catherine up earlier this evening, her father had tackled him on the subject, and he had defended his opinions.

To his astonishment, Catherine had taken her father's side, and the whole unpleasant scene had become so heated that he had left in a huff, saving his dignity as he left by telling her, stiffly, that it would be better if he came back when she was more reasonable. As he drove away he had felt in no mood to return to his parents home, for that would cause questions, and so he had driven for a while, fuming, then stopped at this unknown pub.

A fine thing to happen, he thought, and their wedding scheduled for this July too. Was he to marry her or her father? He would not tolerate this kind of thing when they were married. He had a career in front of him, and already he was becoming recognised by people higher up the ladder than that fossil Haig. Hadn't McIntyre himself listened to him most attentively?

It would have surprised Sinclair deeply, had he been able to listen to the conversation that had taken place following his departure.

"Too clever sometimes, too clever by half," had been her father's brief judgement, before he withdrew behind his newspaper. Catherine had not answered him, for she thought it wrong to criticise her fiancée in his absence, yet she was inclined to agree. Ralph offended people needlessly, and increasingly she was forced to bend her own thoughts to accommodate his crassness. But that was men, and as her mother later said: he was so like her father, and she would have to learn to put up with it, and if only she had held her tongue, then there would have been none of this upset. Catherine had made no reply to this advice, but her lips grew thin and tight.

At the pub, Sinclair found that he had slipped into conversation with a stranger, a cheerful type, who had an easy manner of speaking, and had made some genial comment on the weather. This was unusual for Sinclair, for he was a man who moved within a narrow circle of friends, confining himself to the right kind of people; by that he meant those who he knew to think as he did, which was the right way to think. But he had a grievance within him, sour and burning, and it struggled to be out. The world had not on this occasion treated him justly, and he needed to explain this to someone, and the man had an open, attentive manner.

But it turned out that his new friend was not really the kind of person that he could discuss Catherine with. He was amiable and sympathetic, and listened well, but he did not grasp the seriousness of the offence to Sinclair's dignity. Instead he laughed mildly, and made a vulgar comment on women in general, so that Sinclair talked instead of the source of their quarrel: the ludicrous, outdated institution of the royal family. At first he spoke moderately, then a spurt of deep indignation shot forth.

"Why he should defend people who've done nothing for him, nothing at all, God only knows. Damned useless, no use at all. And her father can't slee it. " Ralph Sinclair had little head for drink, for he had this virtue, that he was an man of clean personal habits, and despised drunks. With so little practice in tipping his elbow, his head tipped instead, rapidly.

"Hey mate, you leave it alone with the King. He did plenty for us in the war, more than you did." It was a man standing at the bar beyond Sinclair's new friend who had spoken, a middle aged, thick set man, balding and grey, yet with a pair of shaggy black eyebrows that caught Sinclair's attention as they bristled at him, adding force to their owner's words. For an instant the eyebrows paralysed Sinclair, as the eye of a snake is said to do, then anger surged up in him at this man with his red butcher's face, and her spoke rapidly.

"What does someone like you know about what the King does, or what I do for that matter?"

"Ee did 'is best for us when the bombs were falling, and 'ee got bombed 'imself," came the loud answer, the speaker reddening and swelling visibly. "Ee came around and talked to them as lost their 'omes, that's what he did. That was worth something, what he did, more than what you've got to say."

"I'm an officer in his army" began Sinclair, "and I do worthwhile things..."

"You pillock, you weren't more than a lad when the war was on," bawled the eyebrows, stepping forwards menacingly.

"Hey hey hey, that's enough," the landlord joined in. "Don't start Eric, or you're out of here again. I think you'd better finish your drink and leave Sir," he continued, turning his attention to Sinclair.

Sinclair was fuming within, but he saw no other course. This place had suddenly turned sour, and he had not wanted to be here in any case. He downed the last of the whisky wordlessly and turned to the door with a brief nod at his late companion, who nodded affably back, being an easy going sort.

"That's right, be on yer way. Don't need your type in here."

Sinclair spun on his heel; did the man think he was speaking to a dog, with his face sneering and triumphant? "My type. What do you think your type is, but nothing." He turned again and thrust his way through the door, seething with contempt, hearing a chorus of indignant voices raised behind him. Best not to waste any more words on that kind of person, what did they know but their own back street ignorance. He strode out for his car, but behind him the door burst open and Eric charged out.

"Hey you, you little twat, I haven't done with you yet." Sinclair felt alarm penetrating the heat of his fury. The man was hefty, and an obvious brawler, and his hands were raised. Be calm and take command, his reason told him, and he stepped forward a pace and spoke with authority.

"Any more, and I'll get a constable and have you taken in charge," he declared, and was instantly knocked his length onto the pavement; the man had struck him a single swinging blow to the jaw.

"Get yer constable," jeered Eric, turning away.

"Not in here, no more tonight Eric," Sinclair heard the landlord's voice through a haze, saw his upraised hand at the door, denying Eric entry. He sat up; there was blood in his mouth, and he felt the coldness of the pavement wet beneath his palms.

Eric was lumbering away down the street towards the next pub, not troubling himself to look back, talking to the night as he went. "Little twat," drifted back to Sinclair's ears, then someone was steadying him as he climbed to his feet.

"You alright sir?" It was the landlord.

"Yes." Sinclair felt far from all right, but he could stand.

"Best be on your way sir. Very unfortunate, but nothing to be done. Nobody here'll want to know anything. Sure you're all right?"

"Yes." Sinclair turned and walked unsteadily to his car, groping in his pocket for a handkerchief.

The landlord watched him go. Silly bugger, he thought. Can't talk that way around here, there's too many bombs fell. Eric's going to end up in trouble before he's done, but its nothing to do with me, as long as he doesn't come back here tonight. Bad temper our Eric, but he's a regular, and this bloke isn't, and the landlord turned back in at his door, shooing the little crowd of spectators before him.

Chapter 23. Cake

It was on the morning of the twenty-third day that the girl first mentioned Helen. It was early, and Stuart was re-fixing the multiple points of his spear while she told some story of the Institute's little intrigues. By now he was pretty familiar with the names of a whole cast of people that he had never met: Silly Betty, the mysterious Rosaline, Sister Agatha and more, but Helen was a new name to him. "Who's she," he asked, pulling hard on the bindings of the spear.

"She's a stupid girl."

"Stupid like Betty?"

"No. Betty's nice but she's a bit silly. Helen's stupid. She's a big fat lump, and she's always eating. They keep having to let out her uniform. She knocked a bun off the table once, and then she fell out of her chair trying to pick it up. Her dress split all up the side. We all heard it. When she got up you could see her skin all white here, and she was eating the bun with one hand and covering the hole with the other."

Stuart laughed. "At least she got her bun." He wet his lips. "What kind of bun was it?"

"I don't know. Sort of a big round one with sugar stuck on the outside, and a big blob of jam in the middle."

They worked in silence for a while, both mentally devouring the sweet sticky pastry.

"I liked them too. We had them every Thursday."

"None here dear. So you're saved from getting fat like Helen."

"I'd never get as fat as her. Her legs wobbled when she walked. She was – spherical. And she used to get colds, and wipe her nose with her hand. I'll never get fat." Tania rose in the dignity of youthful certainty.

Stuart grunted in distaste. At least he was spared that. Horror! A runny nosed kid, and fat, and stupid to boot. God knows how she would have held up here. In Stuart's mind, fat usually went hand in hand with stupid. He glanced at the kid as she pocked playfully with one sandaled foot at the woodpile. A pleasant feeling of appreciation cheered him, for the girl's slender body glowed with health, and as the days had passed she seemed to have gained in lithe assurance.

Was it perhaps the shedding of the dull cotton dress, he speculated? Shedding it, had she shed much of the tomb-dreary conditioning that had gone with it? All this swimming and digging more likely. She would be a beautiful young woman someday, he thought. Her features were smooth and regular, framed beneath curling dark blond hair, her eyes green and clear. Already her shoulders were firm and square, and her limbs were well proportioned, her legs emerging like the smooth new shoots of some exotic plant from the drab khaki of her borrowed shorts. And although it was somewhat naughty to take note, her derriere was round and firm.

As though in response to his thoughts, the girl bent to root amongst the woodpile, the full roundness of her backside swelling out the material, and unexpectedly a thrill of lust leapt panther-like to the fore of his mind. As she straightened, Stuart dropped his eyes, embarrassed, realising with consternation that his hidden part had stirred, and was now swelling rapidly.

"Ready?"

"Just a minute. This isn't tight enough." He fooled with the binding while thinking hard of polar bears on ice floes. After a minute he rose, and they strode out for the fishing ground, his excited part now lulled back to softness.

Christ, he thought as the girl chattered at his side, how did that happen? Now I'm getting a hard-on for an eleven year old. Dammed thing. Doesn't it know where we are? But it was lying down now, and he replied to her easily, feeling relieved to be immersed waist deep between the reefs. The minor incident had startled him a little, for the girl was of an age where surely no reasonable man would think of her in that way, and he saw himself as a reasonable man.

The appearance of the day's first fish quickly diverted him though, and when it lay flapping weakly on the beach he remembered his qualms, and then dismissed them brusquely. The girl was pretty, and the body of course had no sense of propriety. He had been a long time without a woman, and hadn't he merely been speculating on how she would be some day? No harm done, and away with the silly ghost of shame. A few more years and she would be chasing the boys herself, or more accurately dolling herself up for the boys to chase her, and a great pity that he would be long separated from her by then, and would be an old man in his thirties. And he smiled at the thought.

Their fishing was successful, as on the other days, and they cut the ever-growing sign, as on the other days entertaining each other occasionally with a little juvenile banter. But to Stuart the day was not as the others, for a new, bright, lively creature had entered his mind, and swam casually amongst his duller thoughts, surfacing occasionally to dance tantalizingly in the fore of his mind, beckoning him into warm speculation.

It was a little plaything of a thought, that sent a flavour of joy through his imagination, relieving the dull toil with a promise of rest, with brightness, with release from the yearning that now seemed to be present within him, a restless backdrop to his thoughts, a yearning that asked for relief, and sought relief by toying with this glistening play-dragon of thought, and was consoled by the dragon, yet even as consoled was whipped towards greater longing and pain.

More than once he paused, raising his head a little to watch the girl as she bore the loaded basket to the hillside, her legs, slim yet shapely, seeming to wink with the briskness of her quick trot, her bottom, already round and full, swaying a little as she went. He smiled as he watched her swing the basket as hard as she could, hurling the ripped turf out between the trees in a childish game, then waiting to see how far the sods would run down the slope, before turning turned away with an easy twirl and ambling back amiably for the next load.

At the western descent of the sun they looked on an even larger, clearer sign on the dimming hilltop, and when their evening meal had filled them, and the fire sank towards embers, Stuart felt satisfied that they had paid another day's effort to the account of their escape. Yet the day had not for him been quite as the others, for the new creature had come to dwell within him, and showed no sign of leaving.

As they chatted vaguely, the girl lay on her side near the fire, resting her head on one arm to draw with her finger on the red-lit sand, then smoothing it to blankness again with her palm. He noticed, as he had noticed before with grown women, how this awkward posture on unyielding ground elevates a woman's hips, forming a little, rounded mountain that shelters and encloses the valley where muscular thigh meets softer stomach, the valley of mystery leading to....

Enough, he thought, and turning away deliberately he fixed his gaze on the faint, star-lit foam pounding on Tiger Rock. Tania had named it that, he realized, and now she was throwing sand at him and demanding an answer to a question he hadn't heard. Stuart turned back with a sigh. 'What is it now, pest?'

"It's raining Stuart, can't you feel it? You must learn to pay attention or Sister Agatha will be cross."

"Sister Agatha can eat my socks. It's only a few drops, there's hardly any cloud."

But they retreated into the hut, for though the passing sprinkle soon ended, it was time for sleep. Tania sank swiftly into oblivion, but he lay wakeful. The thought-beast that had titillated and disturbed him through the day still roamed in his mind, and in the dark world of the night moved with greater assurance and presence, gaining strength.

At first Stuart tried to think of other matters: of how he would travel home from Singapore, if they ever got there, and of what the speculation must be amongst his friends, if even they knew he had vanished. For a while this occupied him, but then amidst these sober plans the relentless dragon of speculation crept slyly in again, and held before his mind's eye the face of a girl long forgotten, a girl he had known in his teens, and walked in Pillot woods with one long ago summer.

She was a girl he had been very fond of, a quiet, dark haired girl, and they had strolled slowly, too absorbed with each other to care much where they went, content to wander aimlessly, talking endlessly on infinite subjects as the young can, crossing and re-crossing the same trails, oblivious to the people who passed by them on the dappled paths. Only half conscious themselves of their growing purpose, and not speaking of it, they found themselves leaving the beaten path, wading through the woodland grass between the tangled trees, rejoicing in the firm snap of twigs beneath their feet.

Voices came to them faintly, floating through the ever thickening barrier of trees, and his hands felt moist and his voice a little hoarse and unsteady. Yet that didn't matter, for they had ceased to say much, but went on in unstated quest until the distant voices were fainter than the flutter and song of the birds in the branches above, fainter than the close, pressing hum and buzz of the insects.

They passed into a narrow clearing to which no path came, and paused, feeling the warm isolation of the place, and turning to each other came together gently, and embraced softly, but with a rising heat of their own, beyond the summer day's. And he lay with her in the grass where the Blue Bells grew thickly, whilst the shafts of sun and shadow duelled beneath the leaf swathed branches.

They kissed, and her breath fanned his face warmly, and his hands stroked the rounded hillocks of her breasts, and stroked the smooth bareness of her thigh, and rose beneath the thin cotton of her dress to seek the secret, cleft mound, to enter the wet, furrowed cave – he found that he had groaned aloud, and his mast was rigid in his moving hand, and the girl near his side was stirring sleepily at the sound of his voice, and murmuring dully rolled a little to him.

He lay motionless, scarcely breathing, and she sank back into the depths. But across the scant two feet of space her breath brushed warmly on his arm.

He lay still, striving to turn his thoughts to safer areas, but his whole being felt swollen and lively, and he knew well that sleep would not come. Rising quietly, he crept from the hut and made his way down the beach in the soft starlight, heading for the big rock that jutted from the sand a little south of the hut, behind whose shelter they went to dump the refuse of the bodies.

In their early days they had turned into the forest before that point, fetching handfuls of sand afterwards to bury their droppings, but frequent use had fouled the area, and he had suggested that behind the rock was a good place, where they would have privacy, and the ever busy waves would clean it twice daily for them.

This place was denied to him though, for the tide was high, the waves breaking over the rock, and he went to the forest's edge, and at the tree line he dropped his shorts to the sand.

His troublesome part was hard and ready for the touch of his hand, and in an instant he gave himself over to the memory of the girl in the long ago woods - Susan! Yes, that was her name, and it was in the blue bell glade where he had finally got on top of her, when he had fondled every inch of her, and there were some people calling to each other far away in the woods, but they were far away, it didn't matter, and he got on top of her, and he pulled her legs up and apart, and it was wet, but it wouldn't go in, then it went in, and he had hurt his knee on a sharp twig and gasped, and shifted his position, nipping the flesh of her shoulder with his arm as he moved, but she just gasped in her turn and didn't care, and he pushed, and she held him and gasped beneath him, and he pushed, pushed, pushed, Wet! Tight! Hot!

His sperm gushed out thickly, and he groaned to the empty beach as it spattered onto the sand, then grasped weakly at a branch of the tree, feeling drained and unsteady in his relief. God that was better! How long had it been? Weeks! Weeks of it in there, building up like bloody custard. No wonder he was finding himself mooning over the kid, and she so young and unsuspecting.

He peered cautiously through the screen of leaves at the distant hut, its front end a dark bulk against the lighter sand. All was still, save the waves lapping unconcernedly up the beach, and he retrieved his shorts from around his ankles and kicked sand over the glittering drops of fluid.

Yes, weeks. Three of them. And that thing in him had kept silent, that thing that was so much a part of his life, that defined him as a male. Had that part of him been shut down he wondered? When life itself was threatened to such an extreme, is that what it took to make that determined hunger cease its demands for a while? If so, then a good job that there was so much sense in the body, that at real need it would quiet down and leave the untroubled mind free to act. A damned good job, and now he could get some sleep.

He went down the beach to the phosphorescent waves, and washed his hands as they surged about his feet, then returned slanting up the beach to the hut, feeling loose and liberated, feeling a silly urge to dance on the sand. How bright things were beneath the stars! How oppressive the fall of darkness had seemed on that first night, yet now even with so little light the whole bay lay dim but clear before him. Did the sight become sharper with need, or was it that he now knew each faint twist of the tree line, each star edged ridge of the distant cliff?

He entered the hut softly and took his place gently on the left side, lying back to wait the coming of sleep, ruminating placidly on the urge that had been placed in him, as in all men. Strange that he had not needed to empty it for a while, yet reasonable, as it should be, and another lesson on the strange ways of the body. And they used to say it sent you blind! He hadn't noticed that the rest of mankind needed glasses, and they were no different from him. The bloody stupid things that people said, teachers and parsons and the like.

His return must have disturbed the kid, for she rose quietly and crawled from the hut. He listened to the faint crunch of her feet on the sand a she went the way he had gone. Bladder full probably. They both of them did a bit of getting up and going in the night. A good thing he had kicked sand over it. She was an inquisitive thing, full of questions.

He laughed suddenly, for he had got a thought of her gazing at the thick deposit solemnly, and asking if some animal had been sick or something, or was it bird droppings? But of course it would have been dried by daylight, or soaked up. She was a good kid. She had been right, that day when they had first marked the hilltop, and she'd said that if she hadn't been there he would have no one to talk to. She had been very right. How would he have passed the days without her?

The girl returned, and stumbling in the entrance kicked his foot. "Ow," he said gently.

"Sorry." She squirmed back into the comfort of her hollow. "What were you laughing for?"

"I had a funny thought."

"About me?"

"No, someone else."

"I bet it was about me."

"No it wasn't. Nobody thinks about you. I haven't heard anyone mention you in days."

"Very funny. Everyone talks about me. I'm the Queen of the island."

"Quite so Your Highness, quite so. What's your island called by the way?"

There was a long silence, then, "I don't know. I'll name it in the morning. Star Island perhaps. Because you can only see the stars at night when there's no moon."

His ears caught a snuffling, scraping sound coming faintly from the trees behind the hut. "Have you by any lucky chance seen another pig?" he asked hopefully.

"You know there's only Adolph."

Stuart sighed. "That Adolph.... Probably gets very bored at times. He needs a friend. I should get better acquainted with him."

"You leave Adolph alone. Fish are nice."

Perhaps they talked on for a while this way. He did not quite remember, for soon they were both silent, having embarked on the soft journey to morning.

Chapter 24. Special Friend

The following morning was well advanced before Stuart remembered his secretive outing of the night before, and then only when the girl mentioned one Susan.

"Eh. Who was she?" he asked, looking up a little startled from the digging. Surely he hadn't been talking in his sleep?

"Who?"

"Susan. You just said Susan."

"Oh her. She was just a girl who was at the Mal awhile. I don't think she was there long. She went somewhere else."

"The Mal?"

"The Institute. The Malcolm McGraff Institute. We used to call it the Mal. I told you that."

And that was that. A coincidence, nothing more, and he returned to his digging, the girl patiently scrapping the loose clod into her basket as he hacked it free. But a fresh thought had struck him. "How did you come to be travelling by plane?"

"I told you. Sister Therese had to go to the Mal in Singapore. That's the Institute. There's two of them, one in Paa and one in Singapore. And I had to go because the Mal in Paa was overcrowded."

"I know that, but why by plane? I thought these people were always broke and went by boat, or donkey or something. You know, nuns and priests and all that sort. It's a lot cheaper by boat."

"I don't know. Yes I do. Father Colin fixed it. He knew the people who own the plane, and he got them to take us cheap."

"Isaac and Errol. Yes, well everyone knows Isaac and Errol. Or at least they did. But I've never heard of them doing anything for anyone cheaply."

"Well Father Colin got them to. We were going to go in a day or two on the boat, and then Sister Agatha sent for me and said that I had to pack because we were leaving tomorrow on a plane. She gave me a lecture about being grateful. I got a lot of those."

"No more!"

"No. Nooo more. I think Father Colin asked them if they could do it cheap first, and they said no. So we were going on the boat, then they came round and saw Father Colin and said they had two spare seats, but it had to be tomorrow. It was for Sister Agatha really. She'd been ill, and they wanted her to go to Singapore because that would be better for her. They could look after her better. She was old."

"She didn't look ill," commented Stuart, searching his memory, "old though, but she looked pretty healthy. I wasn't really taking notice."

"No, you were too busy looking at the lady with the dark hair."

"I was not!" declared Stuart, flabbergasted again that the girl should have had such an eye for the petty flirtation. "I was talking to Mr. Dawson most of the time."

"Yes but you were looking at her. I saw you. What's her name?"

"Julia. You know what her name was, I told you."

"Yes but you didn't know her before, or you'd call her Mrs. Something, or Miss. How did you get to know her name?"

Stuart felt well cornered. "I heard someone speak to her. The fat man probably, what's his name, her boss."

"Raoul. See, now you don't know his name, but you knew hers. And you didn't know mine either!"

"That," said Stuart with great relish, "is because you are an insignificant squirt who I didn't see. And I did know his name, because I told it to you. So there, I knew both."

"You were watching her all the same. And you must have been listening to them talk."

Stuart rose to move the screen, both disconcerted and amused at this exchange. "You are a monkey. The Malcolm McGraff Institute accidentally took care of a monkey, which like all monkeys sees too much."

"Monkeys are clever."

They worked in silence for a while, for it rode a little on both of them that most of the characters of their wrangle were not only dead, but lost and unburied on this island with them.

"Were you going to see Julia again in Singapore?"

The girl had returned to her subject. Stuart wondered if he should be stern with her. She asked some pretty cheeky questions at times, for a kid, but... well why not. He didn't have to tell her, and there was no harm if he did. Still all the same... Here was a nice little pin to stick in her. "No, probably not," he answered. "I might have though. What about you?"

"Me? I didn't know her."

"No, but you knew somebody else. You were talking about running away from the Institute. If you'd run away, wouldn't you have missed somebody?"

"Yes of course. All my friends were there. Danielle and everybody."

"And somebody else. I mean your special friend."

The girl looked at him in puzzlement. "Who?"

"Father Colin of course. He was your favourite wasn't he?"

"No! No he wasn't! Of course not. He was a priest. He was nice. Just nice." But Stuart saw her colour rise despite her words.

"Yes of course. Just a nice person." And he chuckled wickedly to himself, for the girl had now turned away, flustered, taking her basket to empty, though it was only half full. He had spotted it there alright, he thought, and he nursed his wit until her return.

"Why did they send you to Singapore?" he asked innocently. "Did they want to separate you from Father Colin?"

"No of course not, stupid man," she said indignantly. "They sent me because I was the prize girl."

"You were the prize nuisance, not the prize girl. That's what you said before, so don't change it now. No telling fibs, or you get sent to your room."

She responded with a rude noise. "Silly man."

"Why did they send you though? Do they move you about every so often or something?"

"There were too many girls there. They had to have a number, and they got too many. Sister Agatha always blamed me for everything, and she picked me to go. When she told me I was going to the other Mal, she said I was her prize girl, but she meant it nasty. She said someone had to go, 'cause The Mal had more than its number, and if Sister Therese was going I'd better go too, because I wouldn't listen to anyone else. Then she said she'd like to keep me there till she'd taught me my place, but she had enough work to do already, and nobody could have everything they liked, so I'd better go."

"And now here you are. Do you like this better?"

Tania thought about this seriously for a while. "At least I got away from The Mal," she said finally. "Sister Agatha said she hoped they'd straighten me out in Singapore." She laughed and danced in little stamping steps on the dark dirt. "But I'm not going to The Mal there now, am I?"

"Hopefully not dear, hopefully not. And if I move this screen a bit, we might not get fried here either."

"We are going to England, aren't we? You promised."

"I did dear, and I'll take you there." He squeezed her shoulder reassuringly as he stepped past her. "Just count on me, and keep throwing the dirt."

He resumed his hacking, and she her raking and throwing, and for a while nothing more was said, though he glanced at her occasionally. Damn me if this girl doesn't have some bounce, he thought, God knows what she'll be like when she gets older. He brushed the hair irritably out of his eyes.

"You need a haircut," Tania said.

"I'm overdue for one. I needed one in Paa, but I thought I'd have it done in England." He laughed with some bitterness. "It's a nuisance. Better short in this climate."

"I could cut it," she said brightly, "I'm good with hair."

Stuart was not easily persuaded, but Tania became quite enthusiastic, and he re-learned an old lesson: when children want to do something, only firm, final refusal can prevent it, for logically explaining why it isn't possible is ten times harder than letting them go ahead, no matter what the lunacy.

So it was, that as the late afternoon shadows lengthened he sat on the big log whilst Tania fussed about him. He handed her his nail scissors - instruments of vanity denied to the girls by the good sisters - and reluctantly resigned himself to the ordeal. "Remember, you're next," he warned her sternly, "don't take too much off."

She chattered as she worked, and the dark snippings began to fall about him. She seemed to have less to say after a while, and found it necessary to walk around him occasionally, or have him stand, or lean to one side or the other. "What does it look like," he asked twice, but it wasn't till the third asking that he received an oblique answer.

"That's enough," she said finally, "I'm sure it'll feel a lot cooler."

Stuart ran a hand over the result, finding a texture rather like the turf after his hacking. "Mirror," he said. He looked at the results with forced outward calm, but addressed the deity beneath his breath.

"I think I'll let mine grow till we get to England," said Tania, hurrying to put away the scissors, "girl's hair's difficult if your not used to it." But Stuart continued to look into the mirror with a face like thunder, and she hastened away to the graveyard, finding an urgent need to place flowers on the grave.

"Come back here," he called after her, "it's my turn with the scissors," – but she went all the faster.

It wasn't really all that bad, he thought, as the girl scurried away down the darkening beach. He'd had a lot of makeshift haircuts in Burma, and some of them were worse. It would be cooler, and a close crop by a real barber would quickly cure it. It was amusing to see her alarm though. In truth, he had never intended to attempt cutting her hair, unless his arm was massively twisted, for in his innocent youth he had once succumbed to a girlfriend's desperate request to trim some straggling ends of her hair. He'd felt that he'd done quite a good job for an amateur, but her horror at the result of what had amounted to a few snips was boundless, and of course, it was all his fault.

Since then he had learned wisdom, coming to know that a woman's hair is her glory, too holy to be improved by a man's clumsy hands. Especially Tania's, which was nice, thick and natural – not that a girl of her age should have it any other way of course – and though she brushed it proudly, she didn't fool about with it endlessly, as though all the world hung on its threads. A welcome change.

Jennifer now, she'd been one of these women whose hair was a sort of permanent national emergency, always requiring some kind of repair to be scheduled, though it had always seemed okay to him. He mused on the hairstyles of the various girls and women that he'd known, and their varied ways, and onward to their other more fleshy charms.

Oh dear I've made such a mess, thought Tania as she hurried down the beach. I thought it would be so easy, and now it looks terrible, and I made him let me do it. He'll be so mad forever. We used to comb each other's hair at The Mal, and sometimes we did cut little bits out, but it was the older girl's job really. I didn't think it would be so hard to cut all of somebody's hair.

She stopped a little way from the cairn of stones where Mr. Dawson was buried. It was too dark to go looking for flowers. It felt nice to put something there in the daytime, but it was spooky now, and what if there really were ghosts? She turned hastily back onto the beach, and paused uncertainly; there was nowhere else to go, so if Stuart was really mad, she'd just have to say that she was sorry, and hope that he forgave her.

It had just occurred to Stuart that it was getting too dark for Tania to be wandering the isle, when her figure emerged from the gloom into the light of the fire, making him jump a little, for his thoughts had wandered into the sexual, causing the usual troublesome arousal.

She approached tentatively and sat down opposite him, and he failed to notice anything amiss until he caught the faint gleam of tears on her cheek, reflecting the firelight. "What's wrong," he said, but she did not answer at first. "Don't you feel well?" he continued, puzzled.

"It's a mess," she said timidly, "I made a mess of your hair. I'm sorry, I thought I'd be able to do it really nice."

Stuart laughed in relief. If there were no emergency worse than the state of his hair that had to be good, for any hint of illness reminded him of their utter aloneness. "That's nothing dear," he replied, "you did your best and I needed some off. A week or two and it'll grow back even."

"But I wanted it to be nice for you," she said, her voice catching in a sob.

"Aahh thanks dear, but its nothing to get upset about." He was pleased that she should feel for his trivial injury, for their world had narrowed until it was small enough to rotate around small insults and kindnesses. "Come here and sit by me." She obeyed quickly, and he slipped an arm around her shoulders. "Tell me one of your stories. One about how you used to cut each other's hair," he said in inspiration, "you said you'd had a go before."

"Not really, not proper cutting." She cast him a guilty glance, "just snips. But we used to brush it, and comb it, and put it up." She wiped the tear away quickly, brightening at his attention. "We used to do each other's hair in the evening, before lights out. A sister came round to put the lights out and we had to let it back down again, or we were in trouble. I used to do Danielle's, 'cause she was my best friend" – like you are now, flashed through her mind – "and then she'd do mine. We'd put it up, like this, or like this" – she demonstrated, though Stuart could not have told the difference for the life in him – "and we'd do it like the ladies do in the magazines. We had some magazines, and we hid them so the sisters never found them. They were fashion magazines from London and places."

Stuart laughed.

"Did you ever hide magazines, when you were at school?" she asked.

"Indeed I did dear, I certainly did," he replied, laughing, "but not fashion magazines"

"There were bits on how to use rollers, and advertisements for shampoo to make your hair shiny. We asked for shampoo lots of times, but they told us soap was good enough." She fingered her hair, turning a lock before her gaze. "Mine was getting nasty and frizzy, but it's better now that we've got the pool. Feel." Stuart rubbed the proffered lock between his fingers.

"Its very nice dear, and a nice colour."

Tania wiggled in the sand in pleasure. "It's the best," she declared, and scrambled up to sit unexpectedly on his lap. "It's not all that bad really" she judged, turning his hair between her fingers, "if I took a bit more off just here it'd be quite good."

"Definitely not. I am now extremely happy with the way it is, and do not, repeat not, want any alteration. "

"I could straighten it up a bit, I'm sure I could."

"And I could end up bald. I am determined to stay this way forever, raggy haired but not bald."

"It'll grow long again."

"I'll get some pills to stop it."

"If I just cut this bit…."

"No, no, no. Never."

"Spoilsport. Rotten, rotten spoilsport," she railed at him, pounding his chest in rage. "How am I going to learn to do hair properly?"

"Far, far from me I hope." He slid her onto the sand and stood up; all this bouncing about on his lap had massaged his willy to concrete, and he could take no more; time to consider cooler things, before he burst. "Now let's forget about my untouchable hair, and look at the beauty of these stars, whose names I will teach to you, if I can remember any."

It turned out that he could remember the names of quite a few stars, though whether he always applied the correct name to any particular point of light was a different matter. Tania drank it in though, and her open wonder shamed him into admitting that he was not completely sure if he had it right, but definitely that one was Sirius, and that Betelgeuse, and yes, that was the way to pronounce it, and he wasn't kidding, and they'd definitely check on if he'd got the rest right someday.

Deeper night came, and sleep to the girl, and he lay restless, happy but in pain from his happiness, for he had a friend, a junior member of that strange other half of humanity that fascinates the male race, and he longed for her, whether he should or not, knowing that he should not, yet yearning to do the savage friendly acts of love. And her friendship pleased him, yet his frustration encased him like rusty armour.

Chapter 25. Wall

It would have been difficult to find any part of the island that was flat. The beaches rose sloping from the waters, as beaches must, until their increasing elevation defied the twice daily licking of the salt waves, and the trees took hold. Within the forest the trees confused the eye, but the ground still sloped gently upwards towards the hill. Near the hill, the underlying rock caused a definite ridge between the west and east parts of the forest, that ended a little west of the pool, where the suddenly steepening ground swept up into the hillside, and both fibrous soil and hidden rock were deeply cleaved to form the cleft that channelled much of the hilltop's gathered rain.

Here had lain the shallow pool, as deep as the length of a hand, but so choked with years of fallen leaves that it was little more than a dirty black bog by the ravine's yawning cleft. When days passed without rain, the ravine became a mere wet gully, and this mess of leaves dried out until a thorough squeezing could scarcely have extracted a cupful of water. But when rain fell, the waters tumbled down the gully generously, causing the pool to swell, and the excess obeyed the slope of the land to become a feeble streamlet creeping sluggishly between the trees to the narrow west beach.

That was as they had found it, but that sullen picture was no more. Since their St. George's holiday Tania had turned beaver, scooping the years of filth from the pool until she found a solid earth bottom, into which she dug a little each day, enlarging the shallow depression into a bath sized hollow that the stream obligingly filled. It pleased Stuart that she had undertaken this, for it gave them a reservoir against drought, and a place where they could wash the salt from their limbs and hair.

Tania was the master of this project, and it prevented the boredom that might otherwise have seized her, for she could haul away the sod faster than he could cut it. Her daily digging session allowed him to get ahead, and when she bustled onto the hilltop to tell him triumphantly of the latest measurements of her creation, a harvest of loose sod waited for her to expend her energies on, and she would grimace and make a game of that task too, racing to catch him.

It was also good for them to be free of each other occasionally, for that brief solitude gave time for the taxed batteries of their sociability to re-charge, and when they met again they could entertain each other with the story of some little adventure. Even if it were nothing more than being startled by the racing shadow of a passing bird, yet it was news from afar. Or they might greet each other with a massive pretence of long separation, or tell a lurid tale of having found the island's buried treasure.

Her good nature soothed the sting of his impatience daily, and he knew that well, and was willing to play any little game that pleased her, acting the fool whole-heartedly to defy the despair that could easily engulf them. "I have only two jobs," he cried once in determination to the deaf sky, as he struggled to repair the mattock yet again, "to keep smiling and dig this bloody hill, because one will save us, and the other will save me from going mad."

Tania, scooping nearby, was in a quiet mood, and did not chorus his rhetoric, but it entered the library of her growing mind, and was indexed as wisdom, for his words perfectly fitted the state of their world, and all her former teachers she now saw as mumblers of airy waffle.

As the pool had grown, it had amused Tania to try and divert its outflow from west to east, and she piled the scooped mud into its path, with a view to turning it's course to the bay. This diverted the flow a little to the south, but there was too much slope of land to be overcome, and as soon as the water reached the end of her mud bank it turned again west and soon rejoined its old path.

This minor failure didn't bother her though, and as the rampart of mud dried she topped it with flat, sea-smoothed stones, and named the place Log Pond, for it now had the dignity of a neat, raised place to sit and put things on, just like Log City did when they wanted to sit properly, instead of on the ground. "And" - as she excitedly explained to Stuart - "you can sit there and bath your feet!"

Stuart had cheered this news loudly, cupping his hands before his mouth and bellowing down to the treetops that there were "seats available, with cups of tea and a footbath, for only one shilling and three-pence a head!" But he was wise enough not to mock her enthusiasm with too much wit, and when he later viewed her creation he showered it with lavish praise.

It was a perhaps a couple of days after his haircut that Stuart again declared a holiday, announcing that it was Saint David's Day, which had been moved from its usual time by the special rules governing Star Island. It was not so long since they had taken a day off, but for no reason that he could pinpoint he felt weary, and this troubled him. Beyond his joke, he saw a need to enforce some kind of rest, or treat, to recharge their flagging batteries. But rest was the only treat available, for the island had long ago yielded up its surprises, leaving little means to celebrate.

They sat for a while, until as always they must eat, so they must fish, and both done, how were they to pass their time? Stuart found himself dozing and crawled into the shelter. Tania, having vainly attempted to re-fix the ribbon of her straw hat, decided it made a better decoration to her stick. Tying it in place reminded her of when she had picked the stick up, and announcing that she wanted to try and move the stream again, she marched away, using her now ennobled rod of office to strike her docile subject trees the occasional blow as she went. Stuart waved her a drowsy goodbye before nodding off.

He awoke refreshed. Perhaps an hour or two had passed, for the sun stood at mid-day, and he ambled along the beach to the toilet rock, and returned relieved to Log City. Tania was nowhere in sight, and he remembered she had gone to the pond. Probably she's planning to plant a garden around it next, he thought, or keep an alligator in it. I'll go and take a look.

He turned into the forest and headed northwest. He could have shouted from Log City, for a good shout could be heard nearly the length of the island, but instead he walked quietly, with a vague idea of playing some joke, as it was after all St. David's day. As he approached the pool the sound of splashing came to him through the trees, and he crept forwards more cautiously, halting as he found a line of sea-smoothed stones laid across the path.

Now what game was she playing, he wondered? A little wall, a little row of boundary stones! Was this The Queen's Private Estate now? The pool was as far inland as could be, for further steps would lead closer to the west beach, and, as the endless sighing of the waves was muted by the trees, the sound of water splashing came to him clearly. Is my lady washing her hair, he wondered, or is she excavating again? Excitement shot through him, whether erotic, or simply the urge for some minor devilment, he could not tell. Let's give her a start, he thought: creep in quietly and see what she's up to.

He stepped forwards, but hesitated at the stones; perhaps not a good idea. She takes a bath there now and then, and perhaps that what she's doing. I think about her too much in ways that I shouldn't; why add to it by perhaps seeing more than I should? But the shadow of his butchered hair wavered on the soil before him, as ragged as the reality, urging him to mischief, and strong fascination was on him. He stepped over the wall.

A few quiet paces, and he could see the pool. Tania sat on the stone topped wall, gazing at the ripples cast out by her slowly moving feet, her face relaxed into that calm, pensive expression that tells no shallow thoughts, but mirrors the deeps of the mind lying quiet beneath the skin.

She sat in the shaft of sunlight that fell there between the trees, her clothing folded neatly beside her, naked save for the thin golden chain glinting about her slender neck, complementing the honey gold of her skin, and the light brown hair that fell thick and luxuriant to her shoulders, with curving bays of gentle curls. Her stomach, flat as her chest, showed the rounded muscles beneath the skin, and his eye fell naturally to the plump mound of her sex, its neat slit demurely closed, and her rounded bottom, its softness pressed flat against the warm stone. Her legs though slender were full and firm, and he stood for a moment entranced, for her entire body seeming to glow with a healthy, vital beauty that charmed his soul beyond petty sexual attraction.

Even as he stopped, she raised her eyes from the pool; clear and green, they met his, and she started slightly, then became still again, her face coming to soft life as her lips widened into a subtle smile.

It may have been that in another instant she would have spoken, or placed her hands demurely over her lap, or sprung up and retreated behind a tree, but Stuart was not to know, for he mumbled a hasty 'sorry' as he turned quickly on his heel, averting his eyes, and strode back down the path. The humid heat of the forest seemed to have risen to furnace intensity, but he knew it to be the fire of his own blood, for his limbs were trembling slightly, and his mind too was afire. But it was not the girl's nakedness that had unnerved him: it was her gentle smile.

She is beautiful, he thought as he made his way back to the beach. Young as she is, she is beautiful. I should not have crept in on her like that. I didn't know she was bathing, but I could have guessed, and I should have called out, and now she may be embarrassed and angry. But a mixture of emotions swirled within him, for he suspected that she was neither.

Reaching Log City, he decided to go onward, down to the south end, or somewhere else – anywhere - to let a little time pass and the embarrassment subside. It would be a petty thing normally, he thought, that a man walking in a wood should accidentally see a young girl in the altogether, but this was different, for this was no normal wood, and their situation not normal either, and he was not himself in that area just lately, or more accurately, was a bit too much himself.

Near the barrier rocks he found a shady rock to sit and lean against, the waves creaming almost at his feet. She was a picture of beauty, he thought, and her presence made the plain little pool a place of beauty too, like a garden, like a fairy grove in some old painting, and I would like to tell her that, but I can't: because its all mixed in with the other thing, and she's too young to be talking to about the other thing. And now I do feel all agitated, and I'd better sit here a bit and let that go. Little minx though; I'd swear she didn't give a rap, but then she's got as wild as hell since she got away from the nuns, and she doesn't know any better. I do though, or should do, so here I'll sit awhile and behave.

He lay there for some time, determined to idle, but eventually the rising tide licked his feet, and he decided to head hillwards. He had taken a break, had taken most of the day, and he felt better for it, and was now discontented to lie there longer. There was a sign to finish, and a world to reclaim, and he must be up and about it.

As he started to rise some drops of water fell onto his brow. He had little time to be puzzled about them before an ocean of salt water and seaweed thundered down on him, blotting out all, and he bellowed in alarm as he leaped spluttering to his feet and spun to see Tania haring away down the beach, giggling, the empty water can swinging in her hand.

Chapter 26. Moonlight

It was night, and he lay back against the log, watching the girl poke for amusement at the fire's dying embers.

The sign was nearing completion, and he was weary of it. After weeks of effort it now disfigured the entire hilltop, a great shout for help, but who in all those weeks had come close enough to see it? It would come a last to a raft, of that he had long been sure, but he had ignored the glaring fact and laboured stubbornly on, determined that the sign would be their salvation, and not a raft. A raft could drift them to a better place, but also it might do no more than loose them this secure isle, till drifting in a featureless sea they came to the end of their drinking water.

Was it his imagination, or were the already sultry nights becoming warmer? Here, little north of the equator, there was not the vast difference between summer and winter that Europe knows, but there was some, and it was now heading into March. They had adopted the practice of making the fire farther down the slope of the beach, for it was a troublesome animal whose heat became a nuisance once they had cooked. In their early days they had found it comforting to stoke it into the night and sit around its homely flames, but the constant daytime searching for fuel had broken them of that habit, and the brilliant display of the stars had grown more to their taste.

He knew enough astronomy to identify many of the stars, and the girl had rapidly picked their names up from him, hence her naming their kingdom as Star Island. He had argued that one with her a little, for a vague idea had been running in his head to one day write an account of this tribulation, and call the place something dramatic. Ellis Trial Island perhaps, because wasn't there an Ellis Island somewhere that held a prison? Who knows, he had thought, a few bucks from the Daily Express wouldn't come amiss, and he might some day be famous to boot. But his dutiful care of her had long past ripened into a more genuine feeling of affection, and he denied her little, which was an easy enough task, for there was little available here to withhold or give. So Star Island it became.

Rigel Bay though. That was his naming. They had had quite a few sessions over the weeks, and lots of things got named. He had picked out the bright red dot of Rigel often enough as the great constellation of Orion came swinging up, and one night he had swiftly bagged its name for the bay whilst the girl was still chewing on her choice.

At least, he had often though with wry humour, if Tania had the naming of the island he had the baptizing of it, for that was the night that his youthful drives had clicked back into gear, and he had found a discrete trip down the beach to be a necessary sleeping pill. That had not been the last of such excursions either, in fact it had become a regular habit, for the blasted thing seemed to be firing up daily. Was it all this exercise and healthy living perhaps? That silly little adventure with the pool hadn't helped of course. He'd done it as a vague attempt at fun, and she'd treated it as such and doused him in revenge, but her naked image had stayed in his mind, and mixed with her daily, clothed reality.

Whatever the cause, his desire was an ache that he had come to live with, that like a cruel taskmaster applied the whip for every excuse. Often he looked at the girl and remembered his thought as he had first sought to explore their prison, the girl stumbling silent and shocked behind him: if only the other had been an adult! But he had thought that for a more prosaic reason then. It didn't necessarily fly of course, for who was to know how that theoretical adult would have been.

And now the girl was like.... like family. He would not exchange her bubbly presence for a theory. But if she could still be she, but more of his age? Then what? Trouble perhaps, so best that she wasn't. But after all this reasoning it seemed that even high thinking was not safe, for yet again it had roused the second head a little.

Tania returned from the fire and thumped down beside him. "Stuart, how fast would our boat go?" She was now quite keen on a boat, though he was far less sure.

"Raft dear, raft. I don't think we can manage a real boat."

"Why not?"

"Tools. We need good tools to shape a boat. And you need to know how to do it properly. But a raft's simple. Just get a lot of wood and fasten it together sort of square, and it'll float. Better than a boat really 'cause a boat has to be watertight."

"Why doesn't a raft need to be watertight?"

"Tons of wood tied together, and wood floats. We sit on top. There isn't an inside for water to get into, just plenty of wood. So a raft's safer really."

"Oh. But how fast would it go?"

He didn't know. "We have a sail, so.... Perhaps two miles an hour."

"You said it might be only a hundred miles to Singapore. That means it would take fifty hours."

"Or it could be two hundred. That's four days."

She twisted to him to stare into his face with eyes wide with concern. "What if we fall off into the sea? Or what if we get lost? We could drown!"

"Yes we could dear, that's why we can't just throw one together quickly and sail off just like that. If we're going to try and sail home we have to get everything right first." He spoke evenly enough, but felt as though some distant part of him had formed the sentence, for he was acutely aware that in her anxiety she had laid one soft hand on his thigh, and he felt himself quivered a little, for such a minor eroticism had gained the power to stir him, being long unchallenged by anything greater.

Stuart rose and wandered naturally down to the water's edge till the cool waves lapped his feet. He felt hot and tormented, but the torment was in the mind, not the body, for with a panther's swiftness the urge had seized him to embrace the girl, to draw her to him, to work on her all the force of his masculine vigour and hear her moan with pleasure at the thrust of his hardness.

But she would not of course, and could not, for that was the nature of a woman, and she was a child. How easy it would be to let horseplay slip into fondling, to slide his hand as though helpless between her thighs, and then repent to late as she recoiled in shock from an act that should not happen, that she in her innocence had not even imagined could happen. How would he live with the irreparable ruin of the bond between them, when he was now so fond of her? And how the devil could they endure their days on this island if she shunned him in fear?

"But damn me," he cursed silently, "why do I feel this way so easily?" But he did not need to belabour that question, for he had understood step by step as his desire had grown: she was female, he had grown to like her, there was no one else. The drive that could have freely sought its target in a land of the full grown did not cease just because he had lost that land, rather it still demanded blindly, and in its ignorant wisdom drove him to speculate on ways and means, even as would hunger for food. He was well aware that hunger knew neither morality nor prudence, for he knew men who could no longer look their best friend in the eye after succumbing to this force, and if he pandered to it, he also would be driven to disaster.

Nothing about it was unnatural, he thought, but hellish inconvenient, and he must grit his teeth and continue as a trustworthy friend to the kid till the time of their freedom came. Still, it remained damned unexpected that he could be stirred this way by one so young. "Another matter for wonder in a wondrous world," he murmured to himself, and perhaps that dip into philosophy did the trick, for now he was merely a calm, determined man paddling his feet on a beach, who would soon bunk down sedately for the night, so that tomorrow he would be rested to diligently work on their escape.

Their was one minor detail: a brief walk down the beach would be required later, and would be all that was necessary to quieten some troublesome hormones so that he could get that deserved rest.

The embers faded to ashes, and as the night deepened they retreated to the hut. Most of the nights were dry, and they may as well have slept unsheltered on the sand, or on the hilltop for that matter, but often the clammy rain would fall unexpectedly. In any case their sail carpet was spread in the hut, and it was smoother to lie on than the rasping sand. It was only nine in the evening, but the sun would rise early, invading their shelter with its piercing morning light, and they habitually awoke as the first pale hint of its onslaught lightened the sky.

As usual they lay back quietly, waiting for sleep to take them. They spoke occasionally as some random subject crossed their minds, but mostly they watched the unceasing dance of starlight on the waves and listened to the soft hiss of the surf. Tonight a pathway of silver light ran from the beach away over the rippling sea, for the moon was at its full and rising before them to the height of the sky.

"It looks as though you could walk on it. On the moonlight I mean," said Tania.

Her thoughts must have matched his, for his mind was walking that shining path. "Yes. Walk all the way back to Paa. But when the moon starts to sink in the West we'll see a path going the other way, all the way to Malaya."

"That's better. We'll walk to Malaya in the morning."

A thought had occurred to him. "When we're ready to sail we'll wait till the moon's nearly full. That way we'll have light at night."

"What if it takes weeks?"

"Days. It'll only take a few days. And if we're lucky we might get spotted before then."

"Hhmm."

"Yes hhmm. I know. But we might still be found all the same."

She was silent for a while, then, "Stuart."

"What?"

"I'm scared. What if we drown?"

"We won't," he reassured her. "It's not so far. If it seems too dangerous we'll stay here. Someone's got to see us sooner or later."

The girl didn't answer, but after a moment she shuffled closer to him, until her hair fell on his bare arm. Scared, he thought. She was rarely scared of anything. But water had ended the lives of all who flew here with them, and though the horror had dwindled by now, she would never forget the lesson any more than he would. He hesitated a second, then passed his arm around her shoulders, and she pressed closer as though to share his confident strength.

Surely someone would see them, he thought, surely they must. Over the weeks he had been matter of fact with the girl, saying that the voyage had some danger, but in truth he feared it. Here they were safe, out there on the wide, heaving waters they lost control. But when they were ready they must attempt it, for this was a fool's safety that would last only until illness or injury struck.

Tania had fallen silent, nursing her thoughts, and in his mind he journeyed, for the silver light seemed to pierce deep into his sight, and his imagination travelled through the wood and ascended the bare hill to gaze into the West, where the rising moon would soon fall to join the vanished sun.

A hundred miles? It could be less. And there might be other islands on the way, and if they were any size at all then there must be people, people with boats, boats that they handled with ease. Perhaps there was such an island only a few miles away, perhaps so close that it could be seen after a few hours sailing. Perhaps it was so simple that they would laugh at him for toiling here for so long, and whisk him and the girl to Singapore as though it were nothing.

Singapore! They would be back in the real world, with bustling crowds and shops, and big, sturdy iron ships that could sail ten thousand miles without a problem. And he could go home and pick his life up again, and take the girl with him, and find her father too. But first thing in Singapore, before they got to a ship or 'plane, first thing was some solid food for them both, and ice cream for the kid, as much as she could eat. Next a nice room in a hotel where people did things for you, with a bar where he could have a drink or two, then tuck the kid in and go out on the town, and by God if he didn't plunge it into some woman it wouldn't be for lack of trying. And if he didn't, then at least he would get a night out, and there was a lifetime of them before him.

It would happen. Of course they would get there, it wasn't so difficult. It wasn't as if they were in the middle of the Pacific, thousands of miles from anywhere, or lost at the South Pole. Just that bit too much of water to far, just that bit too much, and the island too small and obscure.

He squeezed the girl's shoulders affectionately, and she pocked him in the ribs in answer. Not yet sleeping then ? But it was time he did, and for all his mental voyage it was standing hard and rigid now, and her closeness wasn't helping things. That was okay though, for soon they would be in Singapore, and though her closeness aggravated his need, it also calmed it with a gentle lotion of companionship. None the less it was hard, and he was restless and wakeful, and he gently disengaged himself from her, chucking her softly beneath the chin before creeping from the hut.

It was cool on the beach, and the moonlight itself seemed to pour down coolness. He walked down to the hissing life of the water and trod the new wet smoothness of the sand, felt the rush of the incoming wave drive the grains between his toes, then drag coaxingly at him in its retreat.

He stepped back a few paces to see the blurred hollows of his steps, and watch the next rushing wave fastidiously wipe them away, then he followed that withdrawing wave and scooped the sand in its wake, gouging deeply with his bare foot to provide the water a harder challenge. This amused him for a while, and he persevered at it, as though to insist that he would not fail to find something of value on this desolate beach.

Presently the sport palled though, and he turned for the shelter of the trees, and there gave himself over to the thought of an unnamed woman who would be pleased to please a handsome young officer, a woman dark, sultry, voluptuous.... Yet as the climax approached the woman's face faded in his minds eye, and that of a brown haired grinning tomboy emerged, and remained with him as his sperm gushed forth.

After the paroxysm ended he sighed and shook his head at his fantasy, as a man does at the folly of the world in general, but he laid no weight of blame on himself, just a weary prayer for their unnatural confinement to be ended. He had grown to accept his obsession without remorse, for he had seen enough of life to know that all men carried their private demons, and he padded patiently down to the surf to wash.

A rustle from the forest made him pause, pricking his ears. Adolph of course. Another male that needed a friend, and if he had one, then possibly Tania would consent to a feast. And there it was again, rustling further north towards the hut. But nothing could be done in the dark, even if there were fifty non-sacred pigs, and he continued on to the waves.

Chapter 27. Sculptress

Stuart had gone for water, and Tania knelt and rooted amongst the sticks of firewood, tossing them aside until one suited her critical eye. She turned the piece of dry wood about in her hands in solemn appraisal, then taking up the Bowie knife shaved a little from the end, pausing occasionally to hold it up in thoughtful judgement. Finally she laid the knife aside and sat back like a samurai on her heels, holding the stubby length of wood erect upon her lap. Yes, just the same, as far as she could remember. Just the same length.

"Carving dolls? I thought you were too old for that?"

Tania jumped with shock as Stuart emerged from the trees, bearing the brimming jug carefully before him, and throwing the stick quickly onto the pile she busied herself with the fire, averting her face from him. "How did you get back so fast? I'm going to tie a bell on you."

"Lot's of people want to tie a bell on me young lady. But nobody ever succeeds, and you're too short."

"I'll be taller someday," she replied with a sad firmness, and wandered down to the waters edge.

Stuart wondered if there was something wrong this morning. Well of course everything was wrong, starting with the minor fact that they were prisoners here, but apart from that? She was usually pretty cheerful, but she had her moods. Just the monotony and uncertainty of it all, he guessed. It got to them both at times, and they had to brush it off and make the best. The tide was retreating down the beach, and he went to mark out the beach signal.

Tania stood looking out at Tiger Rock. She had named it that to herself, but she hadn't told Stuart. Or had she? She couldn't

239

remember. He thought she was a little kid and he laughed at her. When they got back to England he would find her father for her, but then he would go somewhere else. Where would he go to? She hated his wife: she sounded mean and nasty. He should have someone nice, then she could live with them. But she was going to live with her dad when they found him, and she wouldn't see Stuart again. Perhaps they could live close to each other. She stood lost to the world as she pondered the complexities of her future.

Perhaps when they found her dad, Stuart could come and live with them; she was sure her dad wouldn't mind. Perhaps they could get some of her friends from the Mal, and they could start a kind of home like the Mal, only better. They would be glad to get away. They could get Danielle and one or two others, she wasn't sure who. Danielle was her only really good friend, she would want to come, but they might not let her go. Rosalind was nearly grown up, they couldn't stop her if she wanted to leave, and Rosalind was sure to like Stuart. Perhaps she would marry him, and she might want to live with them because she met Stuart through herself, Tania.

But Rosalind wasn't really her friend, she was a lot older, and she ignored her, and Danielle as well. She would laugh at her and Danielle. Her mum would have liked him, but mum was somehow still mixed up with her dad, even though he left her, and anyway her mum was dead. It was too big a problem, and she wandered along the beach to help him with the marking.

"Stuart, where will you live when we get to England?"

"Buckingham Palace," he replied without looking up from the sand.

"No really," she insisted impatiently, "where were you going to? Somebody must have been expecting you."

"Gloucester. That's a city in Gloucestershire. That's where I used to live. My father still lives there, a lot of my friends as well. But I had an idea to live in London."

"Is that where your wife lives?"

"No. She probably went to her parents place in Kent. Maidstone. That's where she said she was going."

"Is she still there?"

"I don't know. She might be somewhere else, I don't know."

"She might have married someone else."

He laughed harshly. "I don't think so dear, she's much to strict with the rules for that. Some of the rules that is."

"What rules? If she wanted to marry somebody else she could couldn't she?"

"No dear. You can only have one husband at a time, or one wife. If you want to stay out of prison that is."

"What if she told the priest she didn't want to be married to you anymore? Then she could marry someone else, and it would be one at a time."

"Jesus Tania," he began explosively, then recollected that she was just a kid. "You can't just get rid of wives like that, or husbands either. You have to go to a court and explain why. When you've got one you're stuck for ages." He had finished the sign, and he threw the stick back to the tree line with a deal more force than was necessary. "Very stuck sometimes."

He stumped back to the fire. "You haven't finished the pans."

"Sorry," she answered, subdued. She had upset him; she hadn't meant to. She just liked to know things, but she had noticed that he sometimes got a bit miffy if she asked about his wife. Not always though.

"Sister Agatha said I asked too many questions," she tried quietly, ready to be completely quiet if he was really angry.

"Sister Agatha is... Sister Agatha is not my favourite person. I'm glad I'm not married to Sister Agatha. Then I would be in trouble."

Tania laughed. It was okay again.

"Who is your favourite person?"

"Winston Churchill of course. Everyone's favourite. Nobody else at all."

"You liar."

"Hey, you shouldn't say that to people. Some people get upset."

"Why not, its true. You had a girlfriend in Paa." Her shot in the dark had risen without thought from some point of quick cunning, and darted from her mouth in the instant.

He looked at her astonished. "You didn't know me in Paa."

"Its true though. You had a girlfriend in Paa. More than one," she elaborated, wagging a finger before his face severely.

"How – do you know that?" he struggled out, now completely flabbergasted.

"I guessed. I guessed and now you've admitted it," she crowed triumphantly, then squealed in gleeful alarm as he pounced on her in indignation and swept her of her feet to deposit her on her back in the sand.

"You, you minx." Torn between anger and hilarity at her witty cheek he drove his fingers into her armpits and administered a vigorous tickling until she howled for mercy, then serenely seated himself on the log as she struggled dishevelled to her feet.

"That'll teach you, brat."

She was not taught though. "It's still true, and you're a bully as well," she said, springing up red and giggling, and falling on him with a flurry of cuffs. He warded her off easily, and seizing her by the wrists swung her face down over his knee and delivered a slap to the offered bottom.

"Don't you dare," came up the voice from about his ankles, now choking with a true fit of the giggles.

"Don't I," he responded triumphantly, and methodically administered a lightweight spanking, first one rounded cheek then the other, much encouraged by the giggle-chocked shrieks that came up from below, and the springy texture of his target.

"Now have you had enough Miss Webster?" He demanded.

"Yes. No. Just you wait."

" Are you going to behave, Miss Webster?"

"No. Never! Let me up. You're a brute!" She could scarcely speak for laughter. He rested his spanking hand on her bottom, feeling the youthful spring of the padded muscles.

"Then you have to stay there," he concluded, none the less releasing the restraining pressure of his left hand. She responded with a rude noise but made no attempt to rise. "In for a penny," he thought and ran his hand luxuriously over the twin mounds of her bottom, feeling their firmness at leisure, conscious of the girl's giggling compliance, then after a final kneading squeeze he regretfully swung her upright to sit her red faced and panting on his knee.

"Brute."

"Shush. You'll wear me out. Now I'm too tired to work."

"Old man. You're an old man." She ran a hand unexpectedly over his chin. "You missed a bit here. And here."

Stuart submitted to the examination.

"And here as well."

"That's because you wore the mirror out peering into it every day" he announced in his best superior manner.

In answer the girl briskly gripped a tuft of his chest hairs and gave a hard yank, then leaped from his knee as he in his turn cried out. She sped away to the water, waved the collection of hairs above her head and threw them out over the surf. "Now you'll never get away. You'll never find them again and they'll always be a bit of you here," she crowed, but her drama was spoilt, for the light breeze carried the drifting clump back into her mouth and she broke off in a titanic fit of choking and spitting.

Stuart convulsed with laughter. "There, now you see! Is there no end to your punishment today?"

Later in the day he wondered at himself for letting his self-discipline slide. The girl's giggles had subsided, but she still seemed in a giddy mood, and feeling that he had succumbed to a dangerous impulse he had firmly assumed a serious attitude, and with a teacher's strictness led the way to their task.

The girl fell in with his mood and quickly sobered up, hauling the earth away with a willing vigour, though she cast him ominous piratical glances from time to time. As they worked he glanced at her frequently. She seemed to have expanded as a person, and though she was not a fraction taller, there seemed somehow to be more of her with him on the hilltop

"Eighty pounds of imp," he murmured to himself at one point, "damn me if I aren't getting besotted with the kid." But when all was said and done, thank God it was her, and not his dreaded mythical snotty-nosed brat. How would he have faced each day with a whiner, or worse still, how would he have faced each day alone?

But definitely he had overstepped the mark today, and it had leaped on him unexpected. A bit of a fun spanking might be nothing much with an energetic youth like her who liked to be a bit of a tomboy, might be now that he knew her so well that is, but even that would be a no-go with many a young girl, and he had gone beyond that bit of horseplay.

Today he had taken a step down the road that should only be walked with a grown woman, and even then was chancy. He had felt her backside up rarely, there was no denying or explaining it away, and he had risked putting the fear of himself into her. Did she know that, he wondered? That is, did she understand his pleasure in caressing her body, did she understand it as the tip of hungering desire? Or was it just another bit of hooligan fun to her, daft stuff that you did in fun, like all kids liked if they had any vim in them at all? And being a little bit naughty made it a bit more fun. Of course. She was too young by years to think any other way, and so he was spared the pain of condemnation that an older girl would have heaped on him. Not just too young to do anything in that area, but also too young to know the area existed.

Or was she? He wondered about that point often. Surely she was as ignorant of anything beyond play as any child of that age should be. But how ignorant was that? He was damned if he could remember when he first understood anything, or precisely what it was that he understood either. Did she understand a boundary? Or was there anything to understand? Who the devil was to say what was and what wasn't proper? It was all a matter of opinion, as in so many things.

But here he shook his head, knowing that he lied with this sophistry. She would not in her excitement have noticed, even if she knew of such a male power, but as he had seated her back onto his knee, his prick had been rigid beneath her weight. And even as he remembered this, his hand remembered the luxurious firmness of her flesh, and remembering it longed for the flavour again. "Discipline Ellis, discipline," he said, "no more or you'll land in a shitload of trouble." But it was with a sigh that he returned to his hacking.

Chapter 28. Strange

"Stuart, what's the date today?"

He didn't need to think to answer that one, "Third of March."

She had made a calculation from his answer. "In six days and six months it'll be my birthday. What are you going to buy me?"

"Nothing. No shops here."

"There's plenty in England. And in Paris. You can buy me something there."

"Oh, we're going to Paris now are we. What are we doing in Paris?"

"My dad might be there. Mum said he liked Paris." She became absorbed in the peculiarity of the two figures. Six days and six months. She'd never worked it out that way before, and the first time she did it was six and six. Six days to go and then she would be halfway to twelve, and funny again because two sixes were twelve. Twelve was special, it was like a sort of end number. After twelve you were thirteen, and that was a whole different set of numbers.

"Now what are you dreaming up?"

"Nothing. It's private," she replied airily.

"God help us. Your private thoughts scare me."

"I was thinking about sums if you must know."

"Sums! About as many schools here as there are shops. You'll be missing a lot of classes."

"I can catch up. The classes were all rubbish anyhow, the sisters were pretty dumb."

"Because they weren't teachers, were they. Or do some nuns study teaching?"

"I don't know. They were all nuts about praying. If you asked them a question about religion they'd go on forever, so nobody ever asked. But we had classes everyday, English and mathematics and geography and stuff. I liked the geography, and the maths."

"That's unusual. I thought girls didn't like maths."

"It was okay. I didn't like geog at first, then I thought that I needed to know where everywhere was to get to England, and then it got interesting. And I got good marks in maths. I came second in the class last year, and some of the girls are a lot older than me, and lots of them are good at maths."

"Well done. I didn't like maths at school, but I got better later on. My father wanted me to be a surveyor, and they need a lot of maths, so I tried hard for a while. It's easier if you have a reason. Who did the classes?"

"Sister Agatha did the geography, and Sister Marie-Clair did the English. All sorts of different people did the history. They kept changing the history teacher, and the new one always did a lot of the same stuff again, so it got boring."

"That's funny, it was the same at my school. It must be a secret method all schools have. Who taught the maths?"

"Father Colin."

"Aha! Now I understand everything! Father Colin was the maths teacher was he, and lots of girls were good at maths, including Miss Webster."

"So? Maths is important. You've got to know maths!"

"Definitely. And definitely if Father Colin's the teacher. Father Colin, *not* Father whatever his proper name was."

"Father Bryne. And everyone called him Father Colin, not just me."

"Everybody!"

"You leave Father Colin alone. He was nice, not like you. You're bad. And you're jealous, so there."

"Of course I'm jealous. I've got this deep longing to be a maths teacher."

"Well that's what Father Bryne was. He was a very good teacher. And that isn't why you're jealous. It's because he was handsome, and you're not. And ...."

"And what?"

"And he had me as his pupil, and I'm brilliant!" she concluded, rising from her morning fire-lighting duty and pirouetting before striding off down the beach. "Put some more wood on."

"Now where are you going to? Are you running away?"

"No I'm going to... fulfil a private function."

"Oh, did Father Colin do English classes as well?"

A loud raspberry was the only reply, and Stuart chuckled over his work. The girl was a one alright. "My monkey," he murmured to himself, "my little parrot." He could well imagine her scheming away, running her fingers over the maps and pretending a deep interest in geography. Would she have really done it, he wondered, got to some age and then struck out for England? Probably not. The dream would have faded as she aged. She'd have got more idea of how to do it in a year or two of course, but that would have meant getting more of a practical idea about the size of things, and as she got more practical, then the whole scheme would have seemed more impossible to her. Still, there was no telling.

But all that was hypothetical now, for she was away from the place, and he had made her a promise for good or worse. "A big promise," he thought ruefully. But then this was a big mess, wasn't it? And if they could manage to get out of this, then perhaps they could manage her problem too.

Strange though, very strange, that a lost girl could get a hopeless idea, conceive a ridiculous plan that could never happen, and then a ludicrous accident like this one could roll the whole thing suddenly into motion as though it was destined to be, and the next thing he knew he was part of it. Strange, very strange.

And that was what Jennifer had called him once when she couldn't get her own way. "You're a strange man," she'd said, and he was blowed if he could remember the reason why. He sighed and rose to fetch another log. As though he'd ever done any thing that was particularly abnormal. "Strange," he murmured, "you should be here lady, helping me dig this bloody sign, then you'd know what strange is. Bloody incredible, that's more like what we've got here."

Tania dropped her shorts and squatted behind the rock. An incoming wave drenched the shorts, but she paid it no heed, and greeted the surging water with a gush of her own while she considered her next retort to Stuart. How did he know she liked Father Colin? Of course she didn't really, he was just so... well not like Father O'Brien, not old and fat. Of course Father O'Brien couldn't help being old and fat, he got old and... well he got fat as well. But he could help being always so strict and grumpy. Not strict really, just grumpy. Sometimes he would make a joke, but it was always a grumpy joke, and then he sort of faded back to normal.

Of course, Father Colin didn't make jokes all the time, but he was nice. And a lot younger of course. He was nice because he didn't go on and on about things if anybody did any little thing that was a bit silly. He was a softy really. Somebody said once he was a softy, was it Betty? Well somebody did. He wasn't really a softy though, he was... shy. She stood and re-tied her rope belt, thoughtfully contemplating the new insight of her growing mind, comprehending for the first time the shyness of the distant young priest. Well really she did like him, didn't she?

And Stuart – the pig – teased her about him. He shouldn't do that, because Father Colin was nice, and Stuart didn't know him. But he didn't mean it really; he just liked to joke. Stuart was quiet a lot sometimes, but he wasn't shy, he was different. He was interesting, sort of strict about doing things right, but if it didn't really matter then he didn't care. He teased her a lot sometimes, but he listened to her as well, and if she had a problem he would try and fix it.

She would stay with him forever, never go back to the Mal, and he would look after her, and he would find her dad. He wouldn't go and live with his wife: she could tell that because he didn't talk about her. He would look after her, and she would look after him. The enigma of how exactly she would achieve living with both Stuart and her dad fluttered through her mind again, but it was a mere vapour of a problem compared to the hard fact of her determination, and she dismissed it swiftly. They just would, that was how.

She wadded out into the waves till they rose about her waist and rubbed her hands together beneath the water. This was a lot better than the smelly bogs at the Mal. There they were always telling you to wash your hands, and don't touch yourself more than you need to, and don't scuff your sandals, and this and that. It was better here, they didn't have to bother with all that stuff, just catch things to eat, and pee in the sea, and don't go in the sun too much.

Why didn't everybody live that way? It was scary here 'cause they were alone, but it was exciting too. Stuart and her had a lot of fun sometimes, and it wasn't as if they were really lost, not lost forever, 'cause now and then they saw a ship way off in the distance, only it was too far off. But when they did get away they would travel all over looking for her dad. They wouldn't let anybody stop them, they'd just keep going till it was all okay again. Now she had to go back to that Stuart, and she'd fix him somehow. She liked him, but he'd get fixed all the same.

Tania stopped and grinned in delight as a thought struck her. What if she were to follow him one night, like she did before? Follow him and then jump out on him, right when he was... She clapped her hands over her face at the thought. He'd go crazy! Yes he would, she realised, a mood of seriousness quickly replacing her hilarity. That wouldn't be a joke; that would be nasty. He went off down the beach because he had something private to do, and if she had something private she would want to go somewhere and not be bothered.

She'd only followed him that one time, and she'd never done it again, though that was really because he nearly caught her. She looked down the beach at the toiling man. Stuart looked after her and did things for her, and he was kind, and when she asked him about anything he told her, if he knew. All the other grownups would tell her she was too young, and she hated that. And she hated his wife too, 'cause she'd been bad to him. He hadn't said she was bad, but she must have been, because when she left him he didn't care, he just let her go, and he wouldn't have done that if she wasn't bad. So now he couldn't really be married anymore, not properly, even though he said that it wasn't that easy. It must wear off or something after a while if you didn't live together, didn't it?

She thought so, because Aggy or somebody said that none Catholics weren't married forever like Catholics were, and so perhaps it wore off. She'd have to ask Stuart to explain it a bit more. He wouldn't mind if she asked him properly like a grownup, and didn't mention his wife. But it couldn't wear off, not really, because he was telling her once that he liked somebody who liked him, but she didn't stay with him because of his wife, and then he sort of stopped and wouldn't say anything more about her.

So he couldn't have a girlfriend because he still had a wife, and he had to live on his own. That couldn't be very nice for him 'cause he was... In her thoughts, Tania hesitated over the forbidden word. Danielle had said it once, and a sister had heard, and Danielle got in big trouble. She said that father Colin was... sexy. Well he wasn't, he was too nice for that, whatever it was supposed to mean. Some of the girls used that word a lot, but only when they were whispering of course, and talking about boys and the stuff they did. They didn't really know anything, 'cause none of them ever saw any boys 'cause they never got out of the Mal, so they didn't know what boys did. She did though.

She smiled quietly to herself. Stuart likes my bottom, she thought. I tricked him about his girlfriends, and he spanked me, but not hard. Nobody ever did that before, and it was exciting. And then he felt my bum all over, so he must like me. That was really exciting, but he only did it that one time two or three days ago. He must really miss having a girlfriend.

Tania had walked down the beach as she ruminated on life's complexities, and arriving back at the growing raft, she gave Stuart a wave of lordly condescension. "I've got my eye on you small fry," she warned him solemnly.

He looked up from the cooking and spread his arms wide to embrace the empty horizon. "I'm glad someone has."

Chapter 29. Horsemen

Colonel Haig was not surprised to be beckoned to a meeting by McIntyre, and although too old a hand to be cocksure of knowing the cause, he felt an anticipated satisfaction.

It was some weeks since his little manoeuvre with the Sinclair situation, which so far had born no visible fruit. Sinclair had if anything carried himself with more confidence for a while, until appearing at a meeting with a bruised jaw, since when he had been a little subdued. But surely that must be some other affair, unless McIntyre was summoning him into his presence to announce that he and Sinclair had duk'ed it out? Haig was not a flippant man, but he chuckled at the thought.

The summons was not an official one, for McIntyre had no direct authority over the colonel that he could wield without treading on the toes of intermediaries. Instead there was merely a friendly call, and a vague request for a chat about certain aspects of the Kenya situation, and Haig with equal casualness suggested that he pop around, rather than shout down the 'phone. Despite his studied calmness Haig felt a thrill bordering on the nervous mixed with his excitement, for the tall man was one of the few people who were capable of making the seasoned colonel feel like his junior.

McIntyre received him at the office with his usual easy charm, and a relevant folder lay ostentatiously open on his desk. Certainly he had questions that lay within the colonel's area of expertise, and certainly they were dealt with, though briefly. Then McIntyre came to the point.

"If this unfortunate situation worsens, Colonel, then we may need to increase the number of officers in the field. Not just the number, but also the quality of experience. How would you feel about a more sunny climate."

"A regular posting?" queried Haig, dubiously. Since he had joined the less defined world of the faceless men he had been a colonel on paper only, without a regiment, but whatever he may now be with intelligence, he was still officially an officer, and officers obeyed orders. He could hardly refuse if they chose to send him to chivvy troops up and down in the old manner.

The Second World War had been hateful, yet it had given final meaning to the years of drill, spit and polish that had gone before, but whilst justifying them, had also ended them. It had halted his slow progress toward the bored success of a rigid, middle-aged career officer, and its challenges had revived his dulling intellect. The formation of the new commando units had loosened his faith in the old structures; he had seen bad, troublesome soldiers transform into warriors, cooks ripen into officers, and raw youths outdo veterans. And regretfully, he had seen supposedly competent career officers go to pieces, wasting lives with their arrogant blunders.

After the war, he had felt his newly sharpened wits wasting in dull routine, and with only passing regrets had abandoned the world of insignia and salutes for that of unseen power. It would be good to be in the field again, but he had no desire to find himself slid into what might become a glorified policeman's job, nagging his officers over trivialities as the years passed and the danger faded, watching himself drift into bored obscurity. Was that what McIntyre had in mind? Had they finally found him a bit too rough grained for their committees, with their smooth considerations and political chatter?

"No Colonel, not in any formal manner. Some more fluid arrangement, where we feel you would be of more use to us." He smiled indulgently, as might a clever, pleasant uncle who reads a favourite nephew's mind. "Something in line with your talents."

It was the word "fluid" that set Haig's mind at rest: fluid, and more use.

"A coordinating role; that's what we see the need for at present. Someone who can keep matters on an even keel, but can be relied on to take action if needed. But only if needed, Colonel Haig, only if needed," he finished with soft emphasis.

Haig felt the warmth of appreciation kindling his spirit. "When would I leave."

"Ah Colonel, this isn't final yet. I thought that I would sound you out before any decisions are made. You understand of course that there would be a number of officers and none military people undertaking this function?"

"Of course." A polite way of telling me that they're not going to make me Viceroy of Africa just yet, thought Haig. Someone else in command of the operation, however it's organised, and I'll be under his orders. Well, I didn't think I was going to be appointed Grand Panjandrum in any case.

"As to your assistant, Captain Sinclair."

"Yes." It was an unfortunate necessity in their line of work that military titles should mate awkwardly with civilian, and Haig was still enough of a regular soldier to dislike it.

"I was fortunate enough to make his acquaintance a little while ago, as you will recall."

"Yes. Carew's farewell."

"He has interesting qualities."

"I have found them interesting myself," responded Haig, finding himself matching McIntyre's leisurely manner.

"Which is why you thought it worthwhile to bring them to my attention I think," McIntyre responded sharply. "Sometimes young men with overly rigid opinions can be guided gently to more useful attitudes, don't you think so Colonel?"

He sees much and gives away little, though Haig. He fishes till he knows everything in the pool. Who's under the microscope now, Sinclair or me? It was time to be direct, but not to bluster, not with this one.

"I had a number of young officers with me in Burma, many of them with next to no experience. If the metal was there you could see it, and usually you had to dig for it. When it came to the test, they turned out well." Haig paused. McIntyre's leisurely manner made him reconsider; was he perhaps being too harsh in his judgement? Was McIntyre telling him that he was loosing patience with youth, as age easily can? "I could of course be wrong," he admitted, "but I doubt it. The man's too pig headed; nothing can be driven in. And we're not dealing with a desperate situation here, where people are forced to learn, or die from their own shortcomings."

"This situation could become very desperate."

"No matter how bad it gets, it's a limited action against an inferior force, not a desperate struggle against an equal, where you have to use every tool you can lay your hands on. This will be containment, in a limited arena. We have the resources, and we don't have to use poor tools for the lack of good ones."

"Yes. That was much my opinion on Captain Sinclair, but like you, I could be wrong, though I doubt it. Thank you for your thoughts on the matter. I take it you would like to be relieved of him. "

"Most definitely."

"Then if this Kenya situation worsens it will be seen to that he does not accompany you there. In the interim it will be convenient if you continue to do what you can with him, and we shall both keep an eye on him."

Colonel Haig left McIntyre's office with a glow of satisfaction, though not from the cause he had expected. Sinclair was gone in substance, and that his annoying presence would continue to hover around for a while was a passing matter. More important was the prospect of Kenya, almost certainly his next port of call. Definitely he needed to talk some more with Brook, and wasn't today Tuesday? So it was; most convenient.

Captain Sinclair was currently less joyous. Since his quarrel with Catherine there was a coolness between them, though neither had mentioned the contentious subject of royalty again. He felt himself treated unjustly, and waited in vain for some word of apology from her that would admit to the rightness of his views. How could she not see that these drones no longer had a place in the world? She was too much influenced by her father.

He had recently bought a television, and had got very much into the habit of sitting stiffly upright as he watched the news, then rumbling out his judgements on the world's doings. It surprised Sinclair that the old man had bought the machine; he was very set in his ways usually, and only the week before his purchase had called them modern claptrap. But now he laid aside his newspaper to view it, and would make his pronouncements at the drop of a hat, as though he was something more than a clerk. At least he was not long winded about it; a few rumbles and then he was done, and it was perhaps this brevity that caused Catherine to take note of what he said, for she also was sparing with words.

The matter might have passed more easily had not his un-avenged flooring of the same evening still rankled, for the two humiliations somehow mixed to become one. They did not discuss the void that was opening between them, and Sinclair seethed and chewed his discontent silently, swinging in his mind from the one sour subject to the other.

Regularly the memory of his beating rose to shame him, and he thought hourly of how much he would like to see the great red-faced oaf hauled away by a policeman, and pictured him in the dock, paling as he was sentenced to a period behind bars. Sometimes he imagined himself meeting the threat with a straight left, clean and scientific, as he had learned in the ring; but often, and this most heatedly, he thought how nice it would have been to have found a brick down there on the pavement, and risen up to smash the swine's head in with it.

When this last image seized him he would clench his teeth in frustrated desire: how he would love to batter the lout! And more than once he twitched as he pictured himself smash, smash, smashing with his brick until the stupid, insolent face was nothing more than a mess of red ruin, blood and shattered bone.

It was impossible to relieve his feelings by talking to Catherine about the incident; he had enough difficulties there already, and would appear a fool. In the innermost chamber of his mind, far deeper than the public forecourt where he kept the proud array of his faultless opinions, he saw himself whipped like a dog that had barked too much, and was thankful that the incident had taken place in some obscure part of London, where he was not known.

Brook was pleased for his fellow colonel. The two men spent the evening talking of Kenya, of its jewel, the seaport of Nairobi, and of the complexity of tribes that hunted and farmed its broad plains. "Will Captain Sinclair be part of this operation?" he asked Haig at one point, a ghost of a smile on his face.

"No he will not. A little while ago he put his foot in his mouth, and consequently will not be blessing me with his wisdom."

"Foot in mouth. That seems to be his main talent."

"This time he did it before an audience. An audience of just one, but one who counted."

"You didn't snatch him back Nigel?"

"I went past that stage with him some time ago Tony. He can't learn by words, so he has to take a fall. Gave a slight push if anything, and he fell over his own shoe laces." Haig shook his head, "this Kenya business – very slippery – could all turn into nothing. Most of the people who know anything about the place think it will turn to nothing, and some think it could be bad. I don't know which, but I do know I don't want to be lumbered with any clowns. Half the concern comes from the royal visit of

Wake of the Raven

course. Prestige. All hot air and whitewash, but we need it, so all the paths have to be made smooth, as the good book says. Or as I believe it does, somewhere."

Brook laughed. "You'd make a good preacher Nigel. You'd have the devil himself in the congregation."

"So I would Tony, if he'd be useful. Matter of fact he is useful; keeps people on their toes. You have to have some kind of threat as well as a carrot."

"To be honest, about this visit" – Brook lowered his voice a little – "I think they'd do well to cancel it. Do we really need this kind of thing, nowadays, all this show? All that fuss about the abdication, for instance. We swear allegiance, but isn't there a lot of sham in it? Like you said, all hot air and whitewash? I mean all this sort of general business about showing the white man's ways to the rest of the world, and the church involving itself in making sure that our head of state is like the driven snow. Does anyone really care anymore?"

He spoke quietly, his voice not carrying beyond the private circle of their armchairs, for many of the club members would have bristled at his words, and he had opened his mind to Haig further than he would have to most other officers.

It was a serious point, and Colonel Haig turned it awhile in his mind before answering. He understood the attitude that had prompted Brook's question, though he was a little surprised that Brook should be infected by it. When the great war machines of Germany and Japan were finally smashed, so much of the old world's ways seemed ripe to go to the junk heap with them, and the exotic scent of a new world drifted everywhere, sometimes stirring hope, and sometimes fear, but always threatening change.

Few were immune. People - who's parent's had scarcely been able to pronounce a foreign name in the newspaper - could watch the newsreels at the local cinema for a few pence, and they saw what a worldwide mess the whole gaggle of politicians and Kaisers had made. Coventry, Berlin, Hiroshima – the list was endless of the rubble piles they had heaped up, and the graves of the mangled dead covered acres. The ancient, furtive mistrust of traditional authority had ripened into loud, active denial. Socialists, communists, economists who saw no God but the force of supply and demand, philosophers musing in print on man's place in the universe, and generally giving a kick to government in conclusion; their voices were strident everywhere, and old ideas like King, Church and Country seemed to stagger, pale and bloodless, before the flush of their vigour.

"Things change, Tony, yet they don't." He hesitated, wondering how to express an understanding whose ramifications vanished into subtlety. "We've always had monarchs, but they haven't held the real power for a long time. Others have it now; you know that as well as I do. But people need something to hold on to, some kind of a standard where they don't have to think, just obey. We don't always know what to do for best, so we pick our way through, and then we need some base to work from that doesn't shift about. People need leaders that they can look up to."

"But people elect leaders nowadays, and when they don't like them they chuck them out. Murder them sometimes, like in Russia."

Haig shook his head impatiently. "Not really what I meant Tony. Not politicians. People don't trust them very far. Half of them aren't fit to run a greengrocer's in any case. Something a bit beyond that, more like... a model. Not exactly a model, more something that embodies."

Brook looked him quizzically. Embody was not really Colonel Haig's kind of word.

"Represents Tony, that's what I mean. Not just represents the country at some jamboree in Kenya, or Canada, but represents how people think about their country. How they think if they're not bolshie that is. Ordinary people, they want someone they can have respect for, look up to. That person doesn't have to be flawless, but he has to be there. To hold a position. Even if he doesn't hold it too well, still the position's being held, at least its there, like a marker, saying 'this is the centre, this is how things should be.' We know things aren't as they should be, but."

"Nigel, I was wrong, you should be a bishop at least."

Haig frowned at his friend's levity. His mind was keen and concise, appreciating and working with the realities that lay beyond the grasp of the dull witted, but he was no philosopher, and it was rare that he would strain to explain what he felt to be at the centre of people. This was one of those rare occasions, and he felt offended that Brook, having tempted him onto the thin ice, should now make a joke of his words. None the less, he kept his patience and tried again. "To put it more simply, before tearing something down, you should be sure that you have something better to put in its place. I don't think that there's something God given about the monarchy, and if the whole institution withers away, then that's how it will be. But they serve a purpose, and they fill a need. As long as people feel that need, they'll be important."

It was Brook's turn to shake his head. "I'm not so sure Nigel, but we'd better leave it at that."

"Yes."

They both knew that it was ground best not trod too freely by men sworn to serve, and Brook felt suddenly that his musings had lead him to accidentally maul a favourite meat of the left, with their class struggle, and suchlike jargon. That was something that he did not want to pursue, for he was not a man of strong opinions, nor did he want to be known as one.

Chapter 30. Bell

"Stuart, is Gloucester a town or a part of the country?"

"A town. A city to be exact. That's means a big town."

"Big like London?"

"No, not so big. But it is one of the biggest cities in England."

"You told me there were woods and fields in Gloucester."

"Gloucestershire. That's the county that Gloucester's in. All the country's divided up into counties and sometimes the biggest city in a county has the same name as the county."

"I remember. York in Yorkshire, Oxford in Oxfordshire. What county's London in?"

"It's spread out over a few counties. London's a very big place."

"Have you been there?"

"Lot's of times, lots of times. Not for years though."

"Will you go to live in London?"

"Perhaps. I've thought of living there."

"Why not live there then?"

"My family are all in Gloucester, most of them."

For a moment she was quiet, then, "Jennifer isn't."

"Young lady, never you mind Jennifer. I shouldn't have told you about Jennifer."

"Why not. She's your wife isn't she?"

"Yes and no. Yes she is, and no she isn't."

"That's a silly answer. What do you mean, 'no she isn't'? Didn't you get married properly or something?"

"I mean she isn't here, so she can't be my wife can she? Probably out at a cocktail party somewhere tonight, eating little sandwiches off a tray, and bits of cheese on sticks. That's enough of Jennifer now. You shouldn't be asking about Jennifer in any case."

A sort of a muffled "urrumph," came from the girl as she rolled away, turning her back, and though he looked at her sharply in the dim starlight, he held his tongue back from any further words. That was easy, for there seemed to be nothing more to say. Dammed kid. Shouldn't be asking grown-up questions like that. An adult wouldn't ask them in fact. But he couldn't really blame her, for she was his fellow cellmate here, and being easy going he had said more than he would to a stranger. Now he was a touch annoyed, and in the silence he thought about her question.

Well yes, he was talking about London, then about Gloucester, and Jennifer was in neither of those places, and thank God she wasn't here either, or he'd never have heard the end of it. When it came to the neat ordering of the world Jennifer had a keen sense of expectancy, and would have demanded daily that someone should arrive to take them off, and someone must be responsible, and it must be somebody's job, and etcetera, till it would have driven him mad.

Once again he pondered the question of how a man who liked things one way should choose to join himself to someone who liked them another, and how a person, so apparently ideal that he should opt to centre his life around her, should transform into something so alien to him that he now detested her. Re his first point, hadn't he noticed? Or was it that marriage was about finding out these things? Surely not, for didn't the wedding service say that marriage was for mutual aid and comfort? That meant a commitment, not a test drive.

Well then obviously he hadn't noticed; love had been blind, just as the proverb said. Or had it not really been love, but just that they were satisfied with the way they liked each other, until one day they suddenly didn't? Hadn't they really just sort of... acted out their roles, like actors who were in a play that they enjoyed, and were satisfied with the other actor, until one day they didn't like the play anymore? Then they had to realise that the player was not the real person.

Stuart disliked too much introspection, feeling that at times he was too much given to it, and....

The girl rolled back abruptly to look earnestly into his face. "Stuart."

"What dear?"

"I didn't mean to be rude, you know, be nosy, but I thought that with it all being years and years ago you didn't mind."

Years and years. Is that what it was? Yes, she was nearly right. It was years, two of them soon, and to her it must seem like an eternity ago.

"That's all right, you weren't really." He lay back, cradling his head on his hands. He knew that he should simply accept the girl's apology, and then find something else to talk the evening away with, but his own thoughts had set him going. Detest? Wasn't that really the thought that had passed through his mind, and about the woman he was planning to be reconciled with? "It's a problem to me," he began, realising as he spoke that he was again feeding the curiosity he had just rebuked. But why not? The kid was as reasonable an audience as he'd found anywhere, and all indiscretions spoken here would go no farther, and affect the greater world as little as the waves smoothing the sands beyond their feet. "She's a problem," he continued, "It's like being tied up."

"How?" The girl listened to him quietly, scratching her toes against the canvas for the pleasure of the scraping sound.

Her earlier question had caught him off guard and irritated him, but now he felt the Alice in Wonderland humour of it all. "Wives that don't want you, aren't with you. Can't have them, can't get rid of them. No use at all." He laughed gently at his joke and the girl wiggled in merriment.

"Wives. You mean wife don't you. How many have you got?"

"I was speaking generally. Just one. One too many."

Tania seemed to have a high degree of mobility tonight. She rolled quickly back toward him and ran her fingers through the tangle of hair on his chest, coiling a hank of them gently between her fingers.

"Don't you dare. I won't have any left."

"You've got tons." He could see her teeth gleam in the starlight as she contemplated some impudence. "Tons of wives too. Or girlfriends."

"Only one at a time dear. Never more than one at a time."

"Well there's none here. Only me." She had discovered some grains of sand hidden amongst the hair and laid her head against his shoulder as she amused herself picking them out. He hesitated a moment, then slipped his arm about her shoulder.

"Just you dear. That's true. But when we get to Singapore..." he added in aloof tones.

She slapped him briskly on the stomach. "When we get to Singapore you're going to be busy. We've got to get to England, we're months late."

"Okay then, I'll be busy. What'll you be doing?" He lay patiently as the girl thought about this, waiting for the process of her thoughts, seeing almost the clean simplicity of her mind as she puzzled on her novel situation: free, and nothing to do, except what came next in her journey home.

But the girl did not answer; instead her fingers moved gently over his skin, exploring the edge of his ribs where they gave way to the flatness of his stomach, and he realised suddenly that a mood had entered the hut, and was living thick and strong in the air about them. It was a beast spirit of joy and menace, that had its own life and purpose, like a warm, confident ghost that had formed from the shadows to stretch soft, sheltering, menacing wings over them.

It was a strange mood-beast that had entered the hut, dangerous, alien and intoxicating, one that could live only in the un-bridged space between two people, and he knew it of old, for it was the midwife of all coupling, the ticket seller for the secret journey. He had not expected its arrival, though he should, for their shared troubles had built it a nest, their shared laughter had beckoned it, and finally it had accepted the invitation. And he understood untold that though the girl had not met this spirit before, yet she too knew its presence, though not its subtle nature; it was the moment when all becomes real and intense, and fantasy has nowhere to hide, and they lay within its jaws, were fanned by its perfumed breath.

The flimsy timbers of the shelter about them, the soft leaves of its thatching; they were suddenly as solid and everlasting as the bronze of a great bell, humming soundlessly, powerfully about them, enclosing them in a private, eternal world greater than the pale, empty beach outside. I should get out, he though, but the shelter seemed as inescapable as the room to which a man is taken helpless to be executed, or be born.

But he remained, for there was no danger, despite all this spirit's strength, for he knew that with a few firm words he could kill it, should kill it, dissolve it forever back to nothingness; for though it had been born from their roving curiosity, yet it lived on only by permission of his laxity.

But he did not, for it was pleasant to lie back like this, pleasant, and more than that, fascinating to be the subject of this half woman's open exploration, fascinating as the extremes of life and death fascinate. Erotic too, not merely because he was coming to hardness, but beyond that physical detail the charm of a human presence was here, and again the door was swinging open to the mystery of another being who was not self, and he would not, could not slam it shut.

Not yet. Let the door stand open awhile, for there were no enemies here, and soon it would close again by itself, for soon the girl would tire of her game and roll away. Then the moment would pass, and she would be merely a child again, and the mood-beast would be gone. But till it was time for it to leave, for God's sake let him hold her awhile.

The girl spoke. "I don't know. I'll find something." Her voice seemed faint and unsteady. "Look after you." He kneaded her shoulder gently, aware that he should push her away, for he was quite hard now and felt that he might start to quiver at any moment, and that wouldn't do at all, for it was all very well to enjoy the child's massaging, but something else to think that it could end in anything but a trip down the beach. But now she was rubbing his stomach, finding more little sand grains to roll about, roll in the darkness and surf-hissed stillness, and the sheer fire of it was sweeping through him.

"Would you like to look after me?" he asked softly to her hair. An affirming grunt came up. "You're a good kid," he murmured, and moved by her affection he kissed her forehead softly.

"I know." She transferred her attention to his thigh, running her thumb over the scab of a scratch above his knee, teasing the finer hairs on the lean muscle. He waited, stroking her hair, running his fingers over the smoothness of her neck. The surf was hissing outside as it steadily ascended the beach, and the fire crackled and hissed at the first touch of a wave. The stars were bright beneath the brow of the hut entrance, and he watched them as the girl's hand ran the length of his thigh, exploring the solid muscle.

This was too much now. This would drive him to do something he would regret, for the pleasant warmth of their intimacy was now passing into painful fire. He stirred slightly and started to sit up, then drew in his breath sharply, for the girl's hand had left his thigh and closed gently on the hard lump swelling out his shorts.

"Tania," he said, feeling his voice strangely breathless and weak, "you have to stop now."

She turned her face up to his, her eyes reflecting the dying flicker of the fire, her expression dim and lost in the faint light. "Let me," she said softly.

He relaxed back. God he shouldn't let her do this. He should have known, had known minutes ago, and he should have stopped her. But what the hell, there was no one here but the two of them; she was his, his Tania, making her own mind up about things. From the strained throatiness of her voice he knew that she did not merely want to please him: she wanted to explore as eagerly as he wanted her to. There was no one here but them, he thought, squeezing her shoulders. What she was happy with, he was happy with.

Her hand ran over the lump, measuring its length through the shrouding khaki, the fingertips probing to define its shape. Her breath like his was now hoarse and audible, ragged in excitement, and liberated by his compliance she sat up suddenly to examine this new thing. He placed one hand gently on hers and rubbed it steadily back and forth. The girl took up the motion quickly, grinning once at him in a shy way, and he saw that she was as besotted as he was. God but this was good, and now he saw his desire clearly: not merely lust for a girl, but this girl, this impish girl, this one whose life was now entangled with his. Suddenly decisive, he surrendered to the rules of this new world they had entered, all his indecision vanishing. He unbuttoned the shorts and as the girl sat quickly back on her heels he pulled them swiftly down. She put her hands to her mouth at the sight of it now standing free: she had desired this, but the reality was a bit more than she had expected.

He put out a hand that trembled and drew her softly down beside him, encircling her in one arm. "Are you okay Honey?"

"Yes." The answer came faint but clear, and she shyly enclosed the column of warm rigid flesh within her palm, rolling it curiously, exploring the way the skin moved loosely over its hard swollen length, her other hand savouring the smooth architecture of stomach and thigh, fingers tracing the joint between the two, curling the already curly hairs.

Stuart pressed her to him, murmuring some broken tenderness; he was afire within, an exalting fire that devoured his senses in victorious flames. The girl wrapped her fingers around the hard length and squeezed, and he gasped and kissed her ear as she began a steady relentless pumping, till it seemed to him that each determined stroke drove him like a willing martyr to a promised paradise. The fire rose in him and came bursting upwards; he gasped her name and crushed her to him, his back arching upwards as his sperm jetted out, glistening silver in the moonlight and falling back warmly to his stomach.

Stuart slumped back limply to the canvas, laying his hand on the girl's to still its motion, feeling the thick warm fluid gluing their hands together, and lay limp as his erratic breathing slowed, feeling the girl quiver.

The unbelievable had happened. Impossible as his desire had seemed, and despite all his qualms and restraints, it had happened, as inevitably and naturally as eating and sleeping. She had performed the friendly, animal act as willingly as he had finally accepted it, though perhaps now she was stunned at what her curiosity had lead to. She sat up suddenly. "Tania..." he said unsurely, but she was turning her raised hand about in the dim moonlight, fascinated by the thick strings of semen that hung in glistening loops between her fingers.

"Sticky!" she exclaimed in awe, and his last anxiety vanished, his back marrying in softness to the sand as his anxious muscles made a final relaxation. What the hell was there to worry about.

"Honey, when you get to twenty-one I'll buy you a bloody Rolls-Royce," he said, and sitting up weakly he passed her his shirt.

Chapter 31. Agatha

The hiss of the surf crept slowly into his consciousness, and he awoke as slowly, rubbing his heels luxuriously on the rough sailcloth. The girl's hair brushed his shoulder; despite the heat of the night she had remained close by him. He lay quietly for a while, contemplating her smooth face relaxed in sleep, then rose softly and crept from the shelter onto the beach.

The high tide was only just beginning to retreat, and he covered the few paces of ruffled sand that it did not reach to stand on the smooth, hard, glittering wetness, and squint into the pathway of golden light that the rising sun threw towards him. He vaguely knew that he should feel concerned, yet he was not, and did not wish to be so. Instead he felt a gentle wonder that things should have worked out this way. The girl.... He could not neatly sum up how he felt, could not have put it into words that would convey any meaning to himself or any other, yet he knew the pleasant flavour of his state.

She was still there, not lost to him, still a part of the world that was not against him, but now was not the unreachable object of a hidden, tormenting, futile desire. She was his. Fate did not, after all, intend to rear an unending series of spikes against him. Part of his inner luminous world, she fitted and agreed with him, stood with him as his little partner in gleeful crime against the grim, dull facts of mere existence. Or at least she had for one heady episode.

He looked back at the hut with a twinge of apprehension as he heard her stir. Was his abandoned restraint really proved to have been laughably unnecessary, or would the pleasant morning be soured with regret? What should he say to her? Has she been a grown woman an enthusiastic morning repeat of something more serious would have been in order, but this was unknown ground, and his mind drew a blank.

After their bit of hanky-panky they had laid quietly together, he feeling drained of all ability to think, astounded by the enormity of what they had just done. There'd be hell to pay for this in England, he thought finally. A damned good job there's no real law out here, just a lot of argument about who gets to rule what bit of jungle. And its damned certain nobody knows who owns this little corner. Some of the coolies might, but they don't count. Tania wanted to do it, so she's okay with it, and that's all that counts. It was just a bit of fun to her after all, just a new adventure to play with, like being stranded her. That was the last that he remembered; would this relentless dawn cause a re-think?

Tania emerged from the hut yawning, and he gave her a tentative smile. "Morning," he tried, feeling his voice a little wooden.

"I've got to go pee!" And she was off down the beach in a stumpy early morning stiffness run, her hair bouncing as she went.

He relaxed again; so that was all. Tania was still Tania, and she was his. How he sun shone on her hair. It was like dark honey flowing behind her. And how long it was getting. Surely it had been much shorter when she first stood before him at Paa airstrip. He ran his fingers through his own ragged mess and found the un-butchered parts to be long, falling down his neck as never before in his life. "Savage of the Jungle," he murmured, and waded into the sea to ease his own bladder.

The girl was back at the hut before him, scooping the ashes into a can. She gave him a grin from a face full of cheeky merriment, and he grimaced a more complex grown man's expression, a mix of humour and embarrassment.

"Come on Honey," he said, taking her by one grimy hand, "let's get the water together."

Later in the day their new-caught fish lay on the beach, and he gutted them as the girl prattled some story of a cheating stallholder in Paa bazaar. She was pleased with herself, that he could tell, but since the morning broke neither of them had said anything in words of their escapade.

"Honey...." She stopped as he broke into her flow of her story. He found that he had now renamed her, and he was pleased at this, for the name was apt. She was his only sweetness on this island, and her hair was lustrous and brown. He would have run his fingers through its thickness, except that his hands were slimy from the fish. He paused in his cleaning and regarding her seriously.

"Honey, when we get back to Singapore and people ask us about how we lived on this island...."

"I know. Sister Agatha would go mad. It's nothing to do with them though, it's our business not theirs. We won't be seeing Sister Agatha again in any case."

Again he felt the easy joy of relief, mixed with wonder that she should be so acute. The kid had grasped his concern even before he brought it up. Pretty smart for eleven. But he had to be sure that she got the full meaning.

"Not just our dear Sister Agatha Honey. She won't be in Singapore in any case. But lots of other people will. There'll be some other nun in charge of the Mal there, and there'll be other people."

"What other nun? There won't be any nuns, we're going to England! You said we were going to England!"

"Yes we are. Listen to me carefully." He threw the knife down and moved closer to her, for her face had twisted in dismay.

"Everywhere we go there will be people, and we need to be very careful or they'll give us a lot of trouble. There will be a nun in charge of the Mal in Singapore, and if you're not careful she'll end up in charge of you."

"How? How can she? We won't go near the Mal there."

"No we won't, but as soon as we arrive the news will spread, and the Mal might come near us. I have to get you out somehow, and if there's any, you know, any kind of difficulty, then they'll stop you leaving."

Tania sat appalled. It had become an article of faith with her that as soon as they arrived Stuart would whisk them onto a plane and away to England. She felt the heavy hand of dark-gowned authority falling on her shoulder like the return of a forgotten nightmare.

Stuart pressed his point further. "There'll be all kinds of people in authority there. The Governor, the police, all the lot. You can't just get on a plane and fly from one country to another, you have to have permission."

"But I'll be with you!"

"Yes. But why, that's the question. What do I tell people if they ask where you belong?"

"With you! I belong with you!"

Stuart didn't answer immediately. It had seemed so clear when he made that promise to her. He had been full of that ready to kill determination that hardship fills the mind with, and confident that a path could be found. Had someone mentioned difficulties to him then, he would have snapped back that he would find a way or force one. Well, those difficulties had not yet come, but their shadow had, and it was time to make good on that mood.

"Let me think about it a bit. I don't know how we'll get past Singapore, but we will somehow."

The girl's face cleared instantly. "Tell them you're looking after me."

"Yes. Yes of course that's the answer. Somehow I have to be officially in charge of you."

"See it's easy. You could tell them you're my dad."

"Yes I'm sure that would be just the ticket," Stuart replied dryly, remembering the events of the night before. This brought him back to his lesson. "And, whether I'm your, your guardian, or your uncle, or whatever I am, everything has to look okay."

"Everything would look alright if you had some kind of paper that said...."

273

"No I mean, you know, nothing ... naughty going on," he stumbled, and wondered if he was reddening. Somehow doing it had been easier than talking about it.

"Oh that's easy. There's nobody I want to tell in any case. All the people I know are in Paa, and they'd all fuss and be mad at me. Apart from Danielle that is, but I'll never see her again."

"Never mind any apart-froms," said Stuart hastily, "you have to remember this Honey, everybody wants to tell you what to do, and everybody talks too much. If anyone important thought that we were like, you know, like... well they'd give us trouble. Lots of trouble. Trouble like you wouldn't believe. No apart-froms," he repeated firmly, seeing the danger of her exception.

"Okay," she said, crawling forward to grin at him a closer range, "its a secret, a big big secret." Like him, she was too pleased with the world to brood on its grimness. She put out a hand quickly and rubbed his chin. "You haven't shaved today. Scratchy."

She was right, he hadn't. Clean forgot!

"What could they do in any case? When we get to England we can do what we want."

Stuart sighed. "Young lady, you have much to learn," he pronounced with dramatic archness. It was enough. The girl understood, and she knew that too much talk would spoil her own plans, so he needn't bother belabouring the point further. Things were all right between the two of them, and that was all he cared about. Matters suddenly seemed simple, and he took an inner vow to worry no more about their little peccadillo. "Fish," he announced, shouldering his spear, "then," he sighed, "the sign!"

They marched down the beach together, and as they went he noticed with pleased amusement an almost swagger in her walk and the poise of her head, and he joked to himself that one could almost say this place got better every day.

Stuart worries too much, thought Tania as they walked down the beach, she trying to match his longer stride. We won't go near the sisters in Singapore, and if we do, we haven't done anything to let them stop us. None of it was any of their business, and I'll make sure it never is. Dumb nuns, always walking about in their robes. They'll never stop me from going to England with Stuart, not even if there's a thousand of them in Singapore.

I won't say anything to them, and it was my idea in any case. Wouldn't it be fun if they did know though? That would really upset them, especially Sister Agatha. Sister Agatha was always going on about men and how they did evil things, but I know more than her, know more than big-blister-Sister Agatha knows, and one day I'll let the big blister know that I know more. One day when we're safe, and then I can write to her from England, and tell her what's what.

Aggy. Old Haggy. She's never done anything like I did, that's for sure. And she never will, she'll just keep on lecturing away at people, and telling them what to do, and being dumb, and if she was here and she was with somebody she wouldn't know how to make them happy. I do though. Stuart needs a girlfriend, that's why he liked that Julia, cause she was nice and pretty and she had a nice voice. But he likes me too, and I must have done it just right, 'cause when his stuff shot out he sort of gasped and held me really tight. I though he was going to jump out of the tent! I did that, and Haggy wouldn't have known how to do it. I must have done it just right. I wonder if Julia would have known how to do it? I suppose so. She was a woman, not like the sisters.

It was a pity Julia got drowned. She was pretty, and she could have told me things like how to dress properly and do my hair. The sisters always wanted you to look – well, ugh! But if she'd been here Stuart might have done it with her, 'cause she liked him, and then I'd never have got to do it, unless he'd wanted to do it with both of us. But he couldn't of course, 'cause you can only have one girlfriend at a time if you really love them, and Julia wouldn't have wanted to share him 'cause she would have really been in love with him, and besides, she was an adult.

I liked her though. I wouldn't have minded sharing him with her till I grow up, but then I'd want him for myself. And that would be fair to him if I'd shared him 'cause she's grown up and she could do the other stuff with him, all the adult stuff where he has to get on top of her, and I can't do that. I can do it with my hand though, and I bet that's just as good for him. It was fun as well, really exciting, and so funny how it was hard and waggly at the same time. I was really nervous at first 'cause I thought he might be mad if I touched it, he's sort of secret about it.

I suppose all adults are though, it's something they're all mysterious about. I never really thought about that before, but they all keep their private bits hidden so you can't tell if they've got one or not, except for women, and they can't hide their bosom things. Men can though, I know 'cause Stuarts shrank after I'd done it. I suppose that's so they can hide it. Or perhaps it's to keep it out of the way. It'd get in the way if it was always big and hard I suppose, and then he wouldn't be able to do stuff like dig. Perhaps that's why he had to keep emptying it, so it wouldn't be a nuisance.

I think he liked it more when I did it though, and it was fun, like, sort of like an adventure. But I got frightened when he pulled his shorts down, cause he did it so fast, and then it looked so big and scary all stuck out. I'd just wanted to feel it first, just to see what it was like, and then it was there all stiff and pointing! But I was going to do it for him if he wanted me too in any case, just like he did it. I knew he'd like me to do it, 'cause he likes anything exciting like that.

He felt my bottom that time when I found out about his girlfriends and we had that big wrestling match. That was fun, nobody ever felt my bottom before. I didn't know that men liked to do that. Father Colin did once, that time when somebody opened the door nearly in my face and I had to jump back, but it was only a little touch and I could tell it was an accident. Anyway, he was a priest and he wouldn't do that, but

Stuart isn't and so it's okay. Stuart's a lot more fun. I'm going to be with him forever and ever, and we'll have lots of fun.

Stuart was not looking at her, but eying the hilltop as they neared the end of the beach. "I'm going to catch the biggest today," she yelled in his ear without warning, and brandishing her spear ran into the water before him. But here her ability fell short of her energy, for Stuart's competitive spirit was aroused, and when later she laid the best of her catch on the beach he wordlessly laid one a good inch longer beside it. That was not too much of an insult, but he rolled his eyes to heaven as he commenced the cleaning, and struck up a tuneless whistling that drove her to fury.

"You wait Stuart Ellis," she told him with forced calm, "I'll catch one so big it'll swallow you and your spear." But Stuart merely whistled the more.

Lately Stuart had taken to examining the sign from the peak of the hill, before hefting his mattock and biting the day's first chunk from the stubborn turf. Before, he had always seized the crude tool as soon as they had ascended the hill, unwilling to waste his time and energy on viewing a sign that he knew fell far short of the mark. Later in the day he might walk to the peak, resting his aching back, and always they would end the day by going to the peak to collect their firepot, but that had other, almost ritual purposes, for the sun fell towards the horizon in the West, and there lay their promised land.

If they had merely wanted to see the progress of the sign more clearly, that would have been futile, for the view from the peak was little better than that from any part of the slanting plateau, but there was a further, subtler reason for going there. To stand there was to be at the highest point of their tiny world, and to know that though the kingdom laid out below them was their prison, they were the lords of it, from the waves that growled beyond the drop by their feet, to the distant ragged scrubland, hidden beyond the tree wrapped slopes leading to the south.

Forced by necessity to be patient, they had adapted as all prisoners do, and coming to see their prison as their home had acknowledged that at least it was a place of beauty. Hence it was a quiet pleasure for them to stand there at the end of each day, and drink in the wild panorama a while before descending to Log City and their campfire.

In recent days he dallied each morning, going with Tania and the firepot to the peak, striding in a zigzag over the sign as he went, considering how few days of effort still remained to complete it, and wondering if it were already time to say finished, and move on to what must inevitably come. Today he did this yet again, eying the shapes of the great letter, noting the few uncut patches that still spoiled their symmetry. Was it worth the final effort to finish that S? It had long been intelligible; the lack was in a sky-born reader. He reached the top and stood abstracted as Tania built the fire.

"That's nearly it," he said, a hint of regret in his voice, as though it were the end of a pleasure rather than a task. "Just that bit there, then we're done."

"We won't finish today," Tania replied, "I'm a surveyor, so I know."

"No, but we will soon. Tomorrow I guess. We arrived on a Tuesday, and we'll finish the sign on one. Then everybody gets ice cream, and I'm buying."

"Not tomorrow silly man," she declared, "day after that. We'll finish on Wednesday."

Stuart shook his head. "Tomorrow. Definitely."

But Tania was adamant. "Wednesday, the day after. You'll see."

"Indeed we will see," he answered purposefully, taking up his mattock and dismissing his thoughts.

Possibly it was his competitive spirit that delighted in their little feuds, or possibly it was the energy that his new cheerfulness gave to him, but he attacked the turf that day with massive vigour, and by the time they descended from the darkening hill his aching muscles were reminding him that he was only flesh and blood. Rain started to fall as they ate, and they retreated early into the hut, carrying their stew with them. Later they tossed the pans out onto the sand, and he stretched out with a sigh.

"You tried to cheat," Tania stated. "We've done tons more today than usual."

"I'm like Moses, I have to get my people across. We great leaders have heavy responsibilities."

The girl sat at his head and began to rub his shoulders, and he rolled face down and luxuriated in the clumsy massage, wondering what the agenda was for winding up the evening. That speculation had occurred to him a few times in the day, and added quite a bit of enthusiasm to a good many of his blows. At the same time he had wondered if perhaps it was a good thing not to repeat their antics. It had all been strangely natural in the end, and Tania obviously regarded it as quiet a lark, but still, she was just a kid. It may have been a one-off with her in any case, something born of curiosity that she would not repeat unless he prompted her to it, and he had told himself that he would do no prompting. Precocious or not, he balked at leading her in further than she wished to go.

"Does that feel better?" she asked presently.

"Much. It's taken a lot of the ache away."

"Roll over."

He rolled obediently, and the girl seated herself astride his thighs, grinning like a fiend.

Chapter 32. Mud

The following day they ascended the slope at a more sedate pace, Stuart stiff and aching, for despite Tania's best massaging efforts his muscles had not forgiven the previous days excesses.

"Tomorrow, tomorrow, tomorrow," crowed Tania as she followed up the slope. She pressed both hands against his bottom and heaved, puffing like a steam engine and digging her feet into the path "Would you like me to give you a push Stuart?"

"Brat. You'll see. We'll finish today if it kills me. Or you better still."

"If it does kill you I'll roll you down the hill, where all the dirt goes. Then I can finish on my own and bury you at the same time."

"You carry on laughing young lady. Today we'll finish, just you wait and see."

"No, you'll see. It'll be tomorrow."

Stuart did see, but he saw beyond his jokes. He saw that whether they came to an end of their task in one day or two, it still remained a poor cause for celebration. The letters had long been large and clear enough to blaze an unmistakable plea for miles, yet they had drawn no eager rescuer. The few planes they had seen were too low and distant, and the near-flat presentation of the hilltop to the sky made the sign invisible to the few ships that passed.

The weeks of manual labour in this high, open place had also served as an intelligence exercise, and over this long time the spies of their eyes had reported monotonously the same disheartening fact: either traffic by air nor traffic by sea passed close to this little isle, and even if they occupied themselves for a further two months, and brightened the great letters with a flower garden, still they were working in vain.

They could not afford to carry on like this much longer, for though there was no dangerous beast on the island, the process of life itself was a threat. If either of them should fall victim to the host of illnesses that snipe at health, to what doctor would they then turn? He shuddered to think of what would happen if some little stomach pain should ripen into appendicitis, or some minor cut become septic. They must leave, and the end of this task meant the end of excuses. Like it or not, they had done all they could on the hilltop, and he must admit to the weakness of their plan, and turn his hand to building a raft. He anticipated the prospect with dread, though he joked and avoided worrying Tania with his fears.

Certainly many people had been forced hastily into the water from sinking ships, and later been rescued, even though they drifted for days or weeks in the freezing waters of the Atlantic, or the endless reaches of the vast Pacific. True indeed, but a heck of a lot besides them had gone into the drink and hadn't been heard of again. He could swim, yes, and so could Tania, but what use was that if they got washed off a raft in the middle of a storm, with not a bit of land in sight? Good for delaying the end a few minutes, that was all.

And if they did fetch up on the Malay coast, were they any safer than waiting here and catching fish? Although it was usually said as joke, the fact remained that the Dayaks still took heads in Borneo, and whilst that was hundreds of miles in the other direction, it was still a good measure of how things could be in these parts.

Malaya he knew, from the early days of the emergency, but he knew it with a rifle in his hands, and a bunch of men with him. After the savagery of the Japs, he had held lesser enemies in contempt, and whether the frightened villagers were friendly or otherwise unimportant, for he feared them no more than their scraggy chickens. Now things were different, for he would arrive alone, unarmed and burdened with Tania.

This had passed through Stuart's mind a thousand times, and always his conclusion had been the same: we may be lost here, but we're living, and that's a surer thing than being out there in one of these storms, so keep on digging till there's nothing more to do.

And soon there would be nothing more to do.

Tania shook the basket beneath his nose and pointed into it suggestively. He had been standing lost in thought. "Today Honey," he declared, striding out towards the last piece of un-mastered turf.

"Tomorrow," she called after him.

Stuart was not to be called on to repeat his Herculean labour however, and Tania to be proved unfairly right, for the sky was thick with cloud. Usually they worked through the frequent rains, but this afternoon the wind rose suddenly and sent down such a driving storm that they retreated hastily through the streaming trees to Log City. Even in a rainstorm it was hotter than an English summer's day in these regions, but the barrage of rain felt cold by comparison, and he hauled off his dripping shirt and threw it outside.

"Wash day," he shouted, for the rainstorm thundered deafeningly on the thatch.

"Too – morrow," crooned Tania, creeping back to the door. She pulled her shirt off over her head, and screwed it up to ring it out. Stuart watched quietly; he had never seen her naked except for that one time, and to see her now stripped to the waist was a pleasant rather than a sexual experience. Her skin was smooth, unblemished, clean of the wrinkles and flab of age, the colour of pale honey.

Odd, he thought. They go on the beach and strip down to knickers as kids, and it means nothing. Then when they're older and there's still nothing there, they have to cover up and get ready to be young ladies. When they are young ladies and we'd be interested in looking, by then they're all covered up. Then we go to a lot of trouble to get them uncovered in private, so we can have some shenanigans. Funny business. And miss here keeps her shirt on in front of me for two months, even though she's got nothing yet, but takes it off now 'cause she's seen my dick. Strange the way it's all set up. And to what purpose? If people look after each other, and give each other some respect, isn't that all that counts?

"Bad man, you shouldn't be peeping," Tania said, looking back over her shoulder. He leaned forward and drew her back, and she stretched out softly for his inspection. Her body was firm and regular, the shoulders square, the faint pattern of her abdominal muscles an echo of his own. Other than the rounding of her pectoral muscle her chest was flat, the tanned skin marked only by the tiny pale nipples.

What will they be like one day, he wondered? She had none of the scrawny child about her; rather there was a fullness in her limbs that suggested the possibility of an athletic build. How much of that was from nature, and how much from all these endless baskets of earth?

She watched him with an amused smile, perhaps a little uncertain, waiting to see what he would do with her. Bouncy with curiosity, she had so far experimented on him; he realised that he had never attempted to give her any pleasure, other than she enjoyed lying beside him, being close to him. Did she need more than that? Could she enjoy more than that?

He ran his fingers over her shoulder, onto the rounded muscle of the chest, tickled the slight point of her nipple. She giggled, and he saw that the nipple had risen slightly, felt it gain hardness beneath his fingers. She giggled, and he bent closer, kissed her skin – how smooth it was – kissed the nipple, nibbled on it playfully. She giggled again, stirring her hips and passing her hands behind his head to press gentle onto his hair.

For long minutes Stuart savoured the girl, running his lips over her slight body, burnishing it with gentle kisses from waist to neck. Her hands ran over his hair, his shoulders, her fingers probing the spurred bones of his spine. Finally drew back and looked into her face. She smiled up at him, loving, trustful, yet faintly nervous – or was it excitement? She loves me, he realised. It's can't be just the wildness in her; she's never done anything like this before, and she doesn't know what I'm going to do.

"Do you like this Honey," he asked softly, unnecessarily, wanting as men do to hear the thinking mind confirm the animal body's wants.

"Mmm Hmmm," was her sufficient answer.

He bent forward and brushed her lips with his, and for a while they played clumsily, the tomboy girl who had one night boldly slid her hand onto his fearful part, enjoying her first natural kiss from him, stepping yet another step from the receding world of girlish chatter to the actuality of flesh joining with flesh. He ran his tongue softly between her lips and her tongue responded, the two slippery little animals sliding back and forth eagerly. She giggled and pushed him away; "wet," she said, wiping her lips with the back of her hand.

The mood for that kind of play was not on her, Stuart realised, and though he became acutely aware of his arousal it did not matter much, for it carried none of the pain of disappointment. She had pulled the gnawing teeth of his guilty frustration, and to desire her had ceased to be a torment, and now was part of the fascinating dance of emotion that envelopes two people bound up in each other. Her affection met a need in him of which the sexual mischief was only a part, and he was happy to let his roused desire simmer, and wait for its shuddering moment.

Later Honey, he thought, summing up his feelings more simply.

They sat in the entrance of the hut for an hour or more, watching the rain pound the sand into a dimpled mud, talking of the odd things that came to mind. The storm slackened and died away, and they emerged onto the fast firming beach and crept cautiously through the dripping forest and up the now treacherous slope, slipping in the new mud.

The day seemed to pass slowly, and Tania wished that the sign were finished. It was horrible up here after a lot of rain. A lot of the time it was like an adventure, but she hated days like this. The rain made the earth all thick and sticky, and it was twice as hard to get it into the basket, and when it was in, then it wouldn't come out. It was always like this when it rained. Stuart had said Tuesday, so she had said a day later, sort of like a bet, but if someone would come along and finish it for them today it was okay with her. They hadn't seen even a far-away plane for ages, and next they had to build a big raft.

What a big job it was to get to England! But she had Stuart, except today he seemed fed up with all this mud too, and didn't want to talk much. What a long day, and now she had carried the basket – twice as heavy – full of nasty dirt to the edge of the hill again, and when she tried to tip it off it hung on. Usually she liked that bit, because if she tipped it right at the edge, it all went rolling down amongst the trees, and that was fun, but now it just slithered of slowly, and sat there in a big lump. This was no fun at all. She'd ask Stuart if they could leave that bit in the corner. He could win his bet if he wanted, she didn't care. She went back to Stuart's side, where he had hacked up a whole lot more for her. "Stuart," she started as he hacked at a half-cut bit, and the mud flew up into her mouth, causing her to splutter and spit. Disgusting, "Urgh," and now he was laughing.

"That's what happens to little girls who talk too much," he called after her as she ran to the water can, but she was too busy spitting out mud to answer.

"Pig," she yelled, when she could speak.

"You like pigs," he shouted back, still amused, "me and Adolph." He threw the mattock down. "Enough for today. We can't finish."

"I win. And we're taking Adolph with us when we leave. You can stay here."

They were spattered and caked with the rich dark earth, but the ever-present sea quickly washed the plastered mud from them and their clothes. Again it was time to cook, and eat, and to her joy the cloudy skies cleared, promising a star clad evening.

On the hilltop, a few scant yards remained uncut.

"How will you build the raft Stuart?" she asked him later as they sat before the evening fire.

"Trees. We'll have to cut a lot down, as straight as we can find them, then lay them all out flat and tie them together." He held out one flattened palm. "We make a sort of mat, the same as this, longer than it is wide, the same size that we want the raft. Then we make another on top of it," he laid a second flattened palm on the first, "and tie them together, and keep doing that until there's enough timber to float without sinking under our weight." Stuart had thought his way through this several times, and he illustrated the succeeding layers enthusiastically, laying one palm on the other repeatedly as though playing a game.

"Where will we build it?"

"On the beach, by the old hut where the water gets deep quickly. I want to make the first layer there at least, and the second as well, but I'll have to get it into the water before it gets too heavy to move. When it's in the water I can work on top to make the next layers. I hope I can get at least two layers before I float it, 'cause one might bend a lot, but with two it should be stiffer."

"Stiffer. Why do you want it stiffer?"

"Cause then it's finished. I don't want it bending and shifting in the water so that I have to keep pushing bits back into place and retying the ropes, not with the waves throwing everything about. And we need a long, straight trunk for a mast."

"Long and straight. Does that have to be stiff too?"

"Of course."

"Very stiff?"

"Well stiff enough...." He noticed the grin that had appeared on Tania's face. "No not tremendously stiff, just stiff enough to carry a sail," he said determinedly, cooking his wit for a retort, "I...."

"What if it breaks? Can you use something else?"

"Yes your neck. And I can polish your brass face to shine ahead of us." He picked up a twig to hurl at her, but threw it into the fire instead. No sense encouraging dangerous habits.

"Now be serious Stuart. What else will it have?"

"A hut on top, perhaps, but an outrigger, definitely. Sticks out to the side to stop it rolling over."

"Long ones?"

"Medium ones, out to the side to stop the whole thing rolling over. Here I am planning seriously...."

"Rolling over!" This alarming picture had recaptured Tania's attention. "Why should it roll over?"

"It'll be long and narrow, and if a wave gets under it, it could roll. So we have some, some sticks out to one side, and a bundle of tree trunks tied to them. That makes it stable. You'll see."

"How do you know all this? I mean, how to build boats. Did you have to make them during the war?"

Stuart laughed. "No. We had to learn a lot of new stuff in the war, but not building boats. I've seen it done that way though. There's a lot of boats like that, the natives use them all over. Outriggers, that's what they're called, 'cause they have this float thing out at the side. Sometimes they use regular boats instead, but that's too hard."

"Will it float? What if the water gets in?"

"There won't be any inside for the water to get into. Just a lot of wood, and we go on top, us and our stuff. We need some kind of a shelter from the sun, and something like a box that we can tie down for some food and water. Not much, just enough for a few days."

"You know lots of things. Useful things I mean. They never taught us anything useful at the Mal, just boring stuff."

"They taught geography."

"Yes that was okay."

"And maths."

"I liked maths. And English, but they made it all boring somehow. I'd like to go to a real school."

"Yes." Stuart thought about this. He'd hated school, couldn't wait to get out of there. They all had really, it was sort of normal. You accepted things at that age, because you hadn't any choice. When you were old enough to get away from it, then you got away. He'd thought a few times since that some more education would be useful. What would he do when he got back? A job obviously, but he'd never had a real job, other than working in his father's store. That wasn't like working for somebody, or having a trade. "Surveyor," he murmured. That wouldn't be too bad really, and he had the school certificates, but at his age, it was too late to think of training for it. He knew all about buying and selling, and he had been doing all right except...

He threw a stick into the fire pensively. If he weren't careful he'd be too old to do anything. The thought troubled him occasionally that he knew nothing but trading out here, and the army. He knew a lot about all sorts, but how would any of it cause someone to give him a job, or help him to set up for himself? Perhaps he should have stayed in the army. He could have worked up to captain, or major, or even colonel, who knows? But that would have bored him to death. Once the war was over, it was all bull.

"You'll go to a real school in England Honey. Learn as much as you can, and don't go wandering about doing daft stuff, thinking you know better than any body else. My dad used to tell me to pay attention at school, but I couldn't wait to get away."

"Were you a dum dum at school?" she asked, poking him in the ribs.

"No. I could do the stuff, but I wanted the army. That was exciting because of the war. After the war I wanted to do something else."

"I'd like to be a teacher," she volunteered unexpectedly, "then I could teach people properly, not like at the Mal."

"Yes. That's good. Teaching's a good job, and there's lots of women teachers. We'll have to get you to a good school. Wasn't your mum a teacher?"

"Yes. She was."

Tania fell quiet, and drawing her knees up to her chin she sat staring into the fire. After that she said little, and he realised that he had again put his foot in it. He made some conversation, but the evening was marred, and she responded in a withdrawn way. A wet day, and a wet ending, he thought.

As they settled for the night she pressed up to him, and he stroked her arm in the dark. He had felt that with evening there might be a little action, but on occasion the memory of her mother upset the kid, and this was one of those occasions. Never mind, he thought, there's other times. Two nights running's going some in any case, 'cause she's just a kid, and its bloody amazing we got to doing stuff like this at all. Do what you can for her; she feeling a bit down, and she's worth it.

He smiled at the thought of her little tease. For all his hard-acquired knowledge of the world, he was a little in awe of the girl: that he had never met anyone like her before was a certainty.

Chapter. 33. Willis

"Nigel, its Colonel Brook on the 'phone."

This was unexpected. He was to meet with Brook at the club tomorrow evening; surely Brook didn't have to cancel? Haig took the 'phone from his wife.

"Nigel, you remember I mentioned Willis?" Haig grunted in assent.

"Well I just heard... it was in the paper... he's dead."

"Dead. How?" But before Brook answered, Haig knew.

"Shot himself. Went into his bedroom and shot himself. Must have been days ago. They just found him."

"Damnation." What else was there to say? Though it was something that happened, and Willis was the kind that it happened to, it remained a shock, as final as it was nasty, and Brook had been close to the man recently, and was upset. Haig spoke some platitudes – he could not have later recalled what words he said – and confirmed their meeting before he hung up the receiver. His brusqueness had sprung not from indifference, but from a feeling that words were futile, and he sat motionless for some time, rummaging through memories of men who had fallen at the world's fences: some too greedy, some too confident; some stupid, and some just plain unlucky.

The following evening at the club, Brook still seemed shaken, and Haig guessed that some undercurrent of guilt was flowing in him. "I can't but help feel that something could have been done, Nigel."

"Rubbish man. It was his life, and he chose to ruin it. He couldn't come back from it. If he'd had the strength of character to come back he wouldn't have got into such a mess in the first place."

"That's damned harsh Nigel."

"It's often a harsh world Tony, especially for those who make it so for themselves. What could you have done?"

Brook hesitated, uncertain.

"You could have lent him something, but would that have cured it? It's a pattern Tony. Loans like that, they just bolster his kind up till the next crisis, just tide them over so they can go on to make the same mistakes again."

"We don't know his kind, Nigel. I mean we don't know if there is a "his kind". I can't recall him being all that different from a lot of others that we served with. A bit arrogant at times, and a bit too much bluster, but then that's not a hanging matter, is it. Everyone had their quirks. Just that business with the bloody mess room funds, that's all. One silly act, and over not enough money to sole your shoes with at that. He was never quite the same after it. Acted cheerful, still tried to bluster a bit, as though nothing had happened, but somehow it rang a bit hollow afterwards."

Haig grunted. "Did the paper give any details?"

"No. Just the basic facts. 'The body of was found' and 'police not seeking a suspect' - all that kind of thing."

"He never did say why he needed a loan, did he?"

"No, but he did say that his wife had left him. Not straight out, not in so many words, but roundabout. 'They were no longer together' – something like that."

That's why it's nipped him so hard, thought Haig. Tony's very much the family man. Close, him and Pamela, very close, living in their own little rosy pink world. He felt a dull pang of envy move within him, not for the first time. He had missed out on that, had somehow failed to gain that pleasant little garden as part of his man's estate. Were Mildred to leave him, how would he feel? Relieved perhaps, or would he be torn? He did not know, and she never would, so useless to speculate.

"Perhaps something could have been done," he admitted reluctantly, "but you weren't to know that. Weren't to know he was so... desperate, that is. We all have our problems. If we were to bail out every lame duck we met, we'd never come to the end of it."

"Still..."

"Yes," said Haig softly, beginning to acknowledge that Willis had been a man, as well as a fool. "One bloody stupidity, and after that everything downhill. If someone could have taken him by the hand... But he was an officer, and he shouldn't have needed nannying. Still... mistakes get made, even by the best. Sometimes you can patch them, and sometimes you can't, no matter how you try." He hesitated, for there were some points of principle that he would loath to be seen to fudge, "I must admit it's been on my mind since you called. Its appalling how one act so long ago has lead to so much. I don't condone theft – if it was theft, because I'm dammed if I ever got to know the details – but yet I've seen men do worse, and nothing come of it, and felt astounded that nothing came of it." He shook his head. "Rum world."

It seemed to him that with his softening, Brook regained his cheer, or possibly it was the brandy working. Haig raises his glass, for whatever his opinions whilst Willis lived, it was one of their own who had now completed his slow, sad fall. "To Major Willis. Not the worst of men. May he be at the end of his troubles." And their glasses clinked together.

Driving home later, Haig found himself in pensive mood. It was always possible to escape a bad situation, to sum it up, wall it off and walk away. That way you weren't hurt when the building fell in, and those who it fell on – you'd told them before you left, begged them to leave, but they wouldn't listen. When it landed on their heads it was their own fault, and you were unscathed, you and those who'd listened to you, because you used your common sense. Common sense, and the sentimental stuff in its right place, which meant second place. That was how he'd learnt to handle things, and how he'd taught many another to handle things, and how a thousand past generals had done it.

At least, that was the flawless theory of it. If you were in the right, you could feel satisfied at that, satisfied that you'd stuck to your guns, and kept your act clean, and sensible, as well as satisfied that you weren't under the wreckage. But none the less, it was depressing. Some one had fallen, and fallen needlessly, from his own folly. No fault of yours, but no praise to your generosity either, and, as he fell, a bit of yourself fell and died with him. Depressing.

Willis had a moustache, he remembered, a thick one, one of the old cavalry types. Beyond that, Haig couldn't quiet picture his face; darkish, wasn't it, and a bit on the fleshy side? But Raymond's face came to mind instead, and he uneasily felt a connection.

Supposing that he had gone to see the man, gone with Tony, helped drag him to his feet. He could have done that, couldn't he? Not lent money of course, because he'd been right there, that never cured anything, but just given Willis a bit of a boost, helped him to see that it wasn't really so bad? No, not really. If he'd known what Willis was to do, then yes, he'd have been first in the saddle to charge in there; he'd done that before, dispensing firm advice to strengthen wavering purpose, speaking softly where a softer man would have shouted harshly, bellowing effectively where a cleverer would have uselessly tried reason.

It wasn't that he was indifferent; they just hadn't known, neither him nor Brook, hadn't known how close to the brink Willis was. They'd heard he had troubles, but then so did the woman who kept the corner shop, and she didn't die of them. It was a pity, but it was too damned late now. Again Raymond's face came before his mind's eye.

"How is Colonel Brook?" Mildred asked.

"A little upset over Willis."

"I've never heard you mention this Willis before," Mildred continued absently, counting stitches.

"Never had cause to. Met him a few times in Burma, once or twice in '46 in Malaya. Don't think I've met him since

Singapore. Never seen him in England in fact. Now isn't that strange."

"Not really. I've never met a lot of the people you talk about."

"You know Captain Soames. And Tony of course. And Major Lister. You've met everybody."

"I've never met Major Lister, just his wife, once. Sometimes I wonder if you make these people up," she concluded with her usual placid humour.

"Have you heard from Raymond recently?"

Mildred peered at him over her glasses. It was not often that her husband asked that question. "He 'phoned me yesterday," she said.

There was silence for a while. "Don't you want to know how he's doing?" she asked.

"Of course I want to know. If he's doing anything worthwhile that is."

"He's got another job. With a publisher. That friend Richard that he mentioned, he arranged it for him. He's been there over a month now, and he's very happy with it, and doing very well, or so he says."

"A month. You never told me."

"Well, you carried on so when he left the last place..."

"Publisher. What do they publish?"

"Books, of course. Novels, and other things, but Raymond's looking after the none fiction books, and he helps decide if they're good enough to publish. He's in what they call the none-fiction section. History, and travel. That kind of thing. He always did like travel books." She looked over her glasses at Haig again. "He says they're very pleased with him there. He seems very settled with it."

"Yes. He might be. He used to ask me things about Burma, and Malaya, and Singapore. Back when he was just a boy, after the war ended."

"Mmmm. He used to ask things before that, when you were away fighting. He thought his father was quite an adventurer. When he was at school, he used to say, 'my dad's in Burma, fighting all the Japs and killing them.' And he used to open the big atlas, and sit there with it on his knee, as big as he was nearly, and run his finger over the page. Perhaps he'll do well. He always did like maps."

A hot, pulsing mixture of love and pain surged through the colonel's heart, as rich as cream and as searing as acid: he had forgotten these past joys. "I could tell him some things about those places," he said, his voice throaty, unlike its usual self, "things they don't usually tell you in travel books... things you have to have been there to know."

"I'm sure you could Nigel. You'd be just the man."

"It's not just the country you know, not just the weather and how much your moneys worth, and what sights there are to see. That's what people want to know when they go abroad on holiday, when they go to Paris or somewhere, and it's just a cock-stride away. When you're at the other side of the world, and you're there for a war, its different. It's the people, and how things are different, and how it changes you. You go out British, but you don't come back the same."

Mildred nodded agreeably, though she could have contradicted her husband. She was not a clever woman; she knew that of herself, but it did not trouble her. Nigel was half right; the war had changed people; it had taken them away, and shown them strange things, and hideous things, and then it had returned them, changed. But time could change them too, and ambition, and disappointment, whether they left their hometown or not, and it had changed him, and she had lost him.

"You know so much about these places Nigel, you could write a book. All these generals are writing books about what they did in the war."

Haig laughed. "It'll be a long wait for me to be a pen-pusher," he said. "Silly woman," he added. He had called her this before, but this time he said it kindly.

"Nothing silly about it Nigel, nothing silly at all. Stranger things have happened," she said with comfortable simplicity.

Haig chuckled again at the thought, but he did not answer beyond that. Instead he gazed into the fire, the flickering mirror in which many a dream has thrived. He did not see the flames, but a boy, slender and blond, quiet, unlike his father, running eagerly to show him his stamp collection; a boy who he sat with, and patiently explained the difficult sums to. How old was that boy? Nine? no, ten.

And he had left the boy and his wife, for his duty said he must help to fight a war, and he had gone, and had seen men laid dead by the roadside, with gory holes in their bodies, and women, and sometimes boys too, boys no older than the boy he had left behind, dead. And when they were laid in shallow holes, then the dirt was thrown on them, and they were gone, forgotten. He had gritted his teeth, and said no discouraging word of his revulsion, but did his job there in the hot jungle, tirelessly directing his men, his finger tracing the map, his officers intent on his word, his men always their weapons to hand, all to kill those monsters who had killed the men, and the women, and the children, and would kill him, and his woman, and his boy.

Then the enemy had weakened, and faltered, and had no bullets, and retreated, and they drove him back, back, through the endless miles of forest, and heat, and malaria; and finally the enemy surrendered, for the Americans had invented the atom bomb, and had burnt their cities, and their parents lay dead there, and their wives, and their children.

Haig had known it to be just, yet also knew war to be a sickening game for fools, and wanted no more of it, and no duty but preventing it, and he went home. But the years had passed, and the boy was gone, and an older boy was in his place; tall, awkward, in his teens, and a space was between them, a vague barrier, not of anger, but of uncertainty, as though they stood on opposite banks of a narrow river, neither knowing how to leap to the other bank. After a while the older boy became a young man who wanted nothing of duty, neither hawkish nor pacific, and left Haig's house.

If he will make something of himself, thought Haig, then why should it matter what he does, as long as it's something worthwhile. The gas took my father in the trenches, back in the fourteen-eighteen war. I too was just a schoolboy, and he too was past his youth; then he was gone, and grandfather, his father, finished raising me, and he told me stories of his father, who had returned maimed from the Crimea, and died before I was born. Now Willis is dead, and, for all that I couldn't stand the man, didn't he serve in Burma, and wasn't he wounded? Yet was there more than a line on that in the newspaper report?

Enough. Raymond never wanted the army, and why should I have ever wished it for him? Let him do what he wants, as long as it's something decent, and we can hold our heads up. Even let him be a bloody politician if he wants to be – and Haig sat up briskly in sudden enthusiasm. In his study – crammed into drawers, crammed into the battered filing cabinet – there were many stapled sheets of papers, many a pencilled drawing, for he had re-fought a host of ancient battles on paper for no reason but his own satisfaction. That was how things could be worked out, how the lessons of experience could be neatly ordered to guide the future.

But a writer? Someone whose name appeared on a dust jacket, who signed copies at Smiths? Not him. What he knew, what he had learned or looked into, that was for practical use, not for entertaining people at two shillings a copy. It was a different sort of people who did that, soft, civilian people.

McIntyre though, hadn't he written a book? Yes, two in fact, and there was nothing soft about him, for all his polite manners. And now that the world could stand no more real wars, and fought paper wars instead... why not? Just as something on the side, of course, because he was earmarked for Kenya, and that must be his main concern. But at least he could organise his notes. Sooner or later Raymond would be around, and it would be something to show him.

And Mildred, knitting quietly, nodded a little to herself as she watched Colonel Haig smile into the glowing coals.

Chapter 34. I Did That

In the mid-afternoon he tore the final piece from the last square, and straightening his back wearily he gazed over the great sign. There were odd tufts of green in the torn soil, but not many, for they had been thorough in their work. Tania hurled her final basketful of turf down the hillside, and checked her impulse to hurl the shallow basket after it, for it had cost her effort to weave it. She too wandered over the sign, picking at odd tufts as she went. Finally Stuart went to the screen and laid it flat before trudging to the north cliff, the girl falling in beside him. They knew what they would see, but it was impossible to leave without a last look from this high point, and they stood wordlessly gazing down the broad slope.

Once it had been a quiet piece of nature, green, carelessly uneven, mute and indifferent to human affairs. A hilltop where a hill man's foot never trod, a piece of land over which no one would ever contend, too small and isolated to have any purpose but to display its scorched grasses to the empty brilliant sky, or placidly receive the downpour of the dark, rain-heavy clouds. Now under their hands it had become a brother to all the shouting billboards of the world, a great canvas of green slashed with the brown-grey of their urgent plea.

The girl's eyes were searching the sky, her face suddenly puckered. "Do you think it was waste of time," she whispered, and he realized that she was close to tears.

"No dear," he answered firmly, finding a calm acceptance of the wasted effort within him. "It was the best thing to do. It was the only thing to do that made sense. Now it's finished, and no one close can miss it. And just think, even if no one ever sees it, you can always say, 'I did that, and it was my idea'."

But his noble speech somehow missed the mark, for Tania let out a wail. "No one ever will see it! Who can I tell if we're here forever?"

He grasped her hand and laid one arm across her shoulders, squeezing her close in strong comfort. Moral was everything; they had won the battle of the hilltop, and they would win the battle of escape.

"We won't be here forever. We'll get away one day, and when we do, it'll be all of a sudden, here one minute and gone the next. Then when you're a big woman you can tell people what you did, and they'll look at you with their mouths open like this," - and he demonstrated with an expression of near-drooling stupidity - "and they'll be amazed. You'll have a friend called Enid, and she'll say 'Goodness Gracious Tania, However Did You Do It?' and you'll say 'I was with a very wise man, and I did everything that he said, and everything worked out just fine!' Then you'll know it's all true!"

He was pleased with his wit, for the girl was now shaking with laughter. She pulled away and cuffed him across the chest, then made a dart for its hairs, but he was too quick and jumped aside.

"I'll never have a friend called Enid. That's a silly name. No one's called Enid."

"Someone must be dear. I'm sure somebody is. Can't say I've ever met an Enid though. Let's get out of the sun and away from this cliff. I don't like you being here."

"There's some scraggy bits."

"Leave them. They won't make any difference. Straight down the cliff side way to the old hut, we need to carry the screen down there."

"What for?"

"We'll need it. It'll come in useful on the raft."

"The raft! O my God." She followed him down across the great design to the screen. He did want the useful thing for the raft, but also a point of pride within him did not want it laying there, spoiling the perfection of their sign. Before they descended onto the treed slope, he took one last look at their creation, as did the girl. She made no comment, but she too was proud of their accomplishment. As with many things, his half-jesting words had found their mark within her.

It was late in the day to start in earnest, but yet too early to do nothing, and Stuart found himself pottering about behind the old native hut, looking at this tree and that, fetching the rope and running it out to check its length yet again. He would have called a holiday in celebration if there had been anywhere to go, but there was not, and the only celebration was to say "done" to the first endless task, and start the second.

Tania seemed bored and disinterested. She flopped down onto the sand as he wandered about, then sprang up and announced that she was going to put some flowers on the grave. She had done that a few times in the past; it was one of the little rituals that gave variety to their narrow lives.

He watched her go thankfully; there were worse things she could do than put flowers on a dead man's grave. Like him, she occasionally voiced her disgust out loud to whatever powers might be near to aid her – which meant in effect the air and the trees – but she complained little to him, and shirked her tasks never. The Mal must have been a damned boring place if this seems better, he thought.

He watched her dwindle down the beach; trim little figure, nice round bottom. No boobs of course, but so what. They'd look silly on a girl her age, always did when they started growing ahead of their time. She seemed to be filling out though; he was sure she was bigger than when they arrived. Was it the work perhaps, or was she just growing.

Now that the sign was finished, he wondered if he'd asked too much of her? No, not really. He'd done all the digging, although she'd snatched up the mattock and had a hack now and again, and she'd dragged all the sod away. One hell of a load of soil though, he thought, all those square yards, it must amount to tons. If I'd had a platoon of infantry here with me to do it, then there's have been no end of grumbles. But do it yourself, and who is there to grumble too?

"Lieutenant Ellis, your command is considerably shrunken," he murmured, and sat on the sand. Tania looked back as she climbed the little rise that preceded the scrubland; she waved and disappeared around the bend of the treeline. "My troops," he murmured. A long time since he'd had men under him, where they had to obey, yes sir no sir, and then him off and saluting to someone over himself. That had been all right during the war; in war there was no other way but orders and authority. No use in peacetime though; then it was all bull. He'd had a few employees since of course, but that was different. And one wife of course.

Let's not forget the one wife, no indeed. Not that he'd expected obedience. Decency yes, and some kind of sense of reason, but not obedience. In the end he'd had none of the three. Still, what could you expect; she'd been spooning with a major before they met, and she thought her family were God knows what important. "Pampered bitch," he muttered.

Now he had this little bandit, and she had twice the rattle that Jennifer ever had, yet he could trust in her. She was worth ten Jennifers. He smiled at the thought of their antics; he would take her shopping and get her some decent clothes when they got back to Blighty. That big store on the High street, they always had women's and girl's fashions in the front window. He'd fancied a girl who used to work in the lady's department, and he wandered in once to see her, so he knew what it was like, all yes ma'am and no ma'am. Of course she'd have to go in the children's department, and he'd have to go with her; couldn't very well bung a five pound note in her hand and tell her he'd wait outside. That was an interesting thought; what would the assistants say to him?

"Doesn't she look a pretty little girl in this sir? She is a pretty young lady. Is she your daughter, or your niece?" He'd be sure to get the bit about niece, he was too young for a daughter that age. Grow a beard perhaps, put some grey streaks in his hair.

Or why not just smirk and wink, have a bit of fun? No, she wouldn't like that; that would spoil the treat. She was a proper little thing in some ways, very proper, could stand on her dignity quite a bit, but just happened to be as hot as hell when the fit took her.

Not that he'd have done anything so stupid in any case. And ice cream. There'd have to be ice cream that day, and wasn't there was an ice cream parlour on the same street, or did it close down? It didn't matter in any case, they'd have to do their shopping before they got to England; their clothes were a disgrace. She'd probably like to go shopping in her beloved Paris; if it could be managed, he'd do it.

He smiled at the thought of her loose in some Paris store, and shook his head at his thoughts. You Sir, are besotted, he thought to himself, and besotted in a very improper way too. If all this hadn't happened, then there was no way he could have imagined it happening. From officer to married man, onwards to abandoned man, and finally to white slaver, running up and down the China seas with his... his whatever. Woman, he supposed, except she wasn't a woman. Then if he couldn't say woman, what word could he use? What was she to him, what title could he use? There probably wasn't a name for it, just a nasty label. Concubine or something, like Solomon had. But weren't they supposed to be just like wives, only spares? In any case, they were out of Bible stories, and they were all very well there, but no good in Marks and Sparks Ladies department.

He laughed at the thought; why worry, the proper hadn't served him too well, had it? And from what he'd seen so far, it didn't work too well in the whole world. Make laws, make rules, tell people what they had to do and what they couldn't, stuff them into their place; then when the whole thing went wrong, get up an army and kill people wholesale, bomb whole cities, shopkeepers, women, children, the lot. You had to go with it of course. When you were up against Nazis and Japs there wasn't any choice, they had to be dealt with. He'd been eager to do his bit at the time, he'd even found it exciting, but looking at it now, it was ghastly. All over now though, and this wasn't getting a raft built.

Stuart rolled to his feet. Pick a tree and fell it, he thought, make a start, you'll need a bunch. Heavy work, not much Tania will be able to do. Where's my army got to in any case?

He picked his tree, and was hacking at it in a dogged fashion by the time Tania strolled back down the beach. "Ah, my Aid-de-Camp", he exclaimed as she came up, "now don't stand too close, because there'll be quite a thump when this comes down, and I don't want you under it."

"What's an Aid-de-Camp?" she asked, standing back a pace.

"An assistant to a senior officer."

"Did you have one?"

"No. I wasn't at all senior. Just a lieutenant."

"Did you have a regiment?"

"I was part of a regiment. Colonel Haig's regiment. He had a bunch of majors and captains as well as me though. I was very junior."

"Did you help him run the regiment?"

"Sort of. Lieutenants help the captains. I helped run a company in the regiment." He straitened up from his chopping. "When we get to England I'll have to say you're part of my private army. It's either that or I'm your uncle."

"You don't look like my uncle. You don't look like my dad at all, and you would if you were my uncle."

"Shush, nobody might notice."

"Can I be one of your Generals?"

"Certainly you can. You can run a company, and you'll have to be the company as well. That's your official title from now on, Company Commander. Makes sense doesn't it, you're my only companion here."

Tania laughed at that. She liked anything that bound her to him, freed her into the freer world from which he had come to her. Stuart had rested as they talked, sitting within the shade of the tree that was soon to fall. Now he rose and applied the machete vigorously, until the there was a crack, at which Tania cheered, and the tree fell with a swish and crash to the sand, causing her to dodge hastily back a few more paces.

"Told you," said Stuart, rising, dripping sweat, "you'll end up staying here with Mr. Dawson if you don't take more care. Under a tree or falling off that cliff."

Carefree in her nimbleness, Tania pulled a face, "you're supposed to shout timber," she retorted.

"Yes, well don't blame me when you find yourself dead. Now all these branches need to come off, and you can haul them down to the fire. Better make another pile here, and we'll start lighting the signal fire down here."

"Why here?"

"The water's calmer here, and it gets deep more quickly. The beach is steeper, so it doesn't go in and out so much." There were a few rocks projecting from the water close to the hut, and Stuart eyed them speculatively. "I can anchor the raft onto those when it gets bigger." He started to hack off one of the lower branches, but swinging the machete in its short, hard stroke was cramping his already tired muscles, and his energy was ebbing with the daylight. Finally the ache of his cramped muscles was too much, and he threw down the machete in disgust.

"Aren't you tired?" Tania asked, "let's go and eat. It's getting dark."

"Yes. A proper long axe would be nice, then I wouldn't have to bend. It's the bending that's hard. I need a longer thing."

Tania hid her face and giggled, and Stuart forced a tired laugh, thinking how commonplace words could take on a second meaning. "Right monkey, home time. Next one I cut, I'll cut the lower branches off first."

More toil, he thought, as they trudged back along the darkening sands, and nothing more than danger at the end of it. If the big boy in the sky would send a plane I'd consider burning a candle, a bloody big bunch of them in fact.

Chapter 35. Toys

A thousand times Stuart had built the raft in his mind as he had torn at the hilltop's soil. The great palms being useless, the trunks of smaller trees within the forest would have to suffice. He would need dozens of them, and as he had too little rope to bind each one to the other, he planned to make lay them side by side on the beach, until he had a deck twice as long as it was wide.

Then he would lay trunks half the length on top of these at right-angles, binding only the end trunks of this top layer to all those of the lower. On this platform he would lay another layer the length of the raft, and again bind in the ends, continuing like this until he had sufficient timber ridding the waves to easily buoy up the weight of two passenger and their provisions.

When that final layer was in place, lashing four last cross pieces over it would secure it into the design, and the criss-cross of timber should be rigid and unshifting. The cross pieces would extend out to one side to carry a few trunks for an outrigger, and the repeated hole would house the mast. Then their raft would be ready, for good or bad.

A petrol-driven chainsaw would have been useful, or any saw or axe. Having none of these, Stuart hacked with countless strokes of the machete at the small trees of the forest. Selecting one with as straight a trunk as possible, he would hack the branches from it until the lower trunk stood naked and disfigured amidst an untidy pile of its lost foliage. Then, kneeling as low to the ground as he could, he would patiently hack his way through the trunk, and at its fall strip off the higher branches before dragging his fallen victim through the forest to throw it with a pile of its ravished sisters, close by the old hut, well clear of the thieving waves.

Tania doubled as his surveyor and cleaning lady, seeking out the straighter trees for his execution and hauling away the branches to one of several stockpiles within the forest.

This last duty was perhaps unnecessary, but kept her busy and produced a sense of order in the ravished forest. "Firewood, let's have it all piled up in one place, then we know where it is. No more foraging." Stuart had said this briskly, but kept a thought to himself. If their raft proved too rickety to trust, they might need wood for many, many cooking fires.

The forest trees were a maze of frustration, for no two trunks were of the same thickness, and all were bent, but patiently he jig-sawed them into place. Four layers would be enough, by his calculations, and today he would complete laying the second on the first, leaving a space for the mast-hole.

As he worked a variety of emotions pulled at him, but he found himself balanced in a calm space between them, for he saw a clear path to follow, and following it swiftly he outran all feeble worries. He had a task to accomplish, and that the great sign had attracted no rescuers did not dismay him, nor cause him to falter. The sign was there, and its existence gave him a feeling of mastery.

They had struggled bedraggled to shore, to find a mere acre or two of lost greenery, and had made from it their springboard to return. Though their efforts had born no fruit they were victors, for they had not merely survived, but achieved. As a warrior lord might fortify a village to repel invaders, so they had fortified the island to attract them. Short of building a lighthouse, he could do no more in that area. "We were civil engineers, and now we are master ship builders," he commented to Tania in calm jest.

They would escape. That was his determination, but though he worked hard he did so with a patience that now came naturally, for now he found himself in no great hurry, content to take the days methodically. He did not rush or stint any detail, for he was not eager to come to the end of the task, when they would stand before the final choice: to fret idly on the beach awaiting discovery, or to chance their very lives upon the waves. As he worked and planned their voyage, he hoped still that it was the raft building that would prove futile, and that their great flytrap would finally catch its fly.

So though he applied himself to this perhaps final scheme of escape, he did so like a man who attends a daily job, and though he works from need, it is his habit and livelihood, not the centre of his life. Tania now stood at that centre; the young sharer of his troubles, the former torment of his womanless state, she had become the pivot on which his world turned, entrancing him whilst troubling him, like a precious diamond that a penniless man might find, but not honestly own.

They had performed a common enough act together, and a mild one at that, had she been like him a citizen of the adult world. But she was not. She stood firmly at the other side of that vague but yawning canyon that marks the supposedly responsible from the supposedly innocent, and he had crossed that divide in curiosity, and enchanted he remained in the forbidden land, now his only home, finding it a sweet, pleasant country. That it was a land of danger he uneasily knew, yet smiled at, for they had become a lost tribe.

More, the great world of the narrow space of their passion seemed a land free from harm, a place where he need please only himself and the single sprite inhabitant, a place where he, a just ruler, need give no account of himself to any lesser mortal. He would have protested in genuine hurt had some passer-by accused him of arrogance, for in truth he was not consciously arrogant, but the rigors of their near death and confinement had hammered him to a contempt for the opinions of the easier life that they had lost. He felt himself to have been tested and honed as few men are, and being so tempered by adversity, the moderate opinions of the pampered outside world seemed to him like thin mist.

Even the Burma campaign had not tried him as this lost imprisonment in some ways had, for then he had endured the danger and hardships as one amongst many, and of all who had stood with him in the early days, most had survived. But of the Raven's passengers all but he and the girl lay dead, and had it been possible to recover their bodies, then the island's largest dwelling would have been its graveyard. All things on this island lay in their hands or fate's. There was no third person to assist or hinder, therefore they need answer to no one but each other, and they had become each other's delight.

Had someone asked him to justify himself, he would not have put his case in any such rounded manner, for his attitude was a rough and ready reality to him, the practical instinct of a beggared survivor to retrieve the riches of his life, and he felt no scholar's need to classify his feelings. Indeed, he might have roared with laughter at such an asking, for what had they done but the minor tricks of youth's first eager exploration, and who but some fool of the old, passing world did not know that all who breathed yearned for things they had been solemnly forbidden, which most would eventually seize on despite all the nay-sayers.

There was a question in his mind though, springing from wonder, a stronger source than any dry moral theory: the question of how a girl so young could be this way, or more accurately, the fact of how she was this way. Were all young girls like this, he wondered, landmines that lay as dormant as stones, but only because the habits of the world fenced them off well, kept them penned in their place by rule and restriction, so that they may be safe, and not impede the tramping feet of the busy adult world?

Then of course there were no explosions; harmless they had been made, and harmless they seemed, and harmless they were. But this one had schemed hopelessly to flee the coop, and against all odds the coop had fled from her. Like him she had been carelessly lost by the clumsy, clanking system, had fallen from the lists of who is who, and what they are, and where they may confidently be found.

 This girl, was she no different from the rest of the half-pint collection that she had lived amongst, no stronger than the rest of the Danielle's and Betty's and what have you, swapping their gossip, dreaming their early dreams of as yet unknown youths, plotting their minor defiance's, sullenly enduring and longing for the distant escape into adulthood? Would all of them, if given the chance, have revelled in the whispered of naughty as Tania had? Or was she exceptional?

His mind roamed through these questions as he worked, but it was mere idle thought, and the solid reality of his life was the island, and Tania, and escape.

He had stepped over the wall of The Rules, and looking back found it crumbled and useless behind him. He could not step back, for the thing done was done, and there was no undoing. Once or twice he had shaken his head as he wondered at his folly, but he named it folly half in jest, as a man might call himself a fool for some petty mistake, yet in reality have no lower opinion of his self. He was not old, but he was seasoned, and had seen enough of the contradictory world to spare himself the rod.

If he could have gone back and snatched himself from temptation he would not, for the girl had become dear to him, and he had no vicious act on his conscience. He had not cajoled her into their tabooed intimacy, hastening a child too early into adult games, for she herself had given the final push to the crumbling wall that should have separated them, and with its fall he had gained safety from that fall, and he had gained her.

And what world toppling intimacies did they share? Kisses, cuddles, the luxury of touching her smooth, friendly skin, running his hands over her slender shoulders, stroking her back, and her fascination with his male difference, that amused and astounded him each time her deft hand drew the mysterious male fluid from him. How many times now, since that strange night? He had lost count. Two weeks nearly, and not everyday. It didn't matter. It was all pettiness in evil, yet all the world in their affection.

When finally he bound the last of the two cross-pieces into place, it seemed that they would someday have a raft, for when he seized an end of this great cross barred gate, and lifted it, grunting with the effort, his feet biting deep into the soft, crunching sand, the bottom layer held together firmly. Tania cheered, and he lowered it back to the sand slowly.

"Rollers. We need rollers underneath before I go any further, whilst it's still light enough to lift one end," he said, "and some trunks like tracks for the rollers to go on." The shadows were falling long across the raft, and now the hard won timber was committed to the higher part of the beach. "I need to tie it back to the trees."

"The waves don't come up this high much."

"Any's too much, and a storm can drive them up. We don't want to wake up and have to go swimming after it, eh?"

"No. After here, I'm going to live a thousand miles away from any sea."

"Then you'll have a problem if you live in England. It's not that big. Or didn't they teach you that in geography. Who taught the geography, Father Colin wasn't it?"

"You leave Father Colin alone, or I'll use that rope to tie you up."

They ate early, chattering in excitement, for despite their misgivings on the voyage they were heartened by the speed with which the cutting had been accomplished.

"Stuart, how far is it to Paris from England?"

"Twenty-one miles across the channel, and not too far on land."

"Twenty-one miles! That's nothing. We could build a raft."

"This is the last raft that I build. First and last. Look here." He held out his hand to display a raw patch in the fire's red glare. "Blisters on top of blisters. There'll be nothing left of me in a bit."

"Softie."

"You're the softie. Soft in the head. Nothing there but feathers."

A fish bone whizzed past his head. "Hey careful. You'll put me an eye out, then I'll be steering with one eye. Captain Morgan, or something."

As he spoke he felt the touch of raindrops, and they stirred from the fire and went into the shelter. He lowered himself gently into place, for he had collected a different set of aches from those acquired on the hilltop, but the girl thumped down heavily beside him. "You're very rough tonight. Like an elephant. You'll have to leave the island if you go on this way."

"No I'm not, I'm like a fairy. Sister Therese said so."

"Sister Therese was wrong," he said wiggling about to mould the dented sand to a better shape, "what do nuns know about fairies. Fairy stories more like, her and Father Colin."

"Don't you say anything about Sister Therese," she shot back with a sudden sharpness, "she was my friend. She was really good."

Stuart accepted his rebuke in silence, warned by her abrupt change. He teased her often about the young priest, amused by her embarrassment and her smart replies, but it seemed that the elderly nun was off limits to his wit. Tania did not speak again. She was not a sulker, but when upset she was apt to fall silent, retreating into her own thoughts. He lay for a while waiting, but like him she was kneading the canvas covered sand into place. He reached out a hand and stroked her shoulder tentatively. "Do you miss her Honey?" he asked gently.

She moved over to him and slumped down beside him, and he encircled her with one arm.

"Yes. She wasn't like the others."

"I'm sorry. I was only joking."

"You shouldn't joke about Sister Therese. She looked after me. She used to tell me stories."

"What kind of stories," he asked, willing to hear some holy tales of saints, if it served as penance for his offence.

"About when she was a young girl in Spain. She lived there when she was young, before she was a nun, and she used to have adventures."

This was unexpected. "Tell me about them. We've got plenty of time."

"No."

"Why not?"

"You'll laugh, and they're private. You've had lots of adventures, you'll think they're silly."

"Lots of adventures. Not all that many Honey. This must be the biggest, not that I'd call it an adventure."

"You were in the war, in Burma. You were fighting with the Japs."

"So were lots of people. But they managed to stay away from being lost on islands afterwards. I've never heard of any of them getting lost."

"We're not too lost, you said so. And we've got lots of stuff here."

Stuart sighed. "Sister Therese Honey. Let's hear about her adventures. I promise I won't laugh."

Tania wiggled in excitement, often her preliminary to some story of The Mal's inhabitants. "She lived in Spain, not really Spain though, some place on the coast that was like a bit of Spain, only different. She lived in this little village, and they had their own language different from Spanish. Her father was a farmer or something, and he grew grapes. When she was a little girl she used to ride the donkeys, and sometimes they'd have dances in the village, on saint's days. They were festivals or fiestas or something, and they weren't really about dancing, more praying and processions and stuff, but they'd have dances as well. She used to go down the hill from their farm to the village, and she used to ride the donkey. She was always talking about the hills and the woods."

We could have used her here, thought Stuart, but he refrained from interrupting.

"She liked this boy from the village, but he was really shy and she daren't speak to him. He was a blacksmith, and his dad was a blacksmith too. She liked him for years, and one day he spoke to her at one of the dances. After that they used to meet, and they were going to be married. But they went to one of these dance-festival things once, and after that they went walking in the woods. It was hours and hours before they got back, and her father was really mad. Then her parents quarrelled with the boy's parents, and after that both of the families didn't speak to each other."

Stuart waited, but the girl seemed to have come to the end. He knew her too well by now though, knew from the way she had trailed off that there was more, but that it was sad. Tania had a dislike of sad endings.

"What happened after that Honey?"

"Nothing. That was the end of it."

"Didn't she want to marry him anymore?" he persisted.

"Yes. But his parents didn't want her to, because of something her dad said to his dad. And he didn't want to either, 'cause his parents said so. So they didn't see each other again, and they didn't get married."

Stuart stroked her shoulder in silence. How mysterious it must seem to her, this world where a boy met a girl, and then by some strange machination of older people everything ended in ruin. What did they do, those two? Was it just an innocent walk in the woods that offended some strict village propriety? Or was it some deeper involvement? How long ago must this be? Last century probably.

He felt awed at the thought. He was born in 1924, his father sometime in the eighteen-nineties. The old nun must have been a young girl then; incredible to think that such things happened then, as they did today. Jennifer's father. He had never met him, and wondered occasionally what the unknown man must think of his unmet son in law, who now he would never know except through Jennifer's account of him.

"Didn't she meet anyone else?"

"No. She said that she never wanted anyone else but him, and she wondered if she'd done something wrong, 'cause it was a Holy Day, and she upset everybody. So she lived at home a bit longer, and then she decided to be a nun."

"What happened to the young man?"

"I don't know. She didn't say."

Good God, thought Stuart. The things people imagine. And then all those years a nun!

"That's a very interesting story Honey," he said, meaning his words. A sense of the vast passage of time had seized him. "How long did she live at home before she became a nun? You know, after she and the boy... parted?"

"Not long. I don't know. I think she said a few years. She used to see him sometimes, but they never spoke again, or they just said hello or something. She said she decided to give her life to God. That's what she said when I asked her, 'give her life to God'."

"Was she very old? I mean, when she liked the boy in the village?"

"Yes. She was grown up. I think she said she was twenty when they started being friends."

They were both silent for a while, he meditating on the ancient story, she glum for her friend's lost love.

"I asked her once if she wished she'd got to marry him. She said that she wondered later if she ought to have left the village and gone somewhere else, and then she might have found someone else, but it was too late then, 'cause she'd given her life to God."

Stuart lay back speechless.

"But she only told me this last bit once," said Tania, rounding off her story, "she told me about the hills mostly, and when I asked her the last bit she told me, then she said that she was supposed to forget all that, as though she were dead, because she got her new name. Only it wasn't really Sister Therese, I just called her that. Really it was Sister Teresa. I liked Therese better though, 'cause it sounds French."

"That was an interesting story Honey," he said, and waited a little to mark a delicate time of appreciation. "Now I have to go pee before it rains again." He crept from the hut and walked to the ebbing tide. As he went Tania's eyes followed him in appraisal.

What a damned story, Stuart thought as he walked down to the waves. It made him light headed just to think about it. How did people live, that such a minor incident should be the cause of a half-century of dedication? Or was there more to it than that? Of course, the old nun wouldn't have told Tania everything, not all the bits and bats of things that go to ending a relationship, or making a big decision. But the bones of the story, they seemed to be there.

Was that really the cause, he wondered? Was it really the disappointment of a weak lover that drove her to be a nun, or had she some germ of an idea before that, some yearning for a life beyond this world, that her loss had strengthened? So she had left the little village where her life was wasting, and entered the narrower village of the convent. Had that proved to be the gateway to a deeper life? Had it been a dedication to a higher ideal, or just an easy flight from the everyday knocks of life, things that other people got over?

I do not know, he thought, and never will know, so forget about it, and certainly don't argue the point with Tania. Whatever her reasons had been, he found himself more kindly disposed to the old nun. She had been kind to Tania, and Tania's friends had become his friends, and her enemies his. If the good sister had wished to dedicate her life, then that and her reasons were her affair.

Certainly it was not something that he could face doing, not even if he had a head full of beliefs, which he didn't. So she had her own strength, and in the end had shown it, for hadn't she pushed Tania against the inrush of the water? That took presence of mind, and a damned pity she hadn't made it out herself. There would have been none of the recent fun and games of course, but that might have been a good thing, for now there was some watching out to do when they got back to civilisation.

The thought struck him that he might use it as an example, suggest to the girl that if she accidentally said the wrong thing it could get them parted, just as happened to her friend, and that might put her even more on her guard. The thought was distasteful to him, and he rejected it with a grimace. He hated subterfuge, and such a hint reeked of manipulation, even though it was true. They had been through all that. She was a canny thing, she knew when to keep her peace. He finished his contribution to the sea, and dipped his hands briefly into the ever-willing waves before turning for the hut.

"You were a long time," she said as he resumed his place. She snuggled up to him and rubbed his chest, fascinated as always with the thin mat of hair.

"I was thinking."

"What about?"

"It's a very interesting story. Sister Therese's story. What would she have thought of me I wonder?"

"She'd have said you're a bad man."

"I'm not. I'm a very good man."

"No you aren't. You trod on my foot."

"I trod on your foot? When did I tread on your foot young lady?"

"At the place where we caught the plane. You trod on my foot when I was at the window."

"Holy smoke!" He had forgotten; the incident seemed centuries ago, but now he remembered it vividly. "What were you doing there? I turned around and you'd just appeared out of nowhere."

"I only wanted to see what you were looking at, and you trod on my foot. What you were looking at *when* you weren't looking at Julia."

"You minx. Talk about a nosey parker, I didn't even know you then, you squirt. And you call me bad."

"Yes you are, it's getting hard again."

"Well you've got your hand on it. It's you that's bad."

Tania didn't answer, but threw a leg over him briskly and started to unbuckle his belt, making rude faces at him and frowning over the hardness of the thick leather. Story time was over for a while.

Afterwards, the fun over, Tania drowsing at his side, he fell to wondering, impressed despite himself by the good sister's story. This fun and games could not go on forever. Should he too make a sacrifice and somehow try to end this folly, which must eventually reach a serious coupling? Was it right to let a child think that life could be lived this way? Wouldn't that be better, better for the person that he had come almost to love, better, for wasn't he the grown man who should know better?

Chapter 36. Well

The following day Stuart found himself turning Tania's strange story of Sister Therese over in his mind, or as he phrased it to himself, the story of Sister Teresa of the Malcolm McGraff Institute, who was also Sister Therese of The Mall. Who may have been the innocent victim of village scandal, or may have been a little goer who got caught, and who may also have been a foolish woman who fled into a nunnery, or a saintly person who entered a Life of Renunciation. Which of these pictures was true, he wondered?

A careless stroke of the machete narrowly missed taking of a finger, and he forced the subject from his mind with a curse. Enough problems here without wandering in the tangle of a lost history. This, the latest tree trunk, stood on the eastern slope, too close too another to let him work, yet he needed it, for it was tall and straight. It was not until it fell defeated down the slope, and he squatted panting by its stump, that his curiosity got the better of him.

"Honey, what was Sister Therese like?"

"She was nice. She didn't make a fuss about anything. If I asked her anything she'd tell me. Well not anything, I mean... I didn't ask her about just *anything,* you know, 'cause she was a nun, but she used to tell me stories about when she was a little girl. Most of the sisters would say that they'd left all their old life behind when then took their vows, and then they'd tell you something about religion, so nobody bothered asking them anything."

"Hmm... she didn't say if she wished she'd stayed with her boyfriend then?"

"No, never. She couldn't in any case. I told you yesterday." Tania answered, kicking at the scattered chips.

Warned by her tone, Stuart refrained from asking further. Tania didn't know, in fact she wouldn't understand the point of his curiosity, and he felt that she might even resent it. She was a romantic girl, and the dead nun had told her the romantic story of her young womanhood, that might have ended in marriage and a flock of children in a remote, sleepy village, and instead had lead her to the alien streets of Paa, and from there to a modern kind of death. What did it matter if the young woman of so many decades ago had had her fling and dented her reputation, or if it was a plainer story of a romance that didn't work out. Perhaps her decision to seek a holy life had no connection with her village lover. It didn't matter, and it was tacky to probe the young girl's memories to clear up an idle question. She was gone and the girl missed her, along with her parents, so let her lie in peace.

Stuart's wondering about Sister Therese's boyfriend, thought Tania. I used to wonder too, but I didn't dare ask if they did anything, 'cause she was a nun. It's not important in any case. She said she was happy serving God. She'd have been a good wife for him though, she'd have made him happy. I think Sister Therese said once that his name was Anton. Stupid man. Why did he listen to his parents? Some people must have some really stupid parents.

She fell into a muse, thinking about the times many years ago, as far back as she could remember, when she had gone to the cinema with her mum and dad, and once she remembered them playing on a beach, and her dad splashing her and her mum in the waves. She remembered her mum squealing and her dad laughing; he seemed to have always been laughing. Then he was gone, and later her mum was gone. He used to call her a bunny rabbit. She turned away quickly down the treed slope, not wanting Stuart to notice the tears that were pricking her eyes. Stuart called out after her, but she didn't stop.

"Anton," she called over her shoulder, "his name was Anton. Sister Therese told me just the once."

She was upset, he could tell that from the choking of her voice. Not with him though; he knew her well enough by now to know that he was not the offender, and he rose and started to strip the fallen tree. When she returned to gather the branches he let her be, and quietly waited for her moroseness to pass. It was the dead Sister Therese; talking about her had upset the girl. Usually there was little of the over sensitive flower in her, but occasionally there was, and who could say what caused the passing emotion to come and go. Not him for certain, that he knew, so he held his tongue as the day passed.

She said little during the rest of the day, and little as the evening passed, but lay close to him as the fire died, coiled into a small heap that could have been a shadow, and they were quiet, watching the stars.

"Stuart. When we find my dad..."

Then she was silent again, and he encouraged her with a grunt.

"I used to think that... when we find my dad... You wouldn't be able to live with us, would you?"

O what now, he thought. The girl asks me this and I can't tell her what she wants to hear. I don't know myself how it's going to work out.

"I don't know Honey," he said finally, "we don't even know for certain where your dad lives. If he lives near me, then I guess I'll be living near you."

That's lame, he thought. Lame but what else can I say. I've promised her something that I might not be able to do, but I'm not going to lie to her as well.

"I want to be with you," she said simply, as though she had said that the waves washed the beach.

"What about your dad?" he said after a while.

"I want to be with him too."

Stuart sighed. "We'll work it out somehow Honey," he said, "one thing at a time. Off this island first."

"You'll go to your wife. That's why you're going to England." The girl's voice was flat and dismal.

"No Honey, not that. I thought that might be why, but... it isn't anymore. Her and I are over."

"She wouldn't want me to live with you and her."

Stuart laughed at the bittersweet idea. "No indeed I don't think she would. But that's okay because I don't want to live with her either."

"Don't you love her anymore. You got married to her, and she married you. You must have loved her once."

"You know I don't love her. We thought we were suitable, or something like that, but we weren't. We made a mistake."

She wants me to tell her that I love her and we'll always be together, thought Stuart, and it's impossible. Ludicrous, totally ridiculous. She won't be even sixteen for nearly another five years, and when we get off this place it all has to end. I can't run up and down England with her in tow, somebody in charge will ask questions and in the end they'll take her away and put her somewhere, unless I find her father, which I probably can't. If I can't find him she has no one, and if I do find him then there's no reason for me to be around anymore. We got into this somehow, and I refuse to regret it, but its got to end badly somewhere down the line. She's just a child, and I've indulged myself and spoilt her. I never saw this coming, but now it's wake up time. Better to tell her the truth: when we get back to civilisation its over, whether she likes it or not. She has to be in school like all normal kids are, and I've got to put my own life back in order. Tell her now, do it clean, and don't let it drag on and get worse.

"I won't be able to stay with you when we find my dad, will I?" Her voice came muffled from her little clump of shadow.

Tell her no, she won't, he thought. She's growing up, she's thought about it, she's worked it out for herself. Tell her she's right, she'll have to go live with someone else, because you can't fix the world to her likings, and you can't make a life with an eleven year old, its ridiculous, and it's impossible. If it upsets her that's too bad, it has to come sooner or later, and she'll get over it. Get back to reality a bit. Say it now, tell her there isn't a hope, and don't be so bloody squeamish.

He stirred as though the movement could help to shake his words into shape, and she moved closer to him. He saw the gleam of eyes watching him, silver from the starlight, flickering red from the dying embers, and his tongue stuck thick and heavy in his mouth. Tell her now. It was only a child for God's sake; get it done and don't be a softie.

"Honey," he began, then faltered, his fortress of harsh understanding crumbling, useless in this world where just the two of them lived. Better to comfort her as best he could, but not tell her any nonsense or lead her on. He was too fond of her for that. Yes, fond, that was the word, fond. Tell her that. He reached out, and finding her wrist in the darkness drew her close to him. "I don't know what will happen when we get to England, I really don't. I'll try and find your dad, and if I can't, then I'll try and do something else. I really don't know what we'll do, but whatever happens I'll always be somewhere near. I don't want to ever be without you. You're my girl, nobody else. Whatever happens, I don't ever want to be without you."

She pressed close and buried her face in his chest, whilst he sat astounded at his words, having spoken truths that he had not known. He had casually dipped the well of his heart, thinking it shallow, and the bucket had returned brimming to his hand.

They lay quietly after that, content merely to be in each other's company, for the girl's eroticism was not constant, but came in wild and unexpected spurts, unlike the constant duller pressure of an adult's desires, and he felt a tenderness towards her that overrode his sometimes fierce passion.

Besotted, he thought. That is the indeed the word, besotted. And why not keep her with me one way, or another? She's a diamond, and she'll grow. Throw her aside to please someone? Who exactly should I be pleasing? I won't throw away beauty and happiness in order to pick safely at some garbage that I don't want, and play at being like all the other garbage pickers, safe and obedient.

You've said too much to her, came the calm thought from another part of his being, it can't last, for all that you want it to, and for all your feelings. You've muffed the chance of putting the brakes on, you've been weak where you should have been strong.

Yes, he thought, I am weak, weak like most people are, because we all need things, and we do dumb things to get them. So no, I'm not weak, but perhaps that was a pretty weak thing to do, and a pretty dumb thing. I get further and further in, and how can I cope with this when we get back?

He sought in his mind for some time, looking for what he should have told her, and yet not sure that he even need look, for as they lay quietly pressed together she seemed disarmed from any further concern, as though his words were power enough to solve her fears, to melt them away like springtime snow. Perhaps it's best if I leave it alone, he thought. She's happy, and it'll probably turn out all right in the end, so why blather on, getting into gloomy stuff about wanting this, but being forced to have something else instead.

He doubted the firmness of the bog before him, doubted the uncertainty of the path through his future. It was not the first time that his cautious mind had found it necessary to do so, and he knew that it would not be the last. But in his heart the light streamed golden from the open doorway of his treasure house, and again it dispelled the dull, grey ghosts of caution. His eager will had made its decision, and again he told his fears to be silent, and kissed the girl's forehead affectionately.

Tania felt sleep creeping softly forwards; the world turned in harmony. They would never be parted, Stuart and her. Warriors rode through the rainbow coloured world of her mind, strong comforting reliable heroes, one of them her Father, one lesser knight Father Colin, one warrior maiden Danielle, another Rosalind; yet over them all stood Stuart, the Great Chief, the Warrior so strong that he was the world, the Light of the World and the heroic country on which that light fell. At his kiss she hugged him closely. He was Hers, and he would always be with her.

Chapter 37. Orbits

"There seems to be more rain and wind than there was," Tania said. They were sitting in the doorway of the old hut, gazing at the half built raft bobbing at anchor as they chewed on cold boiled yam. The old hut had become their second headquarters as the raft progressed, and though they had never cleaned up all of its squalor, it served to shelter them from the spattering of rain that fell on and off all the morning through the thick, humid air.

"Yes, I've noticed," Stuart replied shortly.

"If the weather gets worse, won't it be dangerous on a raft?"

He would have avoided the question if he could. "It won't be too bad. At least the wind's in the right direction. It's the time of year. There'll be more rain to come, not less."

"What if we get washed off?"

"We won't get washed off." But what if they were? Even Tania could see it, and again a picture rose in his mind of the storm closing on them in fury, of her swept overboard and lost between mountainous waves, and he clinging to the raft, unable to see her, fearful to leap insanely into the raging seas after her. "We'll have to do every thing we can to make sure nothing goes wrong. Some kind of a shelter on the deck, and an outrigger to stop it turning over. That's still to make, once I've got the main bit finished. If it's big enough, the waves won't throw it about too much."

"How much longer will it take?"

He started to reply, but stopped, for suddenly the answer was not clear. He had scratched the sand many times, calculating how much timber it would take to float the two of them, and he saw now that he had worked by the wrong assumptions. He had planned for how little they could get away with, and in answering her question he saw his error.

A ship with only a hundred miles or so of sea to cross would not be troubled by a minor storm, yet he feared them, and all his fears were founded on the tiny size of the craft that he had built in his mind. Build it big; that was the answer. Take time and make it big, so that all but the largest waves would not even mount to its deck. Put a cabin on top even. Then if a gale howled they could stay inside, with plenty of tins of water lashed down. If the winds drove them west, then fine; if they drove them anywhere else, then all this sea was enclosed with major islands, and they would end up somewhere. Just as long as it all held together.

"I did think a few days. Maybe a week, but now I think we should make it bigger. I don't know, maybe two more weeks."

"Two more weeks," she echoed. It had not really occurred to Tania that the raft would also involve a lot of work. She knew that Stuart didn't want to try and sail away unless he had to. He hadn't talked about it much, but when he had he'd never seemed very cheerful, and she had become nervous about it too.

The day seemed to pass slowly, and she wished that the raft were finished. They hadn't seen even a distant plane for ages, and building this big raft went on forever. What a big job it was to get to England. But she had Stuart, only he seemed a bit grumpy today, and didn't want to talk much.

It would be nice when they got to Singapore. She had heard that it was a big city, much bigger than Paa, and very famous all over the world. Not like Paris or London of course, but it would be exciting to see it, and they would keep going to London.

The rain ceased in late afternoon, and by the time the lengthening shadows ushered them down the beach to their own hut the clouded skies had cleared, and as they cooked and ate the star clad darkness bloomed above them.

Tania brightened after that, her spirits springing up swiftly as children's do, and soon was chattering about the moon, saying that it was funny that it had a face, and he recited a slightly rude version of an old rhyme about the man, at which she laughed. Stuart was pleased at the revival of her merriment, and pleased at his own words. He had rediscovered that kindness to others brings joy, a truth only known fully as we act it out, whose theory is swiftly lost in the tangled thicket of our wisdom. Better, he knew a fact that would interest her and enliven the dark night awhile.

"There's something funny about our moon," he began sagely, "it's very big compared with other moons."

"What other moons?" Tania interjected quickly, alert for a possible teasing, "there's only one."

"Yes, we've only got one, but there's moons around other planets. Mars has got two, Phobos and Deimos. And a lot of the other planets have moons, more than one. Jupiter's got a whole bunch."

"You're making it up. How do you knows that? You don't know anything about moons."

"I do," Stuart insisted, outraged, "I learnt it at school. Mars has two, and Jupiter's got... twelve, that's it, and Saturn's got a lot as well."

"Twelve!" now he was definitely teasing her. "How could there be twelve moons? They'd bump into each other."

"They don't, they all go round together. All the planets have more than one, it's only Earth that just has the one."

Tania stared at him, her mind boggling. She searched the sky for the bright star that he'd once named as Jupiter, although he'd said he wasn't really sure. "You wouldn't be able to tell, it's too small," she said.

"Of course you can, you can see them through a telescope. Somebody saw them when they invented the telescope, Galileo or someone."

She turned back to him, determined to sort out his nonsense. "What did you say those were called, those moons around Mars? Bet you can't remember."

"Phobos and Deimos. That means fear and, and rage or something. They're not very big, not like our moon."

"I've never heard that before. I think you're making it up."

"I'm not. We've got a really big moon, and it pulls at the tides, and it makes them go up and down. What do you think makes the tides go up and down?"

This was beyond belief. He told her silly stories sometimes, but never this daft. "They just go up and down, that's all."

"They go up and down because the moon pulls at them, with gravity. That's why we have tides, because we have a big moon, and it's got a lot of pull. Didn't they teach you anything like this?"

Tania realised suddenly that he wasn't fooling her. He never did with anything real like this. She felt the dizzying rush of the world expanding: there was a vast universe of wheels, pushes and pulls that she knew nothing of. "No, they didn't," she said quietly.

"I'm surprised you know the world's round," Stuart continued, triumphant now that his learning was being accepted.

"Perhaps they didn't know," she answered, "don't you dare mention Father Colin."

"I am innocent of all slanders against Father Colin."

"No but you were thinking about him. He probably knew, but he hadn't told us yet."

"Now that you're not there Father Colin will teach everybody about it. He will teach silly Betty, and they will run away together and be married."

Tania leapt on him with a shriek. "Pig."

"He will, he will."

A little trial of strength by wrestling was now necessary, and he should have been easily the victor, except that she bit his arm. It ended with her nestling against him, whilst his hand massaged the roundness of her bottom appreciatively, slapping it lightly to feel the quality of its bounce.

"Nobody will ever marry Silly Betty," Tania murmured, "she'll have to join the circus and be a clown, that's what Danielle said."

Stuart slid one arm beneath her and rolled her on top of him, and from this vantage point applied both hands to her backside. "She'll probably end up the Chief Nun at The Mal," he answered, and transferred his attention to her belt. Tania had long ago abandoned the clumsy rope for a length of twisted cloth, slipped through the loops and knotted in front like a shoelace. He slid his fingers beneath her belly, searching for the cords, and she raised her hips up to allow his hands passage. He pulled the knot undone and slid her shorts down onto her thighs, returning his hands to her rounded buttocks.

"She won't," Tania said quietly, "Danielle doesn't like anything to do with churches."

"Like you."

"They're all right sometimes, but..."

"But what?" Her mind fascinated him: so much perception, so little clutter of content. How strange it was to lie here with her on top of him, telling her early thoughts, her simple understandings, whilst he rubbed the two rounded mounds, probed the creases where they gave way to her legs, ran his palms down the smooth back of her thighs.

"But what?" he whispered. He wanted her to speak, wanted to hear the steadiness of her voice reassure him that he was not frightening her.

"Boring. They make it boring. The little statues are nice though," she said. She nosed into his hair, found his ear, nipped it gently between her teeth.

"Don't you dare," he murmured, "you've bit me once already."

"You're stronger than I am, so I'm allowed," she answered softly, releasing the threatened ear.

He did not answer; their words seemed to be trailing off, fading, unneeded and dying in the hot jungle of their closeness. He returned his hands to her bottom: plump, yet firm and solid, the sides hollowed slightly at her hips. He slid one hand inward and paused; she would tell him if it was unwanted; she had a mind of her own. His fingers slid into the crevasse of her legs, searching gently, until their tips touched the plump little mound, stroked its softness. She gasped slightly, and he paused, but her legs opened a little in the ancient way of compliance, and he slid his hand deeper, massaging the smooth split mound. It yielded to his fingertips; he felt the wetness, ran his finger firmly down and up within the moist slit.

Tania gasped and quivered; she pressed her hips back, thrusting her secret part hard against his gentle hand. She had felt his thing grow hard beneath her as he played with her, and now he had done it; he had touched her Sisi, and it felt hot, good, swollen with a life of its own. This was the heart of the magic kingdom; here there was just the dark, and him, and he was hers, for her to be his, and he was rubbing it gently.

Stuart played with her for a while, gently, but with firm roughness, kissing her neck whilst his palms rubbed her buttocks and his fingers aroused the plump, damp lips tucked beneath them.

Tania did not speak; lying on him as on a magic carpet she rode the delicious moments, her breath sighing raggedly in and out, her hips first pressing down against his hard masculine part, then rising to greet the pleasure of his fondling. She was lost to anything she might have been taught, for having been taught nothing but dark hints, she sailed by her heart, of which he had long been the captain.

Stuart too rode in the quiet joy of their embrace, for the girl was enjoying his caresses, and he felt that masterful pleasure that comes from giving pleasure, that satisfies longer and more deeply than the mere act of sex. His desire for her rose; he grasped her by the shoulders and she rolled onto her back at his pressure.

Stuart slid her shorts down to her ankles, pulled them free and tossed them aside; crouching between her thighs he gazed at her offered vagina in awe; how big and rounded it was! He grasped the inside of her thighs and pushed them upwards, so that it narrow mouth opened to him. He undid the buttons of his shorts quickly.

Tania had rolled onto her back willingly, excited that he was looking at her special part, but she felt a stab of fear. Since they started their big, secret adventure, all the confused whispers of her friends at The Mal had condensed into understanding of the unknown act; Stuart would do it now; he was pulling his shorts down, and he would take his big hard thing and push it into her, and it would hurt.

She wished that he wouldn't. She had got excited when she first saw his thing, and she wanted to touch it, and see what it was like, and make it feel nice for him. She liked it whenever he touched her, and it was lovely when he started playing with her Sisi, but now he was going to put it in her just like he would with a grown-up girl, and she felt scared. She never thought of this, but now it was obvious. She shouldn't have been bad; it was all her fault. Would it last long?

"Stuart," she whispered tremulously, "don't."

He stopped in the act of pulling his shorts over his ankles. "I'm not going to do anything to hurt you Honey," he whispered back, "I'm just going to play with you. It's okay, I won't hurt you. I want to do something nice."

He slid back into place between her thighs, kissed the flatness of her stomach, stroked the fleshy lips so close to his. She was still tense; her legs were pressing his shoulders, as though she would like to close them. She was scared suddenly, but he knew she had no reason to be. She had jumped onto a roller coaster that had proved scarier than desired, but she must ride it to the end. He slid down and put his mouth to the one that waited him, kissed it firmly, probed its softness with his harder tongue.

Tania gasped; she clutched at his hair and pushed, then pulled him to her. The thought of Danielle's solemn whispering shot through her mind, then she was bucking frantically; it was good, good. She made on last heave frantic heave, moaning and shuddering, then she fell back as though stunned. She felt Stuart pull away from her and clutched at his arms; something harder than his tongue touched her, touched her right there, right on the little stump bit, rubbed up and down just as nice but different, up and down, up and down. He's nearly doing it to me, she thought; will he do it? But she was past caring. Then a stream of hot stuff came pouring over her belly, lots of it.

He slumped down beside her and she rolled to him, and they held each other without speaking for a long while, their breath shuddering as though they had both received a fright.

"I'm all wet," she said suddenly, recovering with the quick energy of children. Stuart hauled his shirt out of the corner. It was seeing more than a bit of unusual use just lately, he thought dazedly, and that was a damned close thing; so much for thoughts of restraint.

This can't go on, he thought later, but it was more an expression of wonder than a decision. Apparently lots of strange things can go on, he corrected himself, including us being here for two bloody months, and he stroked the sleeping girl's hand as he drifted contentedly into sleep.

Chapter 38. A Friendly Wave

Tania seemed a little grumpy this morning, and Stuart, though hiding his pain, felt crushed by the complications of his newest task. His creation bobbed at anchor, half complete, but with not a hint of grace in its ugly shape. Despite all the days of careful measuring and hacking, all the wrenching and lashing, the tangled mass of timber resembled nothing so much as a great, square crows nest that had fallen from its place in some gigantic tree to land in the bay, where it clutched desperately with a ropey hand at the nearest rock.

The remaining rope was not equal to his need, and worse, the machete, visibly thinned by constant sharpening on the rock, no longer struck home so solidly. What if – no, what when! – it broke under all this use, he worried increasingly. Yet the raft needed more bulk, and both the outrigger and the mast were still to make and fit. The cabin.... Was that still possible, or something they would have to do without?

They had been too many days without a break, he realised, and they must determinedly take one, before he made some error they could not afford. At mid-day he announced a holiday, it being the day of a saint whose name he claimed to have forgotten, but whose day they would celebrate by telling stories, and forget the troublesome world of rafts and storms until tomorrow.

Later, in obedience to this plan, they sat on the sand before Log City, and Tania told a story of The Mal's intrigues. Stuart, having lost the thread, asked why Rosaline should do such a thing, not that he expected complete clarity from the answer, for Tania's logic had many strange holes and voids. He was not helping her coherence much, for he had assisted the celebration by tickling her into a better mood, and improved on this by nibbling her ears. She, brightening, announced that her suntan was uneven, and performed a brisk strip whilst continuing her story. From there, the shade of the hut was undoubtedly the next stop, but passion had to bide its time, despite his nibbling, for she was in the throes of her story, dancing a naked pantomime on the sand to illustrate its points.

Stuart broke off in mid-question, for a strange, harsh, droning noise was coming across the bay, as though from the rocks at the southern end, and he wondered if somehow the tide's action was causing the sound.

Then incredible comprehension dawned, and he leaped to his feet at the sight of the toylike airplane approaching from the south through the blue heights of the sky. For an instant they stood transfixed; then they were running, shouting, waving their arms, Stuart tearing off his shirt to wave it madly at the onrushing plane. Surely they would see, they must see, they were so close, no more than a thousand feet high and now nearly overhead!

The plane roared over, lashing them and their signs with its fleeting shadow, and passed over unfeeling whilst they bellowed at its very wings and raged madly at its fleeing tail-plane. The drone of its engines faded, and they waited, their lives suspended in agony between joy and despair, trapped in a void likes prisoners awaiting a jury's verdict, neither captive nor free.

"They're going," cried the girl, "they're going away!"

Then slowly it seemed that the plane was turning, its course no longer straight towards the none-existence from which it had come, but bending surely. Yes, bending and turning from its northward path, displaying the sun-bright spread of its glorious wings as it banked and swung in a great circle to return towards the island, and descending as it turned until within seconds it was passing them again, lower this time, but farther out, its shadow echoing it on the blue water beyond the reef. They renewed their shouting and waving, determined by sheer force of their energy to drag the so close plane to them, the girl running frantically back and forth, her shirt like his having become a flag.

As the plane hurtled into the distance, Stuart ran to heap leaves onto the fire, determined to leave no chance untaken when all the sweating weeks of effort hung on this unknown pilot's understanding. "Dammit Tania," he yelled as he stoked, "get some clothes on," for he had realised suddenly that she was buck-naked, and they had returned in an instant to a world where that wouldn't do at all. "There's people here! It's... somebody!"

But his words were wasted. Tania was running along the beach to meet the plane's return head on, and already they could see it swinging back to over-fly them again, but lower, much lower, and approaching fast, faster until it was upon them tiger-like and roaring over the bay so low that it seemed the waters must flinch from the thunder of its engines.

As if in the final throes of a pitched battle they greeted it with a bombardment of waving and shouting. In the tiny cockpit they glimpsed the dot of a face, the hint of whiskers and the glint of sunlight on goggles, and then it was gone, and he threw down his shirt and raised his arms to the sky in jubilation. "He saw us. He's seen us. He's damned well seen us!"

They waited, sweating and near exhausted from the fury of their efforts, Tania grumbling at his cajoling as she writhed on the sand to pull her shorts on as the growing noise signalled a fourth pass over. Again they sprang into their frantic pantomime, and again the incredible glimpse of a face peering down at them through the cockpit window, but this time a hand was raised in a casual wave.

It was perhaps this easy human gesture that staggered them more than all else, and they shouted no more, but watched quietly as the plane turned, and returned to make a fifth and final pass, but higher this time, and as it passed it rolled lazily in the air, wings wagging up and down in signal. Stuart found himself falling like a penitent to his knees on the sand, unable to do more than wave back feebly and murmur a simple, "thank you, thank you."

Then it was gone, the noise of its engines fading slowly until the sky was empty, and the island was again lonely and peaceful, as if a mere mocking dream had faded in the all consuming sunlight.

"Will he come back? Will he come back?" shouted the girl, and without waiting for an answer plunged into the forest, heading for the hilltop, vainly pursuing the vanished miracle.

"We're going home. We're going home," he cried hoarsely after her, "put your dammed shirt on for God's sake," then he ran after her into the forest, as unable as her to resist the plane's magnet-pull.

It would have been impossible to do anything coherent that day, even if he had not declared it a day of leisure, for suddenly the rafts, signs, storms and holidays that had dominated their lives were silly irrelevancies, and even after the passage of an hour he was still in a tremble of excitement.

The pilot had signalled to them, he had signalled! He had made that wagging of the wings that these fly boys used to do in the war, that means I understand, or I acknowledge, or whatever the devil they used it to mean, but he had seen! With a damned enormous SOS on the hilltop that any fool could tell had taken an age of effort to make, and another drawn on the sand with the two of them dancing on it and carrying on like banshees, what else could he be doing but signalling his understanding. They were saved: they were going home. Within days – how many? – two perhaps, a boat or something would come, and it was over! He felt weak with the relief of it.

Tania was unable to contain herself: convinced that the plane would return at any moment; running to the southern rocks almost at the cry of a bird and returning to demand of him again if he were sure that the plane would return.

"Not that plane Honey," he assured her after the third such trip, "but they'll send something. There's nowhere here for a plane to land. Probably they'll get one of the local cargo ships to put in here. It may be a day or two."

"Ohhh..." she stamped the sand in frustration. "Always waiting. It's always tomorrow or soon, never now."

"Come on, we'll fish. We need something to do."

"We've fished today. We've got plenty."

"We might as well. I don't think there's any sense working on the raft."

"You fish. I'm going to the hilltop." And she was gone, plunging into the bushes. "Keep the fire burning," her voice drifted to him from amongst the trees, "there might be another one."

He went alone to the fishing ground, wading past the raft, for he had no patience for it anymore. But even there he felt unbearably restless, as though the furious bombardment of the plane's noisy promise had blasted his calm to rubble, and the fish evaded him easily, until finally he skewered one and waved it on his spear at the lone sentry on the hilltop. She waved back, but stayed at her post, gazing out over the sea. "Don't stay up there all afternoon," he muttered, "you'll get burned and then you'll know."

A damned fine way to be found too, he thought, with her not a bloody stitch on, and that's before we've even got off the island. So much for being careful and saying nothing. What shall I do if it leads to any funny looks? Throw all her clothes in the sea and insist she never had any? Say we were keeping them nice in case of visitors? "Blast," he said out loud, "no end to problems." I'll have to talk to her when she gets back, he thought. It's not her fault, but this place is at an end any day, and from now on we'd better look pukka for the real world. She says she understands; I hope to hell she does.

He waded ashore with his catch, deciding to fish no more, and sat in the cool dark of the old hut, leaning wearily back against the rickety uprights. They had enough to eat already, there was no sense in slaughter for the sake of it, and he felt impatient for the end of this beachcomber's life. They had worked hard in the last few days, harder even than usual, and with the promise of an end, a deep tiredness had leapt upon him.

It was strange, he thought, how they had never moved their base down here to the old hut. They fished here every day and the yam grew here, and if a gale blew up this corner of the bay was more sheltered. It would have made more sense to live down here, and that was why the natives who had built the hut had chosen this place. A few paces down the beach and you were catching breakfast. And this was probably where they had first landed their canoe, lured at a glance by the stiller, deeper water in this corner. Wasn't this where he kept their raft, his and the girl's? This place made more sense – but only to a native.

Their problem had never been the distance of things, but the closeness. It was nothing to walk a couple of hundred yards from Log City, a welcome task in fact, one more little necessary walk to add space to their world. Once he had started the shelter at Log City it was quicker to complete it, so they could get on with their other stuff. Certainly their days had never been empty of work. How many days had it been now? March eighteenth, so over two months. Had someone told him on their first day that he would sit on this speck for so long he would have laughed at that man for a fool, yet here they both were, and even now they were still not escaped, despite all the circling of the plane.

But they would be, of that he was certain. He had not been wrong in fearing that rescue would not come quickly, for had he laughed at that fool it would have been in uneasy denial. Even on that first day the suspicion had ridden him that they would not be swiftly found, for the feeling had hung over him that, like the sunken Raven, they were too deep buried in the wide immensity of things.

Over the months the verdict of his feelings was proved sound. Now he knew without doubt that they were found, for now they were a point of latitude and longitude scrawled down in some pilot's little book, and from that scanty scrap of information signals would spread out, by 'phone, by radio, by words spoken in English in fan cooled offices. Soon the white man's world would see its duty to its own, and stretch out its arm to reclaim him. Soon, he thought yearningly, soon I shall stand on the soil of Singapore, and if not there, then some other place where I exist again as an Englishman, back again in reality, and I can get an iced drink, or a rickshaw, and not hack at logs and dig dirt all day like a coolie. Soon.

He drowsed, and finally slept as he leaned there, but in that sleep a dream came to him, with no story that he could remember, only that a dreadful shape clutched at him, smothering him, and he fled from it. But it pursued him closely, with a face that might have been a young Japanese, and yet was unknown and European.

He awakened with a jerk and a cry to find that chilly unease had thrown a wet shroud over the warmth of his long-awaited joy. He would not go onwards alone, nor could he go unwarily, with an end to his troubles. There was Tania to consider, and that was no small matter. Already, before their feet even left the sand, they'd been seen in a damned embarrassing situation, Tania running about without a stitch on, and all his cautions suddenly forgotten. Had she really taken his warnings as seriously as he'd thought? If anyone got a hint of what they had done here.... His mind flinched from the thought.

Surely he had dealt with that? It was unthinkable that anyone should get to know, impossible, totally not to be allowed. No one must ever know, no one at all. He could not even attempt to coolly itemise the consequences, for suddenly in his mind they reared before him like the countless muzzles of a firing squad, an impassable wall of death before his face.

He sat up abruptly, shaken by the violence of sudden understanding. Suddenly it seemed incredible that the depth of his danger had never fully occurred to him, for now a stream of unfaceable possibilities was pushing relentlessly into his mind.

How many situations would he have to worm his way through before he got the girl to her father, assuming they could find him? And how many petty officials would he have to explain himself to, and possibly not short or avoidable explanations either, for there was a whole plane full of corpses to report to someone in authority for that kind of thing. What if the girl said the wrong thing unthinkingly? She was clever enough and would never let him down, but sometimes it seemed that she lived in a world of her own, and didn't have the sense of having done wrong to make her cautious.

He knew himself to be not the most perceptive of men, and he wondered often at those rare people who could quickly look beneath the skin of a situation and know what was really going on. How easy it would be for some people to guess at their secret. And he knew also that he was not the best of liars, for it was an art that he despised. If he and the girl were calm, then they could go forward with no trouble, but if a stray thread was ever seized by the wrong person, then how quickly it could all unravel.

He had pictured himself a thousand times as arriving home, not a hero, for the time of lionising heroes was past, and there were a myriad greater than he, but none the less as someone who had done his part, who could hold up his head as one deserving like any other to walk the streets of his own country, and work through the business of his own life, whether in joy or sorrow. For he had killed, but it was in service of his country, and with the full approval of society he had guiltlessly struck down the enemy. His war years had been hard and bloody, but with the approved savagery that lays the mantle of worthiness on the shoulders and declares the hands noble and free of guilt.

And he had committed the sins against a mythical God that man had always committed, rebelling like most of the healthy young animals of his time against the restraints of a moral code that many still nodded to, but many others put no belief in. But these were allowable sins, or if not allowed, only criticised by frock wearing clerics and the like, people who's time had passed, people who you could laugh at or ignore.

But the certainty of that state had passed, and had passed without hope of retrieval. He had dipped his hands into a business from which their was no hope of washing them clean, and though his offence still seemed to him petty, the darkness that discovery would throw on him would be crushing and endless.

The picture returned to his mind of the distant pilot waving, his head a mere silhouette in the cockpit, his raised hand scarcely visible. Was he gloved, moustached? It was not possible in that fleeting distant instant to tell any such detail, yet that friendly hand waving, that roar of engine behind the blurring propeller, they had spoken of order, of competence, of the whole weight of civilisation looking down on their little island and scooping it easily into the arena of the empire's authority. The passing over of the airplane had destroyed the frail barrier of the sea and returned them with a snap to the real world.

Suddenly he was no longer the crownless king of this pocket sized place, living as free of masters as any Borneo headhunter, but a minor item of property in a mighty world of rules and codes, that would now re-tuck him beneath the safety of its wing. But that safety had passed, for he had violated one of the most primal of those rules, one so strict and shameful that the very mention of it could halt polite conversation, and there was no soft place beneath that wing for one who was discovered to have broken this rule.

I am a criminal now, thought Stuart, not just somebody who makes stupid mistakes and gets called a fool, or breaks a traffic law and gets fined. A criminal, one of those people they brand as scum and lock up for years, and after that they're always criminals, even when they're not in jail anymore. One of those people you hear about in the newspapers, and when they come out everyone they knew before doesn't want to know them, and it lasts the rest of their lives.

He rose quietly and left the shade of the hut for the beach. The sun had fallen from its mid day height, and the shadows of the trees seemed to reach after him down the beach, grasping at his legs with their dark arms, so that he felt driven to go to the water beyond their reach.

He turned and squinted into the descending sun, looking up at the tiny figure keeping her patient vigil on the hilltop. You have destroyed me, he thought, I'm standing here, but I may be little more than a dead man, just waiting for the undertakers to cart me off. But he was too honest for that. If I'm destroyed, I did it myself, he thought, and he bowed his head away from the hill and walked tiredly down the beach towards Log City, feeling the weight of the sun beating on his back.

A long time seemed to pass before he reached the southern rocks, and his mind roamed wearily over the thousand teeth of the dreary trap that had opened sluggishly before him. How, how had it come to this pass? He started to walk carefully along the barren pier, picking his way over the irregular rock. He had not been here for weeks, but it would be good to browse amongst the flotsam that bobbed and eddied on the waves that clawed at the long rocky arm, passing time until his fit of the blues passed, as he had often done before.

There was a crab nestling in a pool at the water's edge, a big one that moved feebly with the licking waves, and he crept cautiously down to look at it more closely, for it had a strange, irregular shape. It was dead, that he could see even at a few yards distance, for it was somehow broken and twisted, trailing weed or rotting flesh, yet twitching as the moving waters lent it the appearance of life. Dead, and battered by the sea in which it had once thrived, for its legs were oddly to one side as he reached to retrieve it.

Suddenly he jerked back as though bitten, and slipped on the rock, gashing his thigh. It was not a crab, but a hand rotted to a skeleton, mere bones held together by the last shreds of gristly sinews, the stirring waters causing it to feebly paw the wet rock. For some minutes Stuart gazed at it in sick horror, for it was a thing as hideous and unaccountable as if only the gift of the devil could have placed it there. He looked out at the patch of water where the Raven lay. There had been no storm so massive that it could have disturbed that graveyard; the bodies within must lie there still, so how... Sister Therese. The hand was small, the bones delicate. A woman's hand, the hand of the woman he had been unable to bury, the woman who had cared for the girl. And it had somehow found its way here, to be seen by him, to mock him even as he poised to leap from this prison.

He felt himself quivering on the brink of an unearthly terror, and stared at the hand, unable too take his eyes away, half fearful that it would at any instant resume its stern life and raise a finger in hideous reprimand. He rose slowly and backed away, feeling his way by touch up the rocks, fixing the thing with his eyes, retreating from it as a man might from a tiger that may yet stir itself to spring.

Chapter 39. Study

In the rear of the house there was an upstairs room, the third of the three bedrooms that the builder had planned in his design. Since the colonel and his wife came to live there, it had never held a bed, but instead had become his study, furnished mainly with bookcases centered about his desk. Seated at that desk Haig received the light of the south facing window, and when he glanced through the window he saw the upper branches of the great chestnut tree. Through the long, dreary winter these branches had danced naked, lashed by the damp, moaning winds, and as the wind keened through the empty branches the colonel had thought with regret of the hot, green countries that he had know, and donning a cardigan, he turned on the reading lamp on his desk to assist the dim light of the cold grey sky.

But winter was passing now, and the days lengthened. Soon the long days would arrive, the new buds of spring bursting open to greet the bright sunshine that would flood in through the sashed window. Then it would be pleasant to glance up from his desk and see the richness of the broad, green leaves, swaying sometimes in a summer breeze to afford him glimpses of the mock Tudor eaves of the neighbouring house, and the swish of these leaves would come to the colonel's ears at his desk.

But that was yet to come, and this March day was wet and dreary, and the colonel was paying it little heed. He had started enthusiastically to assemble his notes on the countries he had known, but there was a project unfinished that he wished to complete.

His hobby was military history, and he had left behind both the paper conflict of the committee and the dismal weather, and again entered the world of the snorting horse, of the drawn sabre and roaring cannon. Again in his mind he explored the terrain of a distant valley in nineteenth century Russia, and his fountain pen scratched the paper faintly as he strove to fathom the mysteries of Balaclava, an enigma that had exercised many a military mind. Six hundred and sixty men, six hundred and sixty good men on horses, the pride of the British army. When all the evidence was assembled, who was to blame? What colossal madness was it that had caused the Light Brigade to charge the Russian batteries, and litter that distant valley with their torn corpses?

That Lord Cardigan was an arrogant fool who despised Nolan was known. That Raglan had given an imprecise order for Nolan to carry to Cardigan, that too was known. And that friction between Nolan and his lordship had prevented a clarification of the mangled order, that idea had been proposed and discussed endlessly in the near-century since the disaster.

The explanation had long ago been made that a chain of bad communication had resulted in this most famous of military disasters, but the colonel was unsatisfied by this and gnawed on the problem not of the order, but of the man. Why had Cardigan so recklessly obeyed a plainly foolish order, leading the Brigade in a pointless charge down a valley that he could see was guarded by the iron mouths of several batteries of cannon?

Was it misplaced courage, a determination to be seen not to shirk in the hour of trial, that drove him against all reason to charge the enemy cannon? Behind his drawling manner did a fiercer battle take place unseen, as Cardigan strove to show a false calm to the world, strove against his fears to bolster his sense of duty, until so strengthened it strangled all sense of tactics, and he gave the order to advance? And then, as the distant cannon began to roar, did common sense remain so vanquished by honour that he was able to order the advance to a charge, and lead puny lances and sabres into a mile of exploding shell, with no prize at the valley's end but the fact of stubborn obedience?

Or was Cardigan right? Was he right to obey and follow the rule of discipline, that states inflexibly that only commitment wins the final victory? Did he believe in some great act of heroism, which being unthinking and unconditional, was thereby unlimited and finally irresistible? No, surely not. How could a society be worthy of defending if it did not respect reason, and if it respected reason, how could it promote lunacy? And Cardigan's charge was lunacy.

Raglan had intended him to capture a few abandoned guns a little down the valley, not to try and seize the main battery of cannon, an impossible task. The written order had been vague, but did that excuse Cardigan from thinking? Was it not his duty to know that cavalry were handled thus, and infantry so, and cannon so, and did he not flog his men for not knowing their duties?

He did, and Raglan expected him to use his brigade of horse, not to lose it gloriously. Flesh could not compete with explosives, so Cardigan was a fool, and being a fool was an incompetent also. Raglan was often accused for his vague order, but Haig exonerated him on this point. Surely if officers are fit to hold their rank they do not need an essay to direct their every move. And as before he laid the blame on Lord Cardigan and no other.

But yet Haig felt a reluctance to dismiss Cardigan so thoroughly. Had he not after all ridden bravely at the head of the charge, risking his life no less than all of them? The blue blood in his veins had been no guarantee of his safety, and it was by luck only that he was one of the few to ride back from the slaughter of his command. Or perhaps was he just too out of his depth in the whole affair, and when the puzzling order came from his superior he was too scared to say no?

The distant ringing of the telephone excused Haig from a final conclusion on this point. With only a token grumble he rose briskly from his desk and descended the stairs to the hallway where the noisy instrument stood on its own narrow table, its shiny modern blackness ruling amidst the wood panel and regency striped wallpaper. He snatched the handset up in mid ring. "Yes."

"Colonel Haig..." Haig recognised the voice immediately. It was Braithwaite the family solicitor. "Colonel Haig..." Braithwaite hesitated again. That was unlike him. He had the slow measured manner of his discreet profession, but he was seldom hesitant. "I'm afraid that I have some disturbing news for you."

The colonel felt the prickle of fear run down his back, that prickle that comes not from the threat of a blow, or the arrival of a bill that cannot be met, but from the hint of a deeper disaster, that passing by the flesh will bite the soul directly. "What is it," he asked, his voice level and calm.

"You had better go to Camden police station at once. The police are holding your son Raymond."

"Holding. You mean he's been arrested?"

"Yes, he's been arrested." The colonel was dumbfounded. From the solicitor's tone of voice he had expected a death at least. "But on what charge? Raymond's never committed a crime in his life. Has he got drunk?" and the colonel nearly laughed.

"No Colonel, not drunk. It's a serious matter. The officer in charge will explain it to you."

"Serious matter! The man's too inoffensive to kick a dog! What do you mean serious matter?"

"It may be best if the officer in charge explains that to you Colonel."

"Damn it all Braithwaite you're my solicitor!" the colonel barked, angering in his bewilderment. "Do you think I'm driving all the way to Camden wondering what the devil's going on? Out with it man whatever it is! I'm a soldier not a grocer."

Braithwaite was not used to this. His work was mainly the competent transfer of property, the dull and serious business of drawing up wills, and eventually the sombre reading of them. It was in this area that he had served the colonel and his family, not in the messy world of crime. But his client had demanded an answer, and there was no way out, and so he spoke clearly with a forced evenness of tone. "I'm afraid that Raymond has been arrested on a charge of unnatural vice."

The colonel gazed stupidly at the hard, black plastic that had spoken so strangely to him in its little tinny voice. He felt cold; the hallway felt cold and he felt strangely empty and light.

"What do you mean? How could this happen?"

"Your son and another man. They were arrested on a charge of unnatural vice."

"Where."

"In a nightclub in Camden. It was early this morning. Raymond was allowed a call from the police station and he called me. He doesn't know anyone else in the legal profession."

"I see," said the colonel, his voice soft, little more than a whisper.

"I'm sorry to have to tell you this colonel, very sorry," Braithwaite continued, his calm solicitor's manner crumbling a little under the attack of sympathy. The colonel had been a client for a long time and was always very proper in his dealings, very pleasant to deal with. "I can recommend a colleague. I believe that he's very experienced in these matters, however I am not." But the line was dead, for the colonel had gently replaced the handset in its cradle.

For a while Haig stood in silence, his dull gaze fixed on the telephone resting quietly on its polished table, resting on a little cloth of beige that Mildred had placed there to protect the wood from scratches. There were tiny red flowers embroidered neatly on the cloth, and the colonel touched them gently, running his fingers softly over them. The faint winter sunlight from the open door of his study fell in a dim shaft on the staircase, lending a pale blush to the pattern of the worn carpet. Slowly the colonel began to ascend the stairs, one heavy hand resting for support on the dark wood of the rail.

Chapter 40. Sunset

Stuart returned along the causeway with stiff, wooden steps, forcing himself not to look back. It had lain there for months, he reasoned. It would not stir, could not stir, but none the less he felt its existence follow him, felt a strange awareness on his back, as though at any minute he might feel it touch lightly on his shoulder, and wordlessly beckon him to return to its horrid little nook. Lain there for months as they had toiled, rotted and withered in the sun as they sweated on the hilltop, dipped its mouldering fingers into the bay as they fished, blindly gazed across the bay to the hut where they fornicated.

He saw the girl watching him from the hilltop and stopped; how could he tell her of this dead thing that had kept vigil with them, and how could he hold the hideous mystery within him and not tell her? He went to the shelter and sat on the log, fretful and restless.

She returned, skipping merrily through the forest to deluge him with a stream of excited chatter. Why didn't they land, was he sure they would come back, would they come back today, and her questions beat on him until he leapt up with a snarl, and she stepped back hurt and dismayed. He turned and strode away, maddened by the pressure that seemed to beat on him from all sides, unable to still the turmoil of his emotions.

"Where are you going," she called after him forlornly.

"For a walk," he snapped back, not pausing.

"Can't I come with you?"

He spun about abruptly. "No. Stay there for God's sake," he bellowed. "Can't I be on my own for a while?" And he resumed his angry march, not looking back again.

"What's wrong?" she called, but he strode on without answering, and she watched him till he came to the corner of the bay and passed into the hollow between the barrier and the trees, disappearing from her sight. Then she sank wretched onto the log, tears starting to her eyes. What had she done wrong, why was he angry at her? Was it because she went up on the hill and didn't fish with him? It must be something very bad, because he didn't get like this often, and when she made him mad he told her why quickly. It was going to be dark soon and he had nearly let the fire go out, so she leapt up and anxiously tried to coax it back to life, watching with one eye for his return. But when darkness fell the fire was dead, and he had not returned.

Stuart had passed from the bay into the delta of rough land at the island's south, marching with the stiff, clumsy strides of anger: anger at the girl, because he was angry with himself, angry because he was shaken in an irrational way that smacked of superstitious fear, and yet he could not dismiss it. He checked his stride abruptly, for here he was at Dawson's grave, its rough cross another memento of death looming before him. He had forgotten that he must encounter it here. Was there no end to corpses on this island, he thought impatiently, and continued past it onto the narrow western beach. But there was no escape here, for another minute's striding brought him halfway back to the north cliffs.

He stopped and sat heavily on the sand, brooding as he gazed at the descending sun. This should be a day for celebration, and instead he felt worse bedevilled than the day when they crashed here, for then he had been driven to obvious action by honest necessity, and now he felt hemmed in, unable to see his way for difficulty. His good fight was over, his well-earned evacuation was at hand, but he was more bemired with troubles than when he started.

The image of the skeletal hand rose menacing before him. What nonsense! He had seen death and mangled bodies before, and this was just another piece of grisly remains, to be grimaced at and buried. But that was not true, for it was more. By accident or intention the lifeless hand had pointed to him, and he could not hold back his understanding of why it should disturb him so.

I am a criminal. Again the thought arose in his mind, a fact, not arguable, not to be washed away by words or argument. He had a medal in his case, not the V.C. of course or anything like that, but it was a medal. Would they take it from him? Not that it was more than a lump of metal of course, but they gave it to him for doing his duty. Surely they would give him some allowance for error?

A movie started to play slowly in his mind, a movie where he took the starring role. He saw the policeman arrive at some future door, unsmiling and clad in stiff dark-blue authority, felt himself thrill with hidden guilt at the first smooth words of enquiry, saw the false smile with which he answered the quiet questions that lead on, until finally the policeman laid out openly the reason for his visit: he had "reason to believe that an offence had been committed," an offence against a young girl, "below the age of consent," as he sternly rolled out the grim official phrases. Next came the simple request to "come along with me Sir," and the dreary, tacky interviews in grubby little offices, until finally the formal charge was laid.

Or would they arrest him on the spot, with handcuffs and all that paraphernalia? Was that how they did it in England, or was that too American? But in either case it would move from there to a courtroom, big and draughty, with oak panelling on the walls and confident people in gowns and wigs striding about, reading from papers in their hands, with a judge sitting like God elevated from the rest in his pulpit, old, grey haired, robed in crimson, looking out over the seated rows of spectators who sat stiff and uncomfortable as though they were also on trial, staring through his glasses as though at a circus staged by his inferiors, of whom Stuart was the lowest clown.

Then they started with the recitation of dates, the defining of places, the naming of "Stuart Ellis, of this town, who on that day did, contrary to the laws of," and all the rest of their terrifying jargon. Next came the questions: blunt grim questions, asked with all the distaste and contempt of well dressed authority, probing, dissecting his naughty little pleasures into a thousand scrapes of filth.

And he answered from his public cage, twisting, sweating before the eyes of all the room, unable to evade the history that was typed up neatly on their bundles of notes, until finally he stood in the dock stripped of all the respect he had ever owned.

All that he had ever done right was of no consequence, and finally the sentence came, with the judge's scornful comments smiting him as heavily as the blows of a cudgel, and he was lead away to wear the shabby uniform of disgrace, and dwell in some grim, barred fortress that rang to the clanging shut of iron doors.

A bevy of newspapers fell gleefully on the case, national and local, and with headlined paragraphs reported the trial, the summation and last event of a life that had ceased, leaving as its final bowed shadow the stained jailbird that he now was. All who knew him could read his true story for a few pence, and after a grunt of surprise and a few words of contempt could eject him from their minds, together with the rest of those they had seen disgraced over the years.

Stuart closed his eyes against the brilliance of the descending sun, as though to hide from the bright, closing jaws of the world's inevitable vengeance.

But surely this did not have to be; surely he could solve this threat as he had solved all that had gone before.

But this is different, a relentless little voice within him answered, before you were a soldier or a businessman. You were legitimate then, serving your country. Now you are a criminal.

"Then I'm a criminal," he hissed back at that part of himself. "But it didn't bother me much till now, did it? I just didn't think enough. It's that damned plane. Why didn't it come earlier when we'd only been here a day or two, then all this wouldn't have happened. No, they have to fool about for bloody months whilst you nearly drown yourself and die digging bloody great signs and salvaging sunken wrecks; then when you're sick of it all and go your own way and say to hell with you, they come flying merrily in, waving there damned hands as if it's all a lark. Bloody fool. And if he were to be one she blabs too much to, then would it still be a lark? No, it'll be so serious he'll break both his legs running off to blab to someone else as likely as not, with his face set as serious as if the world's ending."

He sat in the cell of his imagination for a while, brooding on the variability of right and wrong, contemplating the bleakness of rough stone walls, until a chink of light suddenly darted into his gloom. What charges? How could there be any charges? They were not in Britain, so why need he care about British law? Who the devil did this place belong to? Indonesia, Singapore? Was it even for certain that it was on anyone's list of territories, and if it was, whose? And did they have laws against fooling about with the under aged? Wasn't that what he had fobbed his fears of with when they were getting down to it, more or less, quickly grabbing that uncertainty as being all excusing.

Which it probably isn't, he now thought gloomily. They were both British citizens, and that still counted for a hell of a lot. Britain had a long arm.

He didn't know much about how the empire was administered, and even less about lawyer's stuff, but he doubted that he could walk into a British court, airily tell them they had no authority, then cheerfully walk out again. Even if he could, the newspapers would be there, and they would go insane. The *Daily Express* would lap it up, and *The News of The* World even more so. His father had liked both, and he had read enough of their scandal stories. If the court didn't convict you once, then they would, twenty times or more, as long as there was still chewing value in the story. It would be a fine thing for the old man to read.

He dropped his head into his hands as the full weight of the realisation came home. "It will kill him," he murmured aloud, "poor old sod."

He rose clumsily and wandered northward, his mind dwelling on his father. The old man deserved better than this. A lifetime spent in a shop, yes sir and no sir all day long, striving to make a profit. Mother dying and him alone with one son, and all he wants is for that son to be a surveyor, like he always wished he'd been. But I couldn't see it, didn't want it, and I went into the army instead and ended up an officer.

He was all right after that. He never really said so, but I could tell he was pleased. "An officer and a gentleman," he once said. He was being a bit sarky really, but he was pleased all the same. He used to say it to his friends, "they made Stuart a lieutenant," and he said it very casual, but he was pleased inside. An officer and a gentleman for a son, and him just a shopkeeper, and his dad the same. Nobody in the family had ever been an officer, never even dreamt of it. I did something different, did what I wanted to do, and it all worked out okay. Now I've done something else I wanted to, and it's all buggered up. He'll read about it in the papers, and so will all his friends. It'll kill him, and I might as well be dead for what I'll have left. I can't let it happen.

He arrived at the end of the sandy strip and slumped down again, his mind churning the dreary scenario endlessly.

It can't be changed now. So how can it be avoided? What if nothing happens, nobody finds out anything? Surely we could pull it off? But that'd be too much like being lucky. Since I got on that plane nothing's been lucky. It'll out all right sooner or later, wherever we are. It's obvious, always has been, but I couldn't see it, like I couldn't see that damned rotten hand, and it was there all along, and God knows how.

A thought rose before him like a doorway of escape: leave the girl in Singapore! It would be easy enough; tip off the nuns as soon as they arrived, and they'd descend like locusts and snap her up, then he could be on the next plane out of there, gone, and the whole mess left behind like the Raven's wreckage. It was so easy, why hadn't he thought of it before? But he had thought of it of course. The vague germ of the idea had floated around in him for some time, finally to take definite shape. Easy to do, but would that be the end of the matter?

The girl would raise hell, and ten to one she would blurt out the whole story in rage. Then what would happen? Nothing perhaps, just a heap of Hail Marys for her to say, and him forgotten as an exorcised devil, gone and good riddance. Or would they? No, not with their rule-the-world attitude. Almost certainly they'd get into a holy rage and made a case of it; who could tell what they could do? Useless to think that seven thousand miles or so lay between Singapore and England: these people often had pull, and they thought they had a right to decide everything. They were always hounding local administrators into despair about this and that, and if they complained loudly enough into the right ears they could easily throw a hornet's nest over the miles in pursuit of him.

Another thought slammed into his mind, leaping in from its own obscure corner: Dawson! He was with Reuters! Dammit, the newspapers were involved even before he considered the good sisters, for they would be interested in the death of one of their own, and they had a good nose for anything they could blow up into a story. One word from an enraged nun, and they'd be frying him in the next edition.

What a hell of a story for the *Express* and the other rags to get hold of: dead reporters, dead nuns, seduced orphan girls and him in the middle. By the time they'd finished scribbling everything would be his fault, even the plane crashing.

"What The Officer And Gentleman Did On The Island." He could see the Sunday headline now. Even if he avoided the courts, he would have to go to Australia to escape being their plaything for the next twenty years, for God's sake. He would be better off keeping her with him, and keeping a zip on her mouth. Throwing her to the nuns could trigger the very disaster he was trying to avoid, so he'd better stay clear of them at all costs.

But that put him right back in the same place, except now it looked even more dangerous. When they arrived in Singapore somebody was certain to make some kind of fanfare, and the local reporters would guess straightaway that he knew the fate of their missing colleague, and possibly enquiries were still being made for two Arab businessmen and a woman. Also, and why had he never thought of this before, wouldn't the nuns want to reclaim the body of their missing sister, so they could say masses and wave incense over it? They must have been bombarding heaven day and night with prayers for her and the missing girl, so certainly they would jump on even a sniff of a rumour that either of them had turned up, and he was guaranteed a whole posse of them swirling their skirts around the scene.

Christ, it was appalling. They'd grab the girl without waiting for a word from him, and she'd expect him to beat them off somehow. What with? He had no authority to tell them what they couldn't do, and they'd get enough paper to light a bonfire, and endless yap to go with it. He might as well take on a platoon of Nips with a walking stick. In fact, if he protested too much they'd smell a rat and ask why, at least they would if they had an ounce of cunning. They didn't even have to suspect anything wrong in fact: with their attitude, if I say two words against them they'll just act as if her being anywhere with me was unholy, and they'll whisk her away and browbeat her for good measure till something comes out. I'm done for! Whichever way I take, I'm done for!

Why the hell did I do it? Blast her to hell, why did she have to be here, and so bloody useful and cute. A bit of fun and games, and it's worse than if I did a murder. And that bloody promise – why didn't I think first. I only meant well, and nothing's gone right since.

The sun met the horizon, and as its setting glory heralded the onset of darkness it seemed to announce to him personally the end of light in his life. It had risen that morning on another day of hope, but it would never again do so.

He was finished. He had been too damned smart for his own good, thinking he could work his way around this problem and that problem, and make stupid promises, but it would all come out, and now he was finished. Was a shopkeeper's son who didn't know his place, was an officer who thought he'd joined his betters, was finally a broken thing of contempt that couldn't be repaired. As soon as they left this island, he was on the final steps of his path to disaster, and she on her way back to the orphanage, blubbering at the end of her little dream of freedom.

A pity lightning didn't come down and fry the two of them, then they could rot away peacefully here, and no one would know anything about it, because neither of them would be here to tell the story when the boat came. God knows they'd come close enough to it a few times; a pity this damned death trap hadn't gobbled them up.

Or just her.

The thought came to him as simply as scratching follows the itching of an ear. If he were to stand on that beach alone when the boat came, then who would know to ask about her? There were seven bodies lost out there beneath the shallow water, or mouldering under the sand; what was strange that there might be eight? One bad landing alone had ended seven lives as quickly and casually as breaking eggs, and the island was full of other dangers besides. How easily a careless child might slip and fall from the northern peak of the hill and die on the rocks below.

The currents that circled the island could easily take the body out, just as they had the nun's, and she would be part of the tally. Hadn't she nearly run off that very cliff edge herself when they had scarcely been here an hour? The pilot had seen her living, but how could that forbid a later accident? It would be a tragic thing to happen after all these months, with rescue only days away, but that was the kind of thing that could happen in these wild places, and a few pious words of regret with the prayers wrapped all such matters up. He would not go Singapore to meet his doom, but would arrive alone, a free man, safe and free. Though she would stay, he would go on.

Despite himself he imagined her standing on the hilltop, on the cliff's edge, overlooking the ragged, dizzying descent, seeing the hacked, foam-bleeding waves retreat from their assault on the cliff's unseen base. She would go there if he lead her, go there without question. If he pointed something out – some silly non-existent flower peeping shyly from between the rocks – then, a firm grip on her narrow shoulders, a hard decisive push – Stuart leapt to his feet in pain. A dark dragon of despair had come to him, hotter by far than its pretty, playful cousin.

A dragon black, ugly and fearful in its menace.

Tania sat gazing dully at the cold ashes of the fire. She had not succeeded in bringing it back to life, though she had tried hard, pushing the smallest pieces of wood that she could find against the last glowing embers and blowing hard on them. There was nothing to cook with, and no light except the stars, for the moon had gone past its last sliver the night before. She didn't care about cooking for herself, for she felt too upset to be hungry, but there would be nothing for Stuart.

Where was he? Where could he be, for there was no-where to go, so he must be close by. She would have gone looking for him, creeping quietly, but he was so fierce that he frightened her. He had told her to stay here, and she would do as he said. She didn't usually do everything that he told her, but this was different, because he was so mad at something.

She had stayed by the cooling ashes, watching as the long shadows reached down the beach to the water, looking around fearfully, anxious for his return as the bay dimmed into night about her. The usual soft sounds of the night came from the forest behind her, but that was nothing, for there was nothing harmful on the island, no snakes, no animal larger than Adolph.

If there was some moonlight I could go looking for him, she thought, but if he doesn't want to be found then I can't find him in this darkness. Why did I think that, she asked herself. It must be because he said he wanted to be on his own. Doesn't he want me anymore, or does he have to do something private that I don't know about. What if he's got hurt or something? She jumped to her feet at the thought and stood listening, ears straining as though a call for help might be drifting faintly through the trees, but there was nothing but the usual faint sounds of the night.

It wasn't quiet here, she realised suddenly. I thought it was quiet because there's no cars and no people shouting, but there's noise all the time here. Not noise though, just sound, always going on faintly. Wherever you go you can hear the sea washing on the beach, all the time, and if I go right to the middle of the forest to get away from it on this side, then before I can't hear the waves on this side I can hear them on the other. Not noisy, not even loud, just this faint hiss that's everywhere. And the leaves on the trees, there's a sort of hiss that comes from them too. Not always, just when the wind blows a bit, but it doesn't have to blow a lot. It's so faint and soft you can forget about it, and you think it's quiet. But if he shouted I could hear him. What if he's hurt, the thought came again. If he's hurt then the people must come to rescue us soon. What if he were to die?

She bit her knuckles at the thought. Not now, not when we're going home. What would I do without Stuart? I can't find my dad without him, it's too much, and I want to be with Stuart. Why doesn't he come back?

Drops of rain started to pitter down, and she retreated into the hut, not so much to avoid the shower as to be in their place, where they slept together and had some fun. It was worse here though, because she was more alone here, and she kept watching the star spattered sky through the doorless entrance, hoping to see his figure loom dark against it as he came home. Tears welled to her eyes and ran slowly down her cheeks. She wanted him to come back and be okay, and not be angry.

I must find him, she thought. He's a big man but he could have an accident all the same. She scrambled from the hut and paused, uncertain where to start, then taking up her beloved stick for comfort she headed south, following his trail.

Chapter 41. Precipice

He awoke groggily, confused to find himself lying on the beach before the old native hut.

His sleep had been full of dreams, wild and contorted, a dreary series of pursuits by skeletal figures, who followed him accusing him of absurdities whilst he vainly tried to light fires. Every time that he got a fire lit they asked him to explain nonsense that somehow was of great significance, and when he answered they didn't like his explanations, and that made the fire go out. The identity of his main tormentor kept changing: at first it was a sailor who refused to tell him where the boat was, then it changed to his father, and finally, horribly, to a broken, twisted-limbed Tania. His head swam with the dreary confusion of his dreams.

He remembered. He had shouted at Tania, and left the shelter angrily to wander the island in the darkness, his mind whirling in anguished. From one weary station to another he had circled the island, finally to see the sun set from the northern extremity of the west beach, and as the darkness closed on him, had thought her continued life would destroy him, unless violently uprooted.

Then he had been no longer able to bear sitting in that place, where they had landed on the day they swum round the point, and arrived laughing and racing each other. He had climbed laboriously up the forested slope, falling and tripping in the dark, and emerging at the hill top made his way cautiously to the edge of the cliff, where he sat listening to the waves crash on the rocks below, seeing their pale foam in the starlight.

Finally he had left this place also, for Tania had stood with him here too often, and he came down to the old hut, a place she disliked for no particular reason. He lay down on the beach before the crumbling hut, still ruminating on the choice of dreary prospects before him, and finally fell asleep from sheer weariness.

Stuart sat up stiffly, feeling his whole body aching and feeble, as though he had endured a beating. There was no sign of Tania on the beach, and the signal fire was unlit, although the sun was high above the horizon. How had he come to sleep so heavily into the morning, and where was Tania? He felt dirty in mind, as though his tormented thoughts had themselves been acts of shameful consequence; where was she? He had left her alone all the night, and since they had arrived here, they had never been parted after dark. True, there was nothing harmful on the island, but she was of no age to pass the night alone.

Nothing harmful on the island but you, came the thought into his head; you are the only beast here.

He flinched at the memory of all that had passed through his mind during the troubled night, and hauling himself clumsily to his feet hobbled stiffly to Log City. Their shelter was empty; the ashes of the fire were still in the firepit. Where the devil was she, he thought uneasily? A picture came to him in vivid detail of himself shouting at her angrily, telling her that he wanted to be alone: she had taken him at his word and left him alone.

"Tania." He shouted her name into the forest, then went down to the water's edge and shouted again repeatedly to the hill, but there was no sign of her, no answering call.

He returned to their hut and sat heavily on the log, his mind desolate, but seeing clearly, without delusion or the fog of convenient excuse. I have betrayed her, he thought, and betrayed myself. I have used her like an adult, but I've behaved like a whimpering child. I have put my cowardly fears before her, killed her in my mind when I promised to save her.

Shame rose thickly to choke him, shame that was not the mere knowledge of having done some external wrong, nor the everyday angry self-contempt that follows a stupid blunder.

This was a hotter, stronger, more engulfing emotion, drowning his inner being like foul reeking mud. This was shame that flooded all of his mind without reprieving any part, leaving no dry compartment to which he could retreat and marshal his neat contradicting arguments.

He had not broken any rule that he felt worth preserving in his frolics with her, for they were both human, and no matter what her age, or lack of it, they had come together in tenderness, and as she said, it was no one else's business. But now he had nearly violated tenderness itself. Better that he had died than lost this deep integrity of his soul. Incredible the stupid, sick ideas that could run through your head, daft stuff that no sane person would do, unless he were drunk enough or pushed over the edge. And people thought that their brains ruled the world! Daft! Insane!

Get the fire started at least, he thought. But it took a long time to ignite the shavings, for his deft skill had deserted him, and anxiety made his fingers into thumbs.

With the fire finally, burning he made his way anxiously through the forest to the waterfall, and from there onwards up the slope, calling out the girl's name as he went, and pausing to listen for any reply. No shout came back, and the hilltop was empty of her presence. "Dammit where are you girl," he muttered to the emptiness, "I just had a bad patch, that's all." She was not to know all that had gone through his mind, was she? Didn't she know that adults had concern's that troubled them? Why had she hidden? She must be hiding surely, for a call could be heard from one end of this island to the other, unless there was a storm.

He began to feel angry, and marched quickly up the sloping plateau of the hilltop, striding across the great letters like a busy ant crossing a child's game board, looking swiftly left and right for a sight of the hiding girl. Impossible that she could evade him for long, he thought. It would make more sense to go back to the shelter and wait for her, get the water, tend the fire, go fishing. She would show up when she tired of her tantrum.

But he could not. The sour aftertaste of his night of despair was with him, and he must act and wash it from him. He had let go of the reins of guidance, and matters were going adrift, and he must put them back in order. It was not like Tania to act in this fashion, but it was he not she that was at fault, and he must find her swiftly. From the hill's peak he would have the widest view.

But his view was caught even as he approached the narrow peak, for there by the cliff's edge lay a sandal, dull and scuffed, the worn strap broken by the buckle.

Stuart halted, struck to stone by fear, and then ran forward to perch recklessly on the ragged brink, his eyes frantically searching the near vertical slope below. There was nothing there, nothing on the steep broken terraces of bare rock but the occasional patch of grass where the thin dirt maintained a feeble grip. But at his feet he saw the dirt newly gouged, as though a stone had broken loose from the last fraying edge of the plateau, and far below, at the edge of the final drop, a stick, with a green ribbon tied around it at the thicker end. Tania's stick.

The brooding evil of the day seemed to condense suddenly into a fist that gripped crushingly at his heart. "Tania," he howled, and springing back from the drop he raced across the plateau and hurtled into the forest of the eastern slope, crashing heedlessly through the trees, his only thought to reach the surf drenched rocks at the cliff's foot. In his haste he caught his foot on the exposed root of a tree, and fell headlong down the slope, slamming hard full length onto the dirt.

He lay there a full minute, winded, gasping, scarcely able to draw air, until finally he was able to rise slowly to his feet. The fall had knocked some calm back into him, and gasping and bent he retraced his steps; it would be quicker to climb down the terraces of the cliff and look over.

At the brink he grasped the treacherous edge and lowered himself painfully over the brink, scrabbling with both feet for the nearest of the narrow outcrops below. It was a lunatic's venture, but terror drove him. His handhold gave way suddenly, and he found himself sliding the last few inches until his feet struck against the ledge, whilst the dislodged dirt slithered past him.

He clung to the steep cliff face, sweating and waiting for his panting to subside, listening to the tiny landslide continued to cascade over the uneven slope below him, imagining it pouring over the final drop into silence. "Steady, steady," he muttered, striving to drive back the nightmare with calm words, focusing on his task in desperate denial of its futility "too fast and that's it. That won't do any good."

The first few feet were the worst. Below that the slope was steeper, but it was also more uneven, with rugged outcroppings for his feet, and he was able to cautiously descend from each one to the next, searching every hidden gully in hope and fear, zig zagging left and right until he found himself crouched over the stick. Nothing. No sign other than the green ribbon, dirty, limp and wordless. Looking over the final drop he saw it was even more sheer than it seemed from below, falling almost vertically a full sixty yards to where the sea surged and foamed between the rocks, rising eagerly to lick them clean and falling back again patiently. There was nothing to be seen but sharp rock and hungry water.

If she and her beribboned stick had fallen here together, then it had caught on this final ledge, and she, heavier, had plunged onwards, past this last rocky lip, out into the airy void. In his mind he hear the thin, high-pitched scream, saw the flailing limbs, and he winced and cowered from the thought, covering his eyes. Anxiety ebbed from him, leaving calm, lonely misery. He was a free man. What he had meanly desired in his fear had been handed to him deftly by fate, and he was saved from all his fear, and left with the cold, empty hole where it had been.

He sat back from the giddy view and felt tears starting to his eyes; he had lost her, he would never see her again. All the longed for ships and planes of the world could not transport him to one sight of her. He was again a free man, but would never be free again. Wherever he wandered in this world, he would not find her bobbing at his elbow. Wherever he ate, be it crouched in rags by a campfire, or be it seated with rich friends before wine and silver cutlery, he would not look up to see her teasing face. He was alone as never before.

Would she come to him in his dreams, accusing him with a look, or merely puzzled that her big, silly friend was no longer with her to make her laugh with a silly, feeble joke? Or would even that comfort be denied to him, wretched and futile, but better than this empty void before him.

'Tania,' he cried aloud, snatching his hands from his face, but only the crash of the waves answered. Below him the swathes of current surged effortlessly between the rocks, and the waves danced there, sparkling in the morning light and creaming in soft music, eternally playing, eternally free of the pain that coursed incurably through his heart. It would be good to go to them. His masterful scampering here had ended in futility and ugliness, while they sparkled and churned effortlessly, stronger and nobler than he. The waves striking the rocks hurled welcoming spray up to him, as if the strong sea agreed. Surely it would receive him swiftly, as it had received her, and make an end to the disgrace of his existence.

"Stuart!"

He twisted around in shock, nearly toppling from his perch, and grabbed quickly for a handhold; twenty yards above him Tania's face was outlined against the blue sky as she looked down, her expression puzzled and alarmed.

"Stuart be careful! What're you doing down there?"

"Wharr?" his heart leapt with joy, relief, shock that was almost anger. He reached quickly for a handhold and scrambled up the rocky face, ignoring his pains, agile in his relief. In a minute he was back at the ledge where he had slipped, looking for a new handhold to pull himself back over the lip, the girl reaching down to help him.

"Stay back," he shouted wildly, waving her off vigorously with one arm, clinging to a narrow cranny with his other hand. "For God's sake stay back from this place."

She backed away timidly as he shuffled a little along the ledge to find a new handhold, then heaved himself back up over the brink, scrabbled frantically as the edge broke away beneath his hip, and rolled away quickly, as if the cliff might reach out to snatch him back.

She stood stiff and fearful, hands covering her mouth as he sat up, filthy, exhausted, shins and arms scratched and smeared with a dark mix of earth and blood.

"Where were you? Where the hell were you?" he panted.

"I was – near," she said simply.

"Near," he bellowed, too full of emotion to know if he was in joy or pain, "why didn't you answer. I was shouting for you. Damn it all I thought you were dead!" he ended with a roar.

Tania snatched down her hands and yelled shrilly in her turn. "You left me, you shouted at me and left me, and you didn't come back, and I thought you might be hurt so I went looking for you. And my sandal broke and I had to go back to Log City on one foot, and the fire was out, and, an, and you shouted at me." Her voice faltered and she burst suddenly into tears and turned away.

The anger left Stuart as abruptly as if a great dam had burst, draining a vast lake in one swift torrent. It was over, and he was glad to his roots. They had thrown out all the hot words of reproach that needed to be thrown, and she was safe. The hellish episode had run its course and ended in the wetness of tears. Stuart rose from the grass cautiously, a bruised knee that he did not remember banging saluting him with a stab of pain that made him grunt.

The girl spun quickly and ran to grab him by the arm. "Come away," she cried, hauling on his arm determinedly, "come away from here. I don't want you here. What were you doing going down there. You frightened me." And she dragged him hobbling and limping down the slope of the hilltop, Stuart groaning as he went, but pleased as a beaten dog is by its master's later kindness.

By the time they reached Log City he could scarcely walk, and was made to sit leaning back against the old log whilst she scurried to light the fire and set water to boil with chopped yam. When the mounting flames started to lick the pot she came and sat before him and looked at him steadily, uncertain as to who was at fault.

"Did you hide Honey?" he asked gently.

She nodded. "You told me you wanted to be on your own, so I thought I'd keep out of your way till you missed me." She looked at him reproachfully. "You didn't come back all night. Pig."

He was quiet for a while; what could he say? Then, "I'm sorry Honey. Sometimes men do that. Sometimes they need to be on their own, especially if they're worried. It doesn't always mean too much. I just got very upset over something."

"It doesn't make sense. What was wrong?"

"Well sometimes.... it makes sense to men," he fumbled out. Sometimes they just need to be on their own. That's one of the things you'll have to learn about men."

"Hmm really. That and other things."

"Come here."

She came over to him readily, and for a little while speech was forgotten as they remade their love in a private world of little caresses, silly, simple words that mean much, soft kisses that heated until Tania slide her hand slightly between his thigh and giggled at the swelling lump. Things might have gone further, but she pressed down accidentally onto his bruised knee, and he jumped with a howl of pain that took his mind off such things abruptly.

"Oh sorry. Sick man, the sick man needs soup," she exclaimed, jumping up to attend to the pan. "Why did you go down the cliff in any case? You didn't think I'd be there did you?"

"I thought you'd fallen. Your stuff was there, and I thought you'd fallen over the edge."

She gave him her wide-eyed look that meant unspeakable horror. "But I'd be dead. Of course I hadn't fallen over. I'd have gone down onto the rocks and been dead. Why should I fall over all of a sudden?"

"That's what I thought. I thought you were dead. Your sandal was there with the strap broken, and then I saw your stick right down by the edge."

"Is that why you ran? I was following you, then and I thought I'd answer if you shouted again, then all of a sudden you shouted and ran off into the trees as though you were going to the old hut, and I thought I'd better run after you. It all seemed so weird, I couldn't understand. I got right back to the old hut and you weren't there, then I wondered some how if you'd gone back, and I ran up to the hilltop again and looked over the edge."

She paused for a while, not comfortable to say what she had thought. He was an adult after all, so much older than she was. "You scared me," she said finally. "You were right down there looking into the water, and it's so dangerous down there. I thought you'd, you know..."

"What. I'd what."

"You know, gone nuts or something."

"I thought you were dead Honey. I was feeling very nuts, not compos mentis at all. The dirt was all broken at the edge and your stick was there. Everything looked as though you'd fallen."

"Oh." She looked at him round-eyed. "I dropped it. I took it with me when I came looking for you. I broke my strap coming up the hill, and when you weren't there I sat on the edge and dropped my stick over by accident. I was pocking out some stones to throw into the sea, and it slipped out of my hand. I just left the sandal up there 'cause I kept tripping on it. Sorry. And you hurt yourself looking for me."

"Its okay now Honey, every thing's okay now."

" But what did you get so upset about yesterday," she continued energetically, bouncing up and down on the sand with sudden impatience. "I was looking for the plane coming back, and I saw you on the causeway looking at some thing, then you went climbing up backwards still looking at it. I wondered what it was, then I'd forgot 'cause you were nasty to me." She stuck her tongue out briskly. The world was as it should be again. "What was it?"

"Nothing." Stuart's face had gone sour at being reminded of the inexplicable little horror crouched out there on the causeway. The sheer unexplainable spookiness of the whole thing had thrown him as much as anything, and now when everything was okay it was coming back again: a rotten hand that should have sunk and didn't, couldn't be where it was and yet was there. Bloody impossible. Nothing so bad about a severed hand, ugly as it was. Nothing to him at any rate: he had seen a cut off head in Malaya, and that was appalling, but it least he knew who cut it off, and it didn't wander about. He shuddered without thinking and looked up to see Tania regarding him steadily.

"What was it? It was something horrible wasn't it?"

"No. Forget about it. It was just something nasty, and I thought about it too much."

"What? It must have been really nasty 'cause you told me you've seen a lot of nasty things in the war."

"I told you Honey, just something nasty. Something I couldn't understand. It was nothing."

"Tell me. Is that what got you so upset you left me all night?"

"Yes. I suppose it was. But I don't want to talk about it to you, you'd get upset too. Just leave it, another day or two and we'll be gone."

"I won't get upset. What is it?"

"Honey, forget about it please. Its not very nice, and I can't explain it."

Tania jumped up suddenly. "I'm going to go look!" she exclaimed and ran off down the beach.

"Tania," he cried, struggling to his feet.

She halted and spun round. "You stay there, I want to know!"

"Don't go Honey, you don't want to see it."

"Tell me then and I won't go."

He slumped back, defeated by the throbbing of his knee.

"Come back then. I'll tell you but you'll wish I hadn't."

She returned and plumped down by him expectantly.

"There's something on the causeway" he began cautiously, "something from the crash. Something that shouldn't be there. A piece of a body."

"Uurrgh." She clapped her hands over her face.

"I told you it wasn't nice."

"What piece?" She whispered, lowering her hands a little.

He remembered belatedly the fascination that the macabre held for children. "A hand."

"What, just a hand or a whole arm?"

"Just a hand Honey for God's sake. Cut off and all rotten. Isn't that enough?"

"Don't swear Stuart," she said pertly, "you swear too much. Whose hand is it?"

He hesitated. The kid would be upset when she found out. "A woman's. It's a small hand, too small for a man's, and there's a ring on it."

"It must be Julia's," she said in a subdued voice. "How did it get there though?"

"That's the part I can't understand." Tania had fallen silent and perhaps he could now dismiss the gruesome riddle, but having opened the mystery he felt compelled to go on. "Dead bodies sink if they drown because the lungs get full of water. They only float if they have lungs full of air. Bits of dead bodies with no lungs sink all the time. So how did it get all the way there from the plane?"

"Ohhhh," now he had said too much. Tania's eyes were back at supreme horror roundness in earnest. "It must be a ghost or something. Oh Stuart why did you tell me?"

"You asked."

"And there's a ring on the hand? It must Julia's! Urrrgh!"

"No. Julia didn't wear any rings. I noticed that. And she's in the plane. She wasn't injured in the crash, you know, broken up. It's not her hand. But it is a woman's."

"But it can't be Sister Therese's, you said she drifted out to sea."

"Yes. And she wasn't hurt at all, she drown." He fell silent. He did not want to proceed, but Tania now had her teeth well into the mystery.

"But Sister Therese didn't have little hands. She was a big woman. She used to say her mother said she was like a horse. It couldn't have been hers."

"It wasn't just the size Honey. It was the ring as well. It had a sort of, you know, plain religious look to it, like a holy medal or something. It looked like silver."

"Silver!" Tania sat up abruptly. "That native man, you know not the fat one, his brother. He had little hands, I noticed them at Paa, and he had a little silver ring on. It's his hand! I remember thinking it would fit on my finger!"

"What!" Stuart reared back astounded. "That's impossible! How would you remember that?"

"I saw what a pig the big man was, big and fat, and the other one was quiet, and he was skinny and he had neat little hands with a plain ring on. And it was white like silver, and he got all torn up in the crash"

The light of clarity dawned on Stuart. "I thought it was Sister Therese's. It looked so... nunnish."

"You Dum Dum Stuart. Nuns don't wear rings, they don't even wear watches! Oh you are such a Dum Dum!"

Stuart sat abashed. There are times in life when even a clever man must admit to being a fool, and this was one of them. A humble silence was his only answer, for he was a Dum Dum. This he knew for certain, for Tania had just told him so.

Chapter 42. Neptune

He clambered steadily along the barrier rocks, picking his way cautiously along the uneven natural pier. Tania had gone alone to the fishing ground, having declared him still too sick to fish, and though his knee was much improved, he hadn't argued. Tania said he needed to rest it so that it didn't get worse, and though her medical experience was only some past years of treating dolls, she was right, for joints were tricky things, and playing the invalid awhile was better than making it worse.

A mere night had passed since their reunion on the hilltop, yet the day of fear and estrangement was dead, and he had taken pains to bury it. Tania had laughed at him heartily for his ignorance on the jewellery habits of nuns, then become concerned at his increasing pain and lameness, and bustled about the island for water and food, feeding him like a mother and confining him sternly to Log City.

He had obeyed meekly, and lay quietly in the shelter's shadow, feeling himself a fool beyond her knowing. In the evening she fussed over him, and hustled him early to his bed, a weak cripple not fit to look after himself. Here her behaviour became a little inconsistent, for after rummaging him to weariness for tales of spooks and the supernatural she grew in an instant amorous, and he set to work in earnest on her, whilst smothering many a groan as he forgetfully knelt on the injured knee. He held her with a desperate tenderness afterwards, as if by his love to bury deep his near treachery.

She had fallen into deep, easy sleep, worn by the emotions of the day, but Stuart remained wakeful, thinking. He had been on a journey, a hideous, frightening, lost, wandering journey through misery towards horror. He had walked it alone, and it had tortured and shaken him more deeply than The Raven's crash. Quietly, in the darkness by the girl's side, he chewed on the question of his now doubtful worth, knowing that sleep was not for him until he made a peace with his guilt.

When the plane had gone down he had responded, roused his vigour, and done his best as well as he could; done what any real man should try to do, and in his forceful energy of his determination he had cursed the reckless Errol as a half-wit. But now he had been well nigh struck down by vaporous enemies, who were not merely absent, but were no more than the ghostly wailing of his own fears. Why had this rush of fear driven him headlong, trembling like a hunted fox, when he had stood firm to his duty in Burma, and not flinched from salvaging the plane's gruesome wreckage?

Slowly, as the night passed, he had re-walked his thoughts of the previous night calmly, until his steps marked out clearly to him the map of his near disaster.

In those war years that had made him, he had choked back fear, and faced what most men had faced, when they too were obliged to smother their fear, and his manhood had been commended as he stood in line with them to have his gong pinned to his chest. War, imminent death, hardship, defiance of a parent's disapproval, and all the other things that had threatened him; those he had in common with others, and his fear had been measurable and containable, for it was normal and shared.

But this little sin went beyond the common run of things, into a world luminous but strange, and when night had threatened to fall in that new world, he had pictured himself rejected in an outer darkness, for this was not mere adultery, nor war's legalised murder, nor even lining the pockets with a sharp business deal. Those were acceptable horrors that could be bragged of, or brazened out, and if the conscience lay heavy, it could be eased by a little soul bearing to a like-minded friend, preferably over a few drinks.

But this lesser peccadillo placed him outside the world of the pack, beyond its more usual crimes, and so not only beyond the admiration it awarded to a hero, but also beyond the limited chiding it gave to an everyday rogue. And there lay the key: sharp, clean danger he had met head on, and hot anger also, but the threat of his muddy disgrace had crumpled him, for he had long drunk down the applause of others, and not realised how he had savoured it. He had thought of himself as being independent in his ways, and now saw that he merely been more successful, and was as much the puppet of other people's good opinions as any bowing and scrapping sales clerk.

I am less than I thought I was, he had thought, much less. Dad used to say that I should choose something safe for a job, and I thought he was wrong, completely wrong. He was too, but only halfway. He had a point. Safe's worth something, but I couldn't see it then. I went into the army and nearly got killed, but I coped, and I did better than he's done in his life, so he was wrong, but only that time.

Now I've gone my own way again, and I've probably made a mess. Now I have to try and fix it. I stuck to it when I joined the army, and saw it through, and it came out okay. That's what I must do now, see it through and accept the consequences of what I've got into. I've found a jewel in the girl, and I can't keep her, but I mustn't let her down. I made a promise, and at the first hint of a challenge, I got a dose of the heebie-jeebies. That mustn't happen again. I can't keep her, it's crazy to think that I can, and if I could she'll grow up one day, and I'll be an old man by then. But she's mine for a while, and I made a promise, and I can't go through that again.

I must choose, he had thought. I must choose to accept what trouble may come of all this, and swallow it down, like it or not, or I must be driven down that hellish road again by fearing people that don't even know me, until I lose everything, my wits included. I've had a dose of that, and I want no more of it. So whatever comes, comes, and I do my best, and if it all comes out into the open I'll have to endure people's yap, and probably worse than yap. But at least I'll still be me, and I'll still be better than some people I know who did worse, and got away with it. Now I know no more than what I knew before, except now I know it better. No choice to make really. It's made for me, and now I have to live with it and let it be.

With his decision, peace had come, and soon sleep engulfed him.

In the morning he had found that she was again his nurse, and he was still her injured patient. It was a pleasant game to play, and with their sudden unemployment they could afford to play it. She insisted that she could catch enough to feed them, and so he agreed to her prescription, reserving only the right to deal with the unwelcome bit of Andre that still lay out on the barrier rocks. She grimaced at that, and nodded before shouldering her spear and trotting away, and he found a sharp stick and limped off to the barrier.

The ugly little thing was still there. He had half expected it to have been washed away, but whatever wave had deposited it had raised it high, and he was relieved to find it still crouched in its crevasse, relieved that he could confront it again. It looked no better than two days before, and the tide had retreated some hours earlier, allowing it to dry in the heat, so that its stink rose to meet him.

Clambering down to its lair he saw what he had failed to notice before: it sat not directly on the rock, but on a ragged little cushion of some fibrous material. He studied it in repulsed fascination for a while, then speared it on the stick and raised it from its place. As he raised it the cushion came with it, hanging loosely below, and he realised that it was a ragged chunk of the padded material from one of the Raven's seats, into which the tips of two of the fingers were deeply driven.

The seats would float, wasn't that what Errol had said? The mystery dissolved before the memory. A piece had floated, a piece that had been ripped from Andre's seat by the same gouging rock that in one swift impact had torn his body, hacked away his hand and driven his fingers deep into the padding. And it had floated to where all the debris came, bearing its bloody little passenger away from the wreck, only to be washed onto the barrier rocks, and lie there quietly over the months whilst the harmless dead meat rotted. Stuart shook his head in wonder. How such a strange and troubling puzzle should rest on such a simple explanation.

He bore it before him to the end of the causeway and shook it until the padding dropped from the nearly vanished flesh. Thrown out to sea it would join the rest of the Raven's dead, pass honourably back like all other things into the chemistry of the world, and cease to trouble them.

He held it before him a moment, considering the stranger to whom it had belonged. It had been precious to him, a valued part of his warm, fleshy house, and he had adorned it with a simple elegant ring, now buckled, and tarnished with its finger's corruption. He had been a passing nobody, just a quiet subordinate to his vulgar brother. Was he a good man, with someone out there who would mourn his unexplained absence? Or was he some grasping pimp whose disappearance had caused relief?

Stuart did not know, and in any event it was a life that had ended, and he now felt that he understood less of good and bad. Despite his oft-donned cynicism he murmured some soft words of prayer for the lost man, then flicked the crumbling relic out to sea. It raised a last splash, then in a moment the final mark was gone from the restless water. Stuart hurled the stick after it, and turning from the burial, he limped back down the causeway.

At the other end of the bay, nearly the island's length away, the tiny golden brown figure was still plunging energetically for fish, and the sky was of a clear, vivid blue, the deeper green-blue of the bay quivering and sparkling beneath it as its waves licked with cream tongues onto the smooth dark sand. It could be a postcard from some holiday place, he thought, a picture to beckon people to come and spend their money on some peace and quiet, and see something clean and beautiful, that they'll remember forever. And now it feels like that.

We shall never forget this place: it will always be in us, for good or bad, and so we shall always be here. But we've survived and we're going home, just us two, and all these dead people stay here. Why us? Why did we get through, and get so tangled up with each other, and all these others just got scrapped and thrown away. They were going somewhere, some of them at least, and somebody was waiting for them. But now they don't get to go there, and we go on, and something else happens to us, good or bad. They got the hard word and we were excused, lucky.

"Thank you," he murmured. "I don't know if there's anyone or anything out there to thank, but in any case, thank you." He gained the beach and speeded his pace a little, for the sand tried his knee less. Was he hypocritical, he wondered? If there was anything out there, wasn't it better to keep his mouth shut, considering how many of the rules had he broken?

He glanced at the great blueness above, and averted his eyes again swiftly from the sun's glare. It was nothing, he thought, we only had each other, and we were made that way, so what would you expect? There was no one but us, and we hurt no one, and we meant no harm. If you're there, you know that; if you're smart enough to have made that great ball of fire, then you know it, and you don't need any tittle-tattling sky pilot to tell you. And if you know it, what does it matter what any one else thinks, and why should I care what they think?

If they throw me in a cell and lose the key, not to worry. They might have done that in any case some day, for no good reason; why not, they've done it to plenty of others! The world's full of corpses who harmed nobody, and bitter people who were honest and got robbed blind. They'll poke their fingers at me if they can, as though my life's theirs to tidy up as they think fit, all those "theys" with their damned opinions, and then they'll do as they want to in private when it comes to their own affairs.

So to hell with them; we'll get through, the two of us. Just keep throwing us a bit of luck please, and we'll do the work.

Enough of that now, he thought, for in his reverie he had stumbled over a piece of driftwood. You know what comes of too much thinking, and I'd better get down there before she sticks that spear in her foot.

At the fishing-ground Tania waved him off and shook her fist, so he sat on the beach before the native hut, content to be idle, leaning back against the old wall. The ache in his knee was less than the day before, and seemed to be drawing in and defining to a bruised area further down his shin. He could have joined Tania out between the rocks, but she had forbidden him, hadn't she?

He felt relaxed and reflective as he lolled back, watching the naked girl as she hunted enthusiastically amidst the surf. What clothing she still cared to wear was flung in a heap by the logs; like him she knew they were merely marking time whilst rescue ambled towards them, and defying their uncertain tomorrow with a last few todays of liberty. She had transformed in the months that they had been here, not ageing much by the calendar, but expanding from a subdued half-crushed orphan into a sprite of the island. His sprite, his consort in his unwanted kingdom. How could he have done without her? He would rather leave his bones here than leave the island without her. She was his now, his....

But what the devil is she? he thought, and pondered on the riddle that his philosophical mood had set him. Not who, that he knew well enough. Tania Webster, daughter of Roland and Yvette Webster, a British citizen, late of The Malcolm MacGraff Institute in Paa, presently marooned on Star Island, South China Sea, and soon to be returned to civilised society in time for her twelfth birthday. Commendation is made to Stuart Ellis, Lieutenant, Infantry, (retired) for his comfort and assistance to the child in her distress.

That was easy and glib enough answer for a brief report, defining her neatly enough for the world's tidy pigeonholes. But to him – what was she to him? His girlfriend? Preposterous! Girlfriends were women of about your own age, adult women who you could walk out in public with, hold adult conversations with, who might wonder if you were going to pop the question, and might or might not sleep with you if the relationship was strong enough. And if you'd been seen out with them enough times, then friends and aunties might embarrass you by asking slyly when they would hear wedding bells. Those were girlfriends, women who might become wives, young women who it was perfectly in order for your family to be curious about, young women who might some day be part of that family.

Yet hadn't the kid been closer to him than a wife? In all these days that they had been thrown together, hadn't he spent more hours with her than he had with Jennifer in all the year of their courtship? But wife – good God no, that bird could fly even less than girlfriend.

Wives were grown women who had jobs or had children, not children themselves. And wives were women you were tied to by a piece of paper saying that all was in order, plus a ceremony with a man in a frock to say the words. Afterwards everyone congratulated you, and your rowdier friends got drunk at your expense. Then you took your blessed self and blessed new wife home and shagged her good and legal in the privacy of your own home, as often as you wanted, and all was proper, and if she got knocked up, you were congratulated again.

Wife was even crazier than girlfriend, so girlfriend it had to be, and as for the congratulations part, he'd had enough of those at his wedding, and very futile they had turned out to be, so he could do without any more. But as girlfriend still didn't fit, then it looked as though companion was the word after all. "Tania Webster, I hereby declare you my companion," he intoned solemnly to the distant girl.

Remembrance of his wedding brought the thought of Colonel Haig into his mind: what would the colonel think of this affair if he were here, what sage advice might he give?

Stuart had found the colonel to be a tough, practical man, yet tolerant, but surely he would find that this one took the candle. For a minute he considered his former superior's possible reaction. "Bloody Fool's" his most likely verdict, he thought, and burst out laughing.

Companion then. That was a title he had suggested in joke to the girl, and that would have to serve. But there was something too Star Island about that one, and Star Island words would only serve on Star Island. Back to girlfriend then, and that still didn't fit.

"But that's the best I can do, Ladies and Gentlemen," he murmured, then chuckled again at the though of the colonel's possible comments, but affectionately, for he had a deep respect for his ex-commander.

Across the water the girl was still stalking obsessively, spear aloft, fixed in her desire to one day catch a fish bigger than any of his. As he watched she lunged forward furiously and made a titanic thrust into the water, overreaching herself and falling face down to disappear into the waves. Stuart burst out laughing in earnest, for the girl was comic in her determination, and he sat up to clap at her re-emergence.

Her head broke surface, her hair thick and dark with water. Then from the waves before her a fish rose slowly, massive, glittering points of water spraying from its flailing fins as it cleared the waves, scales glistening in brilliant colour as it thrashed on the skewering spear. She grasped the spear with both hands and raised it steadily aloft, then herself emerged as she rose from her squat, and strode steadily through the surging waves towards him, her face merciless in a grin of triumph.

The water streamed from her hair and ran sparkling down the tanned health of her body, passing glittering over the flat muscles of her chest, running on in rivulets over the firm roundings of her stomach, as though a warrior maiden clad in bronze armour had arisen from the sea. Her slender arms seemed stronger than the rocky enclosures of the bay as she held her trophy aloft; her thighs seemed of immense power as they churned the water easily before them, the cleft mound of her sex bold and naked between them.

Stuart sat awed at the sight of her, almost fearing her as she ploughed the waters towards him, a Neptune arisen in power to reveal herself a goddess. She strode through the shallows to him, her eyes fixing his confidently, life itself striding boldly forward to confront him. He rose respectfully to meet her.

Tania halted before him, her face radiant with triumph. "Big one," she announced, thumping the fish down before him and tweaking quickly at the hairs of his chest. "Now you have to clean it, lazy man."

And again she was just a naked girl, standing almost as high as his collarbone, just a child who had caught a fish. He placed his hands softly on her shoulders and kissed her smooth forehead ceremoniously, pleased to concede her victory.

"Big one alright Honey, bigger than any of mine. Big celebration feast tonight!"

Chapter 43. Gamblers

It was the second day since the 'plane had flown over, and on waking Stuart went immediately to the hill's peak to scan the horizon with an expectant eye, reminding himself firmly that he was looking calmly for the assured, not anxiously for the doubted.

Star Island was now part of the known world, of that he was sure. The horizon was empty, but somewhere a vessel of some kind was cutting the waves, diverted from its usual routine to pick up an unusual cargo from this little handful of land. It was not possible that things were otherwise, and the rigors of their days had burnt so much impatience from him that the seas seemed to his mind crowded with boats and waving pilots, all surging forward to dance to his convenience.

Over the months he had gone from angry denial to fierce, determined effort, and onwards through almost contentment and useless panic to arrive at this day. Now he felt himself like a battle-chipped sword that had been re-sharpened, and he would not blunt that edge in futile anxiety. His mind was ready, and to his relief so was his body, for the pain in his knee was almost gone, only a few twinges troubling him as he descended back to the beach.

The raft he ignored, and taking up his spear he waded out to fish, but he did not pursue the fish with his usual determined concentration, or seeking teasingly to top Tania's victory. Instead, his mood was that of a man who arrives at the last day of a holiday, and whiles away the final hours in the last enjoyment of a pleasure that he has pursued eagerly, whilst quietly conscious of an unseen clock ticking away the minutes until he must lay aside his toys, and taking up his luggage say goodbye.

He felt ready, prepared. Singapore, Alaska, wherever they were taken to, he was ready, as he was ready for the fish that was sliding guilelessly towards him. He raised the spear in an easy relaxed movement, then darted it down smoothly, skewering the gleaming body dead centre.

"Got one," he announced, hoisting it out of the water. Tania was fishing close by, and had jumped at his sudden movement; she had seemed nervous since they rose with the dawn, and he could feel her growing anxiety. Two days was an eternity at her age, and now she was looking out to the horizon again.

"It's your turn," he announced. "I'm going up to the hilltop again and taking a look all around. If I see anything I'll shout. If I don't see anything... I think I'll start to invent some light bulbs, and we'll illuminate the sign."

Tania screwed around in the water violently and stared at him open mouthed in horror, then saw through his joke and hurled handfuls of water at him as he waded to the beach.

"Pig!" she shouted after him, "just you wait. If we're still here tonight I'll pull it off!"

"Oooh," he cried, wincing, "then you'll have to go back to dolls!"

He cleaned the fish briskly, tickled with his riposte, and snatching up the water jar he ran with it up the steep hillside behind the old hut, dodging easily through the trees, twice leaping a fallen branch. He arrived at the high peak of the hilltop scarcely winded, exulted by his fitness.

"Come to Star Island, get a body like Charles Atlas," he cried to the faint breeze, and waved to the girl wading through the waters below. It was true, he thought, he felt fitter than he had in years, and freer, despite the uncertainties that still lay before him. He was free of Jennifer, there was no doubt of that in his mind, free of all illusion that there was a marriage worth repairing. That idea had gone, and the piece of paper that said otherwise would soon be gone too, or he was a Dutchman.

The girl saw him waving and waved back, then turned again to stare at the horizon. "Have faith Honey, have faith," he murmured to himself, and keep growing, he thought. Keep growing just the way you are. We'll manage honey. I don't know how the hell we will, but we'll manage. We'll go on, until we find a better place for you. And if I fall, then I must endure without whimpering, and you must go on alone.

He cast his gaze to the deep water beyond Tiger Rock; "I swear it," he said, then remembering his errand, he too ran his eyes over the still empty horizon, before sauntering down to inspect the now redundant sign. "Hopefully we don't need you anymore," he murmured, kicking at the loose dirt, "but if they don't come in a day or two, then there'll be two of us not too happy, and more work on a certain raft."

The sign was already beginning to weather a little, the bared soil rubbed by the rains from its hacked condition to a smoother texture, the encroaching grass already starting to nibble at the edges of the great letters. When we're gone you won't last long, he thought, and headed for the south end to make his way down to the waterfall. He stopped by the trees at the head of the valley, and picked up the mattock that had raised so many blisters on his hands, now lying here discarded amongst the litter of their meals.

"Don't need you anymore either," he announced, and threw it down, but turned to look back over the bare few acres of grass before leaving them behind.

They had worked hard here, so, so hard, and he had cursed the indifferent sun and the stubborn turf, yet it was a just, peaceful place, that had yielded without cheating to their efforts, giving up its green, wild nature in exact measure to their digging, and here they had strained their wits to outdo each other, and sustained each other's spirits with a host of stories. What would happen here when they were gone, he wondered?

When their digging and hacking and fishing had ceased, and there was no longer a nightly fire on the beach, and when they had gone with their thoughts and fears and jokes and words, would the island then be somehow less? Had it a great, green soul of its own which would miss them? He doubted it; that was just the kind of silly thing you thought when you were leaving a place. But he did not doubt that they would not fully leave; Tania had said it in jest, the day she threw the wisp of hair into the sea.

He smiled at the memory, and feeing the drag of sentiment threatening to engulf him, he turned away down the slope, aware that he was pampering himself, building in his mind a bright shield of confidence that might yet prove false. If it did, then there was a growing problem with the water supply to deal with.

Tania found that she could not keep her eyes from straying to the horizon. The plane had flown over; surely this time someone was going to come for them.

She felt tired of the island. It had been a great adventure, but suddenly she found herself longing to go, suddenly it seemed even smaller than ever, and Stuart would be so disappointed if a ship didn't come. He tried hard to be cheerful, she could see that, but he had so much to do, and sometimes he got down with it, like a few days ago, when he hurt his leg. It was harder for him because he had to think of all the things, and he had to do all the deciding. It must be complicated to be a grown up, she thought. Someday she would be grown up, and it was sort of scary, thinking of all the things she'd have to know and be able to do. But he'd help her, and she'd have her dad as well. Stuart would find him. He could do anything.

Stuart reluctantly dipped the jar into the bath, holding back the drifting debris with his fingers. It hadn't rained in the last few days and the trickle of the waterfall was little more than a steady drip. Now he would definitely have to boil the water, and their wood supply was low again. He had neglected things over the last few days he realised, as he set off through the forest to

Log City, following the faint path that their feet had marked over the months. And the raft was not as firmly anchored as he would like to see it, he thought, it was wrong to abandon it, and he needed to.... He halted, listening.

A steady droning sound was growing, filling the forest, but from which direction it came he could not tell. A pain of excitement as keen as that of fear shot through his heart, and he broke into a run, stopping in consternation as the precious water slopped from the jar, and he stood staring vainly up through the leafy branches as the drone grew to a roar overhead, then died swiftly away. Setting the jar down hastily on the path he plunged into the trees, taking the shortest way to the beach, hearing Tania shrieking his name.

Stuart burst out onto the sands to find Tania dancing, waving, shouting at the water's edge. There was a plane, a big one, nearly as big as the Raven, well out, and turning to come in again! And – oh mercy – there were floats beneath it! A seaplane, and clearly taking a careful look at the bay before landing. He stood transfixed on the sand as it flew low over the bay, well out, its airspeed low.

"Mind those reefs. Mind those damned reefs whatever you do. There's bugger all spare water here!" he cried, then Tania was hanging on his arm shouting. "They're landing," he yelled, oblivious to whatever she had said. "They're going to land in the Bay! They're here! Dammit don't foul up on those reefs!"

But the pilot was careful, whoever he was. He came in from the south, well out beyond danger, and settled the great bird slowly onto the rippling sea with twin wakes of foam.

"Tania!" he called, but she was haring for the shelter. He ran after her to find her scrambling her few possessions into her battering case, jabbering in excitement, and he joined in, hurling his own things into his bag. "Razor, money..."

She shot out from the hut with him close behind, but he halted in the entrance, unable to believe the sight of the seaplane moving across the bay with a steady drone of engines, taxiing slowly to a point out beyond Tiger Rock. It was impossible, a violation of the laws of nature. How could it be that a plane could come to this place, here where no one came, and casually land on this bay as though it were a piece of water like anywhere else, here in this bay, where no one came except to die or be imprisoned?

But it had come, and they were saved. They were going home. There was no haste. He felt his heart swell within him in relief, felt it force the pinprick of womanish tears to his eyes. He turned and looked back into the shelter, checking that nothing had been left behind. Nothing. Just a worn canvas sail for a carpet, rucked up by Tania's swift ransacking, just a few steel cans to be left behind in a jerry built thatched hut.

He paused and looked out at the plane. Despite everything, they had sometimes been happy here beneath this sagging thatch, happy with little, and the few miseries that they had endured now shrank and seemed as nothings, mere passing discomforts. What would happen to them back there, what would happen to him?

He felt a timid desire to step quietly into the forest and disappear, hide and let them leave, take her with them so she would be safe where he could not. Tania had halted half way down the beach and turned, dancing on the spot in impatience and excitement.

"Come on Stuart! Come on. What are you waiting for?"

The absurd thought passed – ridiculous, he would manage – and he gave the ridge of the hut a brisk farewell slap and ran down the beach to join her. They ran together to the water's edge and halted, he shielding his eyes from the still rising sun to see the now motionless seaplane better, she dancing in the surf, squealing in excitement.

"Now we can go to England and find my Dad," she cried, and a chill as of threatened loss ran through him. He put out a hand swiftly and possessed her arm, and she looked up at him smiling, not understanding. Or perhaps she did: he did not know.

Then they were both struck to silence, and stood quiet and still, hand in hand at the shore, squinting into the sun, the waves lapping around their ankles. They were silenced by awe, for a door had opened in the side of the plane, and a great fat man with a bush of red beard stood framed in the narrow opening, waving across the waters to them cheerily, stilling the two with amazement at the sight of a human being who was neither of them.

"Do you think its them?" asked the fat man, jovial, sweating, as he turned and started to haul the inflatable to the hatch. "Off the Raven I mean, some of Errol's passengers?"

"Yer," answered the pilot, raising his binoculars to spy the castaways out across the waters. He had lost five buck's on this point, but he took it philosophically. "Yer, that looks like what's left of the Raven there under the water."

He regarded the two distant figures a little longer through the glasses. "They must have been here for months, they're all in rags and brown as hell, but they're white people all right." He lowered the binoculars, finally satisfied that his bet was lost. " If I hadn't seen the writing I'd have thought they were a couple of savages."

The End

South-East Asia
(As 2006)

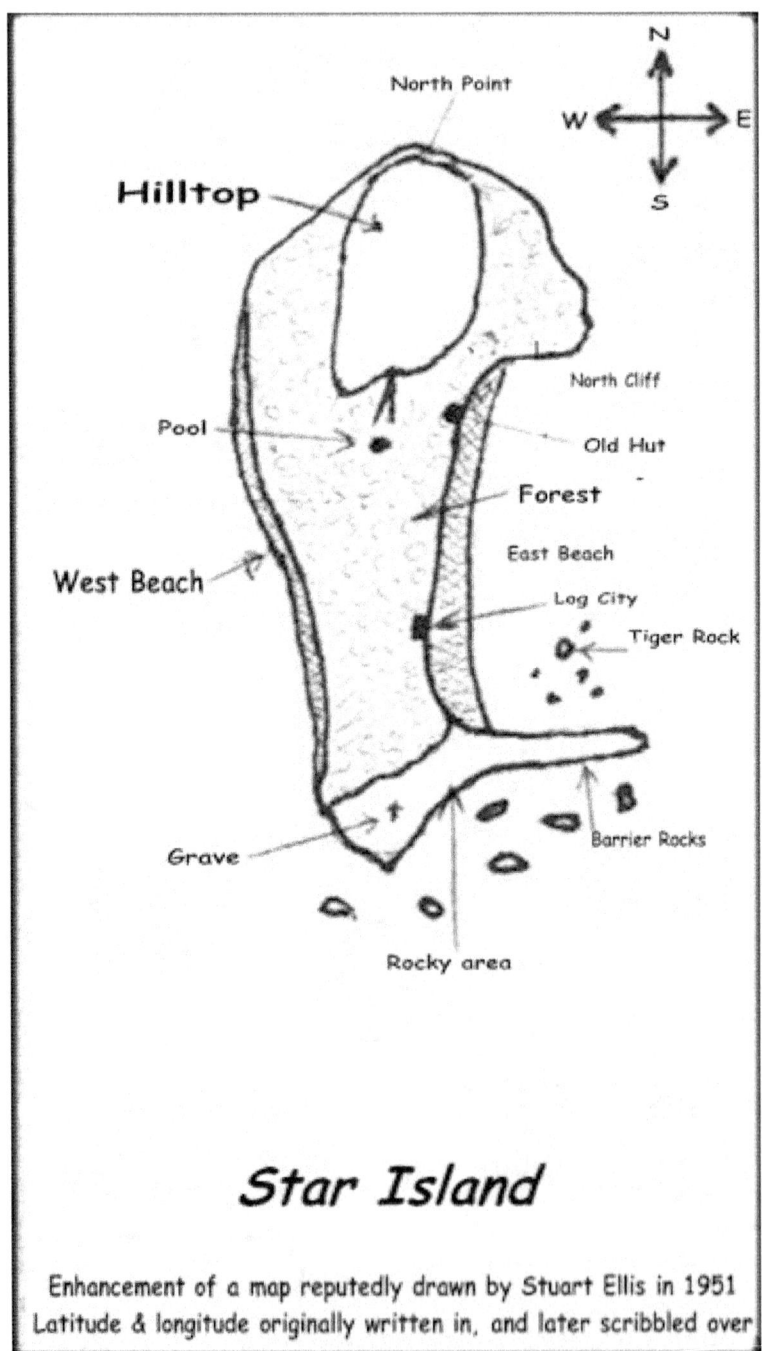

Star Island

Enhancement of a map reputedly drawn by Stuart Ellis in 1951
Latitude & longitude originally written in, and later scribbled over

Actual places and people

Winston Churchill. 1874 - 1965. Prime Minister of Great Britain 1940 - 1945, historically recognised as the great unifier of British spirit during World War II.

Adolph Hitler. Born 1889 in Austria, he rose from obscurity to become Chancellor of Germany in 1933, and in 1939 lead his country into the disaster of the Second World War. Seven days before the surrender of Germany, in 1945, he and his mistress. Eva Braun, committed suicide as in the capital, Berlin, as Russian troops seized the city.

Mahatma Gandhi. 1869 – 1948. An Indian lawyer, spiritual leader and politician, Gandhi is best know for his advocacy of non-violent resistance to oppression, and his role in securing the independence of India in 1947.

Second World War. Fought between the Allied and Axis powers, it commenced on 1 September, 1939 with the German invasion of Poland and ended on 14 August, 1945, with the surrender of Japan.

Singapore, or "Lion City". Originally a fishing village on the southern tip of the Malay Peninsula, it was developed in 1819 as a trading post by Sir Stamford Raffles, and dominated trade in south-east Asia. Captured by Japanese troops in 1942, and repossessed by the British in 1945, its status in 1951 was of a British Crown Colony.

Burma. This country forms the east coast of the Bay of Bengal, across which massive body of water it faces India. To Burma's south is the Malay Peninsula, and to its east, Laos and Thailand. In January of 1942 Japan invaded Burma, driving the British and Indian forces back through the country to India, the longest retreat in military history. In early 1944 the Japanese advance faltered in eastern India, and Allied forces drove them back, reducing their overextended army to a shambles.

Hiroshima. On 6 August 1945, this major Japanese city that suffered the effect of the first nuclear attack ever made. 80,000 people were killed instantly. The attack was purportedly made to hasten the end of the war. However, as Japan was on the point of surrender, it is reasonable to consider the viewpoint that the objective was to intimidate the Soviet Union.

Cold War. A term invented in 1947 to describe the state of tension between the capitalist and communist countries that lead to a massive build-up of nuclear weapons. This fear hung over the latter half of the twentieth century like a black cloud, until the late eighties, when the Soviet Union commenced reforms that lead to its dissolution in 1991.

Malaya. In 1951, a federation of several British protectorates having Malay as a common language. By "Malaya," Stuart is referring to the southern part of the Malay Peninsular. In 1951, Malaya was in the third year of the "Malay Emergency," a military action against communist terrorists.

Kenya. A country on the east coast of Africa, in 1951 a British protectorate. The capital is Nairobi, a sea port whose proximity to big game hunting areas made it popular with wealthy European tourists in the early 1920s. Exploitation of the native tribes by white farmers led to the emergence of the Mau Mau, a secret African society that fought for independence from 1952 to 1959.

Accrington. A small town in Lancashire, a county of north-west England.

Gloucester. The principal town of Gloucestershire, in south-west England.

Charles Atlas. 1893 – 1972. A bodybuilder who marketed the Dynamic Tension method, he was described in 1922 as "the world's most perfectly developed man."

Robert Louis Stevenson. 1850 – 1894. A Scottish novelist and poet. Long John Silver is the villain of his most famous novel, "Treasure Island."

Places in Gary Wilson's account that it has not been possible to identify due to name changes, and possibly other forms of deliberate miss-direction.

Paa. A seaport in the area of the South China Sea.

Panwey. A seaport on the Malay Peninsula, definitely to the north of Singapore, and probably on the east coast, but possibly on the west.

The Malcolm McGraff Institute. An orphanage, set up under a deed of trust that specified administration by the Catholic Church.

Star Island. A small, uninhabited island, probably to the east of the Malay Peninsula.

www.ingramcontent.com/pod-product-compliance
Lightning Source LLC
Chambersburg PA
CBHW072302020726
47501CB00002B/354